COURT OF WHISPERS

REALMS OF LORE: FAE

AMBER THOMA

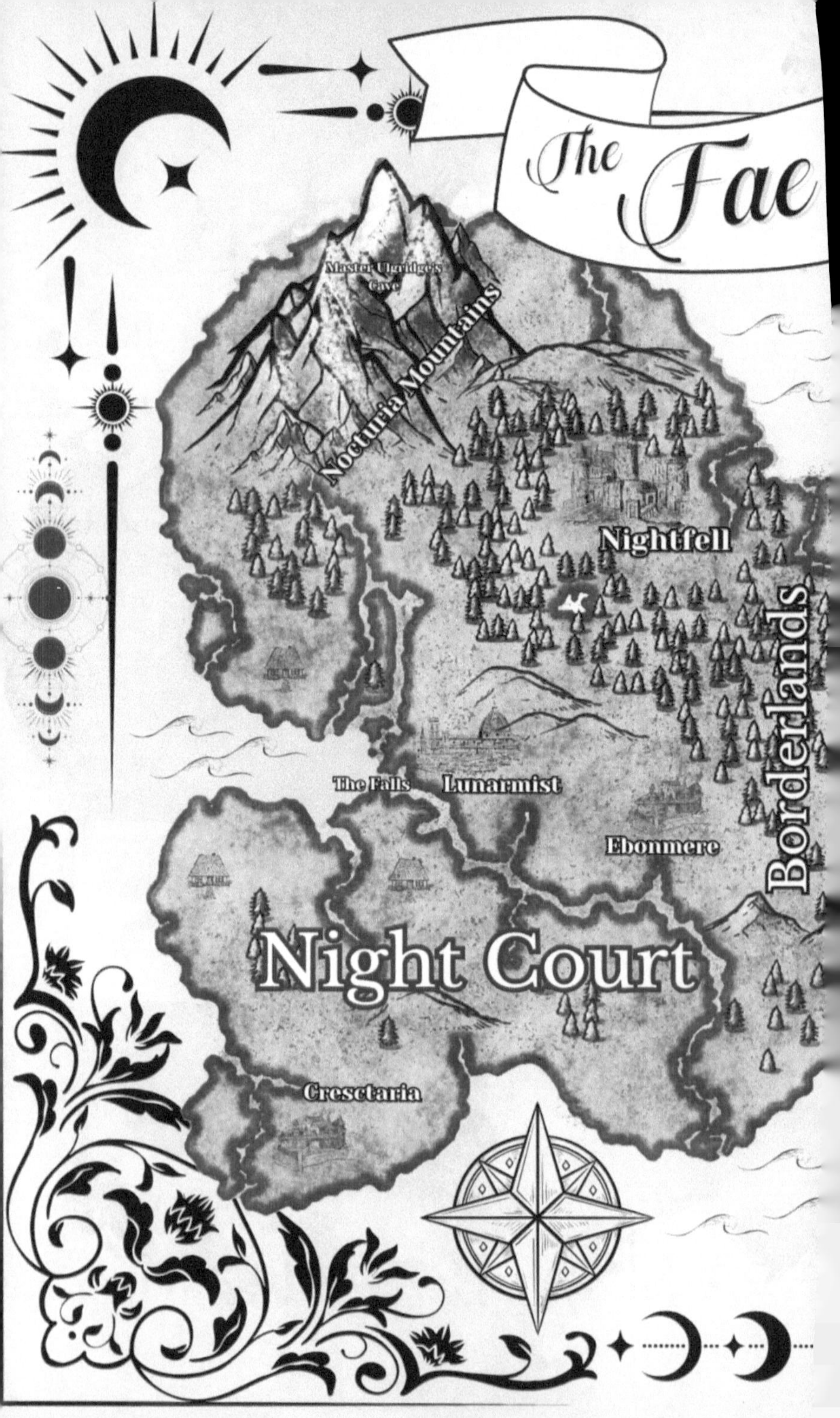

The Fae
Master Uldridge's Cave
Nocturia Mountains
Nightfell
Borderlands
The Falls
Lunarmist
Ebonmere
Night Court
Cresctaria

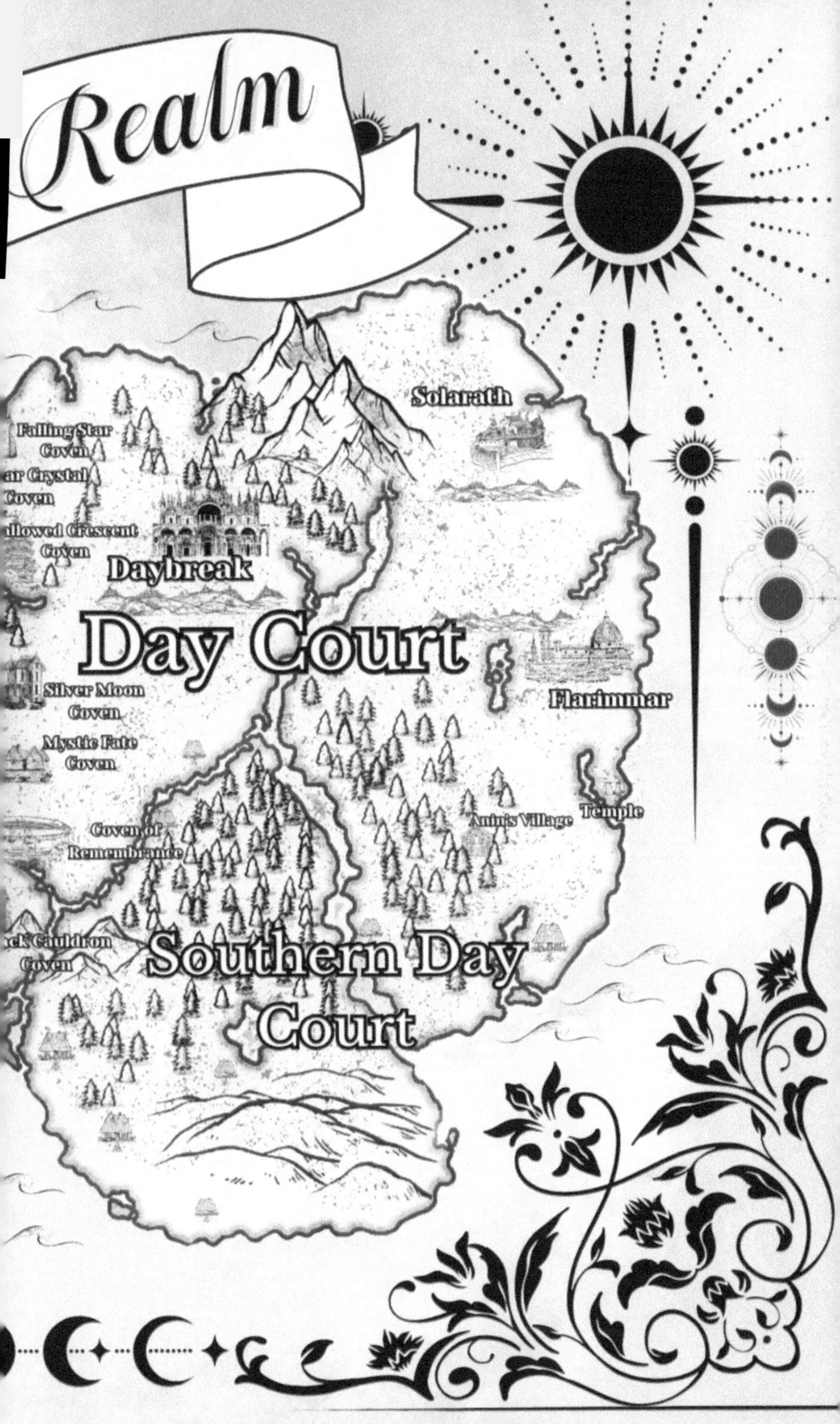

Realm
Solarath
Falling Star Coven
air Crystal Coven
allowed Crescent Coven
Daybreak
Day Court
Silver Moon Coven
Mystic Fate Coven
Flarimmar
Coven of Remembrance
Anin's Village
Temple
ack Cauldron Coven
Southern Day Court

Published by: Author Amber Thoma

www.TwoGirlsOneBookPublishing.com

First Edition Published October 2024

Book Cover By: Rebekah Sinclair

Map, and Interior Designs By: Amber Thoma

For Rebekah,
My hero and the wind beneath my wings.
Shout out to Subway for bringing besties together since 2003
IYKYK

REALMS OF LORE: FAE

READING ORDER:

PRINCE OF DARKNESS

HEIRS OF DARKNESS

QUEEN OF LIGHT

SHADOWS OF LIGHT

COURT OF WHISPERS

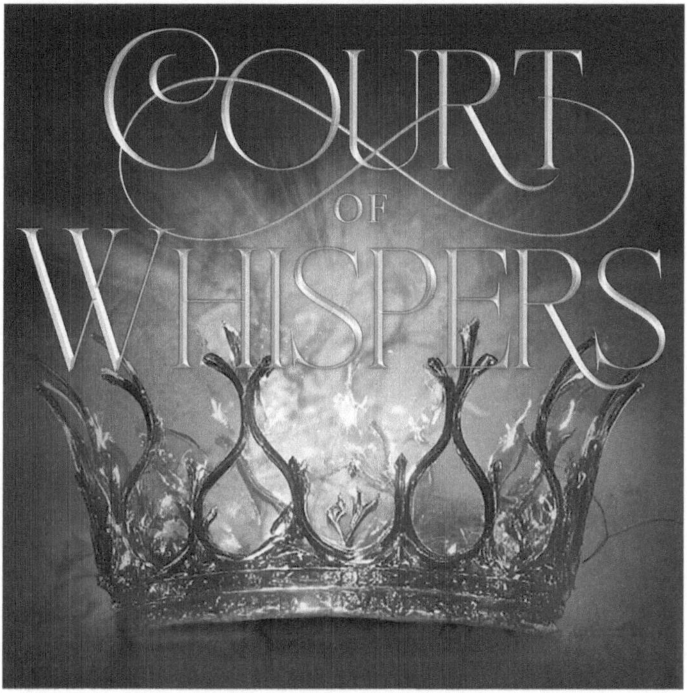

COURT
OF
WHISPERS

Dear Reader,

While Court of Whispers is not as dark as Queen of Light, it does contain heavy topics. As always, please consider your own mental health when starting a new book. I promise there will be laughter in this one, but, per usual, expect some heartbreak. We have one last book after Court of Whispers, so get ready, because here we go!

Welcome back to the realm,

Amber Thoma

This book contains scenes that may depict, mention, or discuss: abduction, abusive relationship, anxiety, assault, blood, death, depression, emotional abuse, fire, hallucinations, murder, physical abuse, PTSD, self-harm, sexual abuse, sexual assault, sexual harassment, slavery, torture, violence, and other mental health issues. Please read at your own discretion.

COURT OF WHISPERS

REALMS OF LORE: FAE

AMBER THOMA

CONTENTS

1. Tatiana 1
2. Lyra 9
3. Ciaran 15
4. Anin 29
5. Etain 37
6. Kes 45
7. Raindal 53
8. Anin 61
9. Panella 69
10. Kes 79
11. Tatiana 85
12. Etain 95
13. Balthier 103
14. Ciaran 111
15. Anin 117
16. Anin 123
17. Tatiana 131
18. Ciaran 141
19. Lyra 153
20. Kes 163
21. Etain 171
22. Balthier 179
23. Anin 185
24. Tatiana 199
25. Balthier 211
26. Kes 221
27. Panella 229
28. Ciaran 237
29. Etain 247
30. Anin 257
31. Tatiana 267
32. Ciaran 273

33.	Kes	285
34.	Etain	299
35.	Lyra	311
36.	Raindal	321
37.	Anin	325
38.	Etain	335
39.	Tatiana	345
40.	Ciaran	355
41.	Lyra	365
42.	Kes	375
43.	Balthier	385
44.	Ciaran	391
45.	Kes	397
46.	Panella	407
47.	Tatiana	413
48.	Lyra	419
49.	Balthier	425
50.	Anin	429
51.	Etain	433
52.	Balthier	441
53.	Kes	447
54.	Raindal	453
55.	Tatiana	459
56.	Ciaran	465
57.	Tatiana	471
58.	Anin	481
59.	Kes	487
60.	Raindal	491
61.	Etain	497
62.	Tatiana	505
63.	Lyra	509
64.	Anin	513
65.	Kes	519
66.	Ciaran	523
67.	Tatiana	529
68.	Panella	535
69.	Anin	541
70.	Balthier	547

71. Kes   551
72. Etain   557
73. Kes   563
74. Ciaran   569
75. Anin   577
76. Panella   585
77. Anin   589
78. Kes   597
79. Raindal   603
80. Ciaran   607
81. Etain   617
82. Leona   627

Acknowledgments   635
About the Author   637
Also By Amber Thoma   639
Also by Amber Thoma   641
Also by Amber Thoma   643
Also by Amber Thoma   645

Chapter 1

Tatiana

Tatiana's rage simmered within her. How dare they betray her? The murmuring of several beings melded into one collective voice. They stared in awe at the disgusting creature in her grasp as they chanted, "Queen of Light!"

"We warned you it would be a mistake to bring her here. Look what you have done," the *whispers* chided. *"What will you do now, Blood Queen?"*

She let the power of her blood magic flood her system and gather strength. She needed more than ever before for something of this magnitude. Control. She had to take back control, and if they could betray her so easily, there was only one way to do so.

"You think *this* shell of a being is your beloved *'Queen of Light'?"* She asked the room before she threw her head back, laughing. She shook Anin with the hand wrapped around her throat for emphasis. The creature had no strength left in her, and when her eyes rolled back,

Tatiana smiled. Yet this was the being they wanted to lead them? She was nothing more than the dirt on Tatiana's shoe.

"I will show you what *real* power is," she said in a quiet, low-tone voice that forced the room to strain to hear her. She watched as the faces of the beings closest to her fell. The ridiculous hopefulness they had trained on Anin shifted to terror as their gazes moved to Tatiana. This made her smile.

She lifted her hand above her head and clenched it, taking control of nearly every being in the throne room. The gesture was not required for her blood magic, but she thought this called for a certain level of theatrics.

She struggled to maintain control and fought to hide her grimace in those first few moments. Many of the powerful fae in the room fought against her hold. Individually, it would not have been difficult, yet together, they posed a challenge. If she had the raw power of a witch feeding her magic, she would never have struggled.

They fought her for a few moments, and then they all were hers. Controlling so many brought her euphoria nearly as potent as the power flooding her veins after a sacrifice.

Almost.

"Yes, feel the power coursing through you. You hold their very lives in the palm of your hand. What will you have them do now?" the *whispers* asked, their echoing voices slithering through her mind.

She thought about it for a breath before the entire room fell to their knees in front of her. She never knew eyes could be so expressive without the control of the muscles around them, but every pair of eyes looked at her in abject horror.

Her gaze slowly shifted to the half-conscious creature that hung boneless in her grasp. She flung her to the ground. Tatiana flicked her hand several times as if she could shake the filth off, along with the female now sprawled on the floor.

"Raindal," she called without looking back, knowing he stood behind her. He was the only other being in the room who had control over their body.

"Yes, my queen?" he asked, stepping forward with his head bowed in deference.

"Take it back to its cage."

"Yes, my queen." He quickly lifted the nymph off the ground and made his way toward the hidden door behind the throne. She listened to his steps retreat as the *whispers'* warning about bringing the nymph to the throne room echoed in her mind.

"Oh, and Raindal?" she called, her voice nauseatingly sweet.

"Yes, my queen?" At least he had learned over the last few decades how to address her properly.

"If you ever suggest such a thing again, you will find yourself on my altar with your throat slit. Do I make myself clear?" The threat clashed with her childlike, sing-song voice, which she had taken to using frequently.

"Yes, my queen."

"Wonderful!" There was a beat of silence before she heard him continue to drag the beast back to her cage, where she belonged.

"He is not to be trusted, Blood Queen." Despite this, she

still refused to think the worst of Raindal. He had been her only companion since the death of her mate, and she was certain he had not meant to suggest something that would end in disaster.

"You silly little creatures," she said, turning her attention back to the Day fae still on their knees. "You would rather have that being—the one responsible for killing your king—sitting on my throne?" She felt their shock reverberate through their minds. "Oh, did you not know? Your king is dead, *murdered* by that worthless creature." She paused and allowed her words to take root.

"Now, what to do with all of you?" she asked in the cadence of the nursery rhymes she learned as a youngling. A flash of something—perhaps a memory? Kind eyes that belonged to a lesser fae female who looked at her with an expression Tatiana was not certain she had ever seen before. Was that what pure love looked like? The female was singing the little rhyme she had just been imitating.

Strange.

This was no memory of hers; she was certain.

She shook her head and cleared it of the distracting vision before she returned her attention to her traitorous subjects. Her fingers traced an invisible path across the faces of each fae she passed until she stopped in front of one of her council members and tapped him on the nose. Leaning down, she peered into his eyes and smiled.

"Silly, you should have known better than to play such a rotten game with your queen." After patting him on the cheek, she stood and continued her stroll, weaving between the stone-like bodies of the Day fae.

"Hmmm, there seems to be only one answer here. You

can each pledge loyalty to me and promise to serve me in whatever way I see fit, or you can go to the dungeons. At least then you can be of use to me in a different way." She stumbled when the will of the strongest fae once again resisted her control. This seemed to encourage them; and they pushed harder, which only enraged Tatiana further.

"You will not win!" she screamed at the room. Despite her control, she could not pinpoint which of the beings had made her look foolish. "None of you are stronger than I am!" Tatiana clenched her fists and squeezed them at her sides as she stomped her feet to emphasize each word she bellowed.

She wanted to break something—she *needed* to destroy something. Tatiana screamed as she ripped hats off the heads of the few fae who wore them. She tore the stupid, ugly things to pieces. After the last one hit the ground, she felt mildly better and plastered on a smile as she continued to skip through the lines of kneeling fae as if nothing had happened.

"Each of you will make a deal with me. I expect you to welcome the chance to bargain with your queen, just as the lesser fae have bargained with you. After all, you are lesser than I am."

She halted abruptly when she came across a rather pretty female. The female's perfect features dissolved the mild peace Tatiana had just found. She glowered at the female. "Do you think you are lovelier than me?" she seethed and leaned down to push her face into that of the beautiful female. "I think we should fix this problem. What do you think?"

The female's head nodded involuntarily, but Tatiana

smiled anyway. "You know what would be fun?" she asked, straightening abruptly to clap her hands together while jumping up and down. "I think we should have an experiment! Let's see what you cannot heal from! Does that sound like great fun to you?" The female's head nodded vigorously as tears streamed down her face.

"Oh, I am so glad you agree!" She placed her hand on the female's shoulder and looked around the room again. "The rest of you, wait here for my return. No one move!" She cackled and slapped her knee as the rest of the room released a strange, breathy laugh she forced from them.

"*You are a foolish queen. Quit playing games,*" the *whispers* admonished. She was tired of their condescension, as if she were not the queen of the Day Court.

"Shut up!" she finally yelled at them. "There's *always* time for fun and games." She realized, belatedly, that she had spoken the words aloud. Tatiana looked around the room and decided it no longer mattered. She did not care what they thought of her anymore and could not be certain she ever had.

Clearing her throat and brushing the invisible filth from her gown, she pasted the smile on once again. She dropped her hand back onto the shoulder of the female who dared to outshine her and then addressed the room one last time. "You will all take this time to consider how lucky you are to have a queen as kind as I am. I am giving you a choice: either go to the dungeons or you can promise me your loyalty."

She smiled down at the female and said, "Now, let's go have some fun." The two disappeared and left hundreds of fae on their knees, trapped in their own bodies.

"Who did you say you were following?" Lyra asked Zandar. Seven of the Silent Shadows-in-training had been tasked with following each head witch without being caught. It had been meant to be an exercise in stealth. She had never thought any of them would come back with tales of porting witches and visits to Day Court temples.

"The head witch of the Mystic Fates Coven. Cordelia, I think her name is. Why are we still sitting here? Let's go get her," he said.

"Calm down, fae-fae. There is likely a valid reason for her actions," Panella said. He rolled his eyes at her. It appeared Zandar was not the biggest fan of his new nickname. Too bad both sisters would never let him forget it.

"A valid reason? She's clearly committing treason!" The wild way he regarded them made it clear that he thought they were crazy.

"You do not understand. Witches do not think of themselves as individuals. We think of ourselves as a collective. The chances of a witch going rogue and committing treason are incredibly slim," Lyra explained. There was no doubt in her mind that Cordelia was completely harmless. A touch scatterbrained? Yes, of course, she always was. However, harmless all the same.

"But not impossible." He crossed his arms and looked down at her. She was not a short witch. If anything, she and Panella were some of the tallest. Yet here Zandar was, staring down at Lyra. It irritated her.

"No, nothing is ever impossible. That does not mean that we need to immediately jump to conclusions and act irrationally. Something you could learn a thing or two about," Lyra said, quirking an eyebrow at him. He could have avoided embarrassment earlier if had practiced a bit of self control and kept his mouth shut. Although, she had to admit, it was incredibly satisfying being able to rile him up so easily.

Begrudgingly, she had to respect him. Many times, when Lyra took a fae down, particularly a male one, they let their pride get to them. It never ceased to amaze her how many of them would sling derogatory things at her afterward. As though their words could somehow erase the fact they were not the big strong fae they thought they pretended to be. Yet Zandar took it in stride. He acted the same way many of those other fae had acted when it had been Kes to leave them flat on their backs.

"I am sure with you as my instructor, little terror, I will learn many things." The smirk he wore as the words spilled from his lips made Lyra's stomach feel strange.

Even worse was the way her hand flitted up to her hair and she nervously patted at the wild blonde curls.

What the fuck?

She scowled at him and heard Panella trying to stifle a chuckle. Opening the link between her and her twin, she let Panella know exactly what she thought about that. Unfortunately, it only made her laugh harder. Straightening her back, she stood as tall as she could and attempted to look as though it were *her* peering down at *him*. It was something she saw Etain, who was much smaller than her, do often enough with Ciaran that she thought she could emulate it.

"Listen here, fae-fa—" Whatever she was about to say next was forgotten when a scroll appeared in front of her face. She opened it and the realm around her came to a standstill. The message was from Kes.

It's time.

That was all it said. There was only one thing it could mean. She jerked her head toward Panella and the two held each other's eyes while they silently communicated. They had both been waiting for this message from the moment they learned that their sister by choice, Anin, had been taken.

"Do you two do that often?" Zandar asked, clearly not understanding the importance of the moment.

"Yes, now we need you to port us to the weapons room immediately," Panella said.

"The weapons room? What's going on?" Lyra did not have the patience to deal with the million questions he would undoubtedly ask. He always had a never-ending stream of them—and opinions—both of which drove Lyra mad.

"Zandar! We do not have time to entertain your curiosity!" She felt a mild pang of regret when his eyes dimmed a little and his jaw clenched tight just before he jerked his head in a nod. She would think about apologizing to him later.

Maybe.

Probably not.

She would rather rip her whole fucking arm off if she were honest.

He put one hand on each of their shoulders, and within a blink, they were standing in the weapons room, looking at Kes, who was smiling from ear to ear. It was a true smile, one she had not seen stretch across his face in over a century. An expression she had not realized, until just then, that she had nearly forgotten what it looked like.

"We have a few minutes to prepare, and then we go get our nymph," Kes said. She had the overwhelming urge to run to the top of Ciaran's tower and scream with joy. A small part of her had begun to think she would never hear those words spill from his lips.

"Where are we going?" Zandar asked, excitement dripping from his every syllable.

"*We* are going to get our sister—his mate. *You* are staying here." His face fell at Lyra's words, but this was no time for her to worry about babysitting anyone. She would never forgive him or herself if he were the cause of them failing to rescue Anin. Failure was no longer an option. Something in her gut told her it was now or it would be never.

"Come on, little terror, I can help." He looked so hopeful, and she was annoyed at herself for the strange feeling in her stomach when he called her "little terror." She told herself she hated the stupid name. Even more so when Kes started laughing.

Just what she needed.

"Little terror, I like it." He laughed even harder when she glared at him.

"That's enough from you, bird," Lyra grumbled. Apparently, everyone else in the room found it highly amusing.

"However, she's right. This is not the time for hands-on learning. I appreciate your willingness to help. The three of us have been planning this for a very long time, and we will not risk anything fucking up our chance." He spoke with a new lightness to his voice and the spark she thought long gone started to flicker back into his eyes.

They had not even gotten Anin back yet; however Kes was already acting as if they had. Worry chewed at the back of her mind when she thought about the state her sister would be in when they finally brought her home. That was something she could worry about tomorrow.

Zandar did not leave, but he did not interject again. He seemed content to watch them plan and Lyra wanted to curse her eyes for the number of times they flicked to where he stood. However, the moment Kes spoke, her attention was solely his.

"Here's the plan."

Chapter 3
Ciaran

Ciaran and master Ulgridge stared in silence at the spot his cousin had been moments before. When Ciaran flicked his eyes back to his old master, he was not surprised to see him gazing into the distance. He was always attuned to the realms around them—if the old fae could be believed.

He would never admit it, but Ciaran was annoyed with himself for not noticing what Kes had picked up after being around Ulgridge for only a few moments. Was he a god? It would explain a lot, such as the sword he carried, which could cut through any magic. Ciaran had searched for such a weapon ever since Ulgridge had cut off his hand to remove the ring that enslaved him, but he had never found one.

If he were a god, the stories he had told Ciaran as a youngling would hold new meaning. No longer mere fairy tales, as he had thought them to be all those years ago, he wished he had paid closer attention.

"You are thinking so loudly, I bet even your cousin might hear your thoughts," the old fae said to Ciaran.

"You can hear thoughts now?" Ciaran was horrified at the possibility and, as always, incredibly jealous whenever he heard of any remarkable power. Ulgridge just laughed, as if he knew exactly where Ciaran's thoughts had gone.

Like he had heard them.

"No, not exactly." Relief coursed through Ciaran. The idea of another hearing his thoughts—except for his mate—was too close to how it felt being controlled by his father all those years ago.

"These missing texts you mentioned—where can I find them? I really do not want to spend another second of my life looking for fucking books," Ciaran practically growled the words out. It was true, though. He felt like his entire life had been spent searching for something, and he was tired of it. He wanted to spend time with his mate, making up for the years they spent apart.

"Sometimes we are fated to do the things we hate or believe ourselves incapable of doing." He still had yet to look at Ciaran and still wore that faraway look as if he were in two places at once.

"Well, fate can be damned." Ciaran did not truly mean the words. Even though he wished he could. He knew deep down that fate was the only reason he had his little witch. Even if fate was responsible for all the misery in his life, he would accept it, as it was also what had brought her to him.

He would always regret the years he spent locked away in his or his father's study, searching for a way to gain ultimate power. Those years were lost to them. No matter how powerful either of them could become, they would never get those years back, and it was entirely his fault. He promised himself he would spend the rest of his life making it up to her.

His mind had not been his own. An intruder had encouraged his spiral into madness. Etain had tried to pull him from the depths of it multiple times. She was the only light in his darkness. Yet when her light could no longer match his darkness and faded, she stopped fighting for him. He knew he had to do it himself or risk losing her forever.

She might have stopped fighting for him, but he knew she never stopped loving him, despite the pain it brought her. Pain he would carry within his heart as a constant reminder of what his selfishness had done to the only being he has ever cared for. The all-consuming love he felt for her was why he never threw his mother's journal into the flames of his hearth.

She had brought it to him and left it for him to read. She had not pleaded with words; however, her eyes—and the pain they held—were louder than any words could have been. He would never admit to anyone, but he had been a coward. He feared what he would learn about his mother within those pages, and rightfully so.

It had been easier to hate her. Easier to believe she was just as awful as his father had been. Now, knowing what he knew, he carried an overwhelming amount of guilt for leaving her to endure his father. Looking at Ulgridge, he could not help but wonder if there was something the old fae could have done for her. Had Ciaran taken his mother with him when he escaped the palace as a youngling, would her presence have influenced him to be a mate worthy of someone as good as Etain?

"It's never helpful to wonder about the past. You cannot go back; you can only move forward." Ciaran wondered what he meant by "not exactly," because it seemed as though he was walking around Ciaran's mind.

"Where are these missing texts?" Ciaran asked, hoping that, for once, the male beside him would give a straight answer. He should have known better.

"You have everything you need to find them," was all Ulgridge said. Ciaran wanted to ask several more questions, but he knew he would only get different versions of the same answer.

Standing, he brushed the dust—of which the cave never had a shortage—off his pants. He looked down at the male that had taken him in when he had nowhere else to go. Without him, there was a good chance he would have still worn the ring, and his father likely would have found him at some point. He owed him his life, and yet the old fae had never called in the debt.

"Thank you for the very detailed answer. It was refreshing." Ciaran rolled his eyes while Ulgridge chuckled. "I better get back to the palace. Apparently, I have more fucking books to find."

"Good luck and farewell," the old fae said. Ciaran paused, and something in the old fae's voice told him this would be the last time he ever saw his mentor.

"Good bye, and… thank you," Ciaran forced the words out. Ulgridge's brows rose in surprise. "For everything." They held each other's gaze for a moment before Ulgridge nodded his head once in acknowledgment. With nothing more to say, Ciaran ported to the palace, and the shadowy expanse of Ulgridge's domain gave way to the inviting, cluttered comfort of Etain's study.

"Ciaran," Etain said while clutching a now-empty vial to her chest, before bending to clean up the substance she had spilled with his sudden appearance. "You would think I would be used to it by now," she mumbled under her breath.

He grinned to himself before appearing behind her as she stood, with the speed only he had, to whisper into her ear, "I hope you never do." When she yelped and jumped again, he laughed.

"You better not be here just to distract me," she admonished him while swatting at his chest. He loved the way her mouth twitched as she tried to hold back her smile while attempting to scold him.

"What if I am, little witch?" His voice was low and promised a particular form of distraction. The bright red flush that enveloped her face and chest was a sight he would never grow tired of.

"Hmm, well then, I would have to tell you to come back later because I now have to start over," she said, gesturing to the floor where she had just cleaned and the empty vial now lying on the table before her. It was the same table he had insisted on taking with them from her little home in that disgusting human village she had once lived in.

"Then I suppose it's lucky that I did not come here to distract you," he said, caging her between his arms against the table. "I took Kes to meet an old friend, and he gave us some interesting information."

"Oh?" she asked, looking all the way up at him. She was so small and yet a larger force than many of the beings in the realm. She did not need him to protect her, and yet, he always would—no matter the cost. "Since when do you have anyone you refer to as an 'old friend?'"

"What else would I call the fae who severed the hold my father had on me as a youngling?" He regretted his words the moment he saw her face fall, and she brought her hand to his heart. He had meant for them to be light, if not comical. However, his little witch's heart was too large. Any reminder of the horrors he endured as a youngling always made her mourn for the much younger version of himself.

She nodded before she asked, "And what did he have to say?" She smiled, even while her eyes remained glassy. He brought one of his hands to her face and tucked an errant hair behind her ear as she leaned into his touch. He picked her up and placed her on a cleared section of the table, making them closer to eye to eye.

Gods, he loved her eyes. He could watch the way the gold flecks within them shifted for nights and never get bored. There was not a thing about her he did not love and he had nearly ruined everything. One side of her mouth curved up after several moments had gone by without him uttering a word as he drank her in with his eyes.

"Ciaran?" she asked, the lightness returning to her voice. He grinned his too wide grin at her and ripped his eyes away from hers so that he could remember what she had asked.

"He was rather cryptic, of course, but he mentioned

there being a collection of elemental books that went missing generations ago. There was even one for shadows. I have never heard of another who had shadows until I read my mother's journal; it had apparently been common enough at one point to have an entire book written about it." He wanted that book and the knowledge it contained. More than that, he wanted it before anyone else found it and could use it against him.

"Naturally," Ciaran continued, "he could not—or more likely would not—tell me where they were. Yet I know he would never have mentioned them if he had not intended for me to find them."

"Wait," Etain said, scrunching her brows and tilting her head to one side. "I think I am missing quite a bit of information. Why were you there to begin with? You are not the type of being who would speak to another without a reason, let alone visit."

She was right, of course. "Panella found it, what we have all been looking f—"

"Ciaran!" she yelled, with wide eyes that filled with anger. "You should have told me immediately, not run off to the mountains looking for books." Her eyes strained around the edges while her voice shook ever so slightly. He had hurt her by not coming to her first.

"Little witch, I took Kes to see him because we also made a discovery that I was certain pertained to his ridiculous quest that many faced b—" he cut the word off and rolled his eyes when she glared at him. "Anyway, he did, in fact, have the information Kes was looking for. I am assuming he is on his way now or preparing to fetch his nymph at any moment. This time he should succeed."

"I cannot believe you came to tell me about books over everything else. I need to go find Panella." She started to slide off the table.

"Wait," he said, grabbing her hands, attempting to pause her movements. "It requires a spell that she has not located yet and a drop of Anin's blood. Nothing can happen until they return. I am sorry I did not tell you first. I saw the connection for Kes and knew that everything else did not matter if he did not discover what it was the b… *goddess* required."

That seemed to quell some of the rage simmering within Etain at his oversight. Her face softened ever so slightly, and he squeezed her hands gently before he admitted, "I am horrible at this, little witch, but I am trying." Her face melted. All anger seeped away, and she squeezed his hands back.

"I know you are," she whispered. "What about these books, then?"

"I do not know. He said I had everything I needed to find them. Whatever that means."

"Perhaps he meant the books were hidden in the underground archive. Or at the very least, you can find the means of locating them."

"Another book to search for," he said with a sigh. "I grow tired of searching for things. First it was the curse, then it was the blood magic, and now it's the elemental tomes. Is it asking too much for just one thing to be simple to find?"

"All the best things are never simple." She looked at him with those gold-flecked eyes that were filled with so much love it nearly stole his breath. He did not deserve her or her love; however, he did not care. She was his, and he would never let her go. He would always be selfish with her.

"No, they are not." Silence hung between them while they each got lost in the other's eyes. Hers flicked to his lips, and he gave her one of his wicked, toothy smirks. He leaned forward and placed a hand next to each side of her again before dropping his mouth next to her ear and whispering, "Maybe I came here to distract you after all."

He watched in smug satisfaction as her skin prickled and flushed the bright red he loved so much. She let out a quick intake of breath, and her heart rate increased as he dragged his lips over the shell of her ear. Her hands fisted into his shirt, and she pulled him closer just as their mouths met.

Their kiss started slowly, each of them savoring the other. He would never tire of the taste of her, the softness every inch of her held. It did not take more than a few moments for their movements to become eager, demanding more from the other.

Hands pulled at clothing, desperate to remove the barrier between them. Etain growled as she struggled with the tie on his shirt, which only made him laugh. She pulled back to glare at him. "Such a needy little witch."

"Ciaran?"

"Yes, little witch?"

"I think you have a better use for your mouth. So stop talking and put it to good use," she said, giving him her own wicked smirk. He did not think it was possible to crave her any more than he already did. Yet as the fear and embarrassment of demanding what she wanted from him dissipated over the years, his desire only grew.

He slowly fell to his knees as he pushed her skirts up. The table put her at the perfect height for him to devour her. With a gentle touch, he grabbed one of her legs and kissed a trail from her ankle to her knee until he could drape the limb over his shoulder and gave the other leg the same treatment. Her little whimpers only made him go slower.

"Ciaran," she gasped out.

"Yes, little witch?"

"Please, I need you." He loved when those words spilled from her lips.

"Oh, little witch, I am only doing what you demanded." He smiled against her inner thigh when she began to complain. The sound morphed into a moan when his tongue slid into her folds. He flicked it over the place she desired his touch most, and her hips flew off the table. He wrapped his arms around her waist and pinned her in place.

He took his time consuming her, savoring each sound that he pulled from her. Etain's nails scraped across his scalp as she gripped his hair when he slid two fingers into her. When he curved them and sucked her in at the same time, she screamed.

He had mapped every inch of her body and knew it better than he knew his own. He knew how to make her soar over the edge, but he wanted to keep her descent just out of reach until she could take it no longer.

She pleaded with him to end her torment in strings of intelligible words. He stood up and flipped her on to her knees before he freed himself and thrust into her before she knew what was happening. The moment he applied pressure to her sensitive nub, she exploded around his cock, gripping him so tightly he thought he might embarrass himself.

"Such a good little witch. How many more do you think you have in you?" He pulled out and thrust fully back into her with his words. She whimpered something else he could not decipher, which only made his ego larger—a feat no one thought possible.

This time, when she came to the top of her pleasure, he let her tip over into oblivion, only to bring her right back up to her peak. He would not last much longer. Each time she flew over the edge, he came too close to his own. He picked up his pace, driving into her harder with each thrust, making the table inch away from him each time.

She screamed out her final release, and he filled her with his own. She collapsed, and he rested his forehead on her still-clothed back. Neither of them moved for several moments, each trying to catch their breath.

When they finally sat up, he grimaced when he saw how many of her containers had fallen off the table and spilled onto the floor. She did not seem to care and only glanced at it while she righted her dress, and he helped her down from the table.

"I have decided you can come and distract me anytime you wish," she said, smiling at him with a gleam in her eyes he enjoyed far too much. He threw his head back and laughed.

"As you wish, little witch," he said, crouching to help her clean up the spilled herbs. "Etain?"

"Yes, my love?"

"Can you ask your goddess where these gods-damned books are and spare me from yet another search? I do not have the time to do so. I have a witch to distract as often as possible." She shook her head at him as she laughed.

"Yes, but you should know she will never tell me anything outright. It's not her way." He assumed as much would be true. She never gave anyone a straight answer, it seemed—not even one of her own.

That many faced bitch.

With each step closer to her cage, her confidence faltered. Anin was desperate to hold on to the powerful feeling that had flooded her moments ago. The fear that a spelled metal box could elicit was embarrassing.

She feared her cage more than she feared her sister's wrath. Pain reminded her she was alive, while spending days locked in the tiny box and unable to move, did the opposite. It took everything in her not to beg the male that dragged her closer to her prison to release her.

When the long hall, which held only her damp stone room and the cage within it, appeared, she could do nothing to stop her body from quaking. The bloody footprints she had left behind on the way to the throne room had dried. She wondered if that would be the only evidence to prove that she had once left her cell. She knew her sister would never make the same mistake again and let her leave the damp little room filled with rows of decaying wings. While she might be losing her mind, she was not too far gone to not have learned from her mistake.

The door to her own personal hell was before them faster than she thought possible, and her vision darkened around the edges. Her head swam, and somehow she felt both hot and cold at the same time.

Raindal threw the door open and pulled her inside. Had she been clear of mind, his gentle handling would have shocked her. Had she been able to think of anything beyond the dread that the golden cage in front of her inspired, she might have heard everything he said.

"—be ready." It was all that managed to seep past the sound of rushing water in her ears. The only thing she thought he was telling her to prepare for was a visit from her sister later. Little did he know she preferred those moments over the long stretches in between. It was the truth, and it disgusted her. How pitiful must she be?

Those visits would provide the only opportunity for her to escape. It would be a long shot at best. She was not delusional enough to believe she would actually get away, but she would be ready, nonetheless. It was not like she had anything else to do.

She tried, she truly did, yet her mouth still opened, and a whispered plea came out.

"Please, no."

If Raindal said anything, the roaring prevented her from hearing it, and she refused to look at him. Every time she saw his face, memories of the pain he had caused her flashed across her mind. She could not handle the looming cage and the memories all at once.

She flinched when he reached out to touch her. She

was not sure when he had let go of her arm. He tapped her shoulder with a single finger, and then she was back in the cage. Watching his back as he walked out the door, she pleaded with herself to hold back her tears until he was far enough away. She did not want to give him the satisfaction of her sorrow.

Has the cage gotten smaller?

She could swear it was smaller. Was it still getting smaller? What if it crushed her? What if it shrank so small that it cut her into pieces tiny enough to fit through the grate of the cage?

A sob escaped, and she could hear nothing beyond the blood rushing through her veins and her thundering heartbeat. There was no way to know if Raindal had disappeared down the hall far enough for him not to hear her. Not without hearing his retreating footfalls. When her thoughts spiraled into horrific scenarios, one after the other, there was no controlling her emotions.

Oh gods, what if she spent another hundred years locked in this box? Two hundred? Just moments ago, she had felt so powerful, and now she felt hopeless.

Was it worse that she had felt the sun on her face again? She had forgotten what it felt like; she thought it would be harder to forget this time. The warmth had chased away the deep chill from her bones, and she felt truly warm for the first time in over a hundred years.

One hundred thirty-seven...

One hundred thirty-seven...

One hundred thirty- seven years.

Anin could not stop replaying the number of years stolen from her in her mind. While she had known a decent amount of time had passed, she had thought half that at most. What had she missed in the last century? What would she miss in the next?

Would Kes keep trying, or would he give up and try to move on? Maybe he could have some kind of life without her. It was not as though she was going to die anytime soon. Or perhaps the Land would finally give up on her and release Anin from this life. She was not sure what hurt more: the thought of Kes dying or the fact she knew she would choose death over another hundred thirty-seven years locked away. Even knowing it would mean the end for Kes as well.

She was selfish. What kind of mate would choose death, knowing it would kill the being fate had chosen just for them? A fated mate was uncommon. It was a gift given to a small amount of fae in every generation. She had never expected to be one of the fae chosen. Honestly, she had thought it a joke when she saw Kes for the first time. There had been no mistaking what she was feeling.

Her mother had died from a mate bond. It had been slow and painful, and the only thing Anin could do was watch. She knew firsthand what happened to the living mate when the other died. Still, she would choose that death for Kes. Given the choice between another hundred years in the cage or death for both of them, she would choose death every time.

It was something Anin had thought about several times over the past... she was not sure how long. It could have been decades or a couple of years for all she knew. Before today, she would have chosen for Kes to live, no matter the price she had to pay. All it had taken was standing tall in the sun and walking on her own to know she could not do it again. She could not survive another hundred years like this. The Land might insist her body continue to live, but everything that made her who she was would die.

Kes had done his best to keep her tethered to herself. Their unique way of conversing was likely the only reason she had been able to make her stand earlier. He had kept her mind sharp with his banter, even if they knew both of them were performing for the other. She could feel the way her absence was affecting him. If he had to live another hundred years like this, she thought it was likely he too would choose death. If he died, would she then finally die too?

She hoped her sisters had finally moved on. If Anin found out they had put their lives on hold for her, it would be another thing she would hate herself for. They both deserved a life full of happiness, not being haunted by the memory of a long-lost sister.

Gods, she missed them all. The few nights Anin had spent with her mate had imprinted deeply on her memory. She could almost recall the way his feathers had felt as she helped remove the damaged ones. She could almost recall his scent and the sound of his voice. She could almost recall the incessant pull toward him that only got stronger the closer they were. Now, that pull had become more of an echo of what it once was.

There had barely been a chance to get to know Etain and yet she was certain fate had destined them to be friends. There had been an instant connection, one she had not even had with her sisters. Anin had always thought that fate could give you three great loves. The love for a mate, a youngling, and the friend that carries the other half of your soul. She often wondered if Etain had been that friend meant for her.

It seemed cruel that fate would give her so much—a mate, a family, and a friend of the soul—only to make this existence her fate as well. Perhaps this was her penance for a wrong she committed in a previous life. Punishment or a cruel twist of fate did not matter; this was simply too much for any one being to endure.

She would not. She refused—a message from Kes interrupted her spiraling thoughts. One she had received before, but never with so much certainty behind it. She tried not to hope. To do so was a dangerous game. Yet, she hoped.

"I am coming for you."

E tain read and reread the passage that Panella had found in the archives about the bloodstones and their potential to protect against blood magic. There was not much to go off of, but she was determined to figure it out. Everyone had been working tirelessly all these years looking for a break just like this, and Etain was not about to let it slip through their fingers.

Most of it was straightforward. They needed either Tatiana's or Anin's blood. According to Ciaran, her friend should be home soon, if she wasn't already. She knew she would not see Anin for a while, let alone obtain a sample of her blood. Regardless of how long Anin needed, Etain would be ready.

They had a plethora of bloodstones that had been stored away in the hidden room. Most of them were now scattered across it by Kes. Apparently, he and Ciaran had gone in there together, and moments later that Panella heard screaming and the sound of metal being thrown. Everyone in the archives had fled to give them privacy. Etain thought it likely they all feared being in either of their warpaths.

Etain could only imagine what Ciaran had said to set Kes off. She knew that was what must have happened. Although her mate had been behaving better since pulling himself out of the dark place he had been sinking into, he was still Ciaran, and finesse was not something he possessed when handling others' emotions. She was the exception, believing it was because he could feel exactly what she felt.

With Anin's blood and the bloodstones, all they needed was the spell mentioned in the passage. She had considered it extensively, reading the surrounding pages several times without finding anything. Finally, she consulted her great aunt, and they spent the last few hours discussing the possible origins of the spell.

"Galetia, what if…" she trailed off, uncertain whether she was about to ask a ridiculous question.

"What if what, my dear?" Her great aunt, an incredibly patient witch, provided everyone the space to speak whatever their minds were reluctant to release in their own time. Several heartbeats of silence passed as Etain thought it through one last time.

"If we cannot find this spell, do you think it's possible to create a similar one? It would be dangerous to test, but it might be the only solution. We do not have the luxury of time to wait for the spell to reveal itself."

Galetia sat silently, contemplating Etain's idea. She considered the logistics in her mind. "I think it's possible.

All things are possible. The only problem is understanding the base of the spell. Blood magic is uncharted territory. Perhaps if we could find even a hint of what the spell was, we could concoct our own."

Etain had not expected there to be even a shred of hope that they could devise their own spell. Although the task seemed daunting, it provided them with another possible path. They could either find the original spell, which was preferred, or create a new one.

She slumped back into the chair next to her aunt. She had recently taken to pacing her study in Witch City while reading, and now felt exhausted. Could anything be even slightly simple or easy? Ciaran had just asked the same question. While she would happily accept the smallest sliver of ease, she knew it was all in fate's hands. If fate wanted it to be easy, she would make it so.

Sighing, she hung her head in her hands. She needed to take a break. The pressure of finding the final key to their protection hung heavy around her neck. Her aunt rubbed her back in small soothing circles, easing some tension. Etain sat back up and stretched, feeling even lighter when her spine gave her a delicious crack.

"Let's give our minds some time to interpret what we've discussed. In the meantime, how about we work on what we know we can create?" Etain suggested.

She had informed her great aunt as soon as she arrived that Anin would be home soon if everything went as planned. After the initial joy and excitement, they discussed the likely condition Anin would be in upon her return. After witnessing her mate struggle with his own mental battles, she wished there was something she could do for her friend.

"I think we can," Galetia had said. However, the conversation quickly shifted to the bloodstones and the missing spell needed to activate them. Now Etain needed something else to focus on. Engaging in a task, rather than merely contemplating it, would provide her with the boost she needed. Sometimes, accomplishing a task can make other challenges seem less daunting.

"There are a few potions that, if we combine certain parts and find the right spell to join them, might help us create something to assist Anin's mind for as long as she needs it," Galetia said, rising and retrieving several books from the shelves around the room, and pulling even more from thin air.

Etain had been in the Fae Realm for nearly one and a half centuries, and she still thought being able to tie things to you was the best part of it. Having anything she might need at hand anywhere, and at any time, was ridiculously helpful. She herself used it at least once per night.

The two witches spent the next several hours selecting which parts of various potions and spells they would combine. There were a few instances where they both had forgotten mixing certain things could have… problematic reactions.

It was during one of these incidents, Ciaran returned to her study just in time for a mini explosion that splattered an orange gelatinous substance across Etain's and Galetia's faces. He threw his head back and roared with laughter. She did not care that goo dripped from her.

Time seemed to slow as she watched her mate and committed the image to memory.

She could recall only one other time when he had laughed so freely. It had been right after Kes and Anin recounted the events leading to the death of the Day King. Etain had been slightly appalled that they were laughing about the death of a living being. However, the fact the Day King tried to kidnap Anin and had been the Shepherd that played a part in making her life miserable for so long, she had been able to look the other way.

Ciaran transformed when he laughed so freely. His eyes squeezed shut, and his mouth, already unnaturally wide, opened nearly all the way, showing off his long, sharp incisors. The casual way he stood clutching at his stomach while his whole body shook with mirth highlighted the intensity of his normal stiff and emotionless persona. Only Etain got to see a different side of her mate.

When his laughter finally subsided, time seemed to snap back to normal, breaking the spell she had been under. She became aware again of the globs of orange goop dripping from her. One glance at Galetia and Etain started laughing just as hard as Ciaran had. Her great aunt was covered in the substance and tried to stifle her laughter, likely to avoid getting any in her mouth.

Galetia excused herself to the bathing chamber, and Ciaran pulled a square cloth from his pocket, beginning to wipe her face clean. It was remarkable how tender he could be with her. Everyone else got the razor sharp version of him while she got a softer one. The Ciaran who cradled her chin in his hand and gently wiped a cloth across her goo-speckled face. Every night she fell more in love with him, and she would be lying if she said she did not also love the fact that he was only this way with her.

"Little witch, I think you might have made a misstep in your," he paused to gesture at the mess on the table, "witch things." She snorted a laugh through her nose. Her eyes widened, and she quickly covered her nose with her hand, inadvertently smashing some of the remaining substance and making his extra wide smile return.

"'*Witch things,*' how eloquent of you," Etain said, giggling slightly as he wiped the last bit of her face clean before handing the cloth to her to clean her hand. "And yes, we definitely made a 'misstep.' Luckily, everything is completely harmless—just messy." She then told him what they were trying to do for Anin and how she wished she had thought of it for him.

He scoffed. "I doubt I would have taken it, anyway." She squinted at him and flattened her mouth, prompting him to quickly amend his statement. "But if anyone could have gotten me to, it would have been you." Etain rolled her eyes while trying to suppress a smile.

She let out a deep sigh as she took in the mess of their failed experiment covering the table. They would have to start over. She had hoped to have at least this potion sorted that night. Yet, it seemed as though everything eluded her, at least for the moment.

"What's on your mind, little witch?" he asked, gently grabbing her chin once again, this time to bring her eyes to his. She cursed the tears that clouded her vision and did her best to keep them from falling.

"I fear I might not find what we need. Not only do I not want to let everyone down, but I refuse to allow anyone else the opportunity to wield that kind of power over you, as your father did. I hate that you have to wear this again," she said, grabbing his hand with the finger wrapped in the bright white metal ring.

"There is a glaringly obvious difference between the two times I have worn this ring. The first time made me a slave to my father, while this time not only was it my choice, but it also sets my mind at ease knowing I can never go too far and lose you. Losing you would be worse than reliving the years under my father's control."

"Ciaran," she said softly, holding his hand in both of hers before bringing it to her heart. She opened her mouth to respond, but before she could say anything, she heard the sound of books falling to the ground, along with her great aunt's surprised shriek.

"I am so sorry," she said as she picked up the stack of books to return them to the side table next to the chairs where they had been sitting earlier. "I came out from cleaning myself up, and it looked as though you both could use some privacy, so I came to see mys—" she stopped mid-sentence, cocking her head to the side as she stared at a book that had fallen open when it landed on the ground.

"Galetia? Are you all right?" Etain asked.

"I think… I think I might have found something." She looked up to meet Etain's surprised expression with her own and smiled.

Perhaps fate had decided to make things a little easier after all.

It was time.

It was long past time.

Panella and Lyra trailed Kes, silently navigating the halls. Over the years, this path had etched itself into their memories; each of them could now traverse it blindfolded if necessary.

"What if the spell is not broken?" Panella whispered the question they all were silently asking themselves. It was, as always, the one thing that could go wrong. A spell placed on the final hallway caused anyone who stepped foot past its threshold to hemorrhage blood. If it had not been for the fucking spell, Anin would have been home over a century ago.

"It will be." Kes had to believe his words were true. He was not leaving without her. Panella opened her mouth to speak again, but whatever Lyra conveyed through their twin bond made her abruptly shut it.

He could not explain it, but this time felt different.

There was no question Anin was coming home. He was getting her out of there that night. Spell or no spell. He already had to place more faith in the rebel leader than he liked. Yet, there he was, trusting a being whose face he had never seen.

His heart thundered in his ears, the sound so loud that he feared it might alert a Day fae to their presence. Although Daybreak Palace was not known for its reliable security, it was still unusual to get as far as they had without seeing a single golden guard. This gave Kes a bit more confidence in the rebel leader.

They held their breath as they approached the final hall. None of them had ever made it more than ten feet without retreating before death claimed them. They said nothing and instead exchanged nervous glances as Kes took a step over the threshold and paused. Nothing happened. He sighed with relief and grinned at the twins.

"Told you," he said to Panella, who returned his grin with a watery smile. "Panella, stay here and keep an eye out. Do that creepy twin thing if you see anyone coming."

She huffed a laugh under her breath and waved them on before mumbling, *"creepy twin thing"* while shaking her head. Kes and Lyra turned toward the single door at the end of the long hall. Over the years he had stared at the door for hours, knowing that behind it, Anin waited for him.

He was suddenly nervous. He knew better than anyone that she was not okay, even if she was physically fine. The scars she bore from her time in the Day Court would not be visible to the eye.

"When we get to the door," Kes said quietly to Lyra as

they hurried down the hall, noticing a trail of dried, bloody footprints as they drew closer. "Stay out here and keep watch, just in case." He did not know what horrors waited for him behind that door. He wanted not only to spare Lyra from seeing any of it but also to avoid overwhelming Anin.

Anin.

He was closer to her than he had been since the night of Ciaran and Etain's coronation and mating ceremony. He was so close that his palms itched to touch her. Once he had her in his arms, he did not think he would ever let her go again.

When he turned the knob, he was surprised to find it unlocked. Was it always left like that? He guessed there was no need for a lock when the hall would kill anyone before they reached the door. Or perhaps it was another gift from the rebel leader. Either way, he was grateful for one less barrier between them.

His palms were slick on the metal knob, making it harder to twist. He locked eyes with Lyra, who gave him a quick nod. If she wanted to argue about being left out in the hall, she had the good sense not to. The twins knew her better than anyone, including him, and likely understood she would need space.

With a deep breath, he gripped the knob firmly in his slick palm and twisted it. As soon as the latch released, he was slow to push the door open, fearing he might startle her. From the moment it cracked open, the room's stench assaulted him.

Anin had no choice but to breathe the rank air. Therefore, he would not show any outward discomfort that might make her feel insecure. As he pushed his way into the room, he had to force himself not to growl. He did not want to frighten her.

Two panels of grated metal squeezed her between them, leaving her unable to move even the slightest bit. She appeared caked with filth. He doubted the bitch queen had allowed her to bathe even once in the last one hundred thirty-seven years. If her thin frame—nothing more than skin stretched across bones—was anything to go by, it was clear she had not received even the most basic of needs.

His vision blurred, and it took him a moment to deal with the fat tears heavy with guilt falling from his eyes. It was far worse than he could have imagined; she had never let him see the true extent of the torture she had endured.

He had been so focused on her that he had not given their surroundings even a cursory glance. When he did, he stopped dead in his tracks. Wings. Anin's wings covered nearly every inch of the walls, from floor to ceiling, each in various states of decay. There was a pair that looked like nothing more than a dried husk. They had obviously been the first of many.

The sound of a quiet, raspy sob came from the center of the room. Kes's eyes snapped back to the cage to find the two beautiful black orbs of his mate's eyes staring at him. It took every ounce of effort he had to control the rage boiling inside him and hide it away. She needed tenderness, and that was exactly what he would give her.

"Are you real?" she asked, her voice no more than a whisper.

"Last time I checked," he said, flashing her one of his

wicked grins. She gave him a small smile, tired and nearly empty of all humor, but at least it was a smile.

"You certainly sound real," she said. Her tone had been light, playful even, in an attempt at the banter that had become their preferred means of communication.

"What do you say, my darling nymph? Are you ready to get out of here, or do you need another minute?" She wheezed out a laugh that turned into a sob. The sound ripped at his heart. She needed him. He spent far too long looking for the lock on the box that did not exist.

"It's spelled. I do not think you can open it," she said, sounding devastated. Clearly, she did not believe she was getting out of here. He doubted she would until they were long gone—maybe not even then.

He reached into his pocket and pulled out a small pouch. "Your sister, Panella, made this powder for me decades ago. Just in case we could ever get to you, we wanted to be prepared for anything," he told her as he sprinkled the powder on one seam of the cage. The powder hissed, and seconds later, the bottom swung open. He caught her long before she could come close to hitting the ground.

"Kes," her lip trembled as she said his name. "I'm filthy. You should not touch me." She attempted to push him away. In her weakened state, it would surprise him if she could stand, even though he had felt her pull on his power only mere hours ago.

He had always been quick to give her whatever power she needed. It had happened so frequently while they were apart that he barely noticed the pull on his well anymore. Even taking in as much of her pain as he could became second nature.

"Silly nymph, you must be mistaken. I think you are the most beautiful being I have ever laid my eyes on, and as we all know, I am never wrong." She gave a breathy laugh as tears created fresh tracks along her cheeks. The little laugh quickly returned to sobs. She buried her face in his chest as her whole body shook and she fell apart in his arms.

He took one last look around the small, damp space she had called home for far too long. He wanted to count the wings on the wall but settled for burning the image into his mind for eternity. There would never come a moment when he would let himself forget the hell he had allowed his mate to endure for so long.

Her sisters would want to at least see her after so long. However, they did not need to see the extent of her trauma, and he doubted Anin would want them to. Lyra made eye contact with him the second he cleared the door, careful not to open it further and reveal the horrific scene beyond.

Her eyes drifted to Anin, and she struggled to look away from her long-lost sister. When she finally looked back at him, he gave her a subtle shake of his head. Now was not the time for words—not here, and not when they could hear her soft sobs muffled by his chest. Lyra nodded and turned around, leading them back the way they had come.

While he was not sure how he would ever forgive himself for her suffering, he was positive he would never let anyone force her into that room or anything like it again. He made a silent vow to himself and Anin as he adjusted her in his arms and shielded her slightly with his wings.

He was going to kill that bitch queen.

Chapter 7
Raindal

He needed to see his mate one last time. It would not take long for Tatiana to find the room with her sister still locked in a tiny cage, now empty. Raindal had stood in the shadows and watched as the bird gently carried his mate out of her prison, shielding her from view with his wings. He hoped it would be worth it in the end.

While Anin was free, Raindal was certain his own freedom was going to be short-lived. He had been the one to make her step into the hall with her bloody footprints and had been the last to see her in the palace. Convincing Tatiana that he could not have known the nymphs' blood would break the spell she placed on the hall a century ago would be easy enough.

Yet he had.

Raindal listened and observed everything. Nothing happened in the palace that he did not know about. If he could not personally witness it, one of the lesser fae rebels he had placed in key locations would be his eyes and ears. They reported the queen's movements in real time while he wove his deception throughout the palace ranks of high fae. When Tatiana slept was when Raindal took the greatest risk and looked through The Book of Blood.

It had been impossible to read—the dialect was ancient. Luckily, Tatiana did not know that a witch resided within the city. She had never made herself known to many, and rightly so. He never knew exactly how—perhaps fate—but she heard about the rebellion and joined right when they needed her most.

She had no trouble reading the text. Witches, as it turns out, can read any dialect their ancestors knew. She said something about the knowledge being stored in their blood. It sounded ludicrous to him, but if he had learned anything after a century of being forced to endure Tatiana, it was that blood can do some ludicrous things.

It was dangerous to keep the book away from Tatiana for too long, and he knew he had fate to thank for never being caught. When she had kept it in its strange stone drawer in the temple, borrowing it had been simple. It became much harder when she began carrying it with her everywhere. He had only been able to take it when she disappeared into her mind, locked in some sort of stasis. This had slowed the witch down considerably.

It was only in the last couple of weeks, when everything had begun to come together, that she found the spell Tatiana had placed on the hall. Almost as if fate had orchestrated the whole thing—which she likely had.

The witch never shared her name with him, and after she found the spell he needed, Raindal never saw her again. She disappeared completely from the city, leaving no trace behind. As though she had never been there to begin with.

Something about her made her seem much more than just a witch. He had never pinpointed exactly what made him think that. Yet there was something unsettling that made the hair on his neck stand on end whenever he was around her. That might have had something to do with her jet-black hair, pale-white skin, and glowing golden-red eyes. She looked nothing like any other witch he had ever seen, though he had seen few.

Although he could easily explain away the spell on the hall, the empty cage would be another story. There were too many coincidences in one day. Not even Tatiana, with her broken mind, would be convinced it had not all been contrived. There would be a reckoning. He only hoped it did not end with him dead and Balthier left to the same fate not long after.

He waited for his mate to join him at their usual meeting place and prayed to all the gods that it would not be the last time. They had discussed the likelihood of something like this happening. Yet, somehow, it had never seemed like a real possibility. At least it had not then, but time has a way of changing everything.

They were on borrowed time. He had one of his spies watching the queen's movements and instructed them to send a scroll the moment Tatiana looked for him, or if she left the palace. With the queen, anything was possible and always unpredictable.

It had not been wise to sneak away right after the true queen escaped. If he had any sense, he would have returned to her side immediately after placing Anin back in her cage. However, when it came to his mate, there was never really a choice.

"What is it?" Balthier asked as soon as he stepped into the room and set his eyes on Raindal.

"I just needed to see you. I might be… unavailable for a while. The true queen has escaped." Balthier sucked in a breath through his teeth as they stared at each other from across the room. Raindal watched as his mate's face paled and he blinked rapidly, attempting to clear the tears pooling in his eyes.

"Why even go back? Stay here with me." It was the closest Balthier would ever get to begging him, and Raindal wanted nothing more than to do just that.

"You do not think she would find me here or that a high fae in the Dayless Quarter would not be noticeable to any of her minions?"

"But—"

"If I stay, it will mean our assured destruction. If I go, there is still a chance that we might make it out of this alive. As I've said before, I will always choose the ending where we have the greatest chance of truly being together." Everything he had done throughout their relationship had been building toward one of two endings—death or a life out in the open with his mate. There was no other option, no matter how much Balthier tried to convince him otherwise.

"And if you die?" The question was barely a whisper. He had not noticed how they had been slowly gravitating toward each other until his mate stood directly in front of him.

"Then I will beg fate to bring us together in the next life," Raindal said, as he grabbed his mate's hands to bring the knuckles of each one to his mouth to kiss.

"You would risk my death?" It was the question he had always refused to answer in the past, but now he felt he owed Balthier an answer.

"I would, and I do not do so lightly. A half-life without you or hiding my love for you is not a life worth living. I hope you agree, and if not, at least forgive me." A tear streaked down Balthier's face. This was typically the part when his mate's rage surfaced, and he stormed away without so much as a glance back.

Balthier made no move to push Raindal away, nor did he glance at the exit. It was clear that the moment was important, and they felt the weight of Raindal's actions coming to a head. Neither would admit it, but they both knew this was likely goodbye. If they were lucky, it would not be forever.

He brushed his fingers across the soft fur of Balthier's skin, attempting to memorize him. Raindal never wanted to forget the way his mate felt, like velvet. He danced his fingers up to his face and traced its planes while brushing away the few slow-rolling tears.

"No matter what happens, I am glad it was you sitting at the table looking down on all of us," Balthier said, attempting humor, but the tremor in his voice betrayed him.

"As am I. I was yours the moment that mouth of yours

started running away," Raindal said, brushing his fingers across Balthier's lips and begging his mind to never forget the curves of his mate's mouth, no matter how long they might be forced apart.

"What am I su—" A spelled scroll appeared between them, effectively cutting off whatever Balthier had been about to say.

The message was urgent, coming from one of his spies. The queen had disappeared from the throne room several moments ago. She had taken one of the high fae with her and left the rest on their knees. There was no sign of her anywhere in the palace, and therefore, there was no knowing when she would appear again.

If Raindal had to guess, he suspected he could find her at the temple. If that were the case, he had anywhere from minutes to hours before she looked for him, unless she got herself worked up and... *needed* him. The thought alone made him sick.

"What does it say?"

"That I must go. Circumstances are unknown, and I must tread very carefully if we are to survive."

"Okay," Balthier said with a stifled sob.

"I will come for you as soon as I am able. This is not the end of our story. I refuse to believe anything else." Raindal put his forehead to Balthier's, and they stood there in silence, holding each other. He took a few more moments to commit his scent to memory.

"I love you," was the last thing he said.

Raindal leaned forward and kissed his mate, pleading again to every god he knew that it would not be their last.

Finally, Raindal stepped away and brushed one last tear from his mate's perfect face before porting back to the palace.

He placed all his faith in fate, even though he knew she was nothing if not fickle.

Chapter 8
Anin

The world outside her cage was overwhelming; everything felt too large and too loud. She must have had a rush of adrenaline during her brief visit to the throne room, which masked the overwhelming sensations. Now, standing in Kes's chambers and facing her anxious sisters, the strength of her mate behind her was the only thing grounding her.

The bond was a constant reminder that he would not hurt her; it also reminded her of his deep love for her. She knew she should trust that these beings would never hurt her. Yet she found it difficult to trust herself and thought it was quite possible that it was all a hallucination. An escape her mind had fabricated to help preserve her sanity.

Lyra and Panella waited for her to speak. She was unsure of what to say or if she could say anything at all. The expressions they wore were understanding and told her it would be perfectly fine if she said nothing at all. It was for that reason that she said the most important thing of all.

"I love you both, and I am so happy to see you again. I was not sure it would ever happen." The tears welling in their eyes made her look away. She could not bear to see the anguish she had caused them during her absence. She knew a time would come when she would have to answer to all her loved ones. It was her fault that they suffered at all.

Her sisters slowly approached, but when they reached out to touch her, she was ashamed of how she cringed away from them. She could not look them in the eyes and see the hurt and disappointment that surely flooded them. It was cowardly, yet she still leaned back into Kes and hid under his wings. The three spoke to each other, but her mind was already too loud with the sounds of life around them to truly hear what they said.

She could smell herself. The pungent odor was even more shocking compared to the fresh scent of Kes. Suddenly, the filth she knew covered her made her skin feel like it was crawling with the little creatures that lived in the damp cell with her. It did not matter if they existed or not. Her mind had already decided they were boring little holes into her skin. She needed to get them off of her.

Now.

Her breathing grew shallow, and Kes quickly noticed. He placed a hand on each side of her face and tilted her head to meet his gaze.

"What do you need?" he asked with so much tenderness that she nearly forgot about the millions of legs dancing across her skin. Nearly.

"Get them off. I can feel them on me. Get them off. Get them off. Please, get them off," she begged.

Somehow, he knew exactly what she meant. He kept her tucked within his wings and brought her to his bathing chambers. Without stopping to remove clothing, he walked her directly under the constant spray of water cascading in the corner.

She stared at the water, which ran brown with the decades of filth that shrouded her. The disgusting water swirled around the drain before disappearing for good. She could not help but feel that, no matter how long she stood under the spray, she would never be truly clean again. The water could run clear, but she would still feel the muck coating her.

Without saying a word, Kes grabbed a bottle from the nook in the wall and poured a generous amount into the palm of his hand. She watched as he rubbed the substance between his hands before working the suds through her hair. The feeling was both comforting and terrifying.

It had been so long since someone had touched her with kindness. It took a few minutes of his ministrations before she could relax into his touch. She had been tense and ready for pain. Following the bond connecting her to him, she used the love flooding her to convince her body that he would not hurt her. He would never hurt her.

Logically, she knew that. Yet her mind had fractured into two: the logical side and the side that trusted nothing. Her body had survived by listening to the side that warned of imminent pain. It had a hard time letting go of that fear.

Kes grabbed another bottle and, after rubbing the new substance between his hands, went to touch her body. She flinched, and he paused without hesitation. Tears poured down her cheeks, mixing with the water flowing over her. She did not mean to do it, and she feared meeting his gaze, not wanting to see the disappointment and disgust she was certain she would find.

How could he want her? She was broken, and she did not see how it was possible to be put back together.

"Hey," Kes said as he gently lowered himself to look her in the eyes. "May I wash you?" The question came out gently, and he was nothing but patient as he waited for her response. Words seemed beyond her and all she could manage was a stiff nod.

He showed her his hands and then slowly reached for hers. She watched, mesmerized, as the fingers from one of his hands laced with hers and the other made gentle strokes up and down her arm. She squeezed his hand ever so slightly, not trusting that anything around her was real. When he squeezed back, she meant to let out a breath, but it came out as a choked cry.

Kes kept working the lather into her skin, and she was surprised to see the golden-green color again. She had nearly forgotten what it looked like. When she blinked, it went back to the filth-covered skin she had grown used to.

She blinked again, and it returned to the golden-green hue. If her eyes could not tell her what was real and what was not, how could she trust anything? Her chest tightened and refused to fill with air, no matter how hard she tried to suck it in. Kes squeezed her hand again and kept doing so until she returned the gesture. Somehow, the action eased the vice around her lungs, and she was able to take a breath.

He never dropped her hand, no matter how awkward it became, and he continued to wash her. She should wash herself, but she was not entirely sure she could manage the task. Standing was already tiring enough. Perhaps she should be embarrassed that her mate had to clean her as if she were a youngling. Yet she could not find it within herself to be.

Time passed, and the water she watched circling the drain ran clear. Even so, she still felt the caked feeling of filth and the millions of tiny legs crawling all over her skin. Would she ever feel clean again? Or would the last one hundred thirty-seven years cling to her for the rest of her life?

She wished for a way to remove the memories. Although she knew it was foolish, no such thing existed. Fate determined your memories, and she would not let you forget them. No matter the horrors she placed in your life. It was not fair.

What had she done to deserve a fate as cruel as the one she had just lived? She knew it was something she would endure for the rest of her life. When she was in the cage, she had fantasized about the moment she would be released and how it would feel to be free. Now she knew there was no freedom—not for her. She did not see how she could ever be free again.

Caged by bars or memories, she was a prisoner of fate

—broken beyond repair and a burden to those she loved. Perhaps she should have stayed in the cage. Everyone would have been better off if she had.

The crawling sensation had become unbearable, and she dug at her skin in an effort to remove them. If words spilled from her lips, she was unaware. She ripped her other hand out of Kes's grip to attack the tiny creatures.

It could have been hours or seconds, but when Kes grabbed both of her hands, preventing her from destroying the legs that continued to march on her skin, she screamed.

"I have to get them off!" She could see his lips moving, but she could not hear the words that should have accompanied them. All she could hear was the rushing of water in her ears and the echoing thoughts that drove her to wage war on the creatures. She thought she might have been speaking those thoughts out loud, but could not be sure.

"Anin," she heard him calling her name through the cacophony in her mind. She focused on his voice and followed it out of the chaos that had taken over her.

"They… they are everywhere. Can you not see them?" He had to see them. How could he not?

"Anin, there's nothing there. Only your perfectly beautiful skin. I do not doubt that you see something, but please… you are hurting yourself." She looked down at the arms that were just covered in millions of tiny creatures and were now covered in torn flesh that her tired body was attempting to heal.

"They were there. They were everywhere," she whispered. She had not been aware she was crying. Maybe she had never stopped once she started, but she watched as tears splashed on her ruined skin.

Every time she blinked, she saw the dirt and crawling creatures, and then it would return to her now-clean skin. She might look clean, but she was not. The soaps Kes used to wash away the grime could do nothing about the filth inside her.

Everything was too much: the sounds, the smells, the space. There was a part of her—albeit small—that wanted to go back into the cage in the small, damp room. How horrible a thought was that? She was... she did not know what she was anymore.

They were on the floor of Kes's bathing chamber, and she had no recollection of how they got there. He held her as she sobbed for the one hundred thirty-seven years she had lost and the countless future years that would be lost to her as well.

The scars of her past would mar her future.

Chapter 9
Panella

She had known her sister would not return the same fae she had been before Tatiana stole her away. However, nothing could have prepared her for the Anin who had returned. It took all of Panella's strength not to break down in tears over the state of her once-vibrant sister.

Panella had been foolish to reach out and touch Anin. She knew it, even as her body moved on its own. She had been unable to resist the need to feel her and make certain she stood before them—that she was real.

Kes had not let them into the small room at the end of the hall that once held Anin. However, Lyra caught a brief glimpse when the door first opened, and the sight horrified them both. Through their twin bond, Lyra conveyed everything: the flash of decaying wings, the small cage, and the pungent smell of the damp room.

She had not thought Tatiana was taking great care of Anin, but she had expected she would have her basic needs met. For one hundred thirty-seven years, her sister had been left to rot—quite literally, with severed wings hanging on the wall, as Lyra had seen. Panella suspected that one wall had not been all the horrors Tatiana forced Anin to endure.

Although she wished Anin would let them hold her, Panella knew it was more for her own benefit than for Anin's. The last thing her sister needed was for anyone to place their needs above hers. Panella was grateful that she allowed Kes to comfort her, at least.

If Panella ever went through something so harrowing, she knew the only being she could truly trust would be Lyra. Their twin bond, like a mate bond, could not lie.

Anin had a long road to recovery ahead of her. Both physically and mentally. Panella was not sure Anin would ever recover from her ordeal mentally. She hoped her sister would still be able to have a happy and fulfilling life at some not-too-distant point in the future.

When they returned, Kes had ported them to his quarters. They all stood there awkwardly, unsure what to say or do until it became clear Anin was overwhelmed and needed space. Lyra and Panella had seen themselves out. She was glad they had started leaving brooms or similar items outside his door. Descending all those stairs would have been exhausting, and they were both already emotionally drained.

They rode their brooms to the weapons room to return their gear, only to find Zandar still waiting for them. She did not miss the way Lyra groaned and, even as devastated as Panella was, she still lifted a corner of her mouth.

Lyra needed someone like Zandar. She was prickly, and if she were not challenged, she lost interest. Zandar was clearly a challenge for her. His ego never seemed to get the best of him, even when a witch put him in his place. Few fae, let alone male fae, could say the same.

Neither said anything to him, even as he stood there expectantly. This was Lyra's path to walk, and Panella was there only to enjoy her twin's discomfort and the confusion that accompanied it.

Oh, Lyra.

She wondered how long it would take for Lyra to realize exactly what she was feeling. Knowing her, she likely already knew and was too stubborn to accept it.

The tension grew thick in the room as they put everything away, and Lyra refused to acknowledge Zandar. This would go one of two ways, and either outcome would provide the comic relief Panella was desperate for.

The twins left the room, where Zandar still stood, to walk home. Witch City was only a few halls from the armory, so there was no need to fly. Besides, the Night fae were not exactly tolerant of witches flying through the halls, and, to be fair, none of the winged fae flew either. Although they could all port, witches could not. Either way, it was best not to incur the ire of the palace-dwelling Night fae.

"Lyra?" Zandar demanded from directly behind them. Her twin did not even slow down and was pointedly ignoring him. It was a struggle not to laugh. Her sister was acting like a youngling, and her usual tactic of pretending away a problem was not working.

The large doors to the city were propped wide open,

and while several witches milled around in the typical hustle and bustle, their "day" hours came to an end as the spelled ceiling shifted from sunlight of the Day Court to moonlight of the Night Court. Many of the witches still out raised a hand and smiled in greeting at the twins, but their faces soon morphed into looks of confusion at the fae they knew still followed them. If Panella knew, so did Lyra.

Ah, here it comes.

Lyra spun on her heels and nearly took a step back in surprise at how close he had been behind her. Her stubbornness won out, and she stood her ground.

Oh no, not the pointer finger.

Panella was going to lose her battle to contain the laugh she had worked so hard to suppress when Lyra poked Zandar in the chest and did her best to look down on him.

"Listen up, fae-fae. My sister and I have a lot to process right now and we do not need you following us around like some lost puppy from the human realm," she seethed.

He looked down at her without expression for a few moments before his mouth lifted into the mischievous grin he always wore when he spoke to Lyra. "First of all, those puppies are adorable. Therefore, I will thank you for the compliment," he said with a wink. "Second of all, what are we going to do about the..." he trailed off, looking around at the many witches that had stopped to enjoy the spectacle. "Information I brought you earlier?"

It took both sisters an embarrassing amount of time to recall the strange behavior of the head witch of the Mystic

Fates Coven he had reported. Lyra's hand dropped, and she let out a loud, exhausted sigh.

"Follow us." They veered right toward the random bridges and stairs that would bring them to Etain's study.

"How do you ever know where you are going? This place is a maze—a cluttered one at that," Zandar asked. She could feel Lyra roll her eyes and then give Panella a sharp look when she huffed out a small laugh.

"He's funny. Although nothing is as funny as your reaction to him," Panella said to Lyra through their bond. Little did Zandar know what a wonderful distraction he was providing from thinking about Anin.

"Shut up," was Lyra's only response, which only made Panella laugh.

"What's so funny? Are you all doing that twin thing?" Zandar asked. Lyra still refused to acknowledge him, so Panella glanced at him, almost apologetically. The smirk he gave told her he was enjoying her sister's behavior about as much as Lyra hated it.

When they reached Etain's study, the door was open, and they could hear voices inside. They both cringed when they heard Ciaran; his presence would undoubtedly complicate things.

Lyra had a way of delivering information that was straightforward and to the point, which was helpful most of the time. The King, however, needed to be finessed, which was next to impossible given his practically nonexistent personality.

Oddly, Panella found she did not necessarily dislike the King. She could not say she particularly cared for him, either. However, she did enjoy figuring out puzzles, and he proved to be the most complicated one she had ever encountered.

"Hello?" Panella called into the room before they entered. The second they appeared, all eyes shifted to them. Lyra opened her mouth, no doubt to dive directly into the real reason they were there. Panella knew they should start with something less... problematic. Before Lyra could say anything, Panella interjected with the one thing they had all been waiting for.

"She's home."

The smiles Etain and Galetia wore were genuine, while Ciaran looked—well—exactly the same as he always did. Insanely wicked and bored all at the same time. It was a strange combination.

"How is she?" Etain asked. The question had come out hesitantly, as if she were afraid of the answer. The way she twisted and pulled at her hands indicated her distress. It was one of those habits beings are not even aware they have until someone points it out.

Panella looked at Lyra, and the two tried to figure out the best way to answer the question before Panella said what they had finally agreed upon: "She's worse than we all hoped and yet exactly the way our worst fears told us to expect."

Etain's face fell, but when she looked at Galetia, it filled with determination. "We have been working on something that will hopefully help her." When she finished describing the concoction they were attempting to create, Panella was impressed. It was an innovative idea, and if it worked, it would alleviate the worst of Anin's distress.

"Is anyone going to say why the fae behind Lyra is standing impatiently and looks like he might need to use the bathing chamber?" Ciaran asked, and they all turned to look at Zandar. Panella had nearly forgotten he was there.

"Well, there is another reason for our visit. The head witch of the Mystic Fates Coven has apparently been behaving strangely," Panella said.

"I gave the Shadows in training the task of following a head witch without being detected, and fae-fae here followed Cordelia," Lyra continued.

"Your name is Fae-Fae?" Ciaran asked. He looked appalled that someone would name their young something so ridiculous.

"Zandar, the little terror here," Zandar pointed to Lyra, "likes to call me fae-fae. I think it means she likes m—" Whatever he was going to say was cut off by Lyra's fist lodging firmly in his gut, causing him to double over. It did not matter, though; Ciaran was already laughing, and Lyra was growling at Zandar, even as her dark skin flushed darker.

Panella had to laugh when Lyra began yelling unintelligibly at Zandar while he smirked at her the whole time, eating up every bit of her fire. Finally, Lyra had reached her limit and threw her hands up in the air as she screamed through her teeth. She took several deep breaths, and composed herself, then slowly turned back around.

"As I was saying," she practically ground out through her clenched jaw, "*he* observed some things we thought

Etain should know." She glared back at Zandar. "Tell them everything you told us."

When he finished telling them about the porting to a random temple in the Day Court and talking to someone who was not there, Ciaran was ready to hunt poor Cordelia down. He and Zandar were both jumping to wild conclusions and wanted her head on a pike.

As Panella knew they would, Etain and Galetia remained calm. "I have known Cordelia for ages, and she would never do anything to jeopardize the covens," Galetia said.

"She's colluding with the Day queen! She must be! There is no other reason she would be there. And how does a witch port? We need to get to her before she causes any more damage than she likely already has," Ciaran said, pacing the room.

Etain calmly strode over to him and placed a hand on his chest, effectively stopping his movement and gaining his full attention. "My love, I will remind you that I am the Queen of Witches and will handle this situation. There is likely a reasonable answer."

Ciaran waged a war within himself to avoid overstepping his mate. Finally, he gave her a curt nod. "I will speak with her tomorrow, as I think we have all had enough excitement for one night." Ciaran was not pleased, but he deferred to her judgment.

It always amazed Panella how a being so tiny could get someone large and formidable, like Ciaran, to heed her. There was no doubt in Panella's mind that no other being in the known realms could do the same. Their queen was powerful in more ways than one, and someone like her comes around only once in hundreds of generations.

"Keep an eye on her until then," Lyra instructed Zandar. He mumbled something under his breath about finding the crazy-ass witch first. Lyra smacked him upside the head and asked if he was having issues following a direct order, to which he bravely replied, "As you wish, little terror."

Lyra had finally met her match, and Panella could not be happier for it.

Chapter 10

Kes

After their shower, Kes sat on the floor in his soaked clothes, holding his mate until she cried herself to sleep. Without waking her, he moved her to the bed, changed into dry clothes, and then slipped in beside her. He could not help but feel the weight of responsibility for everything she was experiencing.

He had not fought hard enough and had let her get taken all those years ago. Even worse, he had not been able to free her until the rebel leader made it possible. All of this made him feel like a failure as a mate and in the eyes of the blood oath.

She was not okay. He had not expected her to be, but he had also not been prepared for the reality of her trauma. He was in over his head and did not know how to help her.

She needed time, obviously, but there was something else she needed. Confidence. Hers was non-existent any more. Everything terrified her, which again was to be expected. There had to be a way that, in time, he could help her regain her strength back—both mentally and physically.

Anin stirred in her sleep and found her way back into his arms. He felt the heat of a tear sliding down his cheek. There was a time—too long a time—when he did not think they would have this moment. Her back in his arms, where she belonged.

There was no realm where he let her go ever again. He would do whatever it took to protect her from her sister, or any other force, even fate herself. Anin had already suffered enough for multiple beings and should never have to suffer another night in her life.

He noticed the way her wings were misshapen and did not need to ask what had happened. He saw the rows upon rows of wings that had filled nearly every space of the four walls surrounding her little box. The only other item hanging on the wall had been a mirror that was positioned perfectly to force her to stare at herself. She could watch herself decay or watch her wings decay.

More tears spilled down his face, dampening the pillow he rested his head on. He took a couple of calming breaths. The last thing he wanted was to wake her with his own emotional distress. She did not need that.

It was a strange dichotomy of emotions. On one hand, he felt elated to have her back, the scent of her filling his space once again. The feel of her soft, golden-green skin under his fingertips as he held her. Perhaps it was selfish, yet he could not find it in him to care.

On the other hand, his wrath made him eager to feel another's skin—the Day Queen's golden neck squeezed between his hands. The rage he felt when he thought about that crazy bitch had taken on a life of its own, begging to be unleashed upon her. That entity fed off his hatred for her and grew stronger each night his mate had been held captive. Finally morphing into a force that demanded retribution.

The largest part of him was suffocated by guilt. Logically, he knew there had been nothing he could have done to prevent her from being taken that fateful night, nor a way to get her back sooner. He had tried with all he had, repeatedly. If there had been a way, he would have found it. Logic played no part, however, when it came to his mate.

He had no idea what they would do the next night. Something small each night to help her acclimate to living outside of that fucking box again. He would never ask her about what she went through, only be there to listen if she ever wished to share her memories with him.

If she told him at that moment, he did not think he would be able to control his actions. He did not know if he would ever be able to control his reaction to that kind of knowledge, no matter how much time passed. The possibility that he would immediately find himself in front of that queen bitch to finish her in a horrific and drawn-out way was strong. Blood magic be damned.

He knew exactly what he would do. It was something he had thought about and even dreamt of often. It had started as a way to control his rage and, at some point, had morphed into a fucked up mantra of sorts.

First, he would lock her in a box and hide her away for a century, with no one to speak to, not even in hatred.

Then he would peel thin, paper-like strips of her golden skin away with his wind and hang the translucent sheets on the walls surrounding her. She deserved to watch herself decay for at least a hundred years. Her death at his hands would be painfully slow and meticulous. She had earned it, and he would be more than happy to be the one to deliver her prize.

The only thing better than killing her himself would be watching Anin take her vengeance. Tatiana had taken more than years and wings from his mate. She had taken too much of what made her—her. That was possibly the most heinous of her crimes. Wings grow back, and Anin has countless years ahead of her. That giant missing piece of her, though? He did not know how she would get that back.

Was it even possible? Perhaps that hole would remain for eternity, and he would need to find ways to fill it until she was whole again. He did not know how, but he would complete her again. The old Anin might be gone forever, but no version of her was anything but perfect to him.

Just as he drifted off to sleep, Anin woke up screaming. The sound shattered his heart and was something he would carry with him for the rest of their lives. He would do everything in his power to ensure she never had something to scream about like that again.

"Shh, you are safe. You are in the Night Court, in our quarters, in our bed. You are being held by your insanely attractive, intelligent, and witty mate."

She huffed out a small laugh that sent his heart soaring and mended some pieces of it back together. "That's questionable," she said in a shaky voice.

"I have no idea what you could possibly mean by that," he replied, sounding baffled by her words. This only made her give one more tiny laugh. This—this he could do. Slowly, he would pull her back out one laugh at a time. The moment was short-lived, yet he was grateful for it. Her body shook as she gasped for breath; whatever she had dreamed threatened to pull her back.

"Never forget: When in doubt, follow the bond; it will never lie to you," he whispered softly into her ear. The words seemed to calm her, and she took a moment to take in several ragged breaths. There was no protecting her from the memories of her trauma, but he could be there to weather the storm with her.

"She was... and then he... but then... I—I cannot talk about it," she finally managed to choke out.

"It's okay, my darling nymph. You never have to tell me anything. Just know that if you want to, I will listen." He stroked her hair until her breathing evened out and she drifted back to sleep.

What male dared to touch her? He knew it was not sexual, but whatever this male did to her, he would do to him tenfold. This male did not have blood magic, and maybe the violence Kes could unleash upon him would suffice until he had the queen in his grasp. All he needed to do was find out who he was. It sounded like the perfect mission for his silent shadows.

The first thing was to help Anin find her light again; then he would take care of the foolish male. Then, finally, he would kill that bitch queen.

Tatiana was fresh off the high of her latest sacrifice. She continued replaying the event in the throne room over and over in her mind.

"If you had listened to us, it would have never happened," the *whispers* chided her.

She grew increasingly annoyed at their constant commentary on her life. Tatiana was the Queen of the Day Court. She could do as she pleased. She was unstoppable. The hundreds of high fae in the throne room—still on their knees hours later—could attest to that.

She needed to do something with them. Her power was already strained, and she doubted she could maintain control indefinitely. There was no doubt that most of them would swear loyalty, which would make it impossible for them to betray her again. The few that did not were the issue.

"Keep them in cages and sacrifice them as needed."

"I already thought of that!" she screamed at them. It

was freeing, not worrying about anyone thinking she was mad. They could think what they wanted; and it did not matter. Perhaps she was mad; either way, she was still their queen.

The Blood Queen.

The title had bothered her for decades, as the *whispers* insisted it was her true title. Now she had embraced it. If they wanted the Blood Queen, that was exactly what she would give them.

The violet blood of the beautiful high fae she had sacrificed a while ago drenched her golden skin up to her elbows. She had drawn violet marks down each cheek, starting just below the center of her eyes and ending at her jaw. There would be no mistaking who she was now that she wore her new title freely.

She returned to her quarters to rummage through her extensive gown collection. She was certain she had one that was the perfect shade of violet to match the dried blood she wore. The powder-blue gown she wore at the moment clashed horribly with it, and that would not do.

There were many things Tatiana loved. She loved the rush of power after a sacrifice and loved having ultimate control. However, something she truly loved was her gowns. There were so many, she had to have an entire room dedicated to their storage. She had always loved her gowns. Even as a...

A youngling, barely a decade old, with skin as golden as hers, ripped the layers off her beautiful gown. "Thachory, if it weren't for the blasted gowns my mother forces me to wear, I would beat you every time!" the golden youngling said to an unseen companion.

The vision faded, and it took Tatiana a few moments to remember what she was doing.

Thachory. Did she know that name?

No, of course not. She would never have ripped such a wonderful gown. What a silly notion to be forced to wear such fine garments. She shook her head to clear the strange, intrusive vision and gazed at the fabric in her hand, almost feeling the layers the youngling had discarded.

Such a strange vision.

She had several gowns in a complementary shade of violet. It was a hard decision to make, and surprisingly, the *whispers* remained quiet. Their silence was strange, considering they liked to make their opinions known at every opportunity. She needed Raindal.

Where was he?

It had been hours since he left to return the creature to her cage. Thinking about her made Tatiana crinkle one of her gowns in her fists, which only added to her ire. She would attend to her next. After finding Raindal, he would help her pick out a gown.

She sent him a spelled scroll, annoyed that she had to even do that. He should have returned to the throne room immediately to wait for her. She had craved him while carving up the pretty fae—well, the once-pretty fae. Not even a fae could have recovered from the things Tatiana had done to her face. It made her cackle as the image of her mangled face floated across Tatiana's mind.

Raindal appeared moments later, and she stared at him in silence. He took in the blood that coated her and showed no reaction. This was another thing that added to her ire. He should look at her with hunger, not the indifference he always wore so casually.

Sensing her anger, he finally spoke. "My queen, how may I be of service?" That was much better. She smiled at him and explained her impossible choice.

"I do not know which one to choose, and I cannot possibly wear them all at the same time. That would be crazy."

"Is there one that you have never worn?" That was a good question. She studied the dozen gowns before her. "This is why I need you with me at all times, Raindal. Where did you disappear to?" Her words sounded playful, but she was annoyed that he had disappeared for so long.

"Nowhere. When I returned to the throne room, I found hundreds of fae on their knees, but there was no sign of you. I knew you would call me when you needed me, so I waited."

"*He's lying,*" the *whispers* sang in their strange, echoing voice. If he were truly lying, he would be a master of deception, because nothing about him hinted at a lie.

"*He is a master of deception,*" the *whispers* had been determined from the beginning to drive Raindal and Tatiana apart. She knew this was just more of their scheming.

"*You only see what you want to see.*"

"Shut up!" she screamed. Raindal, used to her outbursts, did not even flinch.

"*You will see, Blood Queen. You will see.*" She wished she

had never responded to the *whispers* all those years ago. She could not even recall what had driven her to do so.

A field of wildflowers, one that looked exactly like her favorite one from younghood. A golden fae, who looked an awful lot like Tatiana, was on her knees in the center of the beautiful field, screaming and pulling at her hair.

She blinked, and the image was gone. She shook her head and refused to think any more about it. The visions were unsettling, and that upset Tatiana. She changed into the violet gown and then admired herself in the mirror. She should have embraced the title of Blood Queen sooner.

"*We tried to tell you.*" She refused to acknowledge the *whispers*. That was enough of them for one day.

"I am in need of some fun. Let's go pay that disgusting creature a visit." She could feel the palm of her hand itching to hold a knife, while the other craved the feel of her paper-thin skin as she peeled it off in ribbons.

Raindal was as silent as ever as they ported as far as the wards allowed. Not even she could port any closer. She was not taking any risks when it came to her. The only sound was the fall of their footsteps echoing down each hall they walked.

When they turned the corner of the final hall, Tatiana came to a stop. There was something on the floor. She suddenly felt very hot, her mind slower than her body in comprehending what she was seeing.

"Is… Is that blood?" she asked, slowly turning her head

to look at Raindal, who stood beside her with his typical lack of expression.

"Probably. She was bleeding when she fell from the cage." There was no way he could be so obtuse.

"You mean to tell me that you did not find it strange that the creature who never bleeds—or, if she does, then it returns to her body—was able to track blood down the hall?" She was certain her voice conveyed the promise of the violence she felt.

"You are right. That is strange. I do not understand why you are so upset over a little blood. Is it not good news that she can freely bleed now? Perhaps the land has finally seen the error of its ways." She wanted to believe what he said, but she knew the land would never relinquish its "Queen of Light."

"Her blood breaks the spell on the hall!" she screamed, so loudly that the word "hall" echoed back to her multiple times. Raindal continued to look at her as if he had not allowed it to happen.

Tatiana took off toward the single door at the end of the hall. She walked slowly at first, but the fear of what she would find behind that door—or, more accurately, what she would not find—had her running within a few steps. She threw open the door, and even though, on some level, she had expected it, the sight of the empty cage shocked her.

Raindal's footsteps were steady as he came to join her. He said nothing as he entered the empty room. The only evidence of her prisoner's stay was the decaying wings decorating the walls.

"Where is she, Raindal?" she hissed the question

through her teeth as her head slowly cocked to the side as she waited for his response.

"I do not know."

"You do not know?"

"She was here when I left." His tone of indifference was really beginning to enrage her.

"Well, she is clearly not here now!"

"No, she is not."

"What have you done, Raindal? Have you betrayed me?" Had the *whispers* been right all along?

"No, of course not. I am just as surprised as you are." He did not look surprised. If anything, he looked anything but surprised, as if he had known she was not going to be there the entire time.

"We told you that you would see."

"You did this!" When she lunged at Raindal, she finally got him to break his stoic expression, and the one he wore at that moment was one of true shock. She took over his body and then ported them to the temple.

Tatiana forced Raindal to climb onto the stone slab and lie down. Once the shackles were in place, she wasted no time grabbing the knife and positioning it at his neck.

"How could you have betrayed me?!" She still held control of his body, so he was unable to answer her. She pushed the knife into his flesh, and his orange blood began to pool in the canals carved into the stone slab. It would soon flow down to the medallion she stood upon, and she would feel the rush of his power sprinting through her veins.

Except she stopped at the first nick. Doubt began to creep into her mind. What if he had been telling her the truth? Was she willing to lose her only companion on an assumption?

"*Do it. He betrayed you,*" the *whispers* hissed through her mind. That was enough to stay her hand; no, she had another idea in mind.

"*You foolish queen!*"

"I will trust your word, Raindal. You made a mistake—a careless one—but you did not betray me. Do not worry," she said as she caressed his jaw. "*I* will make sure you never make the mistake again. *I* will do you a favor. *I* will keep control of you. This way, you will always do what *I* want." She dragged her hand down his chest and paused at the waist of his pants.

"Am I not a kind queen?" she asked him, then made him nod.

She should have done this from the start.

"Now, Raindal," she said as her hand continued south to explore the body that she now owned. "You need to show me how grateful you are. Show me how much you love me." She made him get down from the slab and pick her up to seat her upon it.

"Do not worry, pet; I will make sure you show me just the way I like it," she said, just before she made his mouth invade her own.

Yes, this was much better.

Ciaran and Etain waited in her study for Galetia and Cordelia to arrive. Ciaran insisted on having this meeting right after breakfast. Etain usually enjoyed breakfast, but today she was forced to listen to her mate plot the murder of a witch she considered a friend.

It did not matter that she had told him not to worry or that the situation was likely a misunderstanding. His past was coming back to haunt him, and she could not hold it against him. Their contrasting natures were sometimes glaringly apparent. Nonetheless, she had learned to accept their differences. With a sigh, she stopped trying to convince him and attempted to enjoy her last few bites.

Galetia entered, looking flustered. It was uncommon for her to be late, and the look on her face concerned Etain.

"I am so sorry to be late. The Lunar Crystal Coven's

storeroom was broken into and everything had been smashed. Several hard-to-find ingredients were destroyed," Galetia said, taking the seat next to Etain.

"Did anyone see what happened? Did a spell go awry?"

"That's the thing. There is no residue of spent magic, and it seems that everything was smashed with a heavy object. Lyra and that male that follows her everywhere are investigating at this moment."

Etain laughed when she thought about the shadow Lyra had acquired. "Fae-fae, I believe she calls him."

"Yes, that's the one," Galetia said with a laugh, before her expression changed. "Who would do such a thing?"

"It's probably this witch you both think is harmless," Ciaran grumbled under his breath. "The one who has yet to show herself. That alone should prove her guilt." Etain rolled her eyes at her dramatic mate. She sometimes wondered who was more dramatic of the two cousins. Ciaran would be appalled if he realized how similar they actually were.

She had asked the head witch of the Mystic Fates Coven to meet them several minutes ago. Ciaran had taken to pacing, and Etain tried to calm him by reminding him that Cordelia was always lost in her own thoughts and perpetually late. Her efforts were in vain.

The head witch of the Mystic Fates Coven often wandered while talking to herself, consumed by her thoughts. She would forget to eat and go nights without sleep.

Although she might be obsessive, she was also incredibly brilliant. She had discovered some long-lost spells and identified ways to improve or update their most-used spells. She was a pillar of their community.

Etain and Galetia knew this about her, but Ciaran did not. Even if he did, she doubted he could look past the perceived betrayal. She sighed, and leaned back in her chair, sharing a knowing look with her great-aunt.

Several more minutes passed in which time she was certain Ciaran had worn a distinct path in her rug, before Cordelia strolled in. She always appeared to float everywhere she walked. Which was fitting, Etain supposed, since her head always seemed to be floating in the clouds.

She mumbled to herself, ticking off thoughts on each finger. Suddenly, she stopped, her eyes widening. She pulled out a book and began writing in it, her handwriting erratic with excitement. Etain wondered what puzzle she had just solved and found the witch fascinating.

Ciaran looked ready to pounce on the unsuspecting head witch. She held him in place with a glance and sent a warning through their bond before saying, "Do not forget who is the Queen of Witches. You will respect my authority."

The rage boiling behind his eyes was temporarily replaced by a wicked gleam. He gave her one of his too-wide smirks and said, "Yes, my queen. Careful, I cannot be held responsible for my actions when you look so delicious asserting your authority."

As she felt the heat of her flush creep up her face, his grin grew impossibly wider. She wondered if he would ever lose the control he seemed to have over her internal temperature. She hoped not.

"Oh, hello," the head witch of the Mystic Fates Coven said with a warm smile.

"Cordelia, please come in and have a seat," Etain said, indicating the open chair across from her and Galetia. Ciaran leaned over the back of her chair. She did not need to wonder if he was glaring daggers at the aloof witch across from her. Luckily, she was certain Cordelia was unaware.

The head witch sat down with a groan. "I just now realized that I have not sat in… Well, I cannot remember how long. Time gets away from me," she laughed as if it were a common occurrence. Galetia and Etain smiled while she heard her mate growl above her head. She sighed, knowing she needed to move things along so he would stop being such a beast.

"I understand that," Etain said. "Sometimes, when I'm working on something, hours pass even though it feels like minutes."

"Yes! Exactly!" the head witch replied.

"I will do my best not to take up too much of your time," Etain continued. "That way, you can return to whatever you are working on."

"Lovely. It's quite fascinating," the head witch said.

"A couple of nights ago, Lyra gave her shadows-in-training a task. They had to follow all the head witches as an exercise in stealth. If discovered, they were removed from the program."

"Oh! That is such a wonderful idea. Lyra has always been inventive," Cordelia said. Her words were irrefutably genuine. "Yes, I agree. The shadow assigned to follow you reported some intriguing details. He said you managed to port and that he followed you to a temple in the Day Court. He also noted that you appeared frustrated, angrily yelling at someone he could not see before you ported away again without him. Do you mind telling us what you were doing?"

"I must admit, the story is rather embarrassing. I found an old book deep within my coven's archives, as I often do. The book described a spell of transport, and my curiosity was immediately piqued. I gathered the necessary ingredients and memorized the spell. The directions instructed me to think of a place while reciting the spell and holding the herbs in one hand. The book also described a temple that I could not stop thinking about.

I intended to travel only a few feet, but once something is stuck in my mind, it is hard to push it aside. I was surprised to find myself in the actual temple. Then I recalled that the book mentioned several elements of our realm. Even the shadows your mate commands."

Etain could feel Ciaran stand up straight. She wondered if the witch was telling them about the text he had only just learned of.

"Unfortunately, they were not where the passage had indicated. I admit, I was quite upset, as I had been looking forward to reading something new. So, I recited the spell and used the remaining herbs to return home. However, I thought of the Mystic Fates Coven in the Borderlands by mistake.

Embarrassingly, I had to fly all the way back. I haven't been that frustrated with myself in a long time," she said, shaking her head.

Etain looked up at Ciaran and waited for his gaze to

meet hers. Then she said sweetly, "You see? I told you there would be a perfectly harmless answer." She smiled and returned her attention to the witch across from her.

"Might I see this book?" Etain asked.

"Of course," she said, calling the book to her before passing the weathered leather tome to Etain.

"Cordelia, what can you tell us about this temple?" Galetia asked. As the head witch described what she had seen and its location, Ciaran hung on every word. Etain managed to keep from laughing; her mate had gone from murderous to attentive as soon as the witch mentioned the texts he craved.

As she spoke, he pulled out a map of the realm and located the general area Cordelia had described. After she shared all her information, she seemed to forget that she was speaking with them. She got up and floated away, mumbling to herself again. Her mind seemed to switch to another thought—perhaps even another realm entirely.

"This must be it," Ciaran said, looking at her with another one of his wicked grins. "Care to go on an adventure, little witch?"

Chapter 13
Balthier

A day. Barely a full day had passed since he last saw Raindal, knowing it would be the last for a long time. He had not even had time to process their last conversation when fae began showing up at the hut he shared with his mother. Some he knew; most he did not.

Beings asked him what they should do. He stared at the first ones in confusion. What did they mean? What should they do? What should they do with what? He did not know them and could not fathom why they were standing at his door asking for… *something*.

But what?

It slowly dawned on him that these were members of the rebel movement. With his mate missing, they were looking to him for their next steps. Gods only knew why. As if he could ever lead the rebels.

He was not Raindal. He had barely supported his mate's ambitions and had not wanted to know his plans.

Ignorance had been bliss, or so he had pretended. It was not, but as long as he knew nothing, he could convince himself that it was.

The disappointed looks were beginning to grate on his nerves. Why did they expect him to step into his mate's role? If they had been having meetings, he had never attended them. It was rude of them to make assumptions.

He could barely think straight. A few hours after he last laid eyes on his mate, the feeling of the bond between them changed. It was still there, so he knew Raindal was alive. However, making his way through the bond felt thick, like wading through molasses. Whereas before, it had been unencumbered.

The fae who came to him and walked away disappointed had no idea what he was dealing with internally. He would like to see them try to walk in his shoes. Perhaps their disappointment would turn to understanding.

Much later, after he had cleaned the few dishes they possessed from the meager dinner his mother had made, a knock came on his door that changed everything. He opened it to find the most striking female he had ever seen. Not only was she a siren, but she was also a lesser fae—nearly unheard of.

"What do you want?" he asked, already knowing what she was there for. The same thing all the others had been looking for. Leadership. From him. What a joke.

"Well, that was rather curt," she said, looking at him with an expression all females seem to possess—the kind that clearly conveys disapproval while simultaneously making you want to rectify the issue. Arms crossed, hip out, and brow raised, it was a variation of the same thing from every female he had ever known, and one his mother had perfected.

He sighed and opened the door, stepping aside. The small home he shared with his mother was nothing more than a large room with a fabric partition separating a sleeping area for her. The rest of the space contained a makeshift table and two stools. There was a basin he filled with water every day to wash with, and then his cot, which he had created by growing vines. It was more comfortable than most had.

The female stepped through the door, and he nearly balked at her fine clothing. She was obviously well-off. He expected her to judge their surroundings, but instead, she seemed to admire them.

"I know why you are here," he said, crossing his arms. He knew he was being rude. However, he was tired of dealing with the expectations of others for one day.

"Oh, you do, do you?" she asked, still looking at him with *that* look. "Then by all means, please enlighten me."

"You want to know what you should do next." It was his turn to give her a look, but when he saw her face, her expression was not the surprise he had expected. If anything, she looked more irate.

"There is nothing I despise more than a male telling me what I want," she seethed. The vitriol she conveyed with each syllable, combined with her being a siren and her attire, gave Balthier a good idea of the deal she had been forced to make. He instantly felt embarrassed for thinking she was living better than he was. More than likely, her life was more horrific than his could ever be.

"Apologies. If that is not why you are here, then why are you?" His words were sincere, and she softened slightly toward him.

"To give you this," she said, holding out a folded piece of paper. There was nothing magical about it, yet he felt the weight of the words it contained before he even read it. "He said this would likely happen. When he did not show for our planned check-in, I knew it was time."

Balthier slowly opened the letter and had to force his eyes to the words. Instinctively, he knew that once he read the contents, there would be no going back.

My love,

If you are reading this, it means the worst has happened. I do not mean death, for I believe that to be a mercy compared to the torture of being trapped in one's mind for an unknown period. I knew this would likely be the case as soon as the true queen was released. Yet, I would still choose this because it is the path that must be taken if we are to finally be together as mates should be.

I know you never wanted anything to do with this rebellion. I also know it was out of fear. Well, my love, there is no more time for you to let your fear keep you frozen. I need you to be brave now.

The female delivering this message, Killia, is my right hand in leading the rebellion. Now she is yours—or more appropriately, you are each other's. She will fill you in on every moving piece we have in place.

However, she will only do so if you agree to take your place in the rebellion. I know you are more than capable of achieving great things. Between your kind heart and your tenacity, you can do anything. Besides, you and Killia are the two most stubborn individuals I have ever met. The two of you together will be a force to be reckoned with.

I hope you will choose to be brave, but I will not hold it against you if you choose not to. I did not give you much choice in the situation we find ourselves in. If I am being honest with myself, I gave you no choice at all, even going against your wishes multiple times. I am sorry for the pain I have put us through, and I do not doubt that we have decades more ahead of us.

All good things come to those who wait, and I would wait a thousand lifetimes for you and then a thousand more after that. I hope it does not take that long for us to finally have our time together without the looming threat of the mad queen. I have held that dream for both of us, and now I need you to be the one to hold it.

Be brave, my love, and always remember that I love you with all that I am.

Raindal

I t was not until he had read the last line several times that he realized tears were streaming down his face. He chanced a glance at Killia and was relieved to find not an ounce of pity on her face. All he saw was the steely determination required of someone chosen by his mate to be his right hand.

"Have you read this?" he asked, his voice barely above a whisper.

"No, but he told me what I needed to know for when this day came."

"I see." It was all he could think of to say.

"Do you?" It was a fair question, and he was unsure how to answer it. "Will you rise to the occasion, or will you continue to bury your head in the vines?" she asked, giving him that look again.

He did not answer her. Instead, he read the letter again. He was grateful she did not demand an answer and gave him time to process everything he had just read.

When he finally looked up, she met his gaze and said, "Your mate has spent every waking moment since discovering your existence fighting for you. Now it is your time to fight for him. I will ask you again, satyr: Will you rise to the occasion?"

He held her gaze for several moments. Yes, he wanted to "bury his head in his vines," as she had said. He wanted to pretend he had never met Raindal the moment he crossed into Daybreak. He cursed the rot—cursed fate herself. Yet, he knew he did not truly mean any of it. He would never trade his mate for an easy life.

No matter how much he wished he could.

He stood up straight and took a deep breath, even though fear threatened to suffocate him. He knew there would be no going back after reading the letter. Perhaps he had known the path he was going to choose from the moment the first fae showed up at his door. Either way, there was only one answer he could give.

"I will. For him, I will."

Chapter 14
Ciaran

"I did not realize you meant right this second," Etain said, looking around at the dilapidated temple Ciaran had just ported them to. He shrugged. She shook her head and chuckled. She should have anticipated that there would be no waiting.

"How long do you think this place has sat, unused?" she asked. He looked around, taking in the signs of life he saw everywhere. Of course, it was hard to tell if the layers of disturbed dust came from that odd witch and the fae who had followed her or from someone else.

His gaze snagged on two cages on either side of a curved stone half-wall. There was no dust inside either of them. Even if they had been used, there would still be a thick layer of dust, as on the rest of the crumbling stone floor.

"I would say recent and regularly used," he added after considering the mostly cleared floor around the flat stone altar in the middle of everything. More than anything, it was the paper-thin strips of multiple shades of skin discarded underneath it that told him the temple was still in use. He would recognize that from any distance, being a fan of carving skin himself. He refrained from pointing out the curled bits of flesh to his little witch.

"Oh. Well, perhaps we had better not—Ciaran, look at this," she said, staring at the curved stone wall. "There are hidden compartments." She pushed on one, and it popped out a small drawer. "There's nothing in here but more dust, but look at the images on the front."

There were several, each representing a fae element. He pushed on the one that looked like it might be shadows and was not surprised to find the drawer empty. He pushed on all of them, and the only one that looked like it might have contained something at some point was the one with the heart. Blood magic, he assumed.

The books Ulgridge had mentioned were likely kept in those drawers at some point in history. He took a closer look at the stone altar and the strange medallion on the floor. It was all connected, of that he was certain; only he could not see how.

Etain ventured toward the edges of the temple, where stone pillars continued to support the ceiling. He kept her within his sight as he dragged a finger down one of the channels, from the stone slab to the intricate design on the floor. He paused when his finger touched something sticky and pulled it away to see the faintest amount of violet blood.

"Ciaran," Etain called. "Come see this." She crouched at the bottom of one of the more intact pillars.

"What is it, little witch?"

"It looks like a story told with simple pictures carved into the stone. Parts have crumbled away, but perhaps you will know what it means." He came to stand behind her and look for himself.

"I have no idea what any of this means. However, do you see how the same image of a flame continues to appear?" He pointed at several of them. "This must have something to do with elemental fire." He moved to the next one and saw the same thing, but this time with water.

"Hmm," Etain said, cocking her head to the side the way she always did when she contemplated something.

He watched her as she studied the images. Something was coming together for her. While he always enjoyed watching her, he truly relished watching her mind work. Sometimes he would sit in her study and watch her mix her strange plants and other witchy things together. She fascinated him.

"This reminds me of something I heard about in the Human Realm. Apparently, at one point in the early history of humans, there was a great flood. The entire land was drowned by torrential rain that did not stop for many days.

The part that I always found hard to believe was that only one man and his family survived and somehow repopulated the entire realm. I know there are many types of people and that the land is vast. According to Hecate, there are many veils, far and wide, that lead to many other realms. So how could one family be able to do that?" She looked at him and rolled her eyes.

"That's highly illogical, but what does that have to do with this?"

"This looks like the tale of the fae who flooded the Human Realm, which gives at least part of that story more credence. It also seems like a cautionary tale. You once said that you cannot run out of magic; however, according to this, certain acts may take all of your magic to accomplish."

"That's impossible."

"Well, I thought it was also impossible to flood an entire realm, and yet..." She gestured to the pillar. He had never heard of anyone losing their magic before. It was just an innate ability all fae were born with. Even the lesser fae had magic.

They moved to the next pillar, which was the most intact of them all. Even Ciaran could interpret this story. It seemed to be another warning: a fae who pulled an entire landmass from the bottom of the sea and turned themself into a dried husk in the process. Once the new land was finished, they became dust.

"Perhaps these tales are much like yours where one man's family repopulated the Human Realm. I find them highly improbable," he said, looking down at his mate. She smirked up at him.

"Who knows? These stories make it seem as if an entirely different Fae Realm once existed—not just the inhabitants, but the rules of the land itself."

"Well, only the land would be able to tell, and it does not like to say much." Etain laughed at that as they moved to the next one.

Shadows.

His excitement was short-lived when he took in the destruction of the pillar. It did not look as though time was the only culprit of its ruin. There were just enough images left behind to indicate the element and that was it.

"I'm sorry, my love," Etain said, grabbing his hand and wrapping her small frame around his arm. His disappointment was expected. He knew fate would never make anything easy for him; she never had, and it was highly unlikely she would start now.

He was about to assure her that he was fine when he heard the sound of a female screeching from where the stone altar was located.

"How could you betray me?" There was no mistaking the voice whose screams echoed from further away. Ciaran did not waste even a second before he ported himself and Etain to their chambers.

"Was that...?" Etain asked, her voice shaking. He did not know why it had not occurred to him who was the likely culprit behind the still-drying blood. It took everything within him not to start smashing anything within reach. How could he have let her get that close to his mate?

"The Day Queen."

Chapter 15
Anin

Anin woke in Kes's arms. She lay as still as possible, afraid to lose the mirage her mind had gifted her. She wanted to pretend she was actually there and not in her small cage hanging in the damp stone room under the Daybreak Palace.

She expected the vision to dissipate as soon as she acknowledged it, yet it did not fade away. She could not allow herself to believe that this was true, the reality of it would crush her.

Kes stirred behind her, and she dared not breathe. The moment was about to end before she had even allowed herself time to enjoy her small reprieve.

"My darling nymph," Kes said, his voice rough with sleep. "Follow the bond. This is real, and you are safe. You are in Nightfell with me, your ridiculously perfect mate." She could hear the smile in his voice, and a tear fell, dampening the pillow beneath her head.

She followed the bond as he instructed, and tears

began to fall freely when she realized he was real. It was all real. She had been rescued; she was safe.

"Wow, I did not know my perfection could move you to tears, but I cannot say I am surprised." She choked out a laugh. The audacity of this male would never cease to amaze her. "That's a sound I could hear a thousand times every night and never tire of."

"If I laughed a thousand times every night, you would never have a chance to speak. And you do love to hear yourself speak," she said. His laughter rumbled out of him, low and smooth, and she felt to the very center of all that she was. She had missed their back and forth. It was so much better hearing his voice than their strange form of communication they had created.

"As it turns out, there are sounds I enjoy even more. Shocking, I know. Yet it does not make it less true." She twisted around to see him. Her eyes were desperate to drink him in for an eternity.

"Hello, my darling nymph," he whispered. They were close enough that she could feel his breath warming her skin. The moment felt fragile, as though one wrong move might shatter their peace.

"Hello, my darling feather duster." A lazy grin stretched across his face as he took one hand and brushed the hair out of her face, tucking it behind one ear.

"I will deny it if you ever tell a living creature, but I have even missed being called a feather duster. Your sisters, Lyra in particular, have been creative, to be certain. Yet, nothing compares to the way your mouth forms the word feather. If it must be followed by duster, then so be it," he said as he stared at her mouth.

"Feather? What is so wonderful about the way I say feather?"

"Well, I suppose it could just be the way your mouth says anything." He dragged his thumb across her bottom lip, and the heat she felt pooling inside terrified her.

He must have felt her discomfort and did not hesitate to create space between them. She did not know if she wanted it or not. Either way, the itching was beginning to return to her skin, and she did not think she would be able to bathe enough to remove the feeling.

She untangled herself from her mate and the blankets that had wrapped around her legs throughout her sleep. Without looking at Kes, not wanting to see the disappointment on his face, she went directly into his bathing chamber.

As soon as she was behind a closed door and under the warm spray of water, she slid to the floor. Not only were her legs struggling to keep her standing, but she also felt the need to make herself as small as possible. She hugged her knees to her as the water pounded into her flesh.

A large part of her refused to believe any of this was true. She wondered if she would ever truly believe it. What she did know was that she was going to try her hardest to be the Anin everyone expected her to be. She did not want to disappoint them.

An ugly darkness coated her now—one that festered in her mind and warned her that if she let them see how broken she truly was, they would leave her. While being around anyone was overwhelming, she never wanted to be alone again.

She picked herself up off the ground and dried off

with one of the soft cloths folded neatly in a pile nearby. Each motion was meticulous. She had to be perfect. It was the only way to conceal the ugliness inside her. It should not be too hard for her to pretend to be the Anin who had been taken from this same palace one hundred thirty-seven years ago. Maybe, eventually, she would no longer have to pretend.

She would not cringe away from another being she loved. All she had to do was constantly remind herself to pretend. Just pretend. Everything would be fine.

Kes had a large mirror on one wall of his bathing chamber, and she stood in front of it. She did not truly look at herself; that was the last thing she wanted to do. Instead, she looked at the garment her wings were attempting to create.

It had once been an effortless task. She did not even need to look to create intricate designs with her wings. The ones that still hung in the small stone room had nearly rotted away to dust.

No. That was not what she would think about.

She tried again.

And again.

And again.

They were too short; this pair of wings had not finished growing in yet. They were ugly and misshapen. Nothing she tried worked, and she was not even certain she was doing any of her designs correctly.

Each time her wings flashed, all she could see was a wall covered with decaying wings. Each one different from the pair before. She blinked several times, trying to clear the image.

It did not matter. All she had to do was look at the thin, gossamer wings wrapping around her, and she was right back in her claustrophobic cage.

She was not even aware that she screamed out her frustration. She wanted her wings to be perfect, yet she could not stand the sight of them.

Perhaps she should cut them off?

She saw the tears splash to the ground and onto her chest before she felt them running down her face. If she was saying anything, she could not hear it. All she could hear were thoughts telling her to cut away her useless wings.

"Anin? What happened?" Kes asked as he approached slowly, keeping his hands up and visible to her, as if she were a caged animal. She supposed that was not far from the truth.

"They are ruined," she finally rasped out. Was it her wings that she spoke of, or was it more than that? It did not matter. She hated her wings; she wanted them gone. Kes's arms wrapped around her, and she knew she would never be able to pretend to be perfect.

They would all see her ugliness.

They would all leave her.

"They are ruined."

Cut them away.

"They are ruined."

Cut them away.

Cut them away.

"I—I am ruined."

It's been months since Kes first brought Anin back to his quarters in Nightfell—or "their quarters," as he liked to refer to them. While he was insistent that his space was hers as well, she could not help but feel as though she were invading his privacy.

She had thought about returning to the room that had been "hers" the last time she resided in the palace. However, every time she thought about being alone— even a room away from Kes's reassuring touches—it became impossible to breathe.

It was strange to crave a space of her own. Yet, she never wanted to be out of reach of her mate again. This was not who Anin was. She had been independent her whole life, and now… Well, she was only grateful that Kes seemed to need her as close as she needed to be to him.

Anin had yet to see anyone besides him, except for the few minutes with her sisters when they had first returned with her. She desperately wanted to see her sisters again, but it had taken her longer than she had liked to become acclimated to basic freedom. It was embarrassing enough to have Kes witness her unmaking. She did not wish to see the inevitable pity—or worse, disgust—on her sisters' faces.

Something she had never anticipated when she dreamed of freedom was the decision paralysis she would suffer. It turns out that going so long without having any say in her life made the simplest decisions next to impossible to make. She had only recently been able to choose her dinner, which was more difficult and triggering than it had any right to be.

Apples.

Once, they had been her favorite food in the entire realm. Now, they were forever ruined. She could not look at one without remembering the lone creature that had given her kindness while she had been locked away. There was no way to think of those moments of compassion without associating them with her captivity and all the heinous things the queen had done to her.

She never wanted to eat an apple ever again. If she were honest, even the smell of bread sent her right back to memories of her small cage in the damp stone room. Once the aroma of the freshly baked bread had dissipated, the unbearable stench was amplified. Eventually, she would become blind to the reek of decay again. At the time, she had thought it worth it. Now, the sweet, buttery aroma of fresh bread made her gag and conjured memories of the foul air she had lived in for so long.

Food itself was difficult to get used to again. Although fae would not perish from hunger for a very long time, they did waste away like any other being. The sharp points of her shoulder bones and the deep hollows of her cheeks had only just begun to soften. Kes was doing his very best to entice her to eat several times each night. His efforts, while effective, made her feel like a stubborn youngling.

It was not that she did not want to; she did, truly. Yet, forcing herself to eat was… difficult. Food was still delicious, but instead of eating it all at once, she found herself hoarding and hiding most of it. The constant fear of going without made her irrational. Kes had taken to keeping a constant array of foods on the table at all hours of the night. It helped.

Mostly.

At some point, she knew she would need to push herself to leave the relative comfort she felt within Kes's quarters. Perhaps "comfort" was not the correct term. Safe —she felt safe. Even when her mind attempted deception, she had taught herself to focus on the movement her limbs could make and the smell of her mate that permeated every corner of the space. She could reach out and touch the downy feathers on Kes's wings; if that was not enough, she would feel down the bond to confirm her safety.

The quieter it grew around her, the louder her mind became. Thankfully, it was never truly silent unless Kes was sleeping. He regaled her with a constant stream of stories, filling her in on everything she had missed. It was both wonderful and heartbreaking at once. She had missed so much—*too much.*

"One night, not long after you had been taken, all the witches showed up," Kes told her. They were sitting on the sofa, turned to face each other. Her hands were encased in his, reminding her she was not alone and that she was safe.

She was safe.

"The entire coven?"

"No, every coven. All the witches now reside within the palace."

"How is that possible?" It might seem like a silly question, but anything was possible. It was hard to imagine the witches leaving their covens in the Borderlands and being content as Night Court members, nor could she see the Night fae being particularly thrilled with the living arrangements.

"Ciaran placed an expanding spell on one of the many ballrooms. It gave the witches the freedom to build whatever they pleased within, without altering the appearance of the surrounding palace. It was a genius idea–do not tell him I said that—and as a result, the city is massive. Yet, when you stand outside the doors, it looks like any other ballroom in the palace."

"The city?" He often forgot that she lacked the basic context for most of his stories.

"Sorry," he said, cringing. "They call it Witch City. Every coven has its own space, but now every witch has their own home built on top of it. I thought the Silver Moon Coven in the Borderlands was wild in its construction, but it does not even hold a candle to the insanity of the City. If it were not for magic, their vertically stacked homes would topple." She laughed at his disbelief.

As surprised as he was, she was not. Having grown up in the coven, she knew that to any outsider, the chaos might appear random; yet, the unconventional design worked for them. Beyond that, they also enjoyed laughing in the face of sensibility.

"I want to see it." As soon as she said the words, that ugliness in the back of her mind reared its head, convincing her that it would not be safe and that Tatiana would find her. She knew these thoughts were ridiculous.

If Tatiana could get into Witch City, she would have already. Something—or someone—prevented her from coming to the palace again. Although Anin thought that if the Day Queen became desperate enough, she might risk it. She had been desperate before Anin's escape. How much worse could she have become since then?

"We can go now, if you are sure," Kes said. The hope in his eyes was enough for her to shove her fear as deep as she could.

She was safe. Right?

"I am not sure about anything," she said honestly. "But what's keeping Ta—her out?" There was no way her psychotic sister had not already attempted it.

"We put wards around the entire city to prevent most Day fae from entering. It was one of the first things the fae and witches collaborated on." Some of the tension released from her shoulders, and the image of witches and fae working together made her smile.

"I think I would like to visit my sisters. Perhaps we can start there and see how it goes," she asked, even as terror's grip tightened around her throat. The smile that lit up his face made her want to try.

She could try.

"You are so brave, my darling nymph," he said, his

voice softening as he slowly released one of her hands to cup the side of her face. She huffed a sardonic laugh and looked away. She was anything but brave.

"Anin." When she did not acknowledge him, he used the hand still resting on her cheek to turn her face and make her meet his eyes. "I mean it. You are incredibly brave. I am so proud of you. You fought to survive, and now you are fighting to live. If that is not bravery, I do not know what is."

Tears filled her eyes, and she blinked them away. She was tired of crying, tired of being scared, and just so very tired. For him, though…

For him, she would try.

"Okay, let's go." She nodded, more to convince herself than him.

Kes pulled out his scroll and sent Lyra a message. Faster than she thought possible, her reply came. They were all on their way home that minute and would be there in ten minutes.

All of them.

Kes had told her about Panella finding love and adding to their family. It only made sense that she would meet them as well. She would be fine. It would be fine.

She was safe.

Kes stood and held his hand out to her. There was no doubt that he could feel the fear within her, threatening to empty the contents of her stomach all over the carpeted floor. She stared at his hand while he waited for her to make the choice to go. She knew that the moment she placed her hand within his, he would port them.

"You are brave." He sounded so sure that Anin nearly

believed him. When she looked up at his face, he wore a patient smile. There was so much love swimming in his gaze and pouring through the bond that, for a moment, she forgot the turmoil raging within her stomach.

She was not brave, but for him, she would pretend. She slowly reached out her hand and nearly pulled it back. It hovered above his for what felt like an eternity, and not once did his hand waiver. It remained steady, waiting for her to close the gap.

She was safe.

Anin took a deep breath and gave herself no more time to think about what she was about to do. She closed the distance, the sound of her heart beating erratically the only thing she could hear. The moment she touched him, he gave her hand one small squeeze before they disappeared.

Pretending to be brave and with her terror in tow, Anin took another step toward recovery. At least, that was what she told herself.

Chapter 17
Tatiana

When Tatiana walked into the Throne Room, she paused. She had forgotten the room full of high fae she had left on their knees. At first, she did not want to deal with them and thought they deserved a few days of penance.

She supposed it had been just a touch more than a few days, not that the traitors in the room deserved anything less. She giggled to herself, as she hung on the arm of Raindal walking to her throne.

Her throne.

Not that disgusting creatures.

She screamed, thinking of the empty cage deep in the dungeon's bowels, and dug her claws into Raindal's arm until his orange blood seeped through his shirt's sleeve. Every time she thought of the nymphs' escape, she felt a need to shed blood—particularly Raindal's. She craved it, and he needed to atone for his mistakes.

Tatiana missed the pleasing sound of Anin's screams echoing in the small stone room and bouncing off the walls as they made their way down the long hallway just outside. It had become her favorite song over the years, and now she was desperate to hear it again.

"You should have never listened to him," the *whispers* chided. It did not matter whether she ignored them or not; they continued to speak to her as if she were nothing but a youngling.

"Shut up!" She no longer spoke to them in her mind. There was no point. The *whispers* laughed at her, their sound haunting as it filled her mind.

She hated it. Hated them. Why had she ever listened to them in the first place?

The golden-skinned youngling with golden hair sat at a table, her eyes unseeing, while a pool of golden blood formed beneath her wrist.

Tatiana blinked several times. Each time she saw one of these strange visions, it became harder to remember who she was, let alone where she was. It could have been minutes or days. She was never certain, and the *whispers* were oddly silent afterward.

At least she got a reprieve from their constant disapproval. It was the only positive aspect of the disorienting visions. Sometimes, she thought about releasing Raindal so he could keep track of how long she lost herself in her mind.

The *whispers* had often kept her trapped in her mind with their relentless demands. Listening to them while also hearing the surrounding conversations was nearly impossible—not that she had tried.

For so long, she had listened only to the *whispers*. Nothing else mattered except the power they helped her gain. Now that she had that power, she was uncertain whether she needed them any longer.

Tatiana looked around the room, trying to recall where she was and what she had been about to do. The fae on their knees had not moved an inch. Not that they could—unless she released them. That was how powerful she was.

She did not need the *whispers*; the hundreds of fae before her were proof of that. What she did not want to admit—and did her best to ignore—was the drain on her power. Holding nearly the entire palace under her blood magic's control was exhausting.

Magic did not draw from the well; it was innate. Yet, it made no sense that blood magic was draining her faster than…

The golden youngling was exhausted; her power could not keep up with healing her constantly bleeding wrist. How could it, when her well was always nearly empty because he...

Where was she?

Had that been her?

No, it was impossible. Those were not her memories. She had a happy younghood. One filled with love and a doting mate. No, that was not her.

What had she been doing?

She looked around and saw the hundreds of fae on

their knees and her throne a few steps in front of her. For a moment, she thought her hands gripped the arm of her mate. The fear that consumed her confused her even more than she already was.

Blinking several times and shaking her head, she attempted to clear her mind. When she looked up at the male she held onto, she sighed in relief. It was only Raindal.

Why was she relieved?

She missed her mate terribly. She would have been overjoyed to see him standing beside her once again.

Right?

Of course she would have. The visions were confusing her; that was all it was. She had no idea who the golden youngling was, but she wished she would leave her alone. Shaking her head one last time, she pushed the memory of the vision from her mind.

She knew she had been about to do something, but she was having a hard time recalling it. These were the times she missed Raindal being in control over himself the most. It would have been nice to have him there to remind her.

"It's your fault, you know?" she said, her smile wide and her teeth clenched.

"Yes, my queen." She smiled. At least he did not make mistakes anymore. She also enjoyed how expressive he was now. No longer did she have to look at his impassive face. Now, he looked at her with adoration.

This was better.

She sat on her throne, observing the room full of

unmoving fae. Perhaps if she looked at them long enough, she would remember—

"Oh!" She clapped her hands in excitement. "I remember now. I am a kind and loving queen, am I not?" Tatiana asked. The room responded with a unanimous, "Yes, my queen."

"Because I am, I will give you each a choice. No other ruler would offer you such a gift."

"Yes, my queen," they responded. She smiled at their now thankful faces.

"You have two options. You can either swear your loyalty to me by promising to obey and remain faithful, or you can rot in the dungeons until I have need of you for… something else."

For a moment, she considered making them all promise while she had control over them. However, she would need some to choose the dungeons. Her power drained faster each day she did not make a sacrifice. She was certain that only a few would refuse the promise on their own.

One by one, she made them rise and march single file to the throne. The first fae, a male with bright blue and green feathers so long they dragged on the floor, stood before her. She released just enough of him so he could answer of his own free will.

"What will it be? Will you promise me your loyalty, or will you reside in the dungeons?" she asked. She was surprised to see his face shift from the thankful expression she had made him wear to one of hostility.

"I would rather rot in the dungeons than promise you anything. You are not my que—" She took control of him before he could finish and forced him to walk to the dungeons. She would deal with him later.

Fae after fae chose the dungeons over her, choosing Anin instead. After the tenth, Tatiana screamed and forced the female to rip out her own long, sky-blue hair in bloody chunks before sending her to the dungeons. Tatiana knew just the gown that would complement her blood beautifully.

By the time she had gone through half of the fae, only a handful had made the promise. Tatiana had expected the opposite. She regretted giving them control over the choice, fearing that without free will, it might not be effective.

All her council members, except for Raindal and another male who had a soft spot for the lesser fae, had made the promise. She had expected the merchant, who had first suggested that lesser fae were mere property, to make the promise quickly.

"I am certain I know what you will pick," she said, smiling as she released him just enough. The smile didn't last.

"My queen, I do not understand why you would make those of us already loyal to you make this promise." He seemed… angry, which only enraged Tatiana.

"You dare question me?" she asked, her voice quiet but carrying a promise of violence.

"You are treating your most faithful subjects as lesser fae!" Not only did he dare question her, but he also made the mistake of yelling. She cocked her head to one side and gave him a wicked smile. There was nothing kind about it.

"Are you not lesser than me? Does that not make you a lesser fae to me?"

"I… that's… I've never heard anything more absurd," the male spluttered. She wished she could recall his name, but realized it did not matter. He would not have it for long. Nor his life. She reclaimed her control and took pleasure in forcing him to stand off to the side, alone.

She could not be sure how long it took to get through the entire room of fae—or how long time had passed in general. What she did know was that she was tired of sitting and enraged that only a few dozen out of hundreds had made the promise.

At least she had hundreds of fae waiting to have their power consumed. That reminded her of the merchant she had kept waiting. She rose and compelled him to approach her.

"You foolish male. You should have just made the promise like a good little fae. At least you have a deep well." She reached out with both hands, placing one on Raindal's shoulder and the other on the merchant. In the blink of an eye, the three of them stood in the temple. Chains snapped out, manacling the merchant and forcing him prone on the stone slab. She leaned in to meet his gaze and patted the side of his face.

"I cannot wait to see the color of your blood." The fear in his eyes was a stark contrast to the smile she forced him to wear. She planned to take her time with him. Of all the fae who had rejected her today, his had been the most infuriating.

"Raindal, I am feeling rather excited. I think I will need you many times while he pays the price for questioning his queen," she said, sliding her hand down to grip the bulge she had forced his body to make as she released her hold on the male on the slab. His screams, though not as wonderful as the nymphs', were still music to her ears. "It's going to be such a good time."

"Yes, my queen."

Chapter 18
Ciaran

Ciaran was still fuming about the council meeting he and Etain had left hours earlier. Members of his court had voiced concerns about his strength as king. They were *troubled* by the way Etain had controlled him at the last Lunar Ball. He was ready to rip Syndari's lizard-like head off right then and there. How dare they question his abilities?

"Syndari, how your king and I decide to rule together is no one's business. We, of course, have created a way to balance each other, as fate no doubt intended. Neither of us is more or less powerful than the other," Etain said, placing one of her tiny hands on his leg underneath the table.

Her touch had taken the edge off and calmed him just enough to prevent the scaly council member across the table from losing their head. That did not mean it had done anything to prevent him from growling at the shifting being.

"You are lucky fate has gifted me my mate. If it were not for her, you would have lost your head no less than a dozen times." He glared at the council members— all of them— to remind them of the violence he was capable of.

If Syndari had opened their mouth one more time during the meeting, Ciaran would have lost control. His little witch would have been powerless to stop him. He would have mounted Syndari's head on a stake in the Great Hall. The more he thought about the meeting, the more he liked the idea of doing it anyway.

He sighed heavily and slammed the dusty book shut, perhaps with more force than necessary. He placed it on the stack of finished books at the edge of the table he shared with Etain. Months had gone by, and he was still no closer to finding anything on the damned elemental tombs.

The temple had been his best clue to finding them. However, it was clear they had not been near it for hundreds of thousands of years. He despised fate for making him nothing more than a procurer of books. Yet every time he looked at his little witch, he was reminded that fate had also given him her. Any ridiculous quests it wished to send him on were worth even one minute of a life with her.

"Are you alright, my love?" she asked, resting her hand on his arm and gazing up at him with concern. Gods, she was so small. It was almost comical to see them side by side; their height differences did present some… logistical issues, but he would change nothing about her.

"Ciaran?" she repeated when he did not answer.

"Perfection," he murmured. The word rumbled

through his chest before escaping his lips as he twirled a strand of her dark red hair between his thumb and forefinger. The color was his favorite, and it reminded him of dried human blood. A slow grin spread across his face as crimson crept up her chest and over her cheeks.

Who knew that something as simple as the flush on his mate's skin could bring such pleasure? Just when he thought his view could not improve, a shy smile lifted the corners of her mouth. He swore that the magnitude of his love for her was almost painful.

She had blindsided him. He hadn't known he was capable of loving anyone else until his entire realm revolved around her. Whether it was love or obsession, he saw no difference. He would always love her—obsessively.

"Ciaran?" she whispered.

"Hmm?" He was so caught up in her that everything else faded away. He could not even recall what he had been doing just moments before.

"Are you alright? You were quite growly just a few minutes ago."

"Was I?" he asked, the spell breaking as he recalled their location and the search he had been engrossed in. Unfortunately, he also remembered the earlier council meeting.

"Yes, there were lots of growls and aggressive book-closing."

"Hmm, if you say so, little witch. I am growing increasingly annoyed at spending all of my time scanning old, dusty books."

"Do you think they contain anything you truly need?" she asked honestly.

"If the ancient fae went to such lengths to hide them, then they must contain information worth protecting." He only wished they had not been so thorough.

"But is there a need? What if you just left them hidden?" There was no judgment in her tone, only genuine curiosity.

"It does not matter whether I need them or not. They hold power unknown to me, and that is unacceptable." She laughed softly and shook her head, as if she knew what he was going to say before he did. It was entirely possible she did.

"Enough," he said, standing suddenly and picking up a squealing Etain from her chair. Ciaran held her against him so that they could see eye to eye. He watched as the shock quickly faded, replaced by mirth as she laughed.

"What are you doing, my love?" she asked, her laughter growing louder.

"I recall promising to show you the city—a promise that is well past due."

"Yes, in fact, it is so past due that I have already been to the city multiple times," she said, grinning at him. While she might not be upset with him for not following through on his promise, he was livid with himself.

"It does not matter; you have not seen it with me." For a moment, he considered discovering who she had gone with and mounting their heads next to where Syndari's should be. However, he knew his little witch would never approve.

"No, I have not," she said, placing a small hand on his cheek. "Show me your city, my king."

"Careful, little witch. If you keep talking like that, the

only place I will be taking you is to bed." She threw her head back and laughed as he ported them to the center of Nightfell.

Ciaran could not have planned a better night to take her to the city. There was a bonding ceremony taking place, and the square in the center of the city was decked out with decorations for the festivities. While this was not something he would normally enjoy, he knew his little witch would, and he was not wrong.

She was on her third glass of fae wine, dancing along with the rest of the revelers. He had been surprised to see several witches in attendance, but he had missed a lot while he had been a prisoner to his own mind and fear. No one else seemed surprised, and the sight of each of their kind mixing together made him oddly... content.

He could watch her dance all night, every night. Her pale skin was flushed from a combination of wine and exertion. The gold flecks in her eyes sparkled, and she smiled freely as she twirled and jumped, stomping along with the others in the circle before they turned and moved their feet in complicated patterns only to start the whole sequence again.

Ciaran had never been one for dancing. It was not that he did not know how to dance; he simply did not see the point in it. However, as he watched his mate move with abandon, he became increasingly jealous of the males surrounding her.

Her eyes found his even though he had shrouded himself in shadows. It had become necessary when beings began to line up to greet him, and all he wanted to do was watch his little witch without interruption. She stopped moving in the middle of the dance, and a slow grin full of mischief rose as she made her way toward him.

Without saying a word, she grabbed his hand and pulled him toward the dance floor. He could have easily resisted and remained unmoving, but he did not want to. He wanted to go with her, always.

"Dance with me, my love," she demanded, and who was he to deny his little witch?

Her eyes widened in surprise when he scooped her up and took them to the very center of the dancers. She stood stunned for a moment when he put her down, grabbed her hands, and waited three counts before he began to dance. He executed the steps perfectly, and when it came time to spin, he twirled her around several times before the next steps began.

Etain laughed as she joined him, her momentary shock melting away. The only time they broke eye contact was when it was time to twirl her around, and with each step, he could feel the desire building between them. It flowed back and forth through the bond, growing stronger with each song that played.

There was no telling how long they had danced before the music began to slow and the boisterous beat transformed into something intimate. He did not care that their height difference made it difficult. He still drew her close, took one of her hands in his, and rested the other on her lower back. Then he led her through the slow, sensual steps the song required.

"I did not know you could dance," Etain said. Several strands of her hair stuck to her face and neck from the perspiration their exertion elicited.

"Just because I do not does not mean I cannot, little witch." He gave her one of his wicked, extra-wide grins. He extended his long fingers down so that he was barely caressing the curve of her backside and felt a surge of male satisfaction when her eyes darkened with desire.

"Looking at me like that will get you dragged into the nearest shadowy alcove and reminded of who you belong to," he growled.

"Hmmm, I think I need to be reminded," she said, returning his wicked smirk.

She did not need to tell him twice. He squeezed her ass and lifted her until she wrapped her legs around his waist. He then moved toward the nearest cluster of shadows he could find. Within seconds, he had her pinned against the stone wall of the garden, enveloped by a shield of shadows. She was for his eyes alone.

"You need to be reminded, do you, little witch?" he asked as he set her down on her feet. Two shadows emerged from him. Etain's eyes widened at the sight of the two perfect shadowy recreations of him, and she could only nod in response. Though he did not often use them in such moments, he began to think he should.

Ciaran leaned back against the wall, nearly laughing at Etain's puzzled expression. His amusement only grew when his shadows began to untie her gown, and her eyes snapped to his, wide and heated.

His little witch seemed to enjoy his shadows coming out to play. As did he. Everything the shadows experienced, he felt. Instead of touching her with a single pair of hands, he could touch her with three or more if he wished.

A shadowy hand skimmed down her front, removing the gown and revealing her naked body before dropping to its knees. She gasped when the shadow threw her leg over its shoulder and buried its face in her dripping core. He could taste her desire as it flooded the shadow's mouth and, irrationally, he was jealous of his own shadow.

The other shadow stood behind her, wrapping a hand around her throat while the first shadow squeezed her breasts and teased her nipples until they were hard peaks.

"Ciaran, oh gods. I—" her hooded eyes widened, and his smile turned devious as the shadow kneeling before her slid a finger into her dripping channel and then coated her puckered opening with her own desire. He had never touched her there. However, based on the loud moan she released as the finger slid slowly into her, this would not be the last time.

"My dirty little witch, you like that, do you?" She nodded, incapable of words. He approached her and grasped her chin, compelling her to meet his gaze. "Tell me, let me hear the words, little witch."

"Oh gods, Ciaran, please, more," she begged, her eyes rolling back as his shadow slid its finger in and out, synchronizing with the motions of its tongue on her core. When his shadow added a second finger and sucked on the little bundle of nerves, she detonated.

No longer content to merely watch his mate writhing

from the efforts of his shadows, he pressed his mouth to hers and devoured her cries of pleasure as his shadow added yet another finger. He loved that he tasted not only her mouth but her desire as it slid down the throat of his shadow.

There was something about having his little witch completely exposed while he remained fully clothed that thrilled him, but now he needed to be inside her—all of her.

The shadow at her feet faded back into him while he kept her legs wrapped around him. The shadow behind her slid into her heat from behind, pumping into her a few times before pulling out. While his shadow slowly pressed into her back entrance, Ciaran pushed into her core.

"I do not think I... Ciaran, it's too much," Etain whimpered.

"You can, and you will. I noticed how your core turned molten when you watched females taken like this at the Lunar Balls. You will never forget who you belong to after I have claimed every inch of you," he growled before he covered her mouth with his own to take every cry and moan she released. Those were his. Her pleasure belonged to him. She belonged to him.

With both he and his shadow fully seated inside her, they paused to allow her time to adjust. As her body began to move on its own, he withdrew his mouth and started a fast, hard pace. Meanwhile, his shadow maintained slow, shallow movements behind her.

His little witch had always enjoyed a touch of pain with her pleasure. Her eyes were tightly shut as moans of both sensations escaped her. His shadow maintained a hand on her throat, applying the smallest amount of pressure. "Open your eyes, little witch. Let me see you fall into oblivion."

Her eyes flew open and met his, wild and glassy. They stared into each other's eyes as the shadow behind him increased its pace. "Little witch, I do not know how much longer I can last. Gods, you are so tight," he groaned. The sensation of filling her completely was almost overwhelming. He had to force himself not to finish too soon, as though he were an inexperienced youth.

Etain's mouth opened in a silent scream as she clamped down tight around him. He finally let himself spill into her damp heat. As they slowed their movements, Etain hung limp. He then let his shadow slide out of her before stepping back into her and ported his boneless mate back to their chambers.

Gently laying her on their bed, he asked, "Who do you belong to, little witch?" Her reply was so soft and quiet that, without fae ears, he might not have heard her.

"You, Ciaran. Always you."

Chapter 19
Lyra

S he looked better. Of course, anything was better than how Anin had looked when Kes stepped out with her from the cell where she had been kept for… well, Lyra did not like to think about the many years her sister had been missing from their lives. Particularly not now that she knew the conditions in which Anin had been rotting away.

She had put on weight, and while she still stood close enough to Kes that their bodies were touching, she seemed to stand a little taller. Lyra wanted nothing more than to squeeze her sister in the tightest hug she could manage, but she did not want to frighten her. More than that, she could not bear to see Anin flinch away from her again.

Lyra had been the first to arrive and the only one present when Kes and Anin ported in. They stood several feet apart in the center of the lounge within the home she and Panella had created and later expanded when Ravyn and Tyne moved in with them. At least this time, Anin met her eyes.

"Little chick," Kes said in greeting after they all stood there for several minutes in silence.

"Pillow," Lyra responded. Kes laughed, and her heart soared when Anin smiled.

"I see you two have—"

"She's really here?" Tyne's loud, and excited voice filled the room before the youngling ever stepped foot into it. The change in Anin was instant. She made herself small and tucked herself in under one of Kes's wings.

As much as Lyra wanted to scold Tyne, it was not her fault, and she would never tell the youngling witch her joy was wrong, even if it was loud.

"Yes, but remember, she has been through a lot, and you need to give her space," Ravyn replied in a soft, even voice.

"Oh, right," Tyne said, much softer. "I am just so excited to finally meet Aunt Anin." Lyra never took her eyes off Anin and smiled when she seemed to peek out curiously from Kes's shelter.

Panella was the first to come up the stairs from the entrance below. She moved slowly, not wanting to frighten Anin, and stood next to Lyra. However, all of Panella's caution was rendered useless when Tyne ran up the stairs and into the room, coming to an abrupt stop next to Panella. The sudden movements spooked Anin, and she hid under Kes's wing again.

"Tyne," Ravyn said with an exasperated sigh. To her credit, Tyne did look contrite, even if she could not pull her eyes away from the aunt she had only ever heard stories about.

"Hey there, baby chaos," Kes said, smiling fondly at the youngling. Tyne was more than halfway to maturity, but if you asked her, she would say she was already grown.

She had lost the roundness that small younglings have and was in that stage where some parts of her grew faster than others. It was not uncommon for her to trip over her feet or run into walls she swore were not there before. When your body is constantly changing, it is nearly impossible to maintain a center of gravity.

Tyne rolled her eyes, which were the exact shade of green as her mother's, at Kes. "I am not a baby," she said, glaring at him, which only made him laugh.

"No, but you are definitely chaos," he said, eyes shining with mirth.

"Well, what did you expect to happen? I spent far too much time around you as a youngling not to turn out a little bit ridiculous," she replied. Her hands were on her hips, and the corners of her mouth struggled to stay in the scowl she had forced it into.

During their exchange, Anin slowly emerged from her hiding place. A softness appeared on her face as she watched her mate interact with the youngling. Kes was good with Tyne; he always had been. Likely because he is not much more mature than she is. Actually, Tyne might be more mature now that she thinks about it.

"Ohhh, your wings are so much prettier than his," Tyne said, as she noticed Anin. She barely stopped herself from reaching out to touch them.

"Normally, I would be highly offended; however, I

happen to agree with you on this one," Kes said with a wink. It was strange—in a good way—to see this version of him again. He had forced himself to wear the mask of the memory of who he once had been. That Kes paled in comparison to the vibrant, full-of-life male who stood before her.

"Gasp!" Tyne said dramatically, clutching at her heart. Goddess, she had really spent far too much time with the bird beast. "Can it be? Is that... modesty? No, it's not possible," she said, wearing a comically shocked expression.

"No, not modesty. It's simply a fact. There is only one other being who is better looking than yours truly," he said, placing his arm around Anin and forcing her to come just a bit further out from hiding. He lifted her chin so that they looked into each other's eyes. "And that would be her." Anin's cheeks flushed a bright green at his words.

"Oh, gross. Go get a room," Tyne said, making fake gagging noises, effectively ending the sweet moment between the mates. Her mother sighed again.

"I am terribly sorry," Ravyn said, looking at Anin. "I am Ravyn, and this excited youngling is our daughter, Tyne," who rolled her eyes at being called a youngling. It amazed Lyra how every youngling was always in such a hurry to grow up and refused to listen when told to enjoy their youth. Life only seemed to get harder and more compli-cated the older one got.

"I am very happy to meet you," Anin said. Lyra knew she was telling the truth, even though her body language suggested otherwise. She kept glancing past them at the wall of windows that overlooked the city.

"It's impressive, right?" Lyra asked Anin, who nodded in response. "It took a while to get to this point, but now the covens have pretty much blended together. I am not sure how we could ever go back to our separate covens in the Borderlands."

"Maybe you are not meant to." Anin's voice, though loud enough to hear, was uncertain. The few words she had spoken sounded more like questions than statements. "Fate does get what she wants in the end." That was a truth they knew all too well.

"Oh, Auntie Anin, I am just so happy you are here," Tyne said, bouncing on the balls of her feet. That should have made it obvious to the rest of them that she was about to lose the barely caged restraint and no one should have been surprised when she bolted toward Anin with arms wide open. She moved so fast, no one could intercept her until it was too late.

Anin made a choking noise and flinched away from Tyne's touch. The youngling stopped in her tracks, her eyes wide as if they were consuming her face. "Oh, no," she gasped, covering her mouth with her hands. "I am so sorry, I forgot." Her words were muffled as she took several slow steps back toward her mothers.

"I—" Anin bawled. "I... am... sorry." Her words were stilted and pushed out between sobs. "I... I just... what I mean is..." She tried to form a complete thought, but panic overwhelmed her. Lyra hated that there was nothing they could do to help her. Even after Kes whispered something in her ear, she continued to look at Tyne with a horrified expression.

"It's okay, Auntie Anin, it's my fault. I forgot. I have been dreaming about meeting you for so long that my excitement got the best of me," Tyne said, her remorse making her sound even younger than she was. Anin groaned, and a fresh wave of tears poured down her face.

"I want to… but touch… it makes…"

"I know!" Tyne said, her excitement returning. "How about this? You can hug me whenever you want, and you can tell me when you're ready for me to hug you back." She looked at her aunt with so much hope as Anin blinked repeatedly, taking in what Tyne had just offered.

It was honestly a brilliant idea. Perhaps if Anin were in control, she could take another step toward healing. Tyne was not the only one looking at Anin hopefully.

Her sobs quieted, and she slowly nodded at Tyne while taking a single step out from the shelter of her mate. Tyne slowly closed the distance, smiling up at her aunt the entire time. She stood before Anin for several moments while the others held their breath.

Just when Lyra thought Anin might back away, she lifted a single hand and rested it on Tyne's shoulder. After a few moments, she seemed to become comfortable with that and then slowly—painfully slowly—wrapped her arms around a very still Tyne.

"Thank you," Anin whispered to Tyne, burying her face in the crook of the young witch's neck.

"I love you, Auntie."

"I love you too." Anin's body shook as she silently cried, holding Tyne. Lyra had never been prouder of her niece than she was at that moment. Several moments passed before Anin unfolded herself from Tyne and stepped back into the safety of her mate.

She whispered something to Kes before retreating again. He looked at them apologetically before porting them away. Although Lyra was disappointed not to have felt her sister's arms around her, she was more than happy to have witnessed the progress made.

No one said anything or moved for a heartbeat or two. When Tyne turned to look at them, she wore one of the biggest smiles Lyra had ever seen grace the youngling's face. Before anyone had a chance to speak, the door opened below and heavy footsteps ascended the stairs.

"Little terror, are you here?" Zandar called up, grumbling under his breath about how ridiculous it was that she made him enter through the door instead of porting in unannounced. He still did not seem to understand the concept of knocking.

Lyra groaned and looked up at the ceiling. She did not feel like dealing with his overbearing presence just now—or ever. She glared at her sister when she heard her fail to contain her laughter.

"Why are you here?" she asked, aware that she was being rude but not caring. His entire existence seemed rude to her.

"Well, hello to you too," he said, with his usual mirthful voice. It annoyed Lyra. Everything about him annoyed her. "While I am sure you have missed me in the past four hours, unfortunately, I bring not the best news."

"What happened?" Panella asked, much kinder than she would have.

"Another coven's apothecary has been smashed to pieces."

"How did you find out before we did?" Lyra asked him as she crossed her arms and eyed him suspiciously.

"I was walking by," he said with a shrug.

"You were just walking by?"

"Well, I may have been looking for someone." When she scowled at him, he had the audacity to wink at her. Wink! "Anyway, they asked us to look into it."

"Us, huh?" Lyra asked, rolling her eyes.

"Which coven was it?" Ravyn asked.

"Black Cauldron."

Shit.

Lyra sighed and looked at Zandar. Somehow, the fae had intertwined his life with hers, and she was more annoyed with herself than anyone. Well, no. She was always annoyed by him—or, more accurately, by her body's reaction to him. However, she wasn't going to linger on that thought.

"Alright, fae-fae, let's get on with it." He grinned at her, his smile turning wicked as he grabbed her hand instead of her shoulder and ported them away.

It was a disaster. After speaking with the head witch of the Black Cauldron Coven, she informed them that theirs was the only stock of Arctic Brittlebush. It came from another realm connected to the human one and was nearly impossible to replace.

If that was not bad enough, whoever destroyed the

apothecary left a message behind. Written in red blood were the words: "The golden queen is coming.".

"It had to be done by a witch," Zandar declared after they had fully surveyed the room..

"What in the realm makes you think something so ridiculous?" she scoffed.

"No fae would know about Arctic Brittlebush," he shrugged as if it were the obvious answer.

"There is no way a witch would do this. Why would they? We all know how important Arctic Brittlebush is, and why would a witch threaten *this*?" she asked, throwing her arm out in annoyance to indicate the bloody warning.

"I had never heard of Arctic Brittlebush until just this very moment and I would have no idea what it looked like if it had not been pointed out."

"So, that does not mean it was not collateral damage. How do we know this coven was specifically targeted and not just chosen at random?"

"How many other covens have Arctic Brittlebush?"

"None," she sighed, deflating a bit. She did not want to think it was possible for one of her fellow witches to wreak such destruction on their community.

"Exactly."

Shit.

Chapter 20
Kes

Over the past few nights, Anin had become braver. She embraced her sisters and Panel-Ola's lover with newfound courage. After each step forward, she exhausted herself and slept for hours, or sometimes for entire nights. However, Kes knew the moment he stepped into the small stone room and saw her hanging in that damned cage that her healing would be more than a battle. Anin had to wage war on her trauma—and she was fighting.

Some nights were better than others. Selfishly, he was glad that she had never pushed him away. At times, he had to remind her to connect through their bond. This mostly occurred during nights when she jolted awake from memories haunting her sleep. Thankfully, these episodes no longer occurred every time she closed her eyes.

Although he knew she was far from okay, he was incredibly proud of his nymph. Her bravery required a different kind of strength than battling another. With one, victories were clear and measurable; with the other, you had to trust yourself to believe in your progress. Trust—especially in oneself—is one of the hardest things to achieve.

He managed to stop her from hiding food in random places. The brownies were surprisingly accommodating of Anin's hoarding. If he were to stuff a piece of fruit behind a pillow on the couch, they would make his life miserable for at least a week. He had been concerned that he would need to spell his tower, much like Ciaran's, to keep them out. It seems the little beasts have compassion, after all.

He had been watching her sleep for an indeterminate amount of time when a scroll appeared before him. As he unrolled it, he expected it to be from one of her sisters, or perhaps even from Ciaran. Instead, it was from someone claiming to be the mate of the rebel leader. He demanded that Kes meet him at the same crumbling tower where he had met his mate.

He was tempted to ignore the message—more than tempted. His mind screamed at him to forget it. Then he looked at his mate and knew she would one day sit upon the throne. Beyond that, he knew he owed the last few months to the rebel leader. For that reason alone, he agreed to go.

He spelled the room to alert him if Anin so much as rolled over in her sleep. He refused to let her wake up alone. If she needed him to stop her from reliving a memory, he would be there. She might never know he had left her by herself, but he would, and the guilt was threatening to overwhelm him. Yet, he knew he had to go.

Porting to the ruins, he was surprised to see a satyr pacing in the light. His mate had never let Kes see his face, while he did not seem to have a covert bone in his body. This could not be good.

He dropped down, and the satyr jumped, clutching his chest before staring at Kes. "I know I am pretty, but I am spoken for," he said, and smiled when the satyr rolled his eyes.

"You are just bigger than I thought you would be."

"I get that a lot," Kes said as seriously as he could manage.

"Oh, for the sake of the gods," the satyr said, looking up to the sky as if begging the gods to give him the patience required to deal with Kes.

Kes instantly liked him.

"So, satyr, where is your mate? You do not seem exactly… experienced." He did not want to offend the satyr, but his lack of decorum was a bit concerning.

"He's the reason I sent you the scroll in the first place, against my better judgment. Killia insisted, so here we are." He threw his arms out wide, as if he were annoyed to be there. Kes raised one of his downy brows at the satyr.

"Sorry," he bit out. "It took me forever to walk here. I could not even send the scroll until I arrived."

"Oh, I would be rather annoyed if I had to walk everywhere, too. I guess it's a good thing I decided to show up." The satyr paused in his pacing long enough to gape at him.

"You thought about not showing? After everything he did for your mate? Oh, I would have been so livid. I would have marched my ass straight to Nightfell just to tell you exactly how furious I was."

"Calm down, Day fae; I am here. It was the fact that my mate slept in our bed instead of that horrifically small cage that ultimately brought me here. Now, what is this about? I need to get back to her in a few minutes."

"You need to get her to claim her throne. I have not heard from my mate in months, and I know the Day Queen has done something to him." His words were bad enough, but the finger he wagged at Kes made his earlier feelings about the fae dissipate immediately.

"Who do you think you are to make demands of not only me but also my mate?" he spat at the satyr while crowding him against a tall, crumbling wall. He had to give the fae credit; most in his position would tend to cower, but he did not back down.

"A desperate mate, that's who!" he yelled in Kes's face.

"I understand you are panicking because your mate is gone," he said. When the satyr opened his mouth to argue, Kes glowered at him and raised a hand to stop him from speaking. "My mate was gone for one hundred thirty-seven years! I fucking know what it feels like to be as desperate as you feel right now." The satyr's mouth snapped shut.

"You need to back the fuck off. Anin is in no position to rule a court, let alone take her throne by force."

"But all she has to do is sit on the throne and then break all the deals that have been forced upon the lesser fae," the satyr said, his brow pinching together in confusion. He really thought it was that easy.

"You fool. You forgot to mention that pesky little

magic the Day Queen has. Not only that, but Anin flinches at the prospect of being touched. She shakes when she hears someone walking down a hall, and she cannot breathe if a room is too large. She hides under my wing when even her sisters enter the room. She. Is. Not. Well!" It was the first time he had allowed himself to say all of that out loud. The more he said, the louder he got until he was screaming in the satyr's face.

He took several steps back from the satyr, who stared at him with wide, devastated eyes. Kes was certain he had once looked the same way. He released a heavy sigh and dragged a hand down his face.

"Look, I am not saying it will not happen. It will. You just have to give her time to heal. One hundred thirty-seven years of torture does not simply vanish. Those memories are forever burned into her, no matter how much either of us wishes they were not.

I do not know how long it will take for her to be strong enough to be the queen fate intended her to be, but I do know it will take years, if not decades. And you stand here expecting her to be fine within months."

"I—"

"When she's ready, no matter how long that takes, I will contact you," Kes said, not letting the satyr speak. The satyr physically deflated and stared at the ground, unseeing. Kes felt for him; he truly did. The memory of what the satyr was feeling was still fresh in his mind. There was nothing he could do about it. Anin would be ready when she was ready, no sooner.

Finally, the satyr looked up and met Kes's gaze. It was like looking in a mirror from a few months ago. He wished he could say something to give the satyr hope, but he knew there was nothing.

"What am I supposed to do?" the satyr asked in a small voice thick with agony.

Kes placed a hand on the satyr's shoulder and ported them close to Daybreak. At least he could spare him a long walk alone with nothing but his spiraling thoughts to keep him company. When Kes met the satyr's eyes again, tears streamed freely down his face. Kes answered him truthfully before returning to his sleeping mate.

"Whatever you must."

Chapter 21

Etain

"Well, that was fast," Etain said as she entered the clearing that held the deceptively small mushroom hut.

She had been looking forward to a long walk in the woods, but instead, she had walked for no more than fifteen minutes. The single door flew open, and in the doorway stood Hecate. Or the Many Faced Goddess, as she was known in this realm.

Every time Etain saw her, with the exception of the first time, it still took her a while to adjust to her ever-shifting face. She had to force herself to stop looking for a glimpse of her mother; she had made an appearance only that first time. As much as she wanted nothing more than to see her again, she would never complain and would cherish that first meeting as the gift it was.

"Hello, my child."

"Hello, Hecate," Etain said as she entered the mushroom hut and gave her creator a kiss on her shifting cheek as she passed.

It was always a surprise stepping into Hecate's peculiar home. Much like her face, the interior was ever-changing. No matter how big or small it was at any given time, it always felt like home.

She did not know if that had to do with the drying herbs hanging from the rafters or the ancient table with marks similar to those on the one she grew up sitting around. Etain thought it was more than likely all of that and the goddess herself; she was the original mother, after all.

"Come, child, sit. The tea is almost ready." Etain sat at the large table directly across from where Hecate sat. "I know why you are here, but why do you think you are?" It was always intimidating speaking to a being as ancient as she was.

"I promised Ciaran I would come and ask you about these missing elemental texts he is searching for. I told him not to expect much," she said, smiling.

"Oh, I would have loved to see his face when he asked you to ask me for help—for him." She must have been imagining it because, a second later, she began cackling.

"I was surprised as well. However, I think he would rather become your closest friend than search for another book," Etain said, laughing with her.

"Unfortunately, you were correct. There is nothing I can do to help him. Whether he likes it or not, he is on the path fate has decided for him; all he can do is continue forward." Etain sighed, knowing Ciaran would be disappointed. She had hoped there would be something she could do to help her mate.

"While I can do nothing for him, there is something I can help you with—something you have been searching for," the goddess said as she poured two cups of tea and slid one over to Etain.

"Shade power," Etain whispered, and the goddess smirked at her and nodded her confirmation.

"It is difficult to learn something that no one else knows. I would appreciate any guidance you are willing to give."

"Do you trust it?"

"Trust what? My shade power?" Etain asked, stopping her teacup halfway to her mouth and furrowing her brows in confusion.

"Yes. Do you trust it?"

"Hardly," Etain said, laughing. "It comes and goes as it pleases and is anything but reliable."

"Are you trying to control it?" the goddess asked between sips of hot tea.

"Yes, I put all my effort into controlling it, but it feels like the harder I try, the more out of control it becomes." Hecate nodded. She set her teacup back in its saucer, folded her hands in front of her, and then leaned forward just a bit. Etain felt herself leaning toward the goddess as well.

"Stop." Etain blinked several times. She had not known what the goddess was going to say, but it was definitely not what she would have imagined.

"Stop what?"

"Trying to control it. If you try too hard, particularly

with little to no trust between you and the shades, they will rebel. Shades are not meant to be controlled. Think of it as though you are creating a spell with another witch: You do not control her; you work with her."

Strangely, that felt right. It had always felt like a separate entity from her— as if she were merely a host. However, perhaps she should start thinking of her shade power as a friend.

"Have your other colors shown up yet?" the goddess asked.

"What other colors? Other shades? I only have dark shade."

"Nonsense," Hecate said, moving her hand as if she could brush Etain's answer away. "If you have shade power, that means you have all the colors. Beyond that, you cannot have only dark shade; it does not exist without light shade."

"What do you mean?"

"Balance, my child. Everything must have balance. If you have shade power, you have both light and dark—and everything in between. If you have full shade power, which is the absence of color, then you must have full color power as well."

"Balance... Why have I never seen the other colors, then?"

"Oh, those things can be rather elusive. They like to hide. I swear they think it's a game."

"You speak of them as if they are living beings," Etain said absently as she finished the last of her tea.

"Are they not?" the goddess asked, lifting the kettle toward Etain in question.

"Please," she said, pushing her cup forward. She watched the steam rise as her cup filled again. "I suppose they might be. They prefer to be asked to cooperate rather than told to."

"Yes, they remind me of pixies—mischievous little things." They were silent for a moment, and Etain wondered if the goddess would give her any more instruction on her untamed power.

"I told you about the human man who got me with child. What I did not tell you was that I did not have just one daughter."

"What?" It might not be what she had been hoping the goddess would say next, but she loved a good story, and Hecate had the best.

"I had three daughters. Walshnee, who was born with the same red hair as you. Grimmsel had hair as black as night, and Sidhe with hair the palest shade of blonde. I had to be able to tell them apart, so I made sure to give them distinctive hair before they were born."

"Walshnee..."

"That is who you descend from. She was the only one to stay in the Fae Realm and was responsible for creating the first line of witches in the realm. Any witch born with her distinctive hair was known as a Walshnee witch.

Generation after generation, the Walshnee witches were always born of the same line. Many witches carried the name simply because their ancestors once did. However, there was only one direct line that descended from my daughter.

When Walshnee gave birth to her first daughter, she gifted her half of her power. Every generation after that received the same. However, power cannot just cease to exist.

When a Walshnee died and came to live within me, her power was drawn to its other half. If that half was spread out between multiple living Walshnee witches, it would split and join each of them.

When your ancestor crossed the veil to protect her child, she took most of that power with her. There was only one other true Walshnee who remained living on this side of the veil. When she passed, like was still drawn to like, and that final bit of power crossed the veil.

Just because your ancestors spent generations in the Human Realm does not mean the power was not there to be passed along. The Human Realm nullifies power, unless you are a god, of course. It does not erase it."

"So when my mother died…"

"You were given the full power. There has not been a Walshnee with the amount of power you contain since my granddaughter Maeve was born. She was the queen of all fairies, but of course, the realm she ruled has long ceased to exist. That's a story for another time."

"How did Walshnee become Walsh?" Etain asked. She was so entranced by Hecate's story that she had yet to process what it meant to have that much power.

She had the power of a demigod.

The goddess smiled at her, as if she knew where her thoughts had just gone. "Time, like all things, has a way of eroding one thing and transforming it into another. When Walshnee left the realm generations after Maeve existed, her legacy was eventually simplified to Walsh.

While Walshnee herself was lost to the history of the realm."

"Does that not make you sad?" Etain thought that if she had a daughter who helped shape the realm as much as Hecate's did, she would be devastated when that realm forgot her.

"It is the way fate intended it to be. She left to travel the realms with her sisters and has had many different histories since."

"Do you miss them?" She felt the sting of tears as she thought about her own mother and how she could never leave her in a realm all alone.

"Do not fret, child. I am eternal, as are they. Time moves differently for us. Sometimes they come here, and sometimes I meet them in a different realm. We are gods; we are not beholden to the same laws as others." She stood and began to clean up their dirty cups and the now-empty kettle.

She stopped and chuckled to herself before looking at Etain. "That shadow mate of yours is on his way. It seems you have been gone too long for his liking." Etain rolled her eyes and made her way to the door before quickly glancing back at the goddess. Did she know about Ciaran and what he, well, *they*, liked to do with his shadows?

No, of course not. How could she?

Hecate winked at Etain and opened the door just as Ciaran stepped into the clearing.

Or maybe she did.

"You are back sooner than I expected," Killia said, as he entered the one-room shack he shared with his mother.

"What are you doing here?" He lacked the energy to respond, and perhaps always would.

"Did he not show? Is that why you are back so soon?" Her sharp tone ignored his need for silence.

"He did. He ported me just outside the city." It felt like he was wading through tar as he dragged himself to his cot of vines.

"That was considerate," she said impatiently, her voice demanding more details. He grunted and groaned as he lay down, exhausted. All he wanted was to sleep for days. Maybe if he slept long enough, Raindal would be with him again when he awoke.

Ever since his deal—and those of many other lesser fae —was severed, he had been working tirelessly to get as many out of the city as possible. Many could not leave their families behind and had to continue maintaining the illusion of being tied to a high fae.

Something was happening in the palace. According to the fae his mate had placed there, the dungeons were filled with high fae who refused to make a deal with their queen. The irony was not lost on him.

Apparently, she disappeared daily with one of them and later returned wearing their blood and a matching gown. She was obviously killing them. This was the only way the deals kept getting severed. It was ironic, in a completely humorless way, that not a single high fae nor the queen herself had considered the deals they had forced the lesser fae to make. Their entitlement would be their downfall.

"Balthier!" Killia yelled. He had forgotten she was there.

"What?" he asked, too tired to put any bite into his question. He threw his arm over his eyes, hoping she would go away if he could not see her.

She did not.

"What? What do you mean, *what?*" she shrieked. He sighed, knowing this would be a long eclipse if he did not get her out of there soon. Balthier sat up and looked at her. His face must have answered for him.

"That bad?" she asked softly, taking the seat next to him.

"Apparently, she is too broken to become queen."

"No. That cannot be. We sacrificed everything to free her so that she could save us," she said, refusing to accept his words.

"He said she just needed time. One hundred thirty-seven years of trauma does not simply disappear in a few months. It was not what any of us wanted to hear, but he's right to stand between us and her."

"What do you mean by that?" she asked, her anger rising. She was always angry, it seemed.

"I mean, I might not know what she went through while imprisoned in the palace, but I can imagine it. There is no realm where she did not make her sister wish for death every day. That is many days wishing to die."

They sat there silently, thinking. All he could think about was being without Raindal for nearly a century and a half. Gods, he did not think he would be strong enough to survive.

"I am terrified," he whispered.

"For Raindal?"

"Yes. I have not felt anything from him in months," he said, his voice breaking.

"He's alive. You would know if he were not," she said, leaning her head on his shoulder and holding his hand. "You would know."

"What if he comes back to me as broken as she is?" He finally put words to the fear that gripped to his stomach and twisted every few moments to remind him it was there.

"Then you have to help him put himself back together. You can face whatever comes later—together." She gave his hand a squeeze.

"I am failing."

"Failing? How?" she asked, lifting her head and staring at him, confusion scrunching her face.

"The lesser fae. How can I possibly protect them? I am no one. I have no elemental powers. I am just one fae."

"Why is it your job alone to protect the lesser fae?" Anger returned to her voice—though it had never truly disappeared.

"Because my mate dumped the fate of our kind in my lap when he got himself into whatever trouble he's in."

"Balthier," she said, standing and then crouching in front of him. "It is the responsibility of all lesser fae to protect the others. We all understand that. I'm not sure how you do not. Leading the rebels is not the same, and even then, you are not doing it alone."

"I have no idea what I am doing."

"Neither did Raindal at one point." He found that hard to believe. His mate had always been so sure of himself. He let out a long, slow breath and met her eyes.

"What am I supposed to do?" It was the same question he had asked Kes, and her response echoed his.

"Whatever you must."

"You look beautiful," Kes said from the doorway as he watched Anin finish tucking her wings to create an intricate, layered effect. This might be Anin's favorite wing creation ever. The results were flattering, while still managing to be casual enough for the occasion.

"Thank you," she said, smiling at him through the mirror. She turned and walked toward him, unhurried, and was pleased when his gaze slowly dropped down her body. When his eyes met hers, they were filled with heat.

"Are you sure you do not want to stay in tonight?" he asked suggestively.

She wrapped her arms around his waist and smiled up at him. Part of her felt guilty every time he alluded to sex. She had been back for years, and she still had a hard time with touch, particularly if it were intimate.

It felt as though every protective wall she had built might crumble and collapse, exposing all of her ugly bits.

No one else seemed to notice the scars covering her body, but they were all she could see.

As Kes's hands whispered across her bare skin, all she felt was the path once carved by Tatiana's knife. It made it impossible to finally go there with her mate and he was too wonderful to ever be anything but supportive and never let her see his disappointment. Yet, she knew he had to be.

"Hmmm, tempting." She tipped up on her toes to meet his lips with her own in a fleeting kiss. "But no. I need this time with my sisters. It has been far too long since we did anything like this, and I am actually excited to go out."

Lyra and Panella had been talking about going out for a "sister night" for a long time. Anin had wanted to, but it was not until recently that she felt ready to be out without Kes and surrounded by beings.

Years of effort had brought her to this point, filling her with pride and deep gratitude for Etain's support. Etain had crafted a tea tailored to Anin's needs, easing the persistent sadness and the gaping void of despair that constantly threatened to swallow her whole. It gave her space to breathe, allowing her to observe them from the edges of her consciousness and learn how to live with them. They would always be there, but now they felt like a part of her instead of consuming her.

"If you need me, I will be there instantly. You know what to do, and there is no shame in calling on me. You are being incredibly brave tonight, my darling nymph." He leaned down and gave her lips another soft kiss. That seemed to be as far as she could manage comfortably.

Even if he was not disappointed in her, she was disappointed in herself. She craved him in the way all mates desire their other halves. It was as if her body and heart wanted one thing and her mind refused to be a part of it.

"I will be fine," she said with a roll of her eyes. "I am so much stronger now."

"It is not weak to call for help," he said, squinting his burning red eyes down at her.

"I will. I promise I will. If something happens, I will call for you." Most of the time, she loved how much he wanted to protect her, but sometimes it made her feel like he did not think she would ever be well again.

"I hope you know how proud I am. You have come such a long way in a short amount of time. It's incredibly impressive."

"It's been years, Kes," she scoffed.

"And you were gone for nearly one and a half centuries. Do not discredit yourself." He gave her a serious look, which looked very wrong on his face.

"Fine, fine," she said as she untangled herself from him. "And do not look at me like that. It's weird." He laughed and swatted her on the butt. Which only made her laugh, too.

She had him to thank for the place she was at now. When he first rescued her, she had lost every ounce of confidence she had ever possessed. It was not until he taught her how to port that she slowly started to get it back.

She had fought hard against his insistence that she learn. When he told her how it was done, all she could think about was getting stuck in the nothing. She had just been freed from one prison; she did not want to go to another.

He had eventually gotten what he wanted, and she would be forever grateful. That first time she did it, she felt a sense of accomplishment that she had not known she was missing. She went from letting life move around her to becoming an active participant in it with that one little success. It also helped that she was able to get anywhere she wished easily, giving her a sense of independence.

"Anin?" she heard Panella call from the lounge. It was the only room in the quarters you could port into, and ever since discovering the porting spell, the two never walked or flew anywhere. Not unless they desired to. Kes said it was something his parents put in place when he was a small youngling to force him to check in with them. After they were gone, he never had the heart to remove it.

She was grateful he had not, for multiple reasons. It gave her a small amount of time to prepare to be around others, providing a sense of control. She also loved that it was a nightly reminder of his parents. Every time he ported into their chambers, he was reminded of them. She thought that was beautiful and could not help wishing that she had something like that to remind her of her mother.

"Be there in a minute!" she called from their bedchamber.

"You are going to have a great time, and there is not a thing you cannot do," Kes said, gripping her shoulders so that he could stare directly into her eyes while he spoke. Once she nodded, he pulled her into his arms and held her tightly. "I will miss you, nymph." His voice had turned gruff, and she had to laugh a little.

"I'm only going to the city and will be gone for a few hours at most. You will not have time to miss me."

"I miss you, even when a single wall separates us. I miss you when you are out of my sight for the briefest of moments. Not a second of my life goes by without wanting you to be all that I see." Tears welled in her eyes. He might be a dramatic fluff ball, but sometimes his theatrics came out in beautiful statements just like that one had.

"Anin! Let's go! The band starts in a few minutes," Lyra yelled. She was possibly the most excited of all of them. The Lunars were her favorite band. The lead singer, a witch named Trove, was one of her Silent Shadows and had become a good friend.

Kes took her hand, and they walked down the hall to greet the twins. He always needed to be touching her, and while it had taken her a while at first to relax into his casual, innocent touches, she took comfort from them now. They were nothing more than hand-holding or an arm around her shoulders, but something about them settled her. She found it strange that one kind of touch could settle her while the other did the opposite.

The moment they stepped into the lounge, Kes made a whistling noise before saying, "Well, I had no idea you could clean up so well, little chick. And Panella, you look lovely as always." She rolled her eyes. He loved to harass

Lyra, and she loved to give it back. Anin was just happy that her mate and sister had become such great friends.

"Oh, shut up, I swear something went wrong when you hatched," Lyra said, dramatically rolling her eyes at Kes. Apparently, Tyne was not the only one who had picked up some of her mate's characteristics.

Kes gasped as if he were offended. "I," he began, "was not hatched. Clearly, I was created by the gods and simply placed in this realm as a blessing. You are most welcome." Anin and Panella tried to hold their laughter in as they looked at each other, shaking their heads.

She said her goodbyes to Kes and quickly ported her sisters to the street outside the bar, where a long line had already formed. Lyra grabbed her arm and dragged her to the front door when she had started toward the end of the line.

"Trove put us on the list. Besides, no Night fae would ever make the mate of their precious pillow prince wait in line," Lyra said, laughing at her own joke.

They did not even have to give their names. The large fae guarding the door to The Winged Prince moved the rope of fire he wielded so they never had to even slow their stride.

The moment she stepped past the threshold, she jerked to a stop. She did not know what she had expected the interior to look like, but this was not it.

Wings—thousands of them—covered every square inch of wall space. Not real wings, of course. Mostly they were paintings with various types of wings made from different metals, hanging sporadically between them. The name of the bar should have given her a clue.

"It's great, right?" Lyra asked, mistaking her shock for appreciation. Anin took a deep breath. She would not let her past dictate her future. These were not her wings; they were not even real wings. She was not going to ruin their first night out because of some decorations. That would be absurd.

"Amazing!" she said, and she nearly cringed at the obviously fake excitement in her voice. It might have been the fact that the bar was so loud, or maybe she had not sounded as fake as she thought, but neither of her sisters seemed to notice. She let out a breath and relaxed, happy not to have to deal with their worry.

The place was packed, and she was grateful that Lyra had asked Trove to reserve a table for them. It was off to the side and set into a small alcove, providing them privacy and space from the rest of the bar.

They sat long enough to have their drinks ordered and delivered before The Lunars took the stage. After that, the next few hours went by in a blur of dancing and shouting along to the songs she knew. Every time her drink was empty, their server was there to replace it. The service was impressive, and the concoction she drank was far better than any fae wine she had ever tasted.

"We will be back after a short break, so do not go anywhere!" Trove yelled into the whirling air in front of her, which helped amplify her voice. Following her sisters, she made her way back to their table and collapsed into the plush cushion of the crescent-moon-shaped bench that filled the small alcove and hugged the round table in front of it.

"I am so glad you both dragged me out here," she told

them honestly. She could not remember the last time she had this much fun. She caught her reflection in the mirror behind Lyra, who sat directly across from her, with Panella in the middle. She was covered in a sheen of perspiration and smiling so widely that she knew her cheeks would be sore later. She looked happy—truly happy.

"Me too," Panella said. "I love Tyne with all my heart, but that youngling's attitude inspires anything but love. I cannot wait for her to be out of this stage, and yet I never want her to grow up. It's happening too fast."

"It does seem like you blink, and she's somehow morphed into an entirely new being," Anin said. In the past few years alone, her niece had started to lean toward maturity and further from younghood.

"She still has decades before she reaches full maturity, and even then it will be another century before she has any sense," Lyra said, and they all laughed, thinking back to the trouble they had caused long after they had reached maturity. "For goddess's sake, you have got to be kidding me." Lyra was glaring across the room, and that could only mean one thing.

Anin followed her gaze, and just as she suspected, her eyes landed on Zandar leaning against the long bar on the wall furthest from them and smirking at a scowling Lyra. Panella and Anin immediately began to laugh.

"Sister," Panella said between laughs, "I think he rather enjoys your fury. I wonder what he would do if you were sweet to him." Lyra's head snapped around to look at her sister in disgust.

"Why would I ever do something as horrific as that?"

Lyra asked before taking a drink from her nearly empty glass. The server arrived, placed three new drinks on the table, and pointed at Zandar.

"These are compliments of the gentlemale over there," she said before hurrying off to take care of another table.

"There is nothing gentlemalely about that fae," Lyra grumbled under her breath.

"Lyra, I am beginning to think you are not telling us what's really going on between the two of you," Anin said, giving Panella a conspiratorial wink. Her sister had already filled her in on Lyra's true feelings toward the Night fae who pursued her relentlessly.

"What?" Lyra screeched, causing Panella and Anin to crack up laughing. Lyra sighed and slouched in her seat. "Ugh, fine. I do not exactly hate the way he looks." That was as close as she would ever come to admitting that she had feelings for the fae.

"Oh, sister," Panella sighed. "You are allowed to find love and be happy." Anin nodded in agreement.

"I know," Lyra snapped before she looked down at the glass of swirling purple liquid and fell quiet. "It's the conversations about what comes after that I do not want to have."

Lyra never wanted a youngling, and for some reason, she thought that meant she was not allowed to find a partner. Witches were already hesitant to form attachments outside of their covens, and Lyra was no exception. Anin glanced at Zandar. His smirk had faded and was replaced by one of concern as he watched Lyra.

"Why not ask him what he thinks about parenthood? Most fae are not exactly interested in the role. You will likely be surprised by his answer. Trust me, Lyra, do not let your fear stand in the way of the rest of your life."

Lyra was quiet for a moment before she inhaled deeply and lifted her head. "Perhaps. Anyway, someone change the subject."

"Etain told me she will have the spell for the blood-stones figured out any night now," Anin said. It would be a relief to have her family protected from the effects of blood magic.

"That's wonderful news!" Panella exclaimed before she raised her glass between the three of them. "To taking down the bitch queen!" Anin and Lyra clinked their glasses with hers.

Anin hated it when anyone brought up Tatiana. It always resurfaced memories best left in the past. That was her own issue, though, and she knew that every witch took her crimes against them personally.

Speaking to Tallon's mother had been terrible. The witch had sobbed, knowing her daughter was truly gone. It was even worse when she learned of the death her daughter had experienced. Anin had told her how brave the youngling had been and that somehow fate had inter-vened, allowing Tallon to return to the realm peacefully. She still felt the sting of tears when she thought about it.

"Does that mean she will need your blood soon?" Lyra asked, a hint of concern in her voice.

"Yes," Anin sighed. "I will not lie. I am nervous. I do no —" A loud crash interrupted her and stole their attention.

A fight had broken out between several fae in the center of the bar. Within minutes, other fae moved to break it up, including Zandar. He was a good male, and she hoped her sister would allow herself to be happy with him.

As the scent of blood filled the air, she turned to her sisters and saw her reflection again—this time as a vision she dreaded. She was once more trapped in the small cage, filthy, with her wings rotting around her.

She blinked, and the image was gone. She shook her head and tried to remember what she had been about to say, but the image reappeared. For a moment, she stared at the image the mirror was showing her. Everything faded around her except for the distinctive sound of footfalls. Terror coursed through her veins, but then she blinked and was back in the bar with her sisters.

"Anin? Are you alright?" Panella asked, reaching out a hand toward her.

"Yes, of course," she said, shooting to her feet before her sister's touch could land. "I just need to use the facilities." Her words came out in a rush as she turned to follow the signs that led her to the door she was desperate to hide behind.

She shoved the door open and immediately shut and locked it behind her. She rested her head on the cool wooden surface and took several deep breaths. She could hear the sound of water flowing and turned to find the source.

A pained, horrified sound escaped her. The walls were covered in a repeating pattern of painted wings in perfect rows. She took a shaky breath and ran toward the basin, into which a continuous stream of water flowed, hoping the water was ice-cold.

It was cool, bordering on warm, but it still soothed her

heated skin. After splashing her face several times, she held on to the edge of the basin and hung her head, counting to three on each inhale and exhale, slowly calming her racing heart.

She could do this. None of it was real. She was safe. Her sisters were with her, and they were in the Night Court. She was safe.

The whole thing felt ridiculous to Anin. She had been fine—or relatively fine—for years. The memories no longer plagued her dreams. She was fine.

When she looked back up and gazed into the large mirror above the basin, each blink shifted between images of her in the cage and her present self. All sense of calm vanished, and her breaths came in short gasps as her vision continued to shift with each blink of her eyelids. The faster she blinked, the faster the images changed, until she slammed her eyes shut and then opened them slowly.

While still wrapped around her body, the wings she had admired only hours ago began to rot.

"Nonononononon…" She threw her wings wide open as they began to shrivel into blackened husks still attached to her. Desperately, she clawed and ripped at them. What if it did not stop with her wings? What if she decayed along with them?

"Please… no… off… off…" Her movements became even more frantic and no matter how much she ripped at them, her wings only continued to waste away. Her wild eyes caught on the wings around the room, which had been vibrant and beautiful when she first walked in but were now in various stages of decay. Just like her own.

Spinning away from the mirror, all she could see was a damp, stone room covered in rows of her dead wings.

Oh gods.

On some level, she was aware she was screaming. Her throat burned from the desperate plea she kept repeating.

"Get them OFF!"

"What to do with so many traitors—Woooohhhhh, what to do," Tatiana sang. She skipped up and down the corridor, between the rows of cells in her dungeon. She stopped in front of one of them where a fae had his eyes clenched shut as he whimpered.

She stood still, and got as close as the bars would allow and waited for him to open his eyes. She did not have to wait long.

"Boo!" she hollered in the fae's face. He screamed, which made her giggle. "Such a silly fae! A traitor fae!" She resumed skipping singing about the scaredy fae who betrayed his queen.

"So many traitors' tears!" she sang at the top of her lungs. "I wonder what could be their greatest fears?" She stopped and realized she had rhymed, which made her burst out laughing. Once she caught her breath, she continued skipping and sang her funny little rhyme over and over.

The *whispers* seemed to do nothing but admonish her these days. She had gotten good at ignoring them.

"You are using up more power than you are taking in. If you do not hurry up, you will lose control of your golden army." Tatiana stopped abruptly.

They were the one group of fae to whom she did not give a choice. She decided it was wiser to control them with her blood magic than to lose the majority of her army.

"You always want to ruin all my fun!" she yelled at the *whispers* while stomping her foot.

"Your fun is foolish," they said in their strange, echoing voice.

"You are foolish—foolish for being no fun!" She decided that would be the next little song she sang as she moved up and down the hall.

Tatiana recently discovered that she loved singing silly little songs. They made the boring things more fun and the fun things even better. She made up songs about every single little thing she did. The *whispers* hated it, which only made her do it more.

"It's time for you to stop acting like a youngling and grow up. You are a queen—act like it!" The *whispers* roared in her mind, causing her pain.

... A hand grips the golden-skinned youngling's wrist too hard and makes her whimper... a male with big white wings, backlit

by the sun... "It's time to grow up and stop acting like a youngling."... "But I am a youngling."... "You are a soon-to-be queen"... The grip tightens...

Had she not just been outside?

Where was she?

Tatiana could not remember what she had been doing. When she glanced around and saw the faces of the fae who had betrayed her, looking at her as if she were the crazy one, rage boiled within her. How long had she been stuck in that vision?

She wished she could figure out who the golden youngling was. She thought she saw her mate in the vision. But why would he be hateful to a youngling? It did not make sense. He was the kindest male she had ever met. At least she thought he was. Her memory was not very reliable these days.

"Do not look at me like that!" she screamed. "I am not the crazy one! You all are for betraying me!"

What was she supposed to be doing?

It made her even angrier that she could not remember the simplest of things, like what she had just been doing before that vision exploded in her mind. It was as if she had paused and lived a different life, and then when that one paused, she returned to this one.

She was beginning to confuse herself with the golden-skinned youngling. How strange that she would have visions of another who looked so much like she once had. Perhaps she—

"I remember! It's time for a sacrifice. How silly of me. Of course, that would be the reason I find myself down here. Why did none of you remind me?" she asked the fae in the closest cell. None of them responded with anything besides tears.

"How many should I take? Hmmmm…" She felt the drain on her power and how low her well had gotten. She had been sacrificing one per day, and that obviously was not enough. She shrugged and picked a random number: "Six!"

"Now, if I point to you and give you a number, step forward to claim your prize!" She giggled uncontrollably. She would make them step forward, and she would be the one getting a prize.

"Let's seeeee," she sang as she twirled around with her finger outstretched. When she came to a stop, she gave the fae she was pointing at the number one. She moved up and down the cells, repeating the process until it was time to pick her sixth.

The other five fae had decent wells, but she needed at least one with a relatively deep well. She scanned each cell, searching for the perfect fae. When she spotted him, she pointed at him and yelled, "Six," before jumping up and down and clapping.

She took control of all six and said, "Will the lucky six please step forward and come with me to receive your prize?" All six fae stepped to the doors of their cells at the same time.

"No! Please, not my mate," a shrill voice begged. "Please!" Tatiana searched for the fae to whom the voice belonged.

A female was desperately pulling the arm of the sixth fae she had chosen. Tears dripped from her chin as she begged her mate not to leave her.

"He is your fated mate?" Tatiana asked.

"Yes!" Her voice shifted from shrill to hopeful.

"How romantic," Tatiana sighed wistfully. "What a shame this is a tragedy and not a romance."

"No, please. I beg you, please do not do this. He is my everything." She could never recall Reminold saying anything as beautiful as that about her; perhaps there was never the right occasion for such declarations.

"If only you had both made the promise. You could be in the palace, happy and together."

"Please, let us make the promise now. We will never betray you again." The female gripped the bars of her cell so tightly that her pale sky-blue skin turned grey. Tatiana approached her and placed a golden hand on her dusty-blue cheek. Such a pretty color. She wondered if her blood was the same shade.

"My dear, it is far too late for that," she said, laughing as she backed away. The female's knees gave out, and she fell to the ground, her sobs shaking her entire body.

What a fun game!

She waved her hand, opening the cell doors. The six chosen fae stepped out. She waved her hand again, closing the cells tightly. She then made the male step toward his mate.

"I am not a monster," she said to the female. Her head snapped up, and her face was once again filled with hope. "I will give you a moment to say goodbye." The female's face crumpled as Tatiana released the male's arms and mouth, allowing him to speak.

"Do not worry, my love. We will be together again in

the next life. I promised to wait for you in every life, and I meant it. We must be fated for a happier life in the next one."

"It's not fair," the female said hoarsely, and Tatiana rolled her eyes at the theatrics of it all. She did not want to admit to herself that she was rather jealous because, once again, she could not recall Reminold saying anything like that to her.

He must have, though, right?

"Time's up!" She took control of the fae once again and had them all hold on to her so she could port them to the temple. The female's scream of desperation was the last thing they heard before they were surrounded by the silence of the temple.

She forced five of the fae to march into the large cage off to the side and had the first one lie on the stone slab. She nearly screamed when she turned around and saw Raindal standing there, right where she had left him the day before.

"Oh! I completely forgot about you. How silly of me," she said with a giggle. She made him smile warmly at her and cup her face.

"I would wait forever for you. You are my everything." It did not matter that she was the one who had forced him to say the words. They still made her sigh. It was just so romantic.

"Do not worry, pet. There will be plenty of time after I finish up here to make it up to you. I have so many ideas." Her core clenched just thinking about all the things she was going to have him do and say to her later.

While she could not stop searching her memories for

the words of devotion Reminold had said to her, the first fae was secured to her altar. Her memory was not what it used to be, but she should still be able to recall at least one instance. When she tried to pull on any specific memory with him, it remained just out of reach and became hazy.

Most, if not all, of the memories from before she had acquired blood magic were the same. She had no recollection of their mating ceremony; it was as though it had been carved out of her mind. Which was most unfortunate; it was when he would have been certain to have made declarations of love.

"Surely he did, right?" she asked the fae, choking on their blood.

Tatiana moved quickly through her first five fae. By the time it was number six's turn, she felt as though she were floating from the fresh power rushing through her veins. She picked the now bloodless female up and began to dance with her corpse as she hummed a tune that kept replaying in her mind.

Where had she heard that before?

... a flash of a lesser fae running her gentle fingers through golden hair as she hummed a tune.

The dead fae in her arms sagged, and her greenish-colored blood mixed with the other colors of blood that had come before her, creating an ugly brown. She definitely did not have a gown to match that. The sound of retching reminded her that she had one more fae left.

Dragging the dead female by a single hand over to the cage, she wrinkled her nose as the fae vomited again. Was he ill or something? She hoped it was not contagious. Her mother had died from an illness.

... a hand holding a chalice as another poured a strange liquid into it...

She shook her head to clear the flash of images from her mind. Those hands seemed familiar. Something about them made Tatiana look down at the hand she held and the limp form attached to it. When she glanced around the temple, she saw splatters of greenish blood everywhere.

It was a hideous color.

"What color is your blood?" she asked the final fae left.

"W-w-what?"

"Your blood. What color is it?"

"Y-yellow." Hmmm. She went through her mental inventory of gowns, trying to remember if she had a yellow one. She knew she had gold, but did she have yellow? If she remembered correctly—and that was a big if as of late—she thought she had two.

"That will do," she said, dropping the hand of the fae with the ugly colored-blood. She needed to clean off her hands before dealing with this last one.

Looking around, she saw that there was really nowhere to clean up. She shrugged, ported to her bathing chamber, and washed away all the dull brown of the mixed blood. She figured that while she was there, she might as well check to see if she had been correct about her gowns.

As it turned out, she had forgotten about one and

actually had three! She picked the one she liked best and dressed herself before porting back to the temple.

"There, that's better. It's time for your prize," she said, giving the mated fae a wide smile and opening the door to the cage. His movements were stilted as she forced his legs to walk to the stone slab and lie on it.

"Now, hold on tight. This might hurt a bit," she said, laughing. The shrill sound echoed throughout the crumbling structure, which Tatiana found even funnier. Her laughter shook her entire body, forcing her to grab the stone slab to keep from falling over.

She never knew how long had passed once she started carving into flesh. However, it was never long enough, and these faceless fae were a cheap substitute for the golden-green skin she truly wanted beneath her blade. When she finished, her arms were covered in yellow blood that matched her gown perfectly, and the male was barely left alive, with only the skin on his back unscathed.

Quickly, she sliced across his neck, and his remaining blood poured from him and filled the medallion beneath her feet. When his power flooded her, she stumbled. It was like the last five fae all at once. It had been a while since she had felt this level of euphoria.

She glanced down at her hand and stared at the yellow blood. It was not far off from her own golden blood.

...The sound of fabric ripping... a large hand around a small golden neck... pain... fear... shock... a small golden hand covered in golden blood...

Tatiana's breaths came in short gasps. It felt so real.

Something way back in the deep, dark recesses of her mind lifted its ugly head. She refused to look too closely at it. She did not want to know.

That golden youngling was not her.

It was not her.

Was it?

Chapter 25
Balthier

Balthier preferred to arrive first for their weekly meetings. It gave him a moment to organize his thoughts. Time was scarce, and they needed to use it wisely to avoid discovery.

One of Balthier's first actions upon stepping into his mate's role was to bring order to the rebellion's chaos. Raindal's tendency to micromanage came as no surprise—he was never good at relinquishing control.

However, when he became incapacitated, it left the rebellion in a weakened position. The rebellion nearly fell apart within the first few days of Raindal's absence. Establishing a leadership structure and chain of command was the first thing Balthier did after his meeting with Kes.

He longed to collapse into his cot and never wake until the whole affair was over. Of course, that was not an option. He had to do whatever it took to rescue his mate. Raindal would never wallow in self-pity if their roles were reversed.

Those first couple of years had been anything but easy. It took far too long for him to get the full picture of everything the rebellion had their hands in. He was surprised to find it was not as impactful as he had thought his mate had made it out to be.

Apparently, Raindal had fixated on freeing Anin from the mad queen's grasp, pinning all their hopes on her. While this plan might eventually succeed, they could not wait around for her to decide she was ready. They had to prepare for the true queen to take her throne—to help her fight for it.

He created factions within the rebellion and assigned leaders to each one. They had a face-to-face check-in every week at a new location to help avoid discovery. With all their high fae allies missing, they would be no match physically if they were caught by a high fae. They had to use their minds and be smarter than their adversaries.

As it turned out, that was not exactly difficult. The high fae thought so little of them that they never considered them a risk. Balthier wanted to keep it that way.

He ordered an immediate halt to the minor acts of vandalism and other activities. To make a real impact, they needed meticulous planning. This strategy protected more of the lesser fae and allowed them to better support their community.

"How long have you been here?" he heard Killia ask from behind him.

"Not too long," he said, turning and smiling warmly at his closest friend. He would never have survived all these years that Raindal had been missing without her. They each healed something within each other.

There were fated mates, and then there were soul-mates. He was lucky enough to have found both. She had been crafted from the same mold as he had been.

It was not the same wholeness of heart that Raindal gave him; it was different. Where Raindal felt like his missing piece, Killia felt like a replica of him. He knew her as well as he knew himself. It was the truest friendship he had ever known.

She wrapped her arms around his waist, and they held each other for a moment. The pressures of life seemed to feel a little less heavy with each passing second. When she pulled away, he draped his arm across her shoulders, pulling her into his side to kiss the top of her head.

"And where are you on the murderous scale today?" They had decided long ago that they would never ask each other if they were okay. They were not, and neither of them knew if it were possible to be okay ever again. So instead, they asked ridiculous questions, like the one he just asked her.

"That bastard on the council came for another visit," she seethed, "so I would say I am feeling rather stabby today." The council member, whose name she refused to speak, had certain tastes that were not for the faint of heart.

"And you?" she asked.

"Oh, you know. Another day, another fuck you to fate." They both laughed. It might be disturbing to others how they coped with their lives, but they could not care less. She was still forced to work in the brothels, and he was still forced to let the queen do as she pleased with his mate.

It was fucked up.

They were fucked up.

Within the next few minutes, the rest of the leaders arrived. They had a lot to get through in the maximum of thirty minutes they allowed these meetings to last. So they skipped the waste of time that pleasantries were.

"Clock starts now," Balthier said. "Lorella, let's start with you."

"Not too much to report from the palace. The queen is as mad as ever. Those spells she's been having are becoming more frequent and lasting longer.

There have been times when she is frozen mid-stride, wide-eyed, for hours. When she returns to herself, she is often terrified and disoriented, which can have disastrous consequences for any fae around her." The female paused and looked at him with the pity he hated to see swimming in her eyes. He knew the next part would be about his mate.

"I happened to come across Raindal, standing in the dining room, forgotten by the queen." It was hard for Balthier not to demand she tell him everything and assault her with a multitude of questions. He had to make himself emotionless at these meetings.

"She seems to be doing that more often than not these days. He's losing weight and looks disheveled most of the time." He wanted to storm the palace and get his mate out of there, even if it meant carrying him over his shoulder. Yet, he could not. There was no escape for his mate until he was free from the queen's blood magic.

"I spoke to him," she said in a rush of words. "I know we are supposed to keep these quick and impersonal. However, Balthier, I need you to know I told him the rebellion is very much alive and well and that you were doing everything you can to get him out of there. He might not have moved a muscle, but I swear his eyes looked fierce, not beaten down and empty."

There was a moment of silence, and Killia reached out to grab his hand, giving him a small squeeze of comfort. Balthier nodded at Lorella. She had given him a gift—one that he would fully dissect later.

"Caraway, let's hear it," Balthier said. His eyes were still locked with the female across from him, trying to convey the gratitude he felt.

"The messengers have been busy. With more of us being freed from our deals and able to move freely, we have rerouted hundreds of migrating lesser fae to the nearest abandoned coven and recruited dozens to join the rebellion."

When Balthier first suggested the covens, the other fae had balked. He described one he had passed on the way to meet with their Night Court contact. The structure showed signs of long-term neglect. Holes in the roof had clearly been there for a while, and the land had already reclaimed a good portion of it. Nothing had made him more certain than the silence.

Typically, you can hear a coven before you can see one. Witches are not known for being quiet; if anything, they are the opposite. Everything about them is loud, from the colors they wear to the buildings they build.

When they asked what happened if the witches

returned, he shrugged. They would deal with that if and when it happened. He thought it was better to ask for forgiveness over permission.

"Great, Brock, what can you tell us?"

"There was a group of fae who work the fields with me and who were recently freed from the bonds of their deal. They knew to carry on as if nothing had happened, and we have been able to redirect enough of the freshly harvested fruits and vegetables to feed the Dayless Quarter for the next few weeks.

With fewer high fae watching over us, we have even been able to tamper with the palace food supply. We have been sending them anything we harvest that is already rotten. It does not seem that anyone has noticed, and it's not enough to look purposeful and draw attention." The burly male gave them all a smug smile while the rest of them tried to control their laughter.

"Diabolical. Well done. Flix, what do you have for us?" He had to move them along quickly; they were running out of time.

"We are still looking for weak spots in the city's plumbing and monitoring the high fae activity to determine which streets would be most pertinent to suddenly become… unavailable," he said, smiling wickedly.

"We have managed to set up a fake supply order that is rerouted to the Dayless Quarter and are working on ways to increase the production of weapons to hoard."

High fae have no need for weapons since they each possessed elemental magic. Therefore, making too many weapons at one time would not go unnoticed. The weapons are a last resort. If they had to actually fight the high fae, it would not go well for them, but it was better to be prepared.

"Keep it up. Killia?"

"Nothing new from the spies. It seems that the queen's requirement for the high fae to make deals with her caused them all to lie low, hoping she would forget they exist. There has not been a council meeting in years.

Although, that might be changing soon. The brothels have remained unbothered for a long time, with only the occasional asshole coming by for a visit. It seems the high fae have licked their wounds long enough, as business has picked up to nearly the level it used to be," she said, disgust tightly wrapped around every word.

The rest of them were smart enough not to let their pity show. That would have only set her off, and Killia was always a hair's breadth away from detonating.

Balthier cleared his throat before he plowed ahead. They had minutes left. "It does not seem as though we need to adjust any plans at the moment. Stay vigilant and back off if any high fae grow suspicious. Does anyone have anything else that needs to be addressed?"

"Yes," Lorelle said, and they all looked at her expectantly. "The queen has taken control of every single high fae in the palace multiple times now. I have noticed something curious: not once has a single lesser fae been held hostage by her blood magic."

"She probably does not see us as even a possibility of a threat," Brock said.

"I wonder if she sees us at all. Like a picture hung on the wall generations ago, you see it without truly seeing it anymore," Balthier said.

"I wonder if it might be even simpler than all of that. What if she is unable to? Would she even know?" Killia asked.

They were all silent as they considered it. If that were the case, what would that mean for the rebellion? Every set of eyes looked at him for the answer. Unfortunately, he did not have one, and, possibly more unfortunate, was the hope that Killia's theory caused to bloom within him. Hope was dangerous, so he said the only true answer he could think of.

"Perhaps."

K es had Lyra compile profiles on the top fifty Silent Shadows. He trusted her to select the best of them. From that fifty he planned to build his own Twenty-Three. After hours at his desk in the study, he had only reviewed a few candidates. He was not cut out for sitting behind a desk.

The Silent Shadows had grown quickly over the past couple of decades. What had started as a team of three—him and the twins—was now a few hundred strong. The list of fae and witches eager to join seemed endless.

Of those who signed up, a small fraction of them actually make it through the basic training. It was better that way; we preferred to have smaller numbers and better warriors.

He and Lyra had created a chain of command and organized all the Shadows into units. Everyone had to start from the bottom, but how quickly they climbed was based purely on skill alone. Occasionally, there were recruits who excelled at strength over stealth. They showed too much promise to let them go.

There were others of the opposite inclination. They became his spies, The Silent Ones. No one knew who they were or that they were part of the Silent Shadows. He had tasked one of them with finding out as much information as possible on the male who hurt Anin while she was being held captive. Barely anything had been found on the male. He was a council member that has rarely been seen since Tatiana took control of him with her blood magic; however, he now had the name of the male.

Raindal.

The Silent Ones who looked into it said the lesser fae of the Day Court are surprisingly tight lipped about him. He was not bothered by this; it was only a matter of time before his hand was wrapped around the mystery male's neck. A wicked smile stretched across his face. The male could not hide forever.

Once the Silent Shadows grew into the hundreds, he began sending smaller units to other cities in the Night Court and creating specialized teams. The Twenty-Three elite would be the final one. Thank the gods. He hated doing it.

Kes flipped to the next profile and laughed when he saw "Fae-Fae Pain in My Ass" as Zandar's name. It must have killed her to include him, yet she was right to do so. The male was skilled, and he took direction well. He did not have an ego that stood in the way of his growth and rose in ranks quickly.

Every time he was due for a promotion, Kes made Lyra do it. Gods, it never stopped being funny. She looked as though she ate something sour while he looked at her as though she hung the whole damn moon. One of these nights, Lyra would admit her feelings to herself. In the meantime, Kes was happy to laugh at her expense.

One good thing was that he had not needed to leave his quarters often and had been able to stay with Anin. He was ready to return to the training facility and kick some ass into shape.

Kes's training might have been horrific, but it shaped him into an impeccable warrior. The Silent Shadows were trained in a similar fashion—without his psychotic uncle's insistence on beating them half to death randomly.

Part of him had resented Ciaran when he tasked him with creating the team. Now it was the only thing he had ever created that he was proud of. Apparently, so was the rest of the court. Over the past several years, he and Lyra had started receiving requests for help.

Sometimes it was to discover who had done something so that the appropriate being could be held responsible. At other times it was beings coming to them out of fear and needing someone to protect them. Whatever the need might be; the requests were plentiful and crime dropped in general around the court. Who knew that when they stopped killing each other, the court would begin to prosper?

He was halfway through the profiles and nowhere near deciding on the final half of the elite team when he felt a moment of fear from Anin. It was not just unease, like he had felt shortly after they left. He had expected to feel that periodically. It was her first time out without him.

The feeling was fleeting, and she seemed to be doing fine again. He looked at the profiles spread out across his desk and knew his concentration was long gone. Anin might be upset with him if he showed up at—whatever bar they went to.

He had never gotten the name. It was not something either of them needed to do. If they desired to find each other, they followed the bond.

Her fear came on suddenly once more and was so consuming that Kes shot up from his seat. He was about to port to her when he realized the fear was overpowering his sense of direction. He had to calm down. She needed him.

After a few deep breaths, he finds her and ports as close as he can. The street he arrives on is filled with fae and witches walking from bar to bar. He can sense her straight ahead at a place called The Winged Prince.

"Fuck."

The fae guarding the door sees him coming and clears the way without hesitation. The moment he steps over the threshold, chaos erupts. The furniture at the center of the bar is smashed, and a few fae sit subdued with slowly healing bloody gashes. If any of them had hurt her, he would kill them all.

"Where's my MATE?!" he bellowed, silencing the bar. When no one replied and continued to gape at him, he tried again, forcing the words through his sharp, clenched teeth.

"Kes," his eyes frantically searched for the voice before landing on Zandar. He was holding down another fae, but he nodded toward a hall off to the side.

As soon as he was halfway there, he heard Lyra and Panella.

"Anin, let us in. What's happening?"

He shoved fae out of the way and followed their voices. He turned down the hall and saw them at the end, banging on a door. Of course, she would be in a room at the end of a long hall.

"Move," he growled at them. He did not slow, and at that moment he could not care less whether they got out of his way quickly or not. As soon as he was in front of the door, he did not hesitate to lift his taloned foot and kick it in.

His eyes found her instantly, and his stomach dropped at the sight. She was attempting to smash herself further into the corner while staring at them with large eyes and whimpering incoherent words. There were rips and tears all over her wings, and for a minute, he thought it had happened during the bar fight until he saw the iridescent pieces on the floor. It had been a long time since she had tried to claw her wings off. He had to grit his teeth and shake out his clenched fists to fight back the rage he felt toward who or whatever had set her off.

"P-p-please... no more," she begged them, her voice shaking with fear. He had already sworn to kill that fucking queen, but it did not hurt to swear it again.

He slowly entered the room, holding his hands out in an attempt to not frighten her any more than she already was. "Anin, my darling nymph," he said in a calm, even voice. "Feel the bond, follow it. You are safe. You are in the Night Court." She calmed a bit, and he crouched down in front of her.

She met his eyes and began to sob. "They are rotting. Please… get them off," she pleaded.

"What's rotting, Anin?"

"My wings," she whispered as tears fell in rivulets down her face.

"I promise you, darling, they are as vibrant as ever." She shook her head in disbelief. He was about to reach out to her, but stopped. "May I touch you?" he asked, even while his mind was screaming at him to get her home that very second. She gave him a single nod, and he gently scooped her up into his arms. Kes stopped as he passed her sisters, who were crying as they held onto each other. They had never seen her spiral so far down, and it was not easy to witness.

"You are safe," he said softly. "Let's go home."

"What the fuck were you two thinking? The Winged Prince? Really?" he seethed. They looked confused at first , but then he watched the horror spread across their faces as it dusked on them.

"Oh, gods…" Panella whispered.

"I-I did not—" Lyra started, stumbling through her words.

"Think? Yeah, no shit," he spat at them while Anin mumbled nonsense through her hiccuping whimpers. He wrapped his wings to shield her from sight and walked them back through the still-silent bar. It was the same way he had carried her out of a small, damp room far below Daybreak Palace. He glared at anyone who stared at them as he made his way to the entrance, while quiet sobs sounded from his arms. This time, anyone in his path scrambled out of the way.

The moment he was past the boundary of the ward, he ported them back to their chambers—not once looking back at her sisters. They would get over it, and maybe in time, he would too. He listened to his mate fight the terrors her mind had created, and not for the first time, he fantasized about all the different ways he would kill that bitch queen.

He took them to their bed and cradled her in his arms while she cried until sleep took her. The entire time, he kept repeating the same words to her as he held back his own tears.

"You are whole."

"Your wings are alive."

"And you are safe."

Kes would fight every battle for her, yet this one she had to face on her own. He was powerless to help her, and it destroyed him more than any physical fight ever could.

"You are whole."

"Your wings are alive."

"And you are safe."

Chapter 27
Panella

Panella could hardly believe how thoughtless she and Lyra had been. Only minutes after Kes questioned their actions, she recalled the decaying wings on the cell walls. How could they have missed that? How could they have forgotten?

Her feet dangled over the rooftop as she gazed at the city below. This was her favorite place to sit and think, especially at that time of night. The ceiling of Witch City had been spelled to mimic the sky in the Borderlands, which shifted every twelve hours. Transitioning from mostly sunshine and blue skies to an inky expanse dotted with stars, as if it had its own tide.

When the two courts clashed above the realm, the result was a beautiful cacophony of colors that spread wide across the Borderlands, casting a warm glow over everything it touched below. She thought it strange that the two courts that despised each other could create something so impressive when forced together.

She loved the city; it represented a new era for the witches. Covens mixed, fostering creativity that produced new spells and a greater sense of community. She never wanted to live anywhere else; however, worry nagged at the back of her mind. She knew it was still a long way off, but she wondered what would happen to Witch City after Anin became queen and Tatiana was no longer a threat to the witch population.

Would Ciaran kick them out? Would enough witches want to stay and keep the city alive, assuming he let them stay? As much as she had loved the Silver Moon Coven, the city felt more like home than the coven ever had. She wanted to stay, but if they had to leave, which coven would they choose?

Hers?

Ravyn's?

What about Tyne? Would she have to say goodbye to most of her friends?

There were fae-witch couples all over the city, which seemed to bother the Night fae more than it ever had the witches. If Lyra could pull her head out of her ass long enough to see what was right in front of her, Panella knew she and Zandar would add to the number. What would happen to all of them? Would the fae live in a coven? Would they even be welcomed?

It was pointless to worry about hypothetical problems; she knew this. Yet, given the choice between stressing over the future of their city or replaying the image of Anin tucked in the corner, hurting herself, she would take the city. How could they have forgotten something that vital? Without intending to, they had set the stage for

Anin's spiral into her worst memories. It should have been obvious not to drag their sister to the one bar in Nightfell that was covered in wings.

The Winged Prince.

What had they been thinking?

How would Anin ever forgive them? She had halted when they first entered, and they stupidly thought she was as impressed as they were with the decor. Goddess, they had been such idiots.

Even if Anin forgave them, there was no way that Kes would. Panella was not certain they deserved either of their forgiveness. She had never seen Kes look the way he did when he charged down the hallway toward them. She knew that if she and Lyra had not moved in time, he would have leveled them while kicking the door in. She almost wished he had; at least then, she could feel as though she had paid some form of penance.

"My heart, why are you up here all alone? How was your time with your sisters?" Ravyn asked, and when Panella turned to face her, she rushed to sit by her side. Ravyn put a hand on either side of Panella's face and stared into her eyes. Goddess, she was stunning. Ravyn would never stop taking her breath away.

"Tell me," she demanded, without letting go of Panella's face. Every time Ravyn stared into Panella's eyes like that, it was as if she could see her darkest depths; there was no escaping her—not that she ever wanted to.

By the time Panella finished recounting the details of their night out, Ravyn still had not released her face. She remained quiet while making sure Panella had finished before commenting on anything.

"Neither of you did anything wrong. Do you hear me?" she asked. Panella's gaze flitted to the side, unable to see the truth of Ravyn's words in her eyes—not when she did not agree.

"Panella, look at me," Ravyn demanded, and Panella's eyes obeyed. "You only wished to give Anin a night to feel normal. It's not for you—or anyone, for that matter—to decide what Anin can and cannot handle. She would have left the moment she stepped foot inside if she did not think she would be fine. Trust her to make her own choices. Just because she experienced a setback does not mean it was not also a victory. What about the hours you spent dancing and having a great time? It was not until the fight broke out that things took a turn." She leaned forward and kissed Panella gently before pulling back to look her in the eyes again. "You did nothing wrong."

When Panella did not look away that time, Ravyn let go of her face and took one of Panella's hands in her own before resting her head on Panella's shoulder. They were both quiet for a while, content to be in each other's presence and watch the city light up one by one as the sky grew darker. It was never fully dark, but the low lighting cast shadows all over the city that needed to be illuminated.

"Kes hates us," Panella whispered, breaking the peaceful silence.

"No," Ravyn said with a sigh.

"You did not see his face." It was a look Panella would never forget.

"He does not hate either of you. He was terrified. We are all guilty of using anger to hide our fear." Panella sat with that for a moment. She knew Ravyn was right—she usually was—yet it did not mean she looked forward to seeing Anin's feathered mate anytime soon.

"How did I get so lucky to have fate bless me with such a wise witch?" she asked, and Ravyn laughed softly. It was Panella's favorite sound—low and husky. It was a sound she could feel roll slowly through her body, never failing to create a burning desire deep within Panella's core.

She leaned back, pulling Ravyn to straddle her while gripping the soft flesh of her perfectly rounded ass. "I love you, Ravyn," she said, sliding one hand up her back to weave her fingers into the roots of her long, dark hair. She gripped it tightly, pulling her head back and exposing the delicate column of her throat. Ravyn let out a breathy moan as Panella kissed and nipped her way up the small stretch of skin.

"I cannot wait to be bonded to you," she said into Ravyn's ear, her voice heavy with desire. She pulled Ravyn as tightly to her as she could with the hand still clutching her ass. They were as close as their flesh could come with the layers of fabric in the way. When Panella felt the heat of Ravyn's core mingling with her own, she groaned and twisted to lie Ravyn down on the roof beside them.

Panella slowly dragged her hands up Ravyn's inner legs, not stopping until the tips of her fingers could graze her core. She lifted a single digit to give her a soft—too soft—caress.

Ravyn let out a frustrated sound as her hips lifted, seeking Panella's touch to ease the ache that her need had created. "Tsk, tsk. Only good witches get what they want,"

Panella admonished, pleased by the way her love's eyes were clouded with desire.

Sliding her hands back down Ravyn's legs, she chuckled when Ravyn tried to hide her needy whine. With both ankles in hand, Panella pulled Ravyn's legs wide to drape one into the crook of each elbow before shoving the skirt of her dress up to bunch at her hips.

Planting a hand on either side of her waist, Panella leaned forward, pushing Ravyn's knees up toward her chest as she pressed her body into Ravyn's. Her back arched off the wooden roof, and as soon as her mouth opened to release one of those delicious sounds Panella could coax from her, she claimed Ravyn's mouth. Their tongues danced together until Ravyn began grinding herself against Panella.

She released Ravyn's mouth, kissing down her body until she could rest Ravyn's legs over her shoulders. One of Ravyn's hands gripped Panella's tight blonde curls while the other pulled her dress aside to watch Panella feast on her.

Panella hooked the fabric hiding Ravyn's damp heat and pulled it to the side before dragging her tongue slowly up through Ravyn's wet folds. She maintained a painfully slow pace until Ravyn pulled at her head and begged.

""Please," the word mingled with her needy sounds.

"That's a good witch," Panella said before burying her face in her love's dripping core. As she sucked and then nibbled on her clit, Ravyn gripped her hair tighter and rode her face.

Panella could hear Ravyn's breath growing frantic,

matching the movements of her hips as she climbed higher. She was right at the peak; any minute, Panella's mouth would be flooded with Ravyn's release.

Suddenly, the front door slammed shut, and angry footsteps marched up the stairs. "Mothers?!" Tyne yelled.

Panella unfolded herself from a groaning Ravyn and sat up. As Ravyn struggled to sit up, Panella stood and extended a hand to help her dark-haired beauty rise. She could feel the need vibrating through her, left at the very edge of euphoria.

She pulled Ravyn roughly against her, invading her mouth again, pulling away with a grin as Ravyn's breaths came in short bursts. "How do we taste?" she asked.

"I feel like my skin is going to catch fire any minute," Ravyn cried.

"Good, I like it when you are wet and needy for me."

"I am always needy for you," Ravyn's breathy voice said.

"Good, because I will never stop needing you," Panella said just as Tyne yelled for them again, even more dramatically than before. "Now, let's go see what new drama has our youngling acting like her entire world is about to end."

Ravyn sighed and passed in front of Panella, who reached out and playfully slapped her ass as she walked by. Panella felt pure satisfaction as Ravyn's yelp of surprise echoed her need. Panella's earlier worries were forgotten.

For now.

Chapter 28
Ciaran

"Are you ready?" Etain asked Ciaran. He let out a long sigh. He was never ready to sit in the council chambers and listen to the idiots across the table attempt to sound intelligent.

"Is one ever ready to share a room with Syndari?" he responded, grimacing. Etain just laughed at him and shook her head, as if she thought he was joking.

He was not.

The shifter was lucky to be alive, and it was all thanks to the tiny little witch who was wrapping her arms around his waist.

"Maybe not, but at least this time we have something wonderful to share," she said, smiling up at him.

"Hmmm. Something tells me the wretch will be able to take issue with your announcement. They would likely find a way to disagree if you said the moon is full at this time of night." Her soft laugh reminded him of the melodic way tiny bells chimed. She had many different laughs, and he loved them all equally.

"Shall we?" he asked her. They had already made everyone wait well over an hour.

His need to make them wait for their arrival was difficult for his little witch to accept. He knew she preferred to be early, but she never complained, and that was the only reason he did not make the council wait even longer.

"Oh, look at that. We will only be an hour late. That's practically on time for you!" Etain exclaimed, her eyes wide and struggling to keep the false surprise on her face. She laughed when he scowled at her and ported them to just outside the Council Chambers.

"Little witch, whatever time we arrive anywhere is on time. Being the rulers of the Night Court means nothing can start without us," he said, smirking when she rolled her eyes and playfully slapped at his chest while mumbling something about being a "big blue oaf."

His shadows shot out and flung the doors open. The scene before them was not what either of them had expected. Multiple beings stood and leaned over the table, pointing at someone across it and yelling. There was so much yelling that it was nearly impossible to hear any word over the cacophony of angry voices.

"Silence!" Ciaran bellowed, and the entire room abruptly quieted as all heads snapped to where they stood. The look he gave them made everyone slowly take their seats. He glanced down at his little witch, who was engaged in some form of silent communication that all females seemed adept at with her great-aunt.

Once they took their seats, he allowed the silence to stretch, daring anyone to speak. "Now, someone tell me what the fuck that was about," he demanded once the fae across from him began to squirm.

There was a brief pause before the room erupted again, with too many voices trying to speak at once. Ciaran was already developing a headache. Gods, he hated these meetings and still was not sure what the point of having a council was. If his mate had not kept up the meetings while he was… occupied the past century, he would have let the entire tradition die.

"Enough," Etain said. She did not even have to raise her voice and immediately mouths snapped shut. While he wished he could get those wasted years back, there had been one good thing to come from it. Etain had spread her inky wings and learned to command the room.

His pants always seemed to grow tighter whenever Etain took control like that. For a few moments, he contemplated picking her up, tossing her over his shoulder, and returning to their chambers to show her just how much he appreciated her.

"If you have something to report, please raise a single hand," Etain said. Lyra and Zandar raised their hands with a reluctant Syndari a few moments later.

The witch glared at the fae next to her, while Zandar looked at her with pure adoration. Everyone saw how gone he was for her, everyone but Lyra. This made him like the witch a little more.

"Witch," Ciaran said, nodding at Lyra to speak.

"What he meant to say was, 'Lyra, will you please

report?'" Etain said, while scowling at him. Not a soul in the room thought that was even remotely close to what he had "meant" to say.

"Another apothecary was destroyed," Lyra said. He could feel the worry growing within his mate through their bond.

He reached under the table and placed a hand on her knee, giving it a soft squeeze. Her hand wrapped on top of his and he laced their fingers together, before he raised their joined hands to his lips and kissed the back of her hand. Some of the tightness around her eyes dissipated, and her shoulders relaxed a fraction.

"This one had a message as well," Zandar said. "She's watching you."

"Which was written in human blood, just like the one from a few nights ago." Lyra looked at Etain sympathetically. She was adamant that humans be left alone. It was something the Night fae were not great at adhering to.

"Was anyone harmed? Which coven was it?" Etain asked.

"Hallowed Crescent Coven, and no, no one was harmed."

"At least there's that. Is this the third one?"

"Yes. What makes it concerning, beyond the obvious, is how there were years between the first and second attacks and only mere nights between this recent attack," Zandar said. Ciaran appreciated how the fae could give information quickly and without emotion.

"Are you any closer to finding out who's responsible?" he asked them.

"No, I think it must be a fae, and *he* thinks it must be a witch—a theory that is totally absurd," Lyra said glaring at the *he* in question.

"A witch would never," Galetia agreed.

"So, it must be a fae, then? Your precious witches are no longer considered suspicious because you say they would never? Do you know it to be a fact? Out of all the witches residing in Nightfell, not a single one of them would do something like this?" Syndari seethed at the head witch. Reluctantly, Ciaran had to agree.

"It is far more likely that a Night fae is behaving wickedly than the possibility of a witch going against the covenant," Galetia snapped.

"Zandar, what makes you think it is a witch and not a fae?" Etain asked the male.

"The second coven to be hit was the only one that had any stock of Arctic Brittlebush—something no fae would ever know the name of or what it looked like," he said.

"Does this latest attack not make you think the previous one was simply dumb luck?" Etain asked.

"Perhaps, but I think whoever is behind it is looking for a specific reaction. Are any of the witches demanding to return to their covens in the Borderlands?" he responded.

"None that I am aware of. If anything, most are concerned about what will happen after Tatiana has been dethroned and they are able to return," Galetia said.

"There is a third option," Georden said, looking at Syndari. When she did not say anything, he continued, "Apparently, there have been whispers of a secret society that has been increasing in numbers over the past several years. They want the witches gone by any means necessary, and they denounce a witch as their queen."

"You only want to blame them because you do not wish to upset your head witch!" Syndari screamed at him. All eyes shifted between Georden and Galetia, whose cheeks turned bright pink.

"You and... really?" Etain asked her great-aunt, who gave her a sheepish smile in return. Ciaran could not care less who his mate's great-aunt spent time with. There was something much more important to address.

"Why is this the first time I am hearing about a secret society?" he asked no one in particular. His voice was low and carried a dangerous edge, making the room feel thick with tension.

"I only just learned of them minutes before you joined us. Syndari should be able to answer any questions you have," Georden said with disgust as he glared at the shifter, who sat there fuming in their seat.

When Syndari said nothing, Ciaran released Etain's hand and stood slowly. He planted both hands on the table and leaned forward, crowding as much of the shifter's space as he could with the distance between them. If his silence and movements were not enough to give away how close he was to detonating, his shadows were. Darkness pooled around Syndari as Ciaran stared them down.

"Tell me who. Who dared to denounce their queen? Who dared to insult my mate? Give. Me. Names," he growled at Syndari. "I will hunt them down and rip their heads from their bodies. It's been too long since I decorated the Great Hall."

A small hand gently rested on his forearm. "My love, as upsetting as it might be that some would rather remain bigoted than help create a better realm, there is nothing wrong with voicing opinions. As long as no violent actions are committed, they should not be punished for voicing their displeasure," Etain said softly, while his gaze never wavered from the shifter across the table.

Her touch always calmed the raging storm within him, but this felt dangerous. He would do anything for his mate, but sacrificing her safety was not one of them.

"And what of the vandalism? Is that not an act of violence?" he asked her as calmly as he could.

"There is no proof of who is behind it. There is not even enough to know for sure if it is a witch or fae at work. I think it is best we gather more information in order to make an informed decision." Ciaran slowly sat, his eyes still locked on Syndari. He wanted to ensure they understood that he had no tolerance for the little club he was certain the shifter was a part of.

"Well, I think it would be nice to end this eventful meeting on a good note," Etain said, looking at Ciaran with a smile. "I have wonderful news to share with you all: Galetia and I are mere moments away from having the bloodstones activated. Soon we will all be protected from the effects of the Day Queen's blood magic."

Everyone, even Syndari, congratulated and thanked Etain and Galetia for their hard work and commitment to protecting the Night Court and the witches. It was a momentary peace that Ciaran knew would not last the moment they all stepped outside the chamber doors.

He would do his own looking into this society of

foolish Night fae. Even a hint of malicious intent from any of them, and he would annihilate them all. Syndari realized that he was staring at them again and quickly averted their gaze.

Ciaran was going to go hunting.

Chapter 29
Etain

These were her favorite moments: when it was just she and Ciaran together in her study. With him reading from another pile of dusty books and her working on a spell or a new way to use one of her colors.

"Dear gods, he was such a fool," Ciaran said as he read about another long, dead king of the Night Court. "Honestly, Etain, how were half of these past kings deemed fit to live, let alone fit to rule?"

"What did this one do, my love?" She had to contain the laughter that threatened to bubble out of her. His very real anger toward these beings from the past was hilarious to her.

"He stole the daughter of a witch who was almost as powerful as you." Well, perhaps she could understand his anger toward them after all.

"That's awful. What happened?"

"Her mother and the entire fucking coven showed up and—" he looked up from his book and grimaced at her. "You will not like this. Are you sure you want to know?"

"Yes. Tell me."

How bad could it be?

"They turned him inside out, and he lived like that for several nights before finally returning to the realm." She nearly dropped the container she had just picked up.

Apparently, it could be quite bad.

"Oh. Well, I suppose that is one way to deal with the situation." Ciaran laughed at her response.

"I like their style. I wonder if it says anywhere in here how to do it," he said half to himself. She shook her head while continuing to prepare all the ingredients and tools she would need.

They had finally done it. She was certain she and her aunt had created the perfect replacement spell for the bloodstones. Now all they needed was Anin's blood.

While Anin had known this moment was fast approaching, Etain knew she was terrified. Her friend confided that she desperately wanted to give her blood to protect her loved ones. However, she did not know how she was going to stomach the sight of her blood or of her skin parting.

Etain could not fault her for it. She did not know much about what Anin had gone through, but during a few of their sessions, she had told her some parts. She had to force herself not to cry or react at all to the horrors Anin revealed.

They met every few months to see if Etain needed to adjust the tea she made for Anin. The longer she took it, the more customized Etain was able to make it. She was only happy she had been able to give her friend something to help her on her healing journey.

When she told her yesternight that it was ready and Anin immediately paled, she came up with a plan. She told Anin that she could make it so she would not see what Etain was doing. Then she could cast a spell that would make her feel nothing, and the wound would be so small her body would heal it before she even knew it had happened. Bravely, Anin had agreed.

"My love," she said as she sat on the arm of the chair he had taken over as his own. "Anin should be here any moment."

"Are you kicking me out then?" he asked with one of his too-wide grins just before he grabbed her and slid her onto his lap.

"Ciaran," she laughed, "no funny business, sir. You know I take her privacy seriously."

"Hmm, I think I like it when you call me sir—almost as much as when you call me my king. Kiss me, and I will go. You can make it up to me later." She leaned in to give him a chaste kiss; instead, he took control and fully invaded her mouth, leaving her breathless. Once he set her on her feet, he ported away, laughing. It was only once he was gone that she heard what he had said, and her face heated, thinking about the possible ideas he had for later.

A knock at the door shook her from her thoughts, and she opened it to find a nervous-looking Anin and a concerned Kes.

"Are you certain you want me to leave?" he asked.

"Yes, I will be fine," she assured him absently while scanning Etain's study.

"Go keep your cousin occupied," Etain told Kes.

"Why would I ever want to do that?" he asked, sounding appalled. He gave Anin a soft kiss and whispered something in her ear before porting away.

"Do you ever wonder if they think we believe the nonsense they say about each other?" Etain asked. They both acted like they hated each other, but it was clear to anyone who spent even a moment in their company that together, they were great friends.

"You never know with them. They both think so highly of themselves that it is likely they think they are convincing." Etain laughed at Anin's words as she guided her to the small area she had set up just for her.

She had Anin sit on one side of a curtain Etain that had fashioned. When Anin stuck her arm through the slot Etain had shown her, Etain could hear her friend's breaths become labored. She needed a distraction. This had helped several of the villagers when she had to stitch them up.

"Have I ever told you about the village I came from?" Etain asked. A few moments went by, and Anin's breathing calmed slightly.

"No." It was barely audible, but at least she had Anin's attention now.

"Well, it was a hateful place, if I am being honest, filled with people who let their ignorance turn into fear, which made them all carry a hatred for me. However, what they hated more was how much they needed me. I only tell you this so you do not think I am a horrible person for my reaction," she felt the need to clarify.

"Okay, but I could never think that you are horrible," Anin said with a slight laugh.

"Well, there was this one man. He had a wife and three daughters whom he was absolutely dreadful to. He always sent them to work the market while he went to the pub to drink away whatever coin they had made the day before. Truly, he was just a waste of a human being.

Anyway, the pub was not known for its hygienic practices, and an illness of the bowels and stomach spread through the pub one fall. He came to the market, yelling to his wife and daughters that they needed to leave and tend to him because he was not feeling well. And then it happened." She paused for dramatic effect. She had already numbed the area and was in the process of collecting Anin's blood.

"What happened?" Anin asked.

"Well, at the exact same time, he vomited and shit himself in the center of the market, where the entire village was sure to be at that particular time of day."

"No," Anin gasped, holding back a laugh.

"Oh, it gets even better. When neither his wife nor their daughters moved to take care of him, he took two very angry steps forward. No doubt, he intended to take his frustrations out on one or all of them. However, fate had other plans for him. He slipped in his own vomit and fell hard on the ground, the motion causing him to soil himself yet again."

Anin could no longer hold her laughter in. Finished

with a small vial of Anin's blood, Etain got up and made her way around the curtain to stand in front of Anin.

"I happened to make direct eye contact with his wife from across the square, and she gave me a slow, triumphant smile. You see, she had come to me not three days prior asking for something to help her use the restroom.

I do not know how she did it; somehow, she must have dosed the entire cask of swill they served at the pub her husband frequented, because every drunkard in the village suffered the same affliction for a couple of days. I could not help it; I laughed. I made sure that I was conveniently too busy to help any of those poor souls who caught the illness." Anin's laughter was contagious, making Etain join in.

"I would love to have seen that," Anin finally said as she clutched her stomach, laughing so hard.

"I will certainly never forget it."

"I think I am ready now. Let's get on with it," Anin said, taking a deep breath and slowly releasing it.

"Oh, I am already done." Etain smiled at her friend's confused look.

"Thank you," Anin said in a near whisper.

"There is no need to thank me. We should all be thanking you, Anin, because of you, we will have protection against the one thing that not a single one of us could do anything about, no matter how powerful we are." She took Anin's hand and squeezed it lightly.

"Am I interrupting something?" Kes asked from behind her. "You know what? I do not think I mind. I will just sit here and watch, carry on." Anin just shook her head at her mate and stood to give Etain a hug before they said their goodbyes, which had become a tradition for them.

"Love you, nymph."

"Love you, witch."

"Well, that was not much of a show," Kes said with mock disappointment.

"My darling feather duster, you, my love, are an idiot. Let's go home," Anin said, and Kes's laughter echoed even after they disappeared.

Shaking her head, she sent a scroll to her great-aunt, and the two got to work immediately. They had spent many nights prior making sure the wording was just right. When they were certain they had everything they needed, Etain called on her orange power.

She watched as two ribbons of an orange smoke-like substance unfurled from her. She sent it to wrap around the bloodstone that sat on the table before her. Galetia added the powder they had created from dried bloodbane blooms and a drop of Anin's blood, and they said the words together.

By the sacred blood of kin entwined,
in these stones, our power aligned.
Through ancestral ties, let strength arise,
guard me now from deceitful lies.
With the essence of my blood,
I invoke, activation swift,
as ancient oaths spoke.
Shield my spirit from those who betray,

> *with kin's blood binding,*
> *I shall not sway.*

The spell took exactly one hour to set, and within that time, Ciaran reappeared. Apparently, he reached the limit of an acceptable amount of time away from him. Not that she was complaining.

When the spell was finished, Etain was certain it worked solely based on the way her power had felt at the one-hour mark. She pulled the orange ribbons back into herself and held up the stone.

"Did it work?" her aunt asked.

"It worked; I know it did. However, there is only one way to find out."

"Absolutely not," Ciaran said, plucking the stone from her hand. He ported away for a few minutes, and she shared a confused look with Galetia.

"What was that about?" she asked Etain.

"The blue oaf likely thought I was going to test the stone, as if he would ever let me." The two laughed when Ciaran returned.

"Kes is sending one of his Shadows to test it," he announced.

Etain smiled to herself. They were now protected from the mad queen and the effects of blood magic; well, at least one of them was. She looked at the box filled with bloodstones and sighed, pulling out another one.

"Maybe we should try doing more than one at a time?" Galetia asked.

"Yes, that would be great if it worked. Let's try two this time; then we can add one each time until we hit a limit."

Galetia nodded her approval, and the two witches began preparing everything all over again.

"Don't you want to wait to see if it worked?" Ciaran asked.

"It worked."

Anin sat alone on the parapet at the top of Ciaran's tower. From this height she could see the beginning of the lightening of the sky of the Day Court.

Her court.

The one she was supposed to be the queen of. The thought was laughable. She could barely take care of herself, yet the Land and Fate expected her to rule an entire court? One that was filled with real beings whose lives she could forever damage with one wrong move.

She did not think she could live with herself if she caused as much turmoil in another's life as Tatiana had done to hers. Anin could barely tolerate herself as it was. If she were honest, she was surprised that everyone else could stand to be around her.

There were times when she could forget that she was different. They were few and far between, but they did happen. She wished those times would become her reality and was tired of being afraid of everything. She just wanted her old self back, even though she knew she was long dead.

More than anything, she wanted the touch of her mate not to trigger a memory better left forgotten. She wanted him to touch her, craved the feeling of their bodies moving together as one. She was starved for intimacy, yet her mind rebelled each time.

Kes, of course, was always wonderful. He always stopped the moment he could tell she was no longer there with him. Instead of losing each other to pleasure, he wrapped his arms around her as he whispered reminders to feel the bond and that she was safe. If it were not for their bond, she could release him. He did not deserve to be burdened by her troubles.

She let out a loud sigh and looked up at the stars, searching for answers to her problems. They must have seen enough to know everything. If only they could tell her what to do.

A throat cleared behind her, causing her to nearly lose her balance as she jolted. When she looked over her shoulder, she was not entirely surprised to find Ciaran standing there. She figured he might show up to tell her to get off his tower, like the prickly fae he was.

"Why are you sitting alone up here? You know this is my tower—my private tower—right?" There it was: the way he said "my" made it clear that he didn't think she had any right to sit there. She did not respond; she would not leave until he specifically told her to.

After a long moment of awkward silence, he made a noise of annoyance, grumbling something under his breath that she couldn't understand. Movement out of the corner of her eye made her think her vision was playing tricks on her. It would not be the first time.

Ciaran surprised her by taking a seat on the short wall beside her—more like near her. There was still enough space for at least two more of him to sit between them. Even so, she could not help but gape at him.

"Are pigs flying?" she asked.

"How should I know?" he asked, looking at her as if she had grown another head—or six.

"Is that not what humans say? Whatever, it does not matter."

Neither of them said anything for a while. Eventually, the awkward silence turned into an easy one of companionship. Never in her wildest dreams did she think Ciaran would be sitting beside her, keeping her company. She must truly be pathetic if even he took pity on her.

"When I was a youngling," Ciaran began, "around a decade old, something happened to me. My father imprisoned me. He tortured and experimented on me while I had no control over my body.

He did something akin to blood magic, holding my body prisoner for over a decade. Although it was not nearly as long as your suffering, being so young... well, let's just say it left a lasting impression."

She stared at him for a long moment, feeling that she understood him now. So much about him suddenly made sense. Remorse flooded her for the youngling he had been and the fae he might have become.

"She couldn't control my body, so she controlled everything else. I—" She was about to admit something to him that she had never voiced out loud. He gave her the time and space to finish what she wanted to say on her own terms. Yet she was terrified of him, confirming her fears of being just as insane as Tatiana. Perhaps it was a family trait.

"I almost looked forward to the torture, just to feel something," she whispered the words in a single breath. He nodded as if he understood, and she thought it was possible that he just might. "How did you move on from it?"

He shrugged and then said, "I never did. I pushed it away and controlled everyone and everything around me."

Control.

She wished she had even a small amount of it in any part of her life. It might help her feel a bit more stable. At the very least, it could help her believe the lies she told herself. Saying she was okay was the biggest lie of all.

She was not.

"That was until Tatiana showed up with her blood magic," he said, turning to look out over the city. She thought he might lose his nerve to share a piece of himself if he looked at her. "Then I spiraled into a very dark place —one that not even Etain was willing to follow." She recognized the look on his face; it was one she wore regularly.

Self-loathing.

"What happened?"

"Ultimately, she's the one thing I am unwilling to sacrifice—not even for what I want. I will always want her more than anything else I might desire."

He was silent, whatever he needed to say next, making

him pause. Weighing the decision to give her another piece of him or not. Before then, she did not think they had ever had a conversation that did not stem from necessity. She returned her gaze to the stars, waiting to see what he would ultimately decide.

"I gave her something that allows her to hold me to her moral standards. She has ultimate control over me since I trust her more than I trust myself.—especially after hearing thoughts that were not my own whisper to me for decades."

She snapped her eyes to meet his. "You heard whispering?" Her heartbeat quickened, and she felt as if something monumental was about to fall into place. Several times, Tatiana had referred to the voices in her head as *whispers*; Anin had always assumed it was an illness. If it wasn't, had Tatiana been a different being at some point?

Was she a—

No.

After everything Tatiana had done to Anin, it did not matter how she became who she was now. Maybe she had been a victim, but she chose to become a monster. Ciaran sitting here next to her, clear of mind, was proof of that.

He squinted at her, as if he were reevaluating her. "Yes," he said, his evaluation apparently concluded. "The same thing afflicted my father and his father before him. I had always thought it an illness of the mind, passed down from one generation. However, something happened, cutting me off from my power and, subsequently, from the *whispers*. They never returned."

"Tatiana hears whispers. Do you think they could be a..." she trailed off, afraid to finish her sentence.

"A being?" he asked, finishing it for her. "Playing with the minds of the leaders of the realm? Yes, I just have no idea who it could be or who might possess the power to do it."

"If it is a being, how does one plant themselves in another's mind without some kind of bond between them?"

"That's what I have been asking myself. If we can find the how, we can then narrow down the who."

"You said your father had something similar to blood magic and that he heard whispers?" she asked.

"Yes." When he looked at her, she could see the thoughts turning in his mind.

"Someone… someone must be to blame for all of this," Anin said softly.

"Perhaps, but *who?*" Ciaran asked.

Anin looked back over the city, thoughts churning in her head. "What if it's not a who but a *what?*"

"Anything is possible. I am more concerned with the amount of power that would take and therefore the being must have."

"And who else are they in the minds of?" The possibilities were endless. She almost wished she could go back to thinking Tatiana was simply mad. Who could possibly be behind all of this? And what kind of influence do they wield? She tried to avoid the next question floating around in her mind. Did Tatiana deserve to be… she refused to finish that question.

"Anin?" Ciaran asked after a few minutes of silence.

"Ciaran?"

"If you ever tell anyone what I just told you, I will kill

you," he said, and when she turned to meet his gaze, she knew he meant it. Still, she could not help but laugh. There was the Ciaran she knew. When he scowled at her, she threw her hands up, palms facing out.

"I believe you. Do not worry, your secret is safe as long as you keep mine as well," she said with a grin.

"Not even my cousin."

"You have never told him?" she asked him, cocking her head to the side.

"No."

"Hmm, I think you need to." His wings snapped out in warning, and she once again held her hands up.

"Explain." Ciaran was clearly an intelligent being, yet sometimes she questioned whether he had any common sense. It seemed to be an affliction most males suffered.

"How else is he supposed to know about both Tatiana and your father hearing whispers and having access to a form of blood magic?" To her, it was obvious. If they were ever going to find the powerful being behind the *whispers*, it would take all of them.

"Why would he need to know?" She stared at him in disbelief. Was it possible he could be even denser than her feather duster?

"Because we need to find out who is behind all of this, and to do so, you need to trust your cousin—at least with some of the story." He glared at her, and she thought he might be contemplating her death.

"I will not be the one to tell him," she said. "However, you do need to come up with some version of the truth. He needs to know. I take it Etain does?"

"Of course she does," he snapped.

"Well, I am not sure if you have forgotten, but I am mated to Kes, and I will be the Queen of the Day Court." He nodded slowly, and she watched him realize that his cousin would be a king.

In that moment, when they looked into each other's eyes, they were no longer just the beings they had always known. They were two rulers acknowledging one another. There, on the parapet of the highest tower in the Night Court, sat the two beings who would shape the future of the realm.

As long as she had the courage to take her throne.

Chapter 31
Tatiana

Tatiana seethed with rage—pure, unrestrained fury. How dare they do this to her? She would hunt them down and deliver a wickedly creative punishment. They would know the torture they had put her through before she returned them to the realm.

This was personal.

It had started so long ago that she had not even been aware. The offenses had been minor. A book that was not put back in its place. Or an object that was just slightly off. Annoyance flickered in her memory, but nothing more. Perhaps she had taken it out on a lesser fae, yet it was likely one of the high fae in the dungeons that felt her wrath.

That was another problem she would have to face soon. However, it was not an immediate concern—not like this was.

Framed paintings hung askew throughout the palace as she walked. Paintings that she had fixed nearly every day. Perhaps she was mistaken; her memory was unreliable, and confusion had become her constant companion.

If it had continued to be just one here and there, she likely would never have noticed. Today, however; someone declared war.

It was not just a one-off painting, random book, or object. It was all of them. Every single thing she passed was not where it was supposed to be.

Tatiana craved the order that came from things being put back exactly where they belonged. She needed it. Everything had a proper place.

When she turned down one of the halls earlier that day and saw a dozen or so frames shifted at various angles, she screamed. In a fury, she ripped each and every one of them off the wall and smashed them to the ground. If they were no longer there, they could no longer be off of their perfect center.

Even her throne had been shifted ever so slightly to the right. She was ashamed to admit that at first she had not noticed. She had not been looking at her throne when she finally sat upon it. When she looked up, everything was wrong.

It turned out that having her throne shifted made the entire room look out of place. An entire room! The disorder made her head spin and darkness threatened at the edges of her vision. She left at once and sent a council member to ensure it was fixed.

Possibly the greatest offense of all had been when she returned from a sacrifice. Her arms had been freshly coated in a delicate shade of pink.

When she went to dress in a gown that she knew

would match perfectly, she walked through her room of gowns and screamed. Every pink gown she knew she had was missing. She had been forced to wear a red gown, which she thought looked awful. Eventually, she washed everything away because she could not handle the way the blood and gown did not match. She would rather wear only the gown.

A few days later, it happened again. The pink had been returned, yet another color had been taken. Enough time passed without incident that she thought it might have been in her head all along.

That was until it started again a few days ago and had not stopped since. Today, she had been forced to resort to wearing black with the burgundy that splashed up her arms.

She threw open the doors to the Council Chamber and stomped in. "Someone must answer for this!" Tatiana seethed as she waved to her lack of a matching gown.

The looks of confusion they gave her only irritated her further. If they were not careful, they would be the first she chose from when her dungeons emptied. One of them—the female whose name Tatiana had long forgotten—was the first to look as though she comprehended.

"They are causing mayhem all over the city. They have destroyed several roads and bridges throughout the city, effectively cutting off entire districts. It has made trans-porting goods complicated at best," she said.

"The food supply to the palace has been diminishing every day, and what arrives is half-rotted," another said. Why should she care? She could not remember the last time she had eaten. Fae could live a long time without food.

"They have even gone as far as tampering with the plumbing throughout the city, but mostly in the palace. It has led to a rather unfortunate situation." The words caused all the council members to cringe, their faces pulled in disgust.

"Yes, yes. That's horrible, but who is 'they,' and what have *they* done with my gowns?" she shrieked.

"The lesser fae have started a rebellion. Th—"

"The lesser fae?" she asked in disbelief. When they all nodded in confirmation, uncontrollable giggles escaped her. "Truly?" More nods. Her giggles morphed into maniacal laughter. The absurdity of it all was astounding. Her stomach began to ache, and she had to double over while she attempted to catch her breath in between errant giggles that refused to stay put.

When she could finally speak without bursts of laughter interrupting her, she asked, "And what have you all been doing about it?"

Her smile, which only moments ago had been impossible for her to get rid of, fell quickly. They all tried to speak over one another. Blame was volleyed by a few, while others argued over who had the best idea.

She ported to stand on the table. When half of them did not take notice, she jumped up and down, stomping her feet on the table. "DO SOMETHING!" she screamed.

That got their attention. The room fell silent, and she basked in the peace of it for a moment. She let out a loud, long sigh. Their company bored her, and she wanted to play a game with Raindal.

She liked to call the game Fated Mates. They pretended to be mates, and she had him say all the words she was beginning to feel certain Reminold had never said. However, she did not want to look too closely at that.

"I know!" she exclaimed in her now youngling-like voice. "Kill them! Kill a lot of them!" she squealed, thinking about what a sight that would make. A rainbow of blood. She gasped and looked at them with wide eyes.

"I just thought of something. How fun would it be if it were all at once?" She clapped her hands while bouncing on the balls of her feet.

"Yes, that sounds perfect!"

Ciaran was annoyed that he could not stop thinking about his conversation with Anin. Even more so, a couple of nights later, it replayed in his mind. Worst of all, he knew she was right. There were many things Ciaran hated—honestly, most things he hated—but nothing more than being wrong.

When he thought about his past, he focused only on how it affected him. It had never occurred to him that his cousin might have been affected as well. Of course, on some level, he had always known that their shared past had scarred Kes just as deeply as it had him; only their scars looked completely different.

As right as he knew she was, a large part of him wanted to avoid telling Kes—not for the same reasons he had not in the past, but because he wanted to make the nymph feel as annoyed as he was in that moment.

A scroll appeared before him, and he snatched it out of the air with a huff. He was not in the mood; all he wanted was to find his little witch and see how many times he could make her scream his name in one night.

He opened it and scoffed. Panella thought she had found something and demanded his presence—demanded, not requested. He was going to go, but he was not going to like it.

Ciaran ported to the staircase that would take him down to a secret room that was no longer much of a secret—another thing that annoyed him greatly.

"She's lucky she is under the protection of my mate, demanding that I, the King of the Night Court, go anywhere. Her head would look nice on a spike in the Great Hall," he grumbled under his breath the entire time.

He knew he was being ridiculous, and that he was in the foulest of moods. He could not help it; every time he thought about his father, his mood soured for nights.

"Oh, good," Panella said the moment he stepped out in a blur from the shadows of the stairwell. "I was hoping you would come sooner rather than later." He glowered at her as he made his way over to the table she occupied.

"What's wrong with you? You know what? I do not even want to know," she said, putting her hand up and looking toward the ceiling, mumbling something about a goddess giving her strength.

"Well? What did you *demand* I come to look at?" he asked, not bothering to hide his displeasure.

"Oh my goddess! Is that what all this"—she waved her hand at him in general—"is about?" She rolled her eyes and dragged a giant book. It had sat dusty for so long that the book itself could never be entirely clean.

"Any time I send you a message, I try to use as few

words as possible. I assumed that was what you would prefer, but in the future I will consider your delicate ego," she said, sounding just as annoyed as he was before opening the book to a marked page.

Try as he might, he reluctantly had begun to respect the witch. She never backed down from him, and while that would normally set him off, she managed to do it in a way that did not dig under his skin. She did not linger on it either. She spoke her mind and then moved on as if nothing had ever happened. Unlike Kes, who liked to poke at him until he exploded and then laugh as if it were all a game.

"If you look right here, there is something strange about the power of three. For there to be true balance, there must be three sides: three to lead, three to teach, and three to protect—which is oddly specific and was the reason I thought it might be worth looking into when I got to the passage on this page that spoke of a temple of the three, this one to lead."

"Where is—"

"I already located it for you," she said as she pulled out an old map. This was one of the other reasons he begrudgingly respected her: she was always prepared.

"I looked on the map of the realm we all use now, and there was nothing on it in the vicinity that the book said it was located. So then, I thought it was obvious I should have started with an old map that might have been made closer to the time this book was written. And sure enough," she said, pointing to a small icon. It was in the southeast part of the Night Court, nearly to the Borderlands.

"Oh, what do we have going on here?" Kes asked from behind him, making Ciaran groan. Ciaran looked at Panella and silently begged her not to mention the temple.

"I was just telling Ciaran about this forgotten temple that might be promising for his search," she said, smiling at Ciaran.

Suddenly, it dusked on him: she had summoned both of them. His reluctant respect was evaporating quickly.

"Count me in," Kes said, just like Ciaran knew he would. Kes enjoyed exploring; he had ever since they were small younglings.

"You were not invited," Ciaran said, just as Kes put his arm obnoxiously around his shoulders.

"Oh, cousin, you can be so funny sometimes." He laughed as he leaned over the old map to see where they were going. There was no getting out of it now; Ciaran was going to be stuck with Kes for the next few hours. Maybe he could lose him in the temple. "Let's go!" Kes exclaimed.

Ciaran had to smile back at his cousin. He sounded so much like the small, grey, fluffy feathered fae he had spent every moment with as a youngling—until his father made that impossible.

Before they could port, Panella lightly put her hand on his arm and leaned forward to whisper, "Anin said to tell him. Whatever that means." Her words confirmed his suspicions.

He had been set up.

They ported to the general location Panella had pointed to on the map. The entire area had been taken by the land long ago, which meant they were going to have to search for the remains of the temple. He sent several of his shadows out to speed the search along.

"Well, those are nice to have, I'm sure," Kes said. Ciaran just made a sound of agreement and started walking. Several minutes of silence went by, and Ciaran was starting to think this might not be so bad after all. "You ever... with Etain—"

"If you value the appendage between your legs, you will not finish that question," Ciaran growled, while Kes just laughed.

"Message received, cousin." They walked on in silence, again lulling him into a false sense of peace. "But if you have, good on you. Just saying, glad one of us is having a healthy sex life," Kes said with a chuckle.

Fuck.

Here was the moment.

Ciaran sighed and looked at his cousin. He had the mask he wore so well on, but Ciaran had long ago learned to see beneath it. He looked... lost. Which was not surprising; he would look the same way if it were Etain. Then again, he would have destroyed the realm—and everyone in it—if it had been.

"Control" was all he said, reluctant to say anything else now that the door was opened. It had been easy enough to tell Anin, but for some reason, it felt like he had something sticky in his mouth when he tried to tell Kes.

He had not killed Anin's parents.

Kes had never asked what happened to him or how Ciaran had been able to behead both of his parents—how he had been able to make his mother's death particularly...

Maybe it was because he now had proof that his own mother had loved him, but thinking about what he had been forced to do to Kes's mother left a foul taste in his mouth. It was not remorse; he felt nothing for her. Perhaps it was the fact that he had not chosen to kill her, and if he had been given the choice, he never would have.

Choice was a form of control, and when choice is taken by force, it feels particularly assaultive.

"What?" Kes finally asked.

"She needs control. If she had complete control over one aspect of her life, it would give her some confidence."

This was it.

"How do you know?" Kes asked.

"It worked for me. Of course, I might have gone a touch too far," he said with a laugh. He hoped that if he cracked a joke—even a poor one like that—Kes might be distracted.

"What do you mean, it worked for you?"

"I mean," Ciaran sighed, "Do you remember when we were young and... Well, my father had access to some kind of blood magic and controlled me for about a decade? I might not have been locked in a physical cage, but I was locked away in my mind. That was why I left; I saw an opportunity, and I took it," he said, rushing it out all in one breath.

"So when you...?"

"I think they knew." He did not need to say who they were; they both knew Ciaran meant his parents.

"They knew." It was not a question but a statement, and it sounded like things that had never made sense for Kes had just clicked into place.

"There's more. Did you ever hear my father talking to himself?"

"Yes, I enjoyed taunting him with his illness," Kes said, laughing.

"It was not an illness. I thought it was as well, but that is not the case. The same *whispers* spoke to me." Kes nodded his head.

"I had figured the same illness had taken root in you, but then you seemed to have gotten better."

"There was something that happened that cut me off from my power briefly. The moment that happened, the *whispers* were no more."

"The bitch queen… Anin mentioned something about her talking to herself often. Someone is manipulating the rulers of the realm." His eyes were wide as he considered the implications.

"Yes, and she seems to have been doing so for a very long time. So if you hear whispers…"

"Yeah, got it. If your father and Tatiana had access to blood magic, did you as well?"

"I think that was the power the *whispers* constantly tried to bribe me with. I never got that far." Ciaran hated having the conversation, but he felt lighter for it. They walked in silence for so long that he thought they might find the temple before Kes spoke again.

"So control? That will help her?" Ciaran had to laugh as he nodded. He was thankful Kes was just as uncomfortable with thoughts of their younghood as he was. "Good, because I think I *personally* can guarantee her complete control," Kes said, giving Ciaran a sinfully wicked smirk.

"Disgusting," Ciaran groaned. "Keep that to yourself.

That was not an image I wanted burned into my memory forever."

"You, cousin, are most welcome." Kes was giving a theatrical bow, but then tripped and fell midway. Ciaran burst into a fit of laughter, having to wipe tears from his eyes as Kes picked himself up.

"Now that, cousin, was an image I am happy to have burned into my memory forever," Ciaran said before cracking up again. This time, Kes joined in.

"What is that?" Kes asked, pushing away the brush to see what he had tripped over: a stone step. They looked at each other and grinned. They had found the temple. Well, more accurately, Kes's foot found it.

Ciaran called his shadows back to him as they followed the crumbling stone steps, which were not really steps any longer. After so long, they had become more like a trail of broken stone.

When they pushed aside a particularly thick wall of vines, there it was. It was as if it appeared out of nowhere. There had not even been the slightest hint of the temple; yet just beyond a wall of vines, the massive structure loomed.

"Should we take a look around before we enter?" Kes asked, already moving off to one side.

"Why? I think I will just go in and look for these fucking books and then get back to my mate. I am not expecting this to be anything but a waste of time." Without waiting for Kes, Ciaran flew up to the entrance of the temple.

With all the stairs nothing but a smattering of broken-off stones, it was that or climb. He could port, he supposed, but he did not know for sure what was up there. The last thing he wanted was to land in some unknown pit of ancient muck.

He heard Kes land seconds after his feet touched the stone platform just before a tight, thick stone entryway. It looked like there was a short, narrow hall that opened into one larger room.

Easy.

"You know," Kes said as Ciaran made to step through the entrance, "You really should take a look around and make sure there's no—" Not three steps in, Ciaran heard a click and had a fraction of a second to get out of the way as one side wall of the short hall smashed into the other. Had it not been for his speed, he would have been dead.

A fact that Kes seemed to find hilarious.

"You—you screamed," Kes wheezed.

"I do not scream." There was no way—his thought was interrupted by the sound of mocking blooms repeating one yell over and over before they began to repeat him, saying he does not scream.

"See!" Kes was hysterical and struggling to catch his breath. Good. Perhaps he would suffocate.

"It was a yell, and I would like to hear what you would sound like trying to get out of the way of that contraption. Oh, that's right; the only sound would be your slow ass squished between two walls." The wall in question was still firmly against the other and did not budge when Kes walked through.

Unfortunately, he had not suffocated.

"Do not worry yourself, cousin. I am certain there are plenty of males who scream," he said with a grin Ciaran wanted to wipe all over the floor. He patted him on the shoulder and walked away, chuckling.

Ciaran did not know when, but he would get his revenge on his cousin. If he were lucky, it would be in front of Anin. That would shut him up, and then they could see who was laughing.

"Is that what you are looking for?" Kes called from further into the large room. When Ciaran got there, he was ready to curse fate and every single god.

Before them was a stone box with several symbols and a dial in the middle. As if nearly being smashed to death were not enough. Now he had to figure out the correct combination.

"I swear, if we get this open and the books are not in there…"

"I do not know why you are so upset. I, for one, am having a great time," Kes said honestly.

"This is all my life has been for… ever. Searching for elusive items. I grow tired of it," Ciaran said with a sigh that he felt deep in his bones.

"Well, do not forget that one of those elusive things happened to be your mate. So even if all Fate ever has planned for you is more of this, she still gave you Etain." Gods, he hated when Kes was right.

"Fair point." There was not a single thing he would not do for his little witch.

"Does any of this make sense to you?" Kes asked, pointing to the strange images.

"Not at all."

"That's unfortunate. Do you just want to start trying different combinations until one works?" Kes asked, reaching for the dial. Ciaran snatched his hand back before he could touch anything.

"Normally, I would say yes. However, after nearly being made far too familiar with a wall—"

"And screaming." Ciaran regretted not letting Kes touch the dial.

"I think we should at least look and make sure nothing is going to behead us or something."

"I am rather fond of my head."

"Wait. I have an idea," Ciaran said, as shadows descended on the box. "I'm going to see if I can get my shadows to get into the mechanism and unlock it from the inside."

"You know, that is twice now in one night that I have envied your shadows. What's next? Will I start the Shadow King fan club? Perhaps the secret word to enter the club will be a scream." They heard a faint click and the sound of stone sliding across stone.

"You are never going to let that go, are you?"

"Never." They both peered over the box, and Kes reached out to pat Ciaran's shoulder. "Well, looks like fate intends to keep you searching, cousin."

Inside the box was a single sheet of parchment, words scrawled across it in a language he did not know. He picked it up and put it in his pocket before they ported back to the palace.

Fucking fate.

Chapter 33
Kes

"You do not have to go," Kes said to Anin. She paced their bedchamber, biting one of her long nails. "You do not have to do anything you do not want to. I can go for you, or we can tell him to fuck off."

"No," she gasped, horrified by the idea. "I told him I would be there. I have to go." He hated seeing her like this and feared what might happen if she pushed herself too far.

She had overcome so much in the last few decades, and he did not want this stupid meeting to risk her progress. However, he knew it was ultimately up to her, and he would never tell her what she could and could not do.

"All I am saying is that you owe no being anything." Her face softened at his words, and she strode to where he sat at the end of the bed. He spread his legs so she could stand between them, but was careful to keep his hands firmly on the bed as her arms wrapped loosely around his neck.

It was torture not being able to touch her in the way he desired. Yet he would endure without complaint or pressure her to move faster than she was prepared for; this was his penance for not protecting her in the first place. If she suffered, he would as well.

When she was ready, he would trace every inch of her body. His touch would replace the painful memories with pleasureful ones. It was his life's mission, one he would make sure to do a very thorough job of, happily, and as often as she would allow him to.

"Are you thinking naughty things again?" Anin asked, laughing. He wore his obsession for her freely upon his face, making no apologies for it.

"Anin, you are within my sight; of course I am," he said with a wicked grin, showing off his razor-sharp teeth. One night, he would scrape them across every sensitive part of her body, reveling in the sounds that escaped her.

She rolled her eyes, trying to hide the pleasure his desire for her inspired. "I do, though," she said. Kes's downy brows creased, the conversation momentarily forgotten.

"Says who?" he asked, recalling their current debate; she was entirely too distracting.

"Me. When I touched the throne the day you came to get me, it felt right. I knew, in that moment, that the responsibility for all life in the Day Court was mine to bear. So, at the very least, I must answer to myself," she said.

Anin had been gaining more confidence every night,

and he loved watching her regain her sense of self. When she spoke like that, he was mesmerized by her determination and saw a glimpse of the Anin who was rising from the ashes of her past.

He had always thought her incredible, even when he had left her hanging in a cage down in Nightfell's dungeon the night he captured her. She had enchanted him with every acidic word she spat.

"I will always support everything you want to do, even if that means my power diminishes while living in the Day Court. I would rather be as powerless as a lesser fae than spend a single night without you." His hands itched to caress her, but he gripped the fabric beneath his palms and forced them to remain where they were.

She must have felt how much he craved her skin against his, for she brushed a thumb across his lips before leaning in to kiss him; her mouth lingered for a moment, soft and unhurried. She pulled back far enough to whisper against his mouth, "We will find a way."

"We will," he responded, speaking just as quietly as she had.

"But first, I must take this step." She looked more sure of herself than she had just a few minutes earlier.

"Just remember to take each step at whatever pace feels right to you," he said, staring into her black eyes. He could get lost in the abyss of those dark depths and had gotten lost in them several times, in fact. "Do not let anyone, including me, dictate how and when you take another step forward."

"Deal."

"If you are ready, we should go," he said, finally lifting

his hands from the now severely crumpled bedspread. He clasped her hands and waited for her to make the final decision, and when she nodded, he ported them to one of the higher vantage points in the ruins.

He pointed down below to where Balthier paced, something he seemed to do every time Kes saw the satyr; only this time, he was not alone. A siren stood off to the side in a less-than-modest gossamer gown, looking calm enough for the both of them.

"The satyr is Balthier, and I have no idea who the siren is," he said, scowling; he did not like that there was an unknown.

"Well, let's go find out," Anin said as she squeezed the hand she still held before stepping off the ruins, forcing him to do the same.

"You came," Balthier gasped, halting his movements as both Day fae bowed to Anin.

"Oh, please do—" Kes stopped her before she could finish her statement by leaning in to whisper to her.

"They are letting you know that, to them, you are already their queen, so let them," he said, and then added after a brief pause, "My queen." He took note of the sharp intake of breath and the desire he felt flare through the bond.

"I am Balthier and this is Killia, we have been attempting to run the rebellion in my mate's absence," when he indicated toward the siren she smiled, yet it did not touch her eyes.

Normally, that kind of insincerity would make Kes suspicious; yet her eyes held an emptiness. The kind that took root when horrible things happened, when all one wanted to do was lie down and cease to exist. Her eyes shifted away from his assessing stare, and her mask of calm indifference was once again firmly in place.

"I am sorry to hear that he is a prisoner of the qu—Tatiana's blood magic." She caught herself before she could call Tatiana the queen; that bitch was no queen to any of the beings present.

"Yes, well, I try not to think about it. Luckily, the rebellion keeps me busy and does not leave much time to dwell on the dark, spiraling thoughts that my mind enjoys flashing at me." The satyr laughed, but it was a joyless sound that Kes knew all too well. He did not envy the male.

"Etain has been making as many active bloodstones as she can. I will ask her to set aside as many as possible for you. I am not sure exactly how they work, but perhaps if you can get one to him, it will break her hold over him." The satyr nodded, and Kes could see him desperately attempting to grasp the hope Anin had just given him while also being afraid to let himself.

"Thank you. We should not need many. The mad queen either does not see us as a threat, or her blood magic is defective against us. We are not sure which one it is. Either way, she has given us no reason to worry about it—at least not yet."

Interesting.

What would prevent blood magic from working on lesser fae? He thought it was more likely that Tatiana thought so little of the lesser fae that she did not bother with them.

"We would still appreciate having as many as you can

get us. We might have pushed too far recently, and I would not be surprised if our luck has run out," Killia said.

"How so," Kes asked.

"Well, the palace has been experiencing some unfortunate sewage problems," Killia tried to keep from laughing as she spoke.

"The Blood Queen might also be experiencing some hardships. I hear several of her gowns are apt to go missing and then reappear just as suddenly," Balthier said, attempting to look forlorn, as if his words were a tragedy.

"Oh, I am sure she has lost her mind—well, whatever of it remains," Anin said, laughter bursting from her. While trying to catch her breath, she placed a hand over her stomach and attempted to wave in apology. "I just cannot help but picture her face when she first noticed," she managed to get out between small fits of giggles. "Thank you for that mental picture. I shall cherish it forever." The two Day fae smiled at each other, clearly pleased with themselves.

"I just hope it does not blow up in our faces," Balthier said, his smile dropping as worry crept in.

"We will face whatever she throws at us. We have endured this long. We can continue," Killia said to Balthier. She might not have intended for her words to make Anin feel guilty, but his nymph was flooded with it.

"Well, if she—" Balthier started, looking toward Anin. Whatever demand he had been about to make of Anin died on his tongue when he saw the promise of death on Kes's face.

"We should go," Kes said quietly to Anin. She nodded,

and he felt her desire to make them promises she was not certain she could keep. "Your pace, Anin. No one else's."

When her eyes met his, he knew she was devastated that she could not give them what they needed, yet it was clear to anyone who looked at her how much she wanted to. She watched the two Day fae while crafting a promise she *could* keep.

"Thank you for meeting with me. Please keep me informed, and I will do whatever I can to help." The two beings tried to keep their faces from falling, but their disappointment was palpable. Quieter, she added, "It's not *if* I will be ready; it's when. I have one chance, and if I —" her voice shook as she thought about seeing her sister again. "Tatiana will seize any opportunity available to her, and all will be lost. Stay strong for just a while longer.

You are both incredibly brave, and I am in awe of the strength you both possess. It is terrifying to stand against your oppressors, yet none of you let fear stop you." The two Day fae nodded with tears in their eyes as Anin held their gazes a moment longer. She squeezed Kes's hand, letting him know she was ready, and they ported back to their chambers.

Anin covered her face with both hands and fell onto the bed as she sobbed the moment they were alone. "I need to protect my people, yet I cannot even handle the thought of seeing *her* again," she said, her words muffled.

He reached out and gently pulled her hands away, waiting to speak until she sat up and looked at him. "Anin," he said the second their eyes met. "You do not need to hide from anyone, but never from me. Say the word, and I will take one of those bloodstones and port to the Daybreak Palace to kill that bitch right now."

He meant it, and it was not the first time he suggested it. Fuck, he had even begged her multiple times to allow him to get rid of Tatiana.

"I know, yet I cannot let you fight all of my battles. As tempting as it sounds, particularly now, I know it has to be me that faces her. I have to defeat her, at the very least conquer the fear she instills in me. It's my fate, of that I am certain."

"I would happily fight every battle, big or small, for you. However, I am just as happy to stand behind you and offer support as you fight them yourself. If it's your fate, then the time to take your throne has already been decided. Do not rush yourself." He was unwilling to risk angering Fate and losing his mate because they tried to force it. Fate was far too fickle for that.

"I know, but I refuse to allow her to sit on my throne longer than I must," she said. The power in her voice was one he rarely heard. However, it had been making itself known more often over the past year. The time was coming; he could feel it. She was capable of facing her tormentor; she only needed the confidence to believe that she could.

He leaned forward, placing his lips so close to the shell of her ear that she shivered. "Yes, my queen," he said slowly. When she reacted, just as she had when he said it at the ruins, he surrendered control. "Take what you need from me," he said, moving slowly down her throat, his lips coming as close as possible without touching her. She tilted her head to the side; each time his warm breath kissed her skin, a little tremor made its way through her.

When he reached her other ear, he said, "Use me, any part of me." He placed his cheek a hair's breadth away from hers. They moved in tandem, staying impossibly close yet never touching.

"You are in complete control." The gasp that escaped her went straight to his cock. He never imagined that not touching could ever be so intimate. By the time his mouth hovered just far enough from her lips, her breaths came in heavy pants.

"Do your worst…my queen." It was as if a switch had flipped within her. Vines shot out, grabbing each of his arms and pulling him up the bed toward the headboard. They gave him just enough time to situate his wings before pinning him flat on his back, spreading him in an X on the bed.

Anin looked down at him, desire making her black eyes impossibly darker. He had never been the one tied down before; usually, he had been the one doing the tying. The only other time had been when Anin pinned him to the wall, but he had to admit the view was better from this angle.

"I guess you liked the sound of that?" he asked, chuckling darkly and voice heavy with arousal.

He sure as hell did.

Gods, he did not think he had ever been so painfully hard before. She only smiled at him seductively. He decided that her—at that moment—was the image he would choose to remember forever. When other memories might slip away with time, this one would remain.

More vines snaked up the bed and gripped his clothing, ripping it from his body in one hard tug. Her eyes zeroed in on the part of him that was clearly the most excited to be there. Gods damn, he was uncertain he would last long enough for her to touch him. Just the heat of her gaze was enough to send him over the edge.

Council meetings...Ciaran's ugly face...brownies...that one fae that always looked like they were melting...

He flashed the images through his mind on repeat until he was certain he would not embarrass himself. Which lasted no more than two seconds.

She stood over him on the bed and untucked her wings, dragging each one slowly—painfully so, if you asked his erection—away from her body. Gods, he was not going to last; all she needed to do was breathe in the general direction of his cock and he was sure to burst.

Fuck. Me.

He had obviously seen her naked form before; however, that had been when she needed him to care for her. Of course, he had not been immune to touching his mate's breasts, but it had been nothing more than a fleeting thought. This vision, though? He groaned, the sound turning Anin's grin wicked. He amended his earlier thought about taking one image with him for life and decided he would take two; honestly, he was prepared to collect thousands of them if they were anything like this.

"Anin, I swear to the gods, if you touch me anywhere in the vicinity of my guy down there waving at you, I will not survive the humiliation," he said seriously, which only made her laugh. "Please, spare my ego and sit on my face. I have dreamt about your taste since the moment you called me an insufferable ball of fluff, so please, my queen, sit on my face."

"I suppose I can sacrifice for the sake of your delicate ego," she said, laughing. For the first time, uncertainty crept in, tightening the edges of her eyes. She bit her lip and looked down at him. "Are you sure you want me to… sit?"

"Gods, yes. I want you to fucking smother me. If I die drowning in your desire, I do so willingly. Now, sit on my damn face; I am begging you." He licked his lips, and his mouth was already watering at the thought of her taste.

She sat down tenderly, refusing to put all her weight on him. It did not last long. After a few minutes of licking and sucking at her, she finally gave in and rode him. He devoured her, noting that his favorite meal was now his mate's dripping core. He nipped at her clit gently with his sharp teeth and was rewarded when she flooded his mouth and screamed his name. Two things he had been dreaming about for nearly two centuries.

She climbed off his face unsteadily and crawled down him until she was nearly sitting on top of his cock. "I need you inside of me. Now. I want to feel the way you stretch me," she said just before she fisted him and guided him to her entrance.

"Oh, fuck," he moaned, watching as he disappeared inside of her inch by inch until she was fully seated on top of him. She sat there without moving, allowing her body to adjust to the tight fit of him.

Two minutes, just make it two minutes.

He begged himself to last just long enough. He could feel her already clenching around him, and he knew she was quickly climbing to her peak. He just needed to last longer than her, yet he doubted himself when she began to rock against him. Especially when she slid her hand down her body and began rubbing her clit firmly.

"Gods, you are so beautiful," he groaned as she picked up her pace. Her movements became more frantic, and he could feel her reaching the very edge of her pleasure. Her body tensed as she clamped down around him and threw her head back, opening her mouth in a silent scream, sending both of them over the edge.

Kes finally gave himself permission to let go, aware that words spewed from his mouth, though he had no idea what they were or if they were even real. He fell over that edge into oblivion harder than ever before. When he came to, Anin had collapsed and fallen on top of him.

"Darling nymph?" he asked, concerned that something had happened, that somehow he had hurt her.

"Hmmm," she hummed.

"Are you all right?"

"So very all right," she said sleepily. His nymph was blissed out but managed to release him from her vines.

"I love you, Anin." He wrapped his arms firmly around her—a touch she could handle.

"Love you," she mumbled.

"Do a mating ceremony with me," he said, suddenly nervous for some reason. He desperately wanted to solidify their bond.

"Okay."

"Okay," he said with a smile.

Chapter 34
Etain

Flying through the woods was a different experience. Her inkblot wings and dark shade power ebbed and flowed in reliability, disappearing mid-flight just when she thought they were under control. Sometimes they reappeared a second later; other times, they did not. But she had learned to weave her blue and orange powers in a specific pattern to catch herself before hitting the ground.

It was still terrifying, and Ciaran refused to allow her to fly alone or without a spelled broom or something else to ride. Now that she had decades to work with her shade power, she never had to worry about that again.

After her initial lesson with Hecate, she took her advice to heart and treated all her powers as if they were individual entities. After that, everything became easier. It turned out that they were all eager to play but required proper recognition. They reminded her of the palace brownies of which her mate was so fearful.

She flew everywhere and rarely ported unless time was essential. Her favorite, though, was flying with Ciaran. He took her all over the court, showing her some of his favorite places. They, of course, frequented their favorite waterfall. Etain could feel the heat rising in her cheeks when she thought of the last time they went to the falls. Between the two sets of wings and the endless shadow-Ciaran's—well, things were never boring.

Just the other night, he had sat in one of the wingback chairs in their bedchamber and watched as three of his shadows ravaged her, feeling everything they did. There was something about him not only being everywhere he could be with her, but also watching it happen, that excited her. The Etain from Havenston would have been scandalized.

Over the past few decades, she had gone to visit Hecate whenever she had a new idea for her powers, yet had no idea where to begin. Sometimes, she just went to see the goddess because she enjoyed her company. Something Ciaran could not fathom.

When she entered the clearing where the strange little mushroom hut sat—looking worse for wear, as usual— she tucked her wings away and gave thanks to her shade. The single door flung open, and there stood Hecate, the mother of witches, smiling with her never-ending shifting faces.

"Hello, my child," she greeted Etain, who kissed her cheek as she stepped past her into the—noticeably larger than last time—home of the goddess.

"Wow, in all the different variations of your home I have seen, this is by far the largest." It is not only larger but far grander as well.

Where the rafters once spanned the entirety of her high ceilings, they had been replaced with a second story. The center of the room opened to the ceiling made of glass and offered a beautiful view of the night sky. A wide, split staircase that connected the two floors took up most of the space. She could see the tops of four doors, one on each side of the second story.

"My daughters are visiting, and when all four of us are under one roof, it's best to give as much space as possible," she said.

"Your daughters are here?" Etain had wanted to meet them since the first time the goddess mentioned her triplets.

"Not at the moment. They stepped out and will likely return in a year or so."

"A year? They just stepped out?" Etain laughed. "The immortal view of time is always something that makes me smile."

"Yes, well, to us, a year can feel like hours feel to you. Tea?" Hecate asked.

"Please." Etain followed her into the lounge, which was filled with plush chairs and rich wooden tables. Three of the walls were covered with a multitude of bookshelves that were near bursting with strange-looking tomes. Some of them felt as if they were looking at her.

Did that book just move?

The fourth wall was the one she could not stop looking at. It had a mural of a landscape with rolling green hills and a sky filled with pinks and soft blues and oranges. It reminded her of the Human Realm at sunset. That was until she noticed the rainbow... bridge?

"Why not keep this all the time? I do not mean the entire place, but this room is beautiful." Etain would never want to leave. Strange books and all.

"Sometimes I do; sometimes I make the home what my visitors need. You always felt homesick, so I made my home resemble the one you once knew. However, because of the spells my daughters left on their rooms, there's no changing it until they have left."

Etain took a seat in one of the plush chairs that the goddess indicated she should take; the leather was so soft it felt almost like velvet. Hecate took the chair next to her, and a kettle of tea now sat on the table between them, with a cup and saucer for each. She poured tea into the cups before sitting back and looking at Etain.

"Well, you have the glow of a...content female," she said with a sly grin, and Etain immediately blushed. She took a sip of tea to hide behind, burning the tip of her tongue.

"Very," she said, still trying to hide behind her teacup.

"I'm sure you did not come to see me to share tales of your... experiences. Unless you did, in which case, I will happily listen." Etain laughed, unsure what the point of feeling embarrassed was. Clearly, Hecate already knew all about every aspect of her life.

"Something tells me every story would be old news to you," she said, as the goddess laughed. "No, I was hoping you could tell me if it is possible to combine my shade power with my colors?"

"Of course it is. Mostly, the shades will act as an amplifier for your colors. However, as you are now well aware, the shades have been known to surprise us all."

"I thought it might. I tried doing it the same way I do with my colors, but nothing happened." She had been trying for years to figure it out. She only called on the goddess when she had exhausted everything available to her. She enjoyed figuring things out for herself.

"Well, did you use your little trinket?" Hecate asked, pointing at the amulet she always wore. She had not taken it off for one night since she and Ciaran went to retrieve it from her small two-room home in the Human Realm.

"No, I thought it was just a conductor for the shades. However, I really do not know much about it." There was very little information in her family grimoire and even less in other books from the covens.

"It is called The Weaver, and it is specifically designed to weave one power with another." Etain cocked her head to the side. The Many Faced Goddess always gave information in a particular way; every word was intentional.

"One power with another?" She had not specified shade power with her color power. Suddenly, ideas of weaving her colors and shade with Ciaran's shadows came to mind.

"There are two ways to combine shade power with another: You can infuse the other power, which is the simplest way, or you can weave them together in specific patterns and see what happens."

"What happens when you infuse them?"

"It amplifies the power and turns the color into a darker, richer tone."

"And if you weave it?"

She shrugged. "No one knows what will happen; it is different every time. Shades are very peculiar, after all."

"So I could accidentally blow up the entire palace by weaving my shade with a color?" Etain asked, horrified at the possibility. It was relatively common for her experiments to explode, but those were always harmless—or most, at least.

"It is a possibility, but that's what makes it so exciting."

"Perhaps for the immortals," Etain said, and they both laughed.

"Why not give it a try with something small? Try infusing one of your colors. All you have to do is channel both into The Weaver. It's quite simple." Etain had never thought to try anything with the amulet. It had not helped much with her shade power, so most nights it was just a trinket, as Hecate called it.

Purple seemed the safest bet. Now, the hard part was calling on both the purple and the shade at the same time. She had only managed it once before and had not been able to do anything with them.

"When my daughters were born, I had not been prepared. God or not, triplets are next to impossible," Hecate said. She always shared stories with Etain while she practiced whatever trick the goddess had just given her.

"I cannot imagine. A woman in my village had twin boys, and she looked like she had waged war daily," Etain said as she coaxed both her powers to come out. They were almost childlike in the way one had to get them excited to do whatever was needed. When she had last gotten them to come out together without anything for them to do, they had not been happy, refusing to do it again.

Perhaps it was being in the presence of Hecate that they recognized her as their creator. Or maybe they had finally forgiven Etain. Either way, she coaxed her purple and shade into the amulet as she listened to Hecate's story.

"As difficult as it was, I had never felt such joy. I had experienced everything else, and while I had been happy to discover I was with child, it had been more about the excitement of something new. When they finally came into the realm and I held them for the first time, I knew that was what I had been created for in the first place. I still think that even today, witches like you are proof of it."

Etain smiled fondly at the goddess, and when she looked back down, her purple was starting to emerge from the amulet as a deep plum. It was beautiful.

"I was completely consumed with being a mother for the first few years. It was not until around their tenth birthday that it occurred to me their father should know of their existence. He should get to experience the love and joy that our girls brought me."

Etain was not exactly sure what to do with her powers now that they were blending together. They started at her feet and began to wrap slowly around her legs. It was an interesting feeling, almost like when stepping outside on a foggy morning.

"I searched for him. I looked everywhere and could not find him. I finally made myself visible to his clansmen, who told me he had disappeared years ago. They all thought he was dead."

The deep plum was up to her thighs; however, it did not frighten her. She was content to let her powers have their fun.

"I felt horrible. They said he had not been himself for a couple of years at the end. He spent most of his time searching for something, and as more time went by without finding it, he became worse. I am certain that something was me; my carelessness meant my daughters would never know their fa—"

As her power wrapped around her head, everything stopped. She was nowhere and everywhere at once—only darkness remained until a veil appeared.

A being stepped through and looked back into the veil, where another being stood in shadow. The one in shadow passed the other something; the being stared at the thing in their hand before consuming it.

She could not be certain whether it happened quickly or if it had taken a millennium, but she watched as the being was unmade. They screamed as their skin dissolved and their bones liquefied. They never stopped screaming until they had been remade into something else.

Her vision shifted; no longer looking at the strange thing the being had become. Now it was as if she were flying way up in the sky, just like she did with Ciaran. She was looking down on what might have been an island. It was surrounded by water, but she had never seen land that was pitch black, bubbling and popping as it mimicked the waves of the surrounding water.

She blinked—or at least she thought she had blinked—

and suddenly she was looking at a horrific scene. A woman stood in a field surrounded by hordes of dead bodies, each of which had been shredded by the teeth of an animal.

The woman's mouth was covered in blood and it rolled down her chin to meet the rest of the red blood staining every part of her. Another woman with jet black hair stood before her and the one covered in blood suddenly looked fearful before she shifted between five other faces and then disappeared.

Etain blinked several more times as she looked around, recalling that she was in the home of the Many-Faced Goddess. She was surprised to see Ciaran sitting in another chair opposite her. The goddess stood next to him, smiling as she pinched his cheek and said, "Such a good boy."

It was so absurd that Etain choked out a laugh. "Ah, welcome back," Hecate said to her. Ciaran, without saying a word, shot up from his seat, picked Etain up, and made for the door.

Just before they stepped out, she called, "Come visit again, Shadow King. A few more visits, and we shall be fast friends!"

"There is no realm where that happens," he grumbled, and they left Hecate's home to the sound of her cackling before he transported them to their bedchambers.

"What were you doing there?" Etain asked, shocked that he would willingly step foot inside the mushroom hut.

"You had been gone half the night. I needed to see you

to ensure you were fine. I do not trust that shifting-faced bit—"

"Ciaran! Stop that. She is the mother of all witches. Without her, I would not exist." He made a noise he often made when he had no good argument, but refused to change his opinion.

"The second I arrived, she told me you had been stuck in a vision for a while. When I began to panic, she told me to sit and wait and that you would come back out when you were ready. So I did, and she tormented me the entire time," he said, groaning as Etain laughed at him.

He squinted his eyes at her, then picked her up and threw her onto the bed. He crawled up her body and kissed her deeply.

"Now, little witch, what did you see?" he asked as he settled beside her and pulled her into his arms.

"I honestly do not know; they were very random."

"They? How many visions did you have?" he asked, pulling away to look her in the eyes. She was uncertain how to answer him. None of what she had seen made sense; she could not decipher where one vision had begun and another had ended.

"Three?"

Chapter 35
Lyra

Lyra finished tying the knot on the colorful ribbon she had woven through her blonde curls, smiling at her reflection. She could not recall the last time she had an occasion to dress up. Mostly, she lived in her all-black leather Silent Shadows uniform.

It was not that she disliked wearing beautiful gowns; quite the opposite, in fact. She simply never seemed to have a reason to. Tonight, however, was one of the best excuses to go all out, even going as far as to dust shimmering powder across her cheeks, making her brown skin glow.

Panella and Ravyn were having their bonding ceremony—finally. It did not matter how many times Lyra told her twin that she did not have to wait for Anin's return. She was glad Panella had not listened to her.

The two witches were going to make history as the first-ever bonded pair of witches the realm had seen. At least as far as they knew, and if the last hundred years had taught her anything, it was that they knew nothing. With every book Panella and her team of witches and fae worked through, they were reminded of how wrong their assumptions about the past had been.

Witches did not keep records of many historical events. Mostly, their libraries consisted of information about all things magical. Working in the secret archives had ignited a passion for history that Panella would have never known had they not been forced to move to Night-fell, nor would she have met Ravyn and Tyne. Lyra could not imagine a realm where those three did not form a family.

There was a loud knocking at her door, and the being waited no more than two seconds before opening it. Lyra sighed as she heard the loud footfalls she knew all too well. For a Silent Shadow, he was anything but silent.

Zandar never gave her a moment's peace. Every time she turned around, there he was—relentless in his quest to annoy her. The worst part was that it was working.

She absolutely hated how she stood a little taller every time he complimented her. She despised how her eyes scanned the crowds when she was out with her sisters and was horrified at how her heart beat faster when his bright yellow eyes eventually found hers. Lyra was reluctant to admit that most of all—she was terrified.

It would be far too easy for her to hand that insuffer-able male her heart, packaged up with a tidy little bow. She could easily fall—hopes and dreams first—into a future with him. The moment he left her, she would become a ruined mess. There would be no fitting her pieces back together after she had shaped every one of hers to fit him.

Lyra did not know how Zandar felt about younglings, but it was something she would never give him. While she doubted that would be a sticking point for him, there was an even bigger concern. At any moment, he could find his fated mate, and there would be no competing with that connection.

No, it was easier to never let him have the chance to own her completely. It was smarter to keep her heart locked firmly away. It was safer to stay alone than inevitably be left alone.

She sighed and smoothed the fabric of her gown one last time before exiting her room. The moment she started down the staircase to the main level, she heard an intake of breath. When she looked up from intently watching to ensure her heeled steps did not get caught in her gown, she found Zandar. He was staring open-mouthed at her, and she could not ignore the way his eyes drank her in. It was as if she were the only thing in all the realms that could quench his thirst. She panicked.

"Why are *you* here?" she snapped, hating herself for breaking the spell her mere appearance had cast over him.

The corners of his stupidly perfect mouth tipped up, and that sparkle of mischief that always seemed to glimmer brighter the pricklier she was made her even stupider heart soar. Every night she attempted to make him hate her, yet he only seemed to crave her more.

She hated it.

She hated him.

She hated that she did not, in fact, hate anything about him.

Shit.

It did not help that he looked far too good for her sensibilities. She groaned internally at the way his silky shirt stretched across his broad shoulders. She definitely did not notice how his pants hugged him in just the right way to hint at the generous length the gods had blessed him with.

Of course, he would have the perfect dick.

He said something, but she was, unfortunately—and to her dismay—noticeably dick-merized. Her skin heated all over when she looked up and saw the smirk that seemed to say, "*I can hear everything you are thinking.*"

Lyra was incredibly agile and graceful after decades of training to become one of the best warriors in the entire realm. She moved with the confidence of someone who knew exactly what each limb in her body could do. So, when her feet became wrapped up in her ridiculous gown and she felt herself teetering forward, she froze in shock.

"While I have been waiting for the night you inevitably fell for me, I did not think it would be quite so literal," he said, his arms wrapped around her from where he had caught her. She looked up into his eyes and...

Fuck. Fuck. Fuck. Fuck!

She was done for. She knew it. He knew it. Gods-damned fate knew it. Resistance seemed pointless, but Lyra was never one to give up so easily.

Pushing out of his embrace, she righted her gown, making sure to keep the mass of billowing fabric at the bottom well away from her feet, and she stood tall. Once she knew she had arranged her face into a look of unaffected indifference, she met his eyes.

"Oh, please. Do not flatter yourself. I would like to see you walk down several steps in heels and all this fabric." The all-knowing smirk he wore only seemed to grow with every word she spat at him.

"Mmhmm," he hummed in mock agreement. "At the request of your sister, I have come to escort you." Those damn lips quirked again. How could she want to kiss them and punch them all at the same time?

"Panella would ne—" She stopped mid-sentence and gasped. Panella would not, but... "I do not care if she will be queen one day; I am going to wring her neck." She stomped away from him, the act far less effective in her dainty little heels. His laugh only made her more enraged. Good. Rage was better than whatever the fuck the past few minutes had just been.

"Have I ever told you," he said as he grabbed her hand and pulled her into him, "that I find your tantrums to be adorable?" She tried to wiggle out of his grasp—she swore she did. Yet somehow, Lyra, one of the best warriors in the realm, could not escape his clutches.

"Shut up, fae-fae," she growled.

"Whatever you say," he grinned down at her, "My little terror." She blinked, and suddenly, they were outside the open doors of the ballroom, which had been transformed for the occasion. Lyra had not missed the addition of the word my. No, she had heard his possessive tone reverberate through her bones. She simply refused to acknowledge it.

When she pushed out of his hold that time, he released

her, and she spun away from him to find her meddling sister. Lyra didn't glance back to check if he was following her; she already knew he was.

"Anin!" she whisper-yelled, spotting the wild, golden-green hair sitting in one of the front-row seats. Her sister had the audacity to look at her with confused innocence. However, the mate sitting beside her gave it all away with his obvious glee at Lyra's expense.

"Why would you send him, of all beings?" she tried to keep her voice low. The last thing she wanted was for other witches to interfere in her business; they were all quite the gossips.

"I have no idea what you are talking about," Anin said before turning to look at their other sister, who had just taken her place at the altar. The conniving smirk on Anin's face did nothing to make her statement believable. Lyra doubted her chosen sister intended for it to be.

She felt Zandar take the seat next to her, and she groaned, glaring at Anin and her bird when they failed to hold back their laughter. Logically, she knew her sister only wanted her to be happy, but Lyra could shake the small twinge of betrayal; Anin knew her fears.

As if sensing the change in her mood, Anin glanced at her with concern. She grabbed Lyra's hand and squeezed before leaning forward to whisper in her ear. "You are letting fear keep you from living a full, happy life. Trust me when I say it is better to have loved, even for a moment, than never to have loved at all." She gave Lyra's hand one last squeeze before pulling away and smiling at her.

Lyra let out a long sigh. No one seemed to understand

how she felt about it; sometimes, she was not sure she understood herself.

"So," she said, changing the subject, "should we all be preparing for another ceremony soon?" She expected them both to make different excuses at the same time, as they had done every other time someone brought it up. Instead, they exchanged soft, loving smiles.

"Gross. I will take that as a yes, then." They all laughed, and while Lyra teased them, she felt incredibly happy for them. Her sister had come a long way in the past few decades, and she could not be prouder.

"You look stunning," Anin said, just loud enough for Panella to hear.

"You really do," Lyra agreed. "Yet everything looks nice when you clean off all the dust." Lyra winked at her twin, happy to see her laugh as some of her nervousness dissipated.

Panella had often voiced her fear that a Chronicler would not show up to document their bonding. Somehow, the appearance of the strange white, tree-like being was the only thing that could lend legitimacy to their ceremony. Lyra had told her that their love for each other was all the legitimacy they needed.

She reiterated those words to her twin in their shared mind when she continued glancing at where a Chronicler should be. Panella gave her a tight smile in response.

"They show just in time and leave immediately. Do not worry," she said, as Anin echoed the same thoughts aloud. Her twin took a deep breath and released it slowly before nodding at her sisters and standing tall.

Just as Panella seemed to release her worry, a Chronicler appeared, standing just where Lyra knew one would. The three sisters smiled at each other, emotions swimming in their eyes. Lyra was once again grateful Panella had not listened to her and waited for Anin's return.

The doors closed. Any minute, they would open again to reveal her twin's chosen mate.

Lyra was not an emotional witch; very few things made her cry, and she was certain this was the first time a tear had ever fallen from her in happiness. She startled when her hand was taken, and Zandar gave her a small, comforting squeeze.

She tried to yank her hand from his, but he only gripped it tighter. She stared at him in disbelief while he smirked and continued to face forward. When she sighed and gave up, he began rubbing small circles on the back of her hand with his thumb.

She looked down at their entwined fingers, marveling at the beauty created by her warm brown skin and his dark grey tone. She snapped her gaze forward, trying her hardest to erase the sight from her mind. If not for his incessant gentle circles, she might have succeeded.

The doors flew open, and a hush fell over the room, filled with both witches and fae. Ravyn stood framed perfectly by the large arched doorway for a moment as she and Panella stared at each other. Then, as if her legs moved without thought, she joined her soon-to-be mate.

The Chronicler led them through the motions of the ceremony, instructing them to do what was required. They were nearing the end, holding their cut palms tightly over the chalice below.

"Blood of my blood," the two said together. "Heart of

my heart, together we share this life. My body is yours, my heart is yours, and half of my soul—"

"FIRE!" someone yelled from just outside the doors. Lyra jumped up, motioning for Anin to stay put and nodding for Panella to continue. She was not going to let anything ruin her sister's dream. A hand gently touched her lower back, and she was not surprised to find Zandar moving to the doors with her.

Smoke billowed from the entrance to Witch City, and Lyra felt icy dread drop heavily into her stomach. She loved her city; they all did. If it were ruined… a small cry escaped her lips, and Zandar grabbed her hand once again. This time, she did not fight it.

Relief flooded her the second they stepped into the city. The coven closest to the entrance had suffered minimal damage. The flames had already been extinguished, and all that remained was an excessive amount of smoke.

Coughing, they entered the apothecary within the coven. Most of the room was blackened, and some of it was still smoking. The damage was extensive, but no one had been hurt, and it had been contained within the apothecary. All things considered, they had been lucky.

The escalation of destruction was troubling; however, the message left behind, somehow unscathed by the flames, sent a chill down her spine.

"You have been warned."

Chapter 36
Raindal

He had lost track of how many days he had stood, forgotten, in the corner of Tatiana's bedchambers. Not that he was complaining. He wished she would forget about him entirely.

The one thing he could control was the bond between him and Balthier. He put every ounce of effort he had into keeping it closed off to his mate. There was no need for both of them to suffer from the way Tatiana liked to use him. At least when it was not his choice, the mate bond did not burn.

Not that it had ever been a secret to Balthier, but he doubted the entire court was unaware by now. He hated that he was unable to spare him the humiliation. Tatiana stopped caring who was around when she forced him to pleasure her.

Sometimes, he spent hours kneeling between her legs, her fingers gripping his red hair as she used his mouth to chase her release. All while she sat on her throne and addressed the few high fae loyal to her. The high fae had no idea a fated mate waited for him, but the lesser fae of the palace did. There was no way Balthier had not heard.

Whenever the rebels in the palace saw him standing alone, they gave him updates. Just as he knew he would, Balthier surpassed his expectations. No one had said it, but Raindal could tell. Balthier was doing a far better job than he ever had. Pride swelled within him every time he thought of his mate. Followed immediately by longing.

He had no idea how Anin had survived as long as she had without her mate. While their tortures might be different, Raindal thought he had a good idea of how Anin had felt. Hope was difficult to hold on to, yet it was just as hard to let go.

It had been so long since he had been able to speak with his true voice. Even the one inside his head had begun to change into the strange, monotone one Tatiana forced through his lips.

He laughed to himself, sardonic. This was no less than he deserved. If he were honest, it was not his own torturous life that bothered him. On some level, it made him feel like he was atoning for what he had done to his true queen. No, it was the torture Balthier was forced to endure because of him.

He knew his actions had been the only way to get Anin out, and it had taken far longer than they had hoped. Yet, he was starting to think it was all for nothing.

She had not shown up. While he could not be certain how much time had passed, he knew it had been decades at the very least. Every day that passed, he told himself it would be the one she came to claim her throne. She never did, and he had begun to think she never would.

Every day she did not show was another high fae forced to die so that Tatiana could feed her addiction. It was another day the rot grew closer. It was another day she allowed her court to suffer.

He knew he was being unreasonable. She had endured the worst for over a century, and he was complaining about a few decades. It was only that she had seemed so strong in the face of her sister that last day she spent in captivity. She had stood up to her. She had practically declared war.

Where was that fae? That had been the fae whom he had bet his entire future on. Perhaps it was selfish to expect her to act because he wanted her to. Only he did not care.

It was her duty.

It was her fate.

Fate would get what she wanted. A thought had only recently occurred to him: perhaps she was not what Fate had wanted after all. He regretted betting on her and wished he had just listened to his mate and lived whatever kind of life they could have together. He knew it would never have been a life worth living, but neither was the one they were both being forced to endure.

Raindal had tried to reach for more than fate had been willing to give him. Now, he would likely never see Balthier again.

He had played the game, and he had lost.

She stood alone before the large doors. In the not-so-distant past, she would have been terrified to stand there alone in the wide-open hall. She searched for the fear that, by now, would have already wrapped tightly around her throat, making it impossible to breathe. Instead, she found nothing but excitement.

This night had felt impossible decades ago; it was something she never thought she would have. She never imagined she would reach this level of peace again.

The Anin Kes pulled from the little cage in the room of decaying wings was not the same Anin who stood waiting for the doors to open. She had not been weak; a weak being could never have survived the unthinkable, and she had survived.

It took her a long time to understand that she had not been broken when she was finally free; she had only been shaped into who she needed to be in order to survive. Once she realized that, she began the work of reshaping herself to be who she needed to be, but also who she wanted to be. She thought she might be stronger than the Anin who had run through the Human Realm, chased by her future.

That was not something she found easy to think about. Knowing everything that had to have happened to get her to where she was—where she knew she was meant to be—would she do it again? She was not sure. She wanted to say yes; maybe she would in the far-off future. Right then, though, she could not give a definitive answer.

She still had her issues, and she knew she always would. When the doors swung open and the hundreds, if not thousands, of faces in the room turned to look at her, she felt the panic she had searched for only moments ago creeping up. Just as it wrapped itself around her throat, she saw him—her future.

Kes stood at the end of the aisle, his eyes locking onto hers. Everything around them seemed to melt away. It was just her and him.

Like a moth to a flame, she went to him—to her future, to her forever.

When she reached him and he took her hands, she knew without an ounce of uncertainty that she was exactly where she was meant to be and with whom. Fate might always get what she wants, but sometimes the rest of them did, too. There was nothing she wanted more—not even her throne—than the male before her.

"You look beautiful," he said. "But then you always do." He raised one of their joined hands to his mouth and kissed the back of hers.

She had nearly forgotten they were in a room filled to bursting with witches and fae until the Chronicler spoke into their minds. The ceremony felt hazy, as if it were happening around her. Later, when asked, she did not think she would be able to recall much beyond brief flashes here and there—most of which were of Kes.

Things finally slowed down when she held an emerald knife and slid it through the skin of her palm. It was a bit like history repeating itself; this was not the first time they had made a blood oath.

They put their cut palms together and squeezed just as they had all those years ago, but this time out of want, not necessity. The bond flickered between them, already feeling stronger.

As they spoke the words that the Chronicler provided, she felt the truth of them with each syllable she spoke. He carried half of her, and she carried half of him; the halves fitting together to make them each truly whole.

The entire time she was locked away, he was always there—her constant. He kept her sane with his stories and the different ways he found to entertain her in the strange way they had learned to communicate. They still used it.

"With my blood, I make it so. With my words, I make it true. With my soul, I am bound to you," they both said at the same time before each drank from the chalice.

Kes yanked her toward him, eliciting a very undigni-fied squeak. He dipped her so far back that she was surprised her feet were still on the ground and claimed her mouth with his. He was never one to miss an oppor-tunity for theatrics.

The Chronicler spoke one last time as the bond burned in their chests before snapping into place, feeling as solid as the floor they stood on. "Let it be known that

Anin, chosen Queen of the Day Court, and Kestrel, Prince of the Night Court, are now a fully bonded pair." They were gone immediately afterward.

The room erupted into cheers. When Kes dipped her, claiming her mouth once again, the cheers were accompanied by whistles and other suggestive sounds that made her cheeks heat a dark green.

The night was going by too quickly. She tried to take in each moment and commit it to memory. Yet, as time is prone to do, the greatest moments flashed by in a blur, while the worst crawled by.

She remembered a long line of beings congratulating them—faces that now blurred into one big nothing. There had been food, at least she thought there had been.

What she *did* remember was dancing. Lyra, Panella, Ravyn, and Etain had pulled her into the center of the room, and they laughed and spun, not always on the correct count, which only made them laugh harder.

Tyne joined them, and finally, time took a breath and allowed her to commit the moment to memory before speeding back up. They all looked at Tyne, laughing at something she had just said. Ravyn's hair flew freely about in long black ribbons, while Panella's arm wrapped around her waist. The pair leaned into each other as they laughed.

Lyra was slightly stooped forward, clutching her stomach as her other hand wiped the tears from her eyes. Etain's head was thrown back, her mouth wide with laughter as she gripped Anin's hand. Tyne, whose mission in life seemed to be making everyone laugh as often as possible, had a proud smile stretching across her face, while her eyes glittered with excitement.

She loved these females and was overcome with emotion when she realized just how lucky she was. They were a family—not one of blood, but of choice. Anin knew that just because one shared blood with another did not make one a family. These females shared something far more significant.

Love.

The moment had only lasted a second, but that second would stay with her forever: her sisters, her niece, and her very best friend in a moment of pure joy.

She yelled when she was swept off her feet and spun multiple times. "Put me down, you male-shaped pile of feathers!" she yelled while laughing.

He put his mouth to her ear so only she could hear when he said, "Yes, my queen." Something about those words and the way he said them made her want to drag him to their chambers and not leave again for several nights.

He put her down and grabbed her hand before spinning her into him so that her back was to his chest. "Are you enjoying yourself, my queen?" She tried and failed to keep the moan from escaping her lips. He laughed as he spun her out of his embrace and picked up the steps to the song playing.

She laughed as she watched him. It was not surprising to Anin that her mate would be a skilled dancer; it was not too far off from fighting, and he did that effortlessly. What made her laugh was the extra little movements he added to each step, making everything far more dramatic.

She did not think she had ever laughed so much in one night.

What felt like mere moments—though it had probably been hours—passed before the music began to slow and the celebration came to an end. Without saying a word to anyone else, Kes ported them to their chambers.

"We did not even say goodnight!" she chided him, even as she squealed when he tossed her on to the bed.

"We will see them tomorrow. Maybe," he said with a smirk as he climbed up her body and kissed a trail the entire way until finally meeting her mouth.

"Oh? And what do you have planned for us tomorrow?" she asked. "A quiet night of reading together?"

"Nothing about it will be quiet," he growled between nips along her neck. She was more than happy that she had finally been able not just to bear his touch but also revel in it. Now, he touched her as often as he could; she did not mind. They had a lot of time to make up for.

"Is that a threat? I have to say, I, for one, do not find pillows intimidating." She tried to hold in her smile; instead, she was sure she looked like she had just eaten something sour. The second he laughed, she lost her hold on it.

"No, my queen. That was a promise." He stared into her eyes and brushed a wild curl away. "I am so proud of you, Anin. You are incredible, and I am in awe of your strength." Tears threatened at the corners of her eyes.

She reached up to where he hovered above her and placed a hand on either side of his face. "You are the one who allowed me the space to heal," she said, covering his mouth with a finger before he could speak. She needed him to hear this.

"You gave me everything I needed to rebuild myself into a version of me that I did not know I was capable of being. You are the one I know will always protect me, no matter if it is my mind or body that needs safe keeping." She felt the tears that pooled roll down the sides of her face.

"You are the one I want to shelter in during the good and the bad." She softened her voice before finishing. "You, Kestrel Prince of the Night Court, are my safe place, and that is why you will always own my heart." He stared at her, and she saw his red eyes battle between heat and tears. Eventually, the heat won out.

He unwrapped her wings from the intricate dress she had created for the ceremony and took his time drinking her in. "You are my obsession," he said, kissing his way down her body. "The center of my everything." She arched her chest into his far-too-gentle kisses when he neared her breasts.

"Everything good in my life starts and stops with you," he said, before pulling one of her nipples into his mouth, making her cry out in pleasure.

"All that I am is for you," he said, before gently biting it between his razor-like teeth. She was not sure what would send her over the edge first: his mouth or his words. "And all that I will be is because of you."

"Oh gods," she cried out when his hand parted her wet folds and his fingers found her core. He stared into her eyes as he moved his fingers in and out of her, while his thumb found her clit. She was close. She felt her body come fully alive as her muscles tensed.

"There is no doubt in my mind that I was created by fate with the sole purpose of loving you." With those words, she dove off the edge into pure ecstasy. When she came down far enough to see properly again, Kes had shed his clothes and was kneeling between her legs. She spread them eagerly for him.

Without their eyes breaking contact, he entered her slowly. He made sure she felt every bit of his length as he spread and stretched her to fit him. His mouth met hers just as he seated himself fully, swallowing her moan.

"Kes," she said in a breath, her lips still touching his. "I love you."

Neither of them said anything else as they moved together, unhurried. They did not need to. They showed each other the depths of their devotion in gentle touches and all-consuming kisses while their bond flooded each of them with the other's emotions.

It was a slow climb to the peak of their pleasure, but when they reached the top, it was together. Then they jumped off together, and all either of them knew was the feel of the other and the bond that tied them together.

Forever.

"You think it's possible?" Ciaran asked after she told him about the idea that had been circulating in her mind ever since her last visit to the Many Faced Goddess. She had practiced infusing her color power with her shade power enough times that it felt as natural as breathing.

"I do not see why not. The worst that happens is nothing," she said, shrugging. They were in the training facility Ciaran had made what felt like an eternity ago. "I think if we each funnel our power into the medallion, it should work."

"This is not going to blow up and cover me in some kind of brightly colored goop, is it, little witch?" he asked, eying her wearily.

"I should hope not," she said, laughing. He had watched her go through too many trials of spells. It was not uncommon for her to be covered in all manner of strange, brightly colored substances several times before she perfected her creations.

"However, I am not exactly sure what will happen," she said honestly. "But I am curious to see what is created when our powers are combined."

"All right, little witch, show me what to do," he said, leaning over her shoulder to look at the medallion she held. His hands wandered the entire time she tried to explain it, distracting her to no end. It seemed to be his favorite thing to do, and she did not exactly mind.

"Does that make sense?" she asked when she had finished explaining how she channeled her power through it. She would not be surprised if he had to modify it in some way. Their powers were wildly different, after all.

"I will be honest, little witch. I was incredibly distracted the entire time, but I think I can figure it out," he said. "Or, we can do something else with our time." His hands roamed lower, and she closed her eyes and leaned back into him. Not even two seconds later, her eyes snapped open, and she pulled away.

"Nice try, my love," she said in a sing-song voice, making him chuckle as he took the medallion from her and studied it. She stared at him, smiling, until he looked at her and his brows pinched.

"What? Is there something on my face?" he asked, immediately wiping at it.

"No, I am just looking at you. You seem happy," she said, moving to wrap her arms around his waist.

"I am always happy when I am with you." He cupped the side of her face with one hand, and she leaned into it.

"No, that's not what I meant. You seem lighter, playful even." He looked offended, and she laughed. "It's a good thing!"

"If you say so, I think I know what to do with this… trinket." She looked at him, trying to keep from laughing again, but she could not help it, and the laughter burst from her. He was going to hate what she was about to tell him.

"Your best friend called it the same thing," she said between giggles. He looked at her as if she had grown another head.

"I do not have a best friend." His face was comically perplexed, which only made what she was about to say even funnier.

"The Many Faced Goddess, that was what she called it as well."

"Etain," he said seriously, and she did her best to keep her lips closed tightly between her teeth as even more laughter threatened to escape. "Let's pretend you never said that." He crowded her space, looming over her. "And if you ever say that again, I will make you scream my name until your voice is hoarse for nights." She patted his chest and shook her head.

"My love, threats work better when it's not something that sounds perfectly enjoyable." He grinned at her, that specific grin she knew meant he was about to pounce on her. "Now, do you think you know what to do with that?" She pointed to the medallion he still held.

"Yes," he said with a long, obviously disappointed sigh. He sometimes gave Kes competition for theatrics.

"Wonderful!" she said, and hugged him tight. "Let's begin."

It took them several tries to get both of their powers to go through the medallion simultaneously. Etain was feeding it her blue power, while Ciaran fed it his shadows. She was about to give up and make another comment about him and the goddess—just to see if he would follow through with his threat—when it happened.

She gasped as she watched the shadow form into a perfect replica of Ciaran. With the blue coloring from her power, it looked more like him than his normal shadows.

"Interesting," he said. "I wonder what has changed, beyond the slight tint of blue."

"I am not sure. Can you control it? My power is not listening to me," she said, looking at the shadow that was their powers mixed together with concern.

"No," he said as he approached the shadow. It did not react to him. "What does your blue do again?"

"Strength and agility. It's the color of the warrior." She watched as the shadow studied Ciaran, and Ciaran studied the shadow. For a moment, she wondered if it was something more than just a shadowy extension of her mate.

"I wonder..." Ciaran walked over to the wall, took down the largest ax, and tossed it to the shadow. Etain once tried to pick that same ax up and had not been able to lift even the handle. Meanwhile, Ciaran just tossed it to his shadow as if it weighed nothing. What was more astounding was when his shadow caught it just as easily.

Ciaran grinned, looking so boyish that Etain nearly swooned. She loved all of Ciaran's looks, even the grumpy, brooding ones. However, there was something about this new playful side to him. It was as if he were finally letting the tight hold he had kept on himself loosen.

He returned to the wall of various weapons and grabbed another ax similar to the one his shadow held before swinging it around a few times. He approached the shadow and lifted the ridiculously large weapon in front of him, with one hand no less, and waited for the shadow to touch its ax to the one Ciaran held.

The second the shadow did, Etain could not see anything beyond a blur of blue and shadow. The only proof that they were sparring was the constant clang of the axes as they connected. It was incredible. The shadow was still Ciaran, yet moved on its own accord.

Etain hopped up on the table off to the side of where they sparred and watched. She wished she could see the way they moved and not just a blur she could barely keep track of. It was a travesty. Just as Etain was starting to grow bored, the clashing of metal stopped.

Ciaran stood there by himself, no shadow in sight. His smile was genuine, and he was breathing heavily. "It seems to have a time limit," he said, bending down to pick up the fallen ax and then moving to hang both back on the wall. "That was amazing. It was like fighting myself, but without knowing what was coming next."

"Well, I am glad you had fun," she said. "I, however, could not even watch the show. Your speed robbed me of that. It's criminal, you know?" He laughed as he stood before her. He placed his hands on the table, one on either side of her hips.

"You know what would be fun, little witch?" he asked, leaning into her until she leaned back onto her elbows.

"What?" she asked, the question barely more than a breath.

"If we tried that again, but this time with your red power…" He kissed the side of her neck and nipped at her ear before he said, "What do you say, little witch? Shall we have some fun?"

She was not sure if she could handle all of *that*. However, there was only one way to find out. Besides, the liquid heat pooling in her core as Ciaran's lips continued to explore every bit of exposed flesh he could find needed to be taken care of. When his mouth met hers, she smiled against his and then nipped at his bottom lip.

He growled and picked her up off the table, bringing their bodies flush together. Without needing to say anything, she pulled away just enough to hold the medallion out, and they both sent their powers into it: her red and his shadows.

"Oh no," she gasped.

"What?" he asked, concern leaching away the heat in his gaze.

"My shade power sometimes has a mind of its own," she paused, watching as one shadow formed, then two. "It slipped out with the red." Ciaran had not taken his eyes off her, so he did not see what was happening around them.

The two shadows split into four, and her eyes grew wide as the four split into eight. There was no way she could handle—

"Why is that a problem?" he asked, still looking only at her.

"It can be…unpredictable," she said absently. When she gasped, Ciaran finally turned to see what she had been watching. Half of the eight shadows became perfect replicas of Ciaran, just as she had expected. The other half took a different form: perfect replicas of her.

"I have to say, little witch, I do not mind this kind of unpredictability." They both watched as the Ciarans reached out and caressed the Etains. The true Etain sucked in a breath. She could feel each of the four caresses, as if the shadows had touched her.

"Oh, my little witch, you are in for a treat," Ciaran said as laughed, the sound low and deep within his chest. It was dark and seductive. The sound was a promise of pleasure that never failed to make her core clench.

The shadows, not needing to bother with clothing, touched and caressed everywhere. Her breaths came erratically and her skin was set aflame, while every little hair stood on end. If this was what Ciaran felt every time he brought his shadows out to play, she had no idea how he could handle it.

Watching their shadows together was incredibly erotic for her. Feeling their phantom touches at the same time was an entirely different experience. She clutched Ciaran, who still held her, moaning loudly as one of his shadow's heads went between her shadow's legs, while another lifted her shadow and slowly lowered her onto his hard length. Experiencing both sensations at the same time had her seeing stars.

It was not long before they watched and felt as their

shadows moved from individual groupings to a writhing mass. One of her shadows rode the cock of one of his, while another filled her from behind. This made the real Etain feel impossibly full.

Another shadow of Etain sat on the face of the Ciaran that the other Etain was riding and took another Ciaran down her throat. She felt the stretch in her throat with each thrust of the shadow, and when the final three came together, Etain screamed her release into Ciaran's chest.

"I have to be inside you, little witch," Ciaran groaned as he sat her on the table and pulled out his impossibly hard length. "I have to feel the real you." All she could do was nod frantically. She needed it, too. She needed something real to clench within her.

Frantically, he pushed aside the layers of her dress. He growled when he saw the soaked fabric between her legs before ripping it off her and filling her at once. She fell right back over the edge and felt her release flood her core and drench Ciaran as he took her fast and hard. She understood why he liked to watch his shadows with her. It was empowering to see the pleasure her shadows brought him written all over his face.

She watched the shadow versions of themselves and knew that even if she could not feel everything they did, she would still be desperate for Ciaran to fill her. Watching the facial expressions of her shadow versions, she wondered if that was what she looked like to Ciaran.

When her shadows began to climax, she tried to hold tightly to Ciaran. Her eyes locked onto the real Ciaran's, and he grinned down at her, knowing what was coming.

She was not sure she would be able to handle five releases all at once.

"Ciaran," she panted. "I do not think I will sur—" Stars filled her vision as pleasure flooded over her. The last thing she remembered was screaming his name.

"Etain," she heard Ciaran frantically calling her name. Slowly, she blinked her eyes open; every movement felt impossible. When her vision finally cleared, she saw a very worried Ciaran staring down at her. She smiled lazily, and he let out a huff of a laugh.

"I lost you there for a moment," he said softly, using his fingertips to brush away the damp strands of hair that stuck to her face. When she finally felt capable of forming words again, she said the first thing that came to mind, her words slurred.

"Well, that was fun."

"What do you mean, it's not working?" Tatiana asked her worthless council. Her voice had a habit of switching from the high-pitched, youngling-like one she preferred to a low, cold, and calculated one every time her council opened their mouths.

"We did as you suggested and started rounding up several low fae at a time, took them to the center of the city, and killed them," one of them said. Had he always been there? She did not recall his face, but then again, it was just as likely she had never cared to remember it.

"We even made their deaths more excruciating by burning them alive when the first few cullings did not seem to have the desired effect. If anything, it had only made their attacks even bolder, as if, once discovered, there was nothing holding them back," the lone female said.

She waited, staring at each of them and watching the color drain from their vibrant faces. That was it? Did they even try? When the silence became uncomfortable and they all began to squirm in their seats, she slammed her hands down on the table and slowly stood.

"I am surrounded by incompetence!" she screamed. "Each of you is worthless to me!" She was pleased when they all flinched. She was going to take one of them to the temple next; maybe they needed a little… *motivation.*

She gathered her golden army with one thought and had them all march to the Dayless Quarter. They could have ported, but she wanted them to fear her arrival. For that to happen, they needed time to let the fear really sink in. She wanted them begging her by the time she got there.

"You should turn back, Blood Queen," the *whispers* insisted. *"This will not end well for you."*

"Do not be ridiculous. They are nothing but a bunch of powerless, worthless creatures. There is nothing to fear." She waved off the *whisper's* concerns and tuned them out.

While this would solve the problem of her missing and misplaced things, it did seem like such a waste. If only they had power, then their pointless existence could fuel her blood magic. It was becoming more difficult every day to keep her well at a safe level. It would take a good amount of her power to collect each lesser fae, and she would get nothing in return. The thought made her even angrier.

They marched through the city, her golden army before her. She saw nothing as she passed through—neither the makeshift bridge that had been quickly assembled nor the walls of buildings that had fallen into nothing but piles of rubble. She did not see any of that.

What she saw were the empty places where four of her perfect grass-green gowns had been hanging until she went to change into one. She saw the frames she had smashed returned to the walls, hung at incorrect angles. She saw every single one of her trinkets mixed up and out of order in her chambers.

When the first of her troops arrived at the entrance, they met resistance. The lesser fae had built a barrier between them and the rest of the city. She smiled, thinking about the ridiculous notion that something as mundane as a little wall could protect them.

She had one of her golden soldiers on the front line throw her fire at the pitiful thing. Only nothing happened. She did it again and again, but still nothing. She had her entire army— all one hundred of them— volley their powers at the little wall mocking her.

"Get rid of it!" she screamed as she stomped her feet, only just realizing she stood in a thin puddle of backed-up sewage.

The hem of her emerald-green dress, not the grass-green she should be wearing, was soaked through with things better left undiscovered. Originally, she had planned to march down there, collect all the lesser fae at once, and kill them. Her plan had changed. She would still collect each of them in the grasp of her blood magic, but instead of a fast death, she was going to make them kill each other.

Slowly.

She felt her smile stretch to an unnatural size as she

parted her rows of golden soldiers. It gave her a straight path to the entrance of the Dayless. Just as she neared the end of her soldiers, the wall crumbled. She stood and waited for the dust to clear.

She laughed. The sound was wild even to her own ears when she saw the fearful faces of the lesser fae. They had brought this upon themselves; they had no one to blame but themselves.

"You should have stayed in your place and been content to live the life you were meant for. Now you will have no life to live," she said loud enough that she hoped the entire Dayless Quarter could hear her.

She gave them all a moment to think about why they were about to die, and by doing so, she hoped it gave them time to fear the end. She was pleased when they all grabbed for their loved ones. It would make it easier to ensure it was a face they loved that took the light from their eyes.

She gathered her power within her, knowing it was going to take a good portion of what she had in her well. When she had enough, she sent it out to every single lesser fae in the vicinity—younglings and all.

She frowned when nothing happened. Her power was still sitting in her well, waiting to be used. She tried again, and… nothing. She let out a frustrated sound and clenched her fists together at her sides before she sent her blood magic out again.

The lesser fae in the very front looked around at each other and then at her. Her blood ran cold when they smiled.

Smiled.

She grabbed even more of her power. That must be the reason it was not working. She had not sent enough out. She might lose control of some of the beings she already had, but she was not thinking clearly. All she could think about were the smiles on the faces of the lesser fae—mocking her.

She tunneled deeper into her well than she had in a long time and was dismayed to see it was not as deep as it had once been. When she had hold of all her power, she sent it out over the entire city.

Let's see them mock her now.

Once she was sure she had stretched across the entire city, she reached for every life source within it.

No.

The only beings in her grasp were all the high fae, which had become a considerably smaller number over the years. Fear dripped down her spine and pooled in her stomach. This was impossible.

She backed away down the same path she had just moments ago walked down with all the confidence in the realm. As soon as she passed the first few lines of soldiers, she had them close the gap, and she ported back to her chambers.

She ripped her soiled gown off and threw it in a corner as she stomped to the table with the drawer where she kept the Book of Blood. She did not care that she was naked; she did not care about anything except finding out what went wrong.

"We told you not to," the *whispers* said as they laughed. She did not answer; instead she vowed to kill them as she sat down and began to flip through the book.

"We both know that will never happen." She refused to acknowledge them.

She stopped when she saw something about the costs of using blood magic. Had she not known there would be a price to pay? Or had she not cared? Either way, it was too late now.

The use of blood magic has many factors to consider. If used, even on the smallest of creatures, a piece of the user's well is taken with it. Every sacrifice to obtain blood magic takes over part of the user's magic. Eventually, the user's well will be unable to hold power of any depth, while their magic is completely replaced by the remnants of blood magic. If used consistently and over a period of time relative to the user's initial well depth, the user becomes powerless and can no longer access blood magic, nor the magic they were born with. It is our opinion...

She scanned the pages, searching for anything about blood magic and lesser fae, and tried not to panic. When was the last time she tried to heal anything? Could she still? Or was her innate magic already gone? She would deal with that later. Her eyes caught on another passage.

Blood magic works in an interesting way. It does not take root in the blood, contrary to the name. It takes hold of the power that flows in tandem with the being's blood, thus rendering it useless on any being without power, such as humans, lesser fae, and most of the realm's wildlife. However, a being with a deep well of power flowing through their veins cannot escape the pull of blood magic. It is worth stating...

Her heart pounded in her chest, deafening the sounds of the palace outside her doors. She could not control the lesser fae with blood magic. Panic threatened to swallow her whole until she remembered she could just have the high fae she was able to control kill them for her.

She was about to close the book when something else caught her eye.

With the recent use of activated bloodstones, it had rendered the use of blood magic practically unusable. One drop of the user's blood or that of their kin, and the one wearing the bloodstone would be impervious to the effects of blood magic.

Bloodstones could only be used against her if she let anyone have a chance to get her blood—Anin. She had forgotten that the creature was of her blood. It was something she had wished she had never learned. Yet now...

What was she supposed to do? It was far too late for her to give up the use of blood magic. She was in too deep. She needed to form a plan and find a way to not use as much blood magic every day.

She could not recall ever reading half of the information in this book. What a foolish fae she had been! Had she only ever looked at what the *whispers* told her? Had she simply not cared?

...the golden-skinned youngling, older now but still young, is thrown across the room... large wings with white feathers looming over her... the golden youngling dragged across broken glass...

Tatiana blinked. Then blinked again. She was back, yet the vision did not leave. Every second a flash of violence against the young fae. Less like a vision and feeling more like a memory.

No.

She just needed more power. Everything would be fine if she could find more power.

Everything would be fine.

She would be fine.

Chapter 40
Ciaran

"You told me not to tell you about it until I knew where to send you next. I think I know where," Panella said.

It was true; he had told her that. He just wanted a bit of time to not worry about the damn element books. He had thought it would be years—possibly decades—until he heard from her. Not a single year, and he was not sure it had even been that long.

"Fine," he sighed. "But if you summoned Kes as well, I am not going." There was no way he was going to do anything like that with his cousin again. Kes had become a fan of randomly screaming when Ciaran arrived or leaving "remedies" for sore throats.

Kes had died hundreds of deaths in Ciaran's mind. He told himself that if it were not for his little witch, his cousin would be nothing but a pile of dust. It was Etain that kept him from following through, nothing more. He almost believed it.

"First, let me tell you what the strange text on the slip of parchment you brought back to me says," Panella rummaged through a stack of loose parchment until she pulled out a specific one. "Here it is. The text says, 'Even leaders must learn,' which is about as vague as a clue can be."

Ciaran was already dreading the night he was going to have. He had planned to sit in his little witch's study while she made more sticky substances explode. He loved watching her work—the way she sometimes stuck the tip of her tongue out of the very corner of her mouth as she concentrated always made him laugh.

"So that led me to look..." she looked up at him and saw his bored expression. "You do not care about any of this. Why am I even wasting my breath?" Ciaran shrugged, and she sighed, flipping through a book.

"I found mention of... well, I am honestly not sure what it is—confusion. But th—"

"What are you confused about?" He was not thrilled about going where she told him to if she was not even sure what the text said.

"This," she said, pointing to the passage she had been showing him. "It's confusion."

"Panella," he growled. "I am losing my patience. What are you confused about?"

"No, you idiot. The word right here translates to confusion." She looked at him with a raised brow, daring him to say anything about her tone. He let it slide because he felt like an idiot. Therefore, her words were true. He still growled at her, which never seemed to have the desired effect on her; she just shook her head.

"Well, whatever this confusion is, I found its location. It's under the palace in Lunarmist."

"Under? Are you certain?" he asked, and she gave him an annoyed look.

"Yes, I am certain," she said, rolling her dark eyes at him. She was lucky he tolerated her attitude.

"The only thing under that palace is the catacombs." He had gone down there once before, following one of the fae from the long line of those who played a role in his father gaining access to the ring that allowed him to enslave Ciaran. It hadn't been his favorite experience.

"Well, start there." She shrugged as if it were obvious, which he supposed it was. He would like to see her traipse around in a never-ending cave that smelled like something was rotting. However, knowing her, she would probably find it fascinating.

He thought about pulling Etain away from her current experiment and getting her to come with him. At least with her there, the task would be enjoyable.

He was just about to port to her study and do whatever it took to convince her to come when he recalled the way he had almost become the dust between two walls. Who knew what annoying thing he would face this time? No, he would go alone. Maybe that way he could get it over and done with faster.

"Oh, and Ciaran?" Panella asked. He looked at her expectantly. "Keep an eye out for anything that hints at the rule of three; that might show you where you are meant to go faster." He nodded and ported to the entrance of the catacombs under Lunarmist.

"What is the point of fae having a catacomb? There is

nothing left for us to bury," he grumbled under his breath as he reluctantly descended the stairs, unwilling to risk porting into something unfortunate.

The power of three.

He had not wanted to say it, but he was not exactly sure what that was. He knew three was important to witches and that it was the number of true balance, but that was about all he knew. He had never cared to find out more.

Gods, it smelled awful. They were fae; they could find a way to make the place smell like flowers if they wished —rather than this moldy, rotten one. Even the dungeons smelled better than this.

He sped through as much of the underground tunnel as he could until the catacombs disappeared behind him and there were nothing but stone walls around him. When he came to a fork, he stopped. He could go left or right, but not straight.

Having learned his lesson at the temple, he inspected the entrance of each tunnel, looking for anything amiss. Finding nothing, he considered his options.

He pulled his shadows from him with the intention of sending one in each direction. The only problem was he could not send them further than ten feet at most.

The tunnels were spelled.

When he tried to port, he was not surprised that he was unable to do so. He considered returning and then coming back later when he was less annoyed. Then he sighed, knowing he would never be anything but annoyed with these tunnels.

Left or right?

He went left and planned to speed his way through to the next fork. He went left again and kept making lefts at each fork until he came to a dead end.

A part of him had guessed it when he came to the first fork, and that must have been why he kept choosing to go left. Panella had said the text called it a confusion.

It was a fucking labyrinth.

He traced his steps back to the last fork and went right. He was going to be so angry if he—another dead end.

This was going to be a long night.

When he got all the way back to the first fork, he took Panella's advice and looked for anything that had to do with the number three; there was nothing. He turned right.

Now that he thought about it, three had been showing up often lately: the original passage that helped Panella find the location of the temple had mentioned something about three. There were three rulers in the realm. His little witch had thought she had three visions. There had also been three attacks on Witch City.

He wondered how much of that, if any, was part of this rule of three nonsense, or was he only finding connections because he was searching for them? He thought it was likely all in his head. You could do that with any—Dead end.

Fuck.

He went all the way back to the start and thought about it: if threes were going to play a role anywhere in his life, it was likely here.

A thought occurred to him: what if he tried going left

three turns and then right three turns? Worst case, he would end up right back at the beginning, trying to think up a new plan. However, if this did not work, he was going home to his mate. He would come back and try again—maybe.

It turned out it was three rights and then three lefts; however, that did not get him to the center. He stood before another fork in the path. Logically, he thought he should go right three more times; yet he would not put it past the beings that created this place to trick him.

He searched the entrance to the right and then the left. There was a strange symbol on both of them; one looked familiar. He stared at it and then it dusked on him what it was. It was the symbol from the parchment he pulled from the stone box in the temple.

"Ciaran..." He could have sworn he heard Etain calling him from the other tunnel. Had she followed after him? What if she was lost? What if he never found her?

He did not consider his actions when he sped off down the wrong tunnel after the sound of his mate repeatedly calling out for him. Somehow, the tunnel felt darker than the others and the oppressive feeling of death lingered in the air. His breaths came faster when all the possibilities of what might befall Etain flashed through his mind. He came to an abrupt stop when he realized that he had not heard her call for him again.

"Etain?!" he screamed into the tunnel. "Where are you, little witch?" He could hear the crack in his voice as panic threatened to overwhelm him. He reached another dead end and the floor beneath him began to liquefy.

"It's okay, Ciaran, we will be together soon," He heard

Etain say. A deep sense of despair washed over him before taking root and wrapping firmly around every inch of him, and he could not understand why. If he were about to be with Etain, he should feel elated.

Ciaran had sunk to his chest through the thick, almost gelatinous-like floor when he heard laughter. It was a sound he knew he should never have had to hear again as long as he lived. His father's laugh felt like nails scraping against his mind.

This is not right.

"I always knew you would be a failure," the impossible voice of his father said, full of dark mirth. *"I think your 'little witch' would make the perfect test subject for my experiments."*

No. This was not real.

Ciaran would never allow his father to even breathe the same air as her. His father was dead, and he knew Etain would not have followed him. He searched through the bond and felt her presence far away from him, and for once, was glad for the distance.

After taking several deep breaths, he closed his eyes and cleared his mind while he blocked everything else out around him. When he opened his eyes again, he found himself huddled in the corner of the dead end, his arms wrapped tightly around his legs, making him as small as possible—a position he had not been in since he was a small youngling.

"Thank fuck Kes was not here to see that," he grumbled out loud as he stood. No one had seen him, and no one needed to know about it, yet even as he thought this, he had the distinct feeling that the maze was laughing at him. He brushed the dust off his pants in an attempt to regain some of his dignity before returning to the fork in the maze and going down the path with the symbol he had recognized.

He turned right and when he came to the next fork, he looked for the symbol and found it on the left. He thought there would be just one last tunnel, but when he reached the end of that one, he stood in front of yet another fucking fork. This time, there were no symbols.

Shit.

He stood there, staring at each side, trying to find a difference between the two, and saw nothing. Then he felt along the arch of each tunnel, and when his hand brushed over something, the wall between the two tunnels swung open. Well, it tried to, at least.

He pushed the door the rest of the way open. It made a horrific scraping sound as it dragged across the stone floor. When he stepped through, he did so with caution. Who knew what kind of nonsense was going to try to kill him this time?

There was no wall to smash him, and it did not look like there were any other possible deadly traps. Perhaps the labyrinth had been enough; it certainly was for him.

In the center of the high-arched-ceiling room was another box, much like the one from the temple, illuminated by the light of the moon. He knew without needing to open it that there would be another piece of parchment with another line of text he could not read.

He took a step forward and heard a click, and immediately backed away, once again saved by his super speed. This would not have killed him, but it would have hurt—

a lot. A spike had shot up through the tile he had just stepped on.

When he examined the floor, he saw a meandering path of tiles leading to the stone box with the same symbol on them that he had followed in the tunnels. Tentatively, he stepped on the first one. No click.

After the sixth or seventh one, he felt confident enough to speed through the rest of them. The moment he stepped into the moonlight, he felt whatever had been oppressing his powers and preventing him from porting fall away.

The box had the same locking mechanism as the first, and he wasted no time and sent his shadows into the little crevices and waited. Finally, stone scraped against stone, and the lid slid open.

He looked into the box, and just as he thought, there was a single slip of parchment with a line of text he did not understand. The only thing that kept him from ripping the paper up and forgetting the whole thing was that this was the second location.

There would be one more; that's where the books would be. There was not a doubt in his mind. He shoved the slip of parchment into his pocket and ported home to his little witch.

One more stupid adventure to go.

Gods, he hated this.

L yra and Zandar stared at the information strewn across the wall. They thought that if they could see everything at once, they might make connections they had never seen before.

Unfortunately, it did not work. Everything they knew looked just as random as it did when viewed separately. Nothing was connected.

The three vandalized covens had nothing in common except that they were all covens. The messages were clearly the work of the same individual or group. The only thing that changed was the fire of the last one.

Ever since that attack, Lyra had been on edge, waiting. She did not have a good feeling about the note left behind at that scene, and her anxiety only grew with time.

"This is pointless," Lyra said, throwing her hands up and walking to the couch before flopping down on it.

"As much as I wish I could disagree, I think you are right," Zandar said, running his hand through his short, dark grey hair as he stared at the chaos on the wall. "I cannot see a single connection or a hint of the party responsible."

"I would not even care that much if they had just kept to smashing containers and leaving their ridiculous notes. It's the combination of the escalation and the finality of the last note that makes me feel like there's an unseen timer. As soon as it ends, something bad will happen." Her voice shook a bit at the end, which annoyed her.

"Hey," Zandar said softly as he walked over to the couch where she sprawled. "We can only do what we can do." He picked up her feet and sat down, placing them in his lap.

She hated it when he was like this. It made it harder to ignore the gods-damn burning pit of desire that was once her core. It had long since melted away; she was certain.

Oh no.

He wrapped his hands around Lyra's foot and dug his thumbs into her arch. The moan she let out was embarrassing; she could not help it. Her feet had been aching all night from pacing and standing in front of the wall, staring at it for several hours.

"Are you going to melt for me, Lyra?" he asked as he dug into her arch again.

Yes, yes, she was.

"Gods, if you keep that up, I will—I'll do anything you want me to," she said, groaning as he kept kneading away the aches and pains.

Wait.

What had she just said? Maybe he had not heard her.

Her eyes snapped open, and she looked at grinning Zandar. He had definitely heard her.

Shit.

"Anything?" he asked and his hands, his stupid magical hands, continued rubbing and she considered saying "yes."

"You know what I meant," she said and waved it off like it was nothing. She kept her eyes closed. If she did not have to look at him, she could pretend that it was anyone else making her feel like she was about to become one with the couch beneath her.

His hands moved up her foot to her ankle, and she tensed—until he started working his magical fingers, and she sighed. If she were to die right then and there, she could go happily.

"Hmmm, I do not think I do," he said, and she swore to the goddess that the tone in his voice made her core vibrate, and she thought she was about to fall right over the edge she had been riding for far too long.

Thanks to the male touching her.

She should have told him to stop and move away, but then he started on the other foot, and she could not go unbalanced. After he finished this foot, then she would sit up.

"I have no idea what you are talking about," she said, and nearly kicked him when he pushed on a spot that felt both horrible and amazing at the same time and made her whimper on her last few words.

She was embarrassing herself, yet she was so relaxed she could not find it within herself to care. His hands moved to that ankle, and she swore to herself she would tell him to stop. After one more minute.

One of his hands traced a path slowly up the inside of her leg as he said, "I think you do, Lyra. Why fight this? I know you want me just as much as I want you." It was like cold water was dumped on her.

"Stop," she said as she pulled her foot out of his grasp to sit up and glare at him—a perfectly wonderful moment that he had to go and ruin.

"No, Lyra. We have danced around each other long enough." He reached his hand out and placed it on her foot. She yanked the appendage away immediately.

"Zandar, you are delusional. I have no idea what you are talking about," she said, rolling her eyes and then refusing to look at him.

She squealed, not her most dignified of sounds, as he yanked her down the couch toward him. He climbed on top of her and pinned her hands above her head. They both knew she could get out of the hold easily. They both also knew why she did not attempt to.

Fuck.

"Am I?" he said with that fucking melty voice. No male should have a voice like that; it was a weapon. One Lyra had no idea how to fight against.

He dragged his lips—his stupidly perfect lips—across the shell of her ear, and a tremor worked its way down her body. Goddess, save her. When he laughed, the sound was low and thick and wrapped around every inch of her like a caress.

"I think, Lyra," he said, her name slowly, rolling each syllable over his tongue. Great. Now she was thinking about what he could do with that same tongue. "You are afraid."

There was no use saying anything; on the contrary. She did not trust her voice at that moment to betray her. Her body was already doing a fine job of that.

"What I cannot understand is why?" he nuzzled into her neck and kissed her right below her jaw. The touch was soft and somehow made her burn hotter than if he had been demanding in his touch.

"Why would you, of all beings, be afraid?" The words came out in hot breaths against her skin, which erupted into gooseflesh all over her body. She hated herself—she was going to give herself a strong talking to later— when she whimpered and pushed her heat into the impressive bulge she felt pressed against her. At least she had the same effect on him. The moment she did it again, he groaned.

"If you keep that up, I will fuck you senseless, and we will never have this conversation." That sounded just fine to her. Then she could ignore him for the rest of their lives. "You are one of the bravest beings I know. What do you have to be afraid of?"

"You," she said. It came out quieter than a whisper. She thought for a moment that he had not heard her, but then he pulled away and looked her in the eyes.

"Me? What about me?" He knew it had nothing to do with them being physical; she could kick his ass—and did so regularly.

She groaned and made a half-hearted attempt to slide out from under him. When she woke up that night, she had not seen this happening. She never saw this happening.

"Tell me." The command in his voice was not one she

had ever heard from him before, and for some reason, she stilled, and wanted nothing more than to spill her entire heart out to him.

What in the actual fuck?

She opened her mouth to tell him… she was not sure what, but it was not the words that fell from her lips: "If I let myself fall into you, I would do so completely."

"I am failing to see a problem here," he said with a smirk.

Gods those fucking lips again.

"I will never have younglings," she said. For some reason, she said it as though it were a threat. Perhaps she hoped it would send him running.

"Okay, is it your choice or is it something you have no control over?" he asked. She wanted to take his words and twist them in a way to use against him, but she could not.

"My choice."

"Good," he said, and her eyes flew wide open. "I would hate for you not to have every option in front of you—and not be able to make every choice for yourself." Fucking Zandar. He just had to go and be perfect.

"Was that it? Because I could not give two shits about having a youngling. I do not even think I like them; they are so… small." She choked out a laugh.

"You do not like younglings because they are small?" she asked, laughing even harder.

"What? It freaks me out. What if I broke it?" His face looked truly horrified.

"First of all, they are far more resilient than you are giving them credit for, and secondly, I do not believe for a single moment that you would ever be anything but gentle."

"I do not know. They still freak me out." They both laughed, and when the laughter faded, he looked her in the eyes, and she knew he was about to ask her what else, and there was going to be no getting out of telling him.

"That's not all, though, is it?" he asked. His fingers skimmed the delicate skin of her neck, and she had a hard time concentrating.

"Your mate." It was all she could spit out with her mind all over the place. He pulled back again and looked at her in confusion.

"I do not have a mate."

"But what if…" she trailed off, and understanding lit within his yellow eyes.

"But what if one day I do?" he asked, nodding his head as if everything in the realm made sense to him.

"Yes," she hissed as she turned her head away. She was so embarrassed, and she could not bear to see the amusement in his eyes when he inevitably laughed at her.

"Lyra," he said, grabbing her chin firmly and forcing her to look at him. His eyes bored into hers and looked… angry? "Listen to me and listen well. The chances of any fae having a fated mate are incredibly slim. Anyone I know who has a mate never fell in love with anyone else, even if a thousand years had passed. It was as if their heart knew it already belonged to another."

Did he just say what she thinks he did?

"Even if my nonexistent fated mate showed up in this room right now, it would not mean that I could just stop loving you." They were both quiet; the only sound was the heavy breaths coming between them.

"You," she said, her voice thick with emotion. "You love me?" The question came out all at once in a single breath; she was afraid she had misheard.

"I have loved you since the moment you first laid me out on my ass and put me in my place." She sucked in a breath. Had she wasted all this time on a stupid fear, just as her sisters had told her she was? However, the fear of being abandoned is not stupid; it's terrifying.

"You have?" she asked. The air seemed to thin, and her head felt too light.

"Yes. Now shut up and let me kiss you." When she did not say anything, he grinned. "Thank the fucking gods."

When his mouth met hers, she was not prepared. She did not know what she had expected, but it was not the full invasion and claiming he gave. She had never been kissed if this was what a true kiss was.

His hand wrapped around the side of her neck in a way that made her feel like he had just declared her his. When he kissed down her body, she let him. When he pulled her pants down, she let him; and when he buried his face between her legs, oh goddess, did she let him.

She climbed faster and higher than she had any right to and fell off the edge— hard. Her body shook, and she screamed his name. There was no telling how long it took for her vision to return to normal, but when it did, he hovered above her, feeling very proud of himself.

When he guided his cock—just as perfect as she knew it was—to her entrance, she stopped him. He looked up at her with desperation in his eyes—one that she decided she liked far too much, particularly since she knew it was for her.

"Now, Zandar, do you not think you should take me out on a date before you jump all the way to the end?" He groaned and tucked himself away. She almost lost control when he kissed her hard and she tasted herself on him, but she stayed strong.

She loved the way he chased her, after all.

Kes entered the training facility quietly so that he could take in his Twenty-Three; these were the best warriors he had ever seen, even better than the group for which they were named.

It had been a joke at first—him making his own Twenty-Three. Yet, after he told Anin about the details of his youth and how he became the perfection he was now, she said he should do it. It could be one more way to say "fuck you" to Ciaran's dad.

It's not that he thought back on the original Twenty-Three with hate; some of those warriors gave him a gift he did not even know he was receiving at the time. There was a group of them that provided him with guidance and companionship and forced him to survive whatever fate decided to throw at him. He would be eternally grateful to them—not that he would tell them if he ever saw them again.

He had hoped that when word of the Silent Shadows

began making its way through the court, some of them would show up to join. He was not surprised when none of them did, however; they were the kind of beings that answered to no one but themselves and would be horrible at taking orders.

In the end, it was for the best: the group that filled the training facility was leagues above any of the originals. He had been surprised when he reviewed the list and saw how many witches made the team. He had known there would be a few, but it was a nearly even split, with only a few more fae. He should know by now not to underestimate a witch.

Once he and Lyra had figured out how a witch could fight while using her powers, she took off with it. She had belts made that strapped across their front and around their waists, with dozens of pouches attached. All they had to do in battle was toss one while saying whatever spell corresponded with the little bag of witch "stuff," and boom—at least, most of them went boom.

Eventually, the witches on his team became adept at moving fluidly between their powers and spells without pausing physical combat. If he were honest, it was more impressive than any fae. All the fae had to do was learn how to wield their elemental powers while fighting. The fae were dancing, while the witches were finely sharpened blades with precision accuracy.

Both were great; one just took more skill. Again, that was not something he would ever tell any of them; Lyra would never let him forget it. However, he was certain that all the fae on the new Twenty-Three thought the same thing he did. He watched their faces as two witches sparred, finding it difficult not to be in awe of them.

"Tyne?" Lyra called to where Kes stood. Sure enough, the little shit had snuck up on him. He often regretted teaching her how to be silent when she was so little; she had been incredibly clumsy and full of energy. In no time, she was sneaking about, scaring her moms, which Lyra and Kes had always found amusing. It was ingrained in her now, and he didn't think she even knew she was doing it. To her, she was just walking.

"What are you doing here, squirt?" he asked her. Her adorable nose scrunched at his name for her. He always tried to come up with something new every so often; it was double points if she thought it was gross.

"Really? Squirt? That's foul, but not as fowl as you," she said, her disgust morphing into a victorious smile as he laughed. She really had spent too much time with him, too early in her life.

"Anyway, I am here to join the team," she said, looking at the elite team training.

"Uh-oh, looks like someone doesn't like the sound of that," he said to her under his breath. When she saw her aunt barreling toward them, she sighed.

"Which means my moms will be here any minute," she responded, just as quietly.

"Good luck," he paused before he added, "Squirt."

"Shut it, bird," he just cackled as he backed away. He wanted to see how this went down. He understood why they were all protective of her. He was too. Something else he would never admit to anyone.

The difference was that he saw her as the mature fae

she was now. She was still young and dumb, but she was not the youngling who knocked Panella on her ass, or the one that tried to explain a fight she was having with some of her witch friends. It made absolutely no sense to him. However, younglings nearing maturity rarely do.

He also thought she would be great at it. She already knew more than most when they started. There was no question in his mind that she would wipe the floor with most of the other beings her age wanting to join.

"Hi, Aunt Lyra," she said in a tone that indicated she knew she was about to have an argument.

"Absolutely not," Lyra said, skipping hellos and getting right into it. "Your mothers—"

"Would never allow it," Panella said, walking in behind them. Tyne sighed loudly and looked up at the night sky.

Poor Tyne.

"Tyne, my beautiful daughter, you are far too young to be joining something so dangerous," Ravyn said, tucking a loose hair behind Tyne's ear.

"I am not a youngling any longer," she said. He was proud of her for not letting her voice tip into that whining thing she used to do. It would help beings take her more seriously, perhaps not this particular group of beings.

"Just barely," Lyra said, crossing her arms. Her gaze snapped to his, and he cursed himself for not moving further away. "Are you going to tell her how crazy she is or how this is no place for someone so young?"

So much for not getting involved.

"No," was all he said as he joined them. All four

witches snapped their eyes to him: three pairs were confused, while one was grateful.

"What? Why not?" Panella nearly screeched.

"Why would I? If she wants to join, she will have to start at the very beginning," he said, looking at Tyne's mothers, "And completely harmless."

"I would not say that," Lyra huffed.

"Listen, she's right. She has hit maturity, and she needs to be trusted to make decisions for herself. I, for one, think she will be more of a badass than her aunt by the time she makes it to the elite teams." Tyne looked at him with watery eyes and mouthed a *thank you.*

"This is ridic—" Panella started.

"No," Ravyn cut in, looking only at her daughter. "Kes is right. It's hard to see you as anything besides the youngling you were, but I will do my best to see you as the witch you have become." A choked sob escaped her, and Panella wrapped her arms around her. "I have to let you grow up." The last words were nearly silent.

"We have to let her grow up," Panella said with a sigh.

Tyne picked that moment to jump around and squeal, reminding them all just how young she was. He cleared his throat, and she stopped immediately and composed herself.

"What I meant to say is thank you for trusting me to step into maturity. It does not mean I need any of you less than I did decades ago." She looked at Kes and added, "Even you, I guess." They all laughed, even though her mothers were desperate to mask the sobs trying to escape.

He put his arm around his niece and pulled her away from her mothers so that they could comfort each other.

"Come on, Tynie. This is not the room you start in," he said, walking her to the door furthest away from them. It led to where the latest recruits were going through absolute torture. She was going to love it.

"I know you did not just call me *Tynie*."

"Sure did, and I think I found your official Kes-gifted name," he said while she looked more than offended.

"It's not a gift if you do not want it," she grumbled. He laughed and pulled her in for a tight hug.

"Thank you, Uncle Kes," she said softly.

"Anytime," he said, smiling and looking down at his favorite being next to Anin. "*Tynie*." She punched him in the shoulder, which only made him howl with laughter.

They had not done this—just the four of them—in a long time. Kes sat at the table between Anin and Etain and across from his cousin, who looked... content? It was disturbing, whatever it was—even if he was happy for him.

"And then, when I came out of the visions, the Many Faced Goddess was pinching his cheek and calling him a good boy!" They had been laughing so hard, and mostly at Ciaran's expense the entire time. Kes was having a hard time breathing, but he would suffocate before he ever stopped laughing at his cousin.

"Gods, what I would not have given to have seen that!" Kes said between choked laughter. When Ciaran scowled at him, he laughed even harder. "Oh, cousin, should I tell them the story about the t—"

"Kes, I swear to the gods, if you finish that statement, you will not know your ass from your head," Ciaran growled. He had not even known what story Kes was about to tell, but Kes had so many to choose from and his cousin was not taking any chances.

"I am not so sure he does now," Anin said, giggling when Kes fell out of his chair, acting as if she had just crushed his heart. Everyone was laughing. It was such a different experience from that first time the four of them sat around the same table nearly two centuries ago.

He still had not forgotten the way Etain had stood up to the two big fae males for the fae female she had just met. Kes was not sure he had ever been put in his place quite so quickly. She was tiny—even for a witch—but she never backed down when others needed protecting. He thought she knew, even then, that Anin was meant to be her closest friend.

"I," Anin started before reaching for Kes's hand. He had to constantly remind her that she was not alone. Whatever she did, he would be there for her. "We have something to share, and I hope we have both of your support."

She looked at Kes nervously. They had talked about this exact moment earlier, and he thought part of her never wanted to make this announcement. However, a larger part of her demanded it.

She took a deep breath, sat up straight, and looked at Ciaran and Etain—not as her friends and family, but as the King of the Night Court and the Queen of the Witches. When she finally released her words, she did so as their equal. He had never been more proud of her.

"It's time." They looked at her, and the silence

stretched before both of their mouths tipped up into smiles—even Ciaran's.

He did not know what happened between them at the very top of his tower, but whatever it was made his cousin see Anin as she was meant to be—not as the nymph he first met. Not for the first time, he wondered what the realm would look like with all three rulers united.

"You are finally going to do it, then?" Ciaran asked. Etain swatted at his arm while she beamed at her best friend.

"Yes, I am claiming my throne," Anin said. Etain squealed, not unlike the way Tyne had earlier. Maybe it was just a witch thing.

"When?" Etain asked, her excitement barely contained.

Anin looked toward Kes. They had talked extensively about their future and what it would look like. She asked him if he would be her general. She knew he was already Ciaran's and did not want to overstep. Kes had laughed and told her that he was her mate and would always put her before everyone else. So when he turned back to answer Etain, he did so as his queen's general.

"That is what we wanted to talk to you about."

Chapter 43
Balthier

Balthier, as always, was the first to arrive at the place they had chosen to meet earlier that day. He knew Killia would join him in a few minutes, giving him a small window of time to sort through his thoughts.

There was not much to go over, but he had something to tell them all—something that would change everything again.

He was proud of how far he and the other leaders had taken the rebellion. They might all call him the leader, but he was just one of the cogs that made it work. It required all of them thinking for themselves and being the expert in their faction. He was just the organizer, and maybe even the liaison, but he was not the rebellion itself.

It was much bigger than himself. It was the fae who bravely marched to their deaths, and their loved ones continued to fight while their hearts broke. It was fae like

Killia, who lost pieces of herself every day yet refused to back down. It was all of them, and they were it.

"Always the early bird," Killia said, showing up just when he thought she would.

"Well, you know how I am," he said. She knew him better than even Raindal.

"Hard-headed? Or were you referring to the inability to take a compliment?" They both laughed. He had not meant either of those, but they fit him all the same.

Moments later, the rest of them filtered in. They decided to keep their meetings to no more than fifteen minutes once everything started getting crazy.

"Is it true?" Flix asked as soon as they had all gathered. There was no time for pleasantries.

"Yes. It's true." They looked around at each other and smiled, wanting to laugh, cheer, and celebrate as loudly as possible. Yet, they could not. They still had to be careful—if not more so than before.

"The blood magic does not work on the lesser fae for some reason," he said. "But that does not mean we can let our guard down. If anything, we need to be extra vigilant. She is unpredictable, and I would not put it past her to lick her wounds and then come back at us with something worse." They all nodded in agreement.

"What can we do to help protect the quarter?" Caraway asked. This was their biggest issue.

"I am not sure there is anything we can do. We have created an evacuation plan and a way to spread messages to everyone in the quarter within moments. We are no match for the high fae and their elemental powers," Killia said.

"We can build another barrier. It will not stop them, but it might give us the few minutes we need to get everyone out," Balthier said.

"Everyone but those still with deals intact," Brock said.

"We will be fine. Do not worry about us. Get as many out as possible." He hated that Killia still had a deal with a high fae. If he could, he would kill that bastard for her.

"Balthier," Lorella called. "I have eyes on him again. We are working to get the bloodstone to him, but he has not been alone." What Lorella meant was that *she* had not left him alone. He wanted the queen dead, sure. However, once he had Raindal in his arms again, he did not care what happened to her, as long as Anin sat on the throne and they were left alone.

"Thank you," he said, feeling as if those were inadequate words to give. The palace spies were doing the most dangerous job of all. No one knew how Tatiana would react, yet they kept going.

"I have news," he said. His stomach was in knots, yet fluttered with excitement. He did not know how this would pan out or if they would all make it to the other side, but it was happening.

"We have all been invited to a meeting to plan the next steps for the rebellion," he said, aware he was drawing it out. They all looked at him in confusion, each of their faces saying, Is that not what we are already doing?

"The meeting will be hosted in the palace." Now they looked at him as if he had lost his mind. "In the Night Court." Gasps echoed around the circle. "I know those in a deal cannot go, and it's too late to make arrangements for a day of leave, but I think the rest of us should go so we can give her the best information possible."

"You mean…she…" Killia said, tears in her eyes as she tried to express what they were all attempting to process.

"The queen is coming."

Chapter 44
Ciaran

Ciaran had not forgotten the secret society of Night fae. After that meeting, he started tracking down each member. He trailed behind them, moving with a quiet, practiced stealth, careful to remain just out of sight. It was funny—in a decidedly not funny way—that their relentless complaints annoyed him more than they threatened. After all this time tailing them, their petty grievances were wearing his patience thin.

It was infuriating.

To him, saying anything negative about the witches was a direct insult to his mate. Yet, Etain believed all beings should voice their *opinions*. A view he begrudgingly respected. She claimed only those who acted out violently deserved consequences. The definition of which, unsurprisingly, varied greatly between them.

He had been sure it would take only a few nights to catch them in something nefarious; he was wrong. In all the decades he had followed them, they had done nothing but complain.

This was... disappointing.

They were grating to listen to and painfully dull. Ciaran caught himself stifling yawns while enduring their meetings. For decades, their complaints had not varied; they had only grown more asinine over time, each grievance somehow duller than the last. According to them, witches were apparently responsible for the most trivial things, their very existence blamed for every minor inconvenience.

If one failed to secure a date with the fae they tried to court, it was, of course, the witches who had cursed them. The sheer absurdity of their reasoning left him shaking his head, and he did not even particularly care for the witches. Well, not that he cared about anyone besides his mate.

Did they truly believe that their romantic failures stemmed from a witch's curse rather than their own shortcomings? He could almost picture their melodramatic expressions, filled with righteous indignation, as they recounted their tales of misfortune, spinning grand narratives from their petty woes.

Another had gone so far as to blame the witches for the small well he had been born with, a complaint so ridiculous it almost made Ciaran laugh. He wondered if the male's well was the only small thing he had been born with. The creature had an endless capacity for self-pity. It was absurd; not even younglings whined as much as they did, and he often found himself rolling his eyes in disbelief.

What made Ciaran certain they were not responsible for the attacks on Witch City was the reverence they had when they spoke of the unknown being after the last attack. They wanted to find out who was responsible and recruit them into their society. Whoever was behind it had become their personal hero.

The worst part was the amount of time he had spent following the sniveling fae with nothing to show for it. Each hour spent observing them felt like a lifetime wasted. They had not even uttered a single word directly about Etain. It was as if they sensed his presence lurking in the shadows and had consciously chosen to hold their tongues, unwilling to lose their heads just to complain.

At least he could multitask. He had sent his shadows to watch them while he sat, watching his little witch make her witchy things. Several of his shadows followed the leaders of this society for what he decided would be the last time.

It was no surprise that Syndari was one of the leaders; after all, they always complained at council meetings and in every other aspect of their life. The incessant whining rolled off their tongue far too easily, while each complaint was more trivial than the last. It was remarkable how they turned mundane inconveniences into epic tales of despair.

How horrifically boring.

One good thing had come from his efforts: during council meetings, he took a certain wicked delight in saying things that hinted at conversations he should know nothing about. The shifter's eyes would widen with surprise, if only for a moment, before they settled back into their placid, unbothered expressions. He relished the subtle shift in their demeanor and the way the shock would ripple through them. It was a fun game in his otherwise monotonous observations.

Yet that too began to lose its appeal. The thrill of watching their reactions dulled with each passing meeting, becoming predictable and offering little more than a fleeting smirk in the oppressive boredom.

His shadows followed them, slipping through the darkness undetected, along with two others, to one of their not-so-secret meetings. Ciaran could not help but smirk at the absurdity of it all; it was laughable how clever they thought they were, prattling on as if their secrecy mattered. He was certain Tyne was more clever by the time she was three than all these fools combined.

He was about to call it quits when one of them said something strange. Ciaran had no context, which meant, clearly, he had missed something crucial at some point in their tedious complaints. Frustration flared within him— had he been so lost in their incessant whining that he overlooked a pivotal moment?

"Did you receive your calling?" one asked.

"I have," Syndari said, while the others nodded in affirmation.

"Will you answer the call?" another asked. A moment of silence while they each considered their answers.

What is this call?

The words echoed in his mind, a puzzling thread woven into their monotonous complaints. It hinted at something deeper—something significant that piqued his curiosity.

"I believe so. There's no reason not to," Syndari replied.

Great, so much for this being the last time.

Ciaran's annoyance began to shift into something more alarming. If their 'calling' could ignite something dangerous, he might have underestimated the society's significance.

He was still no closer to discovering who was responsible for the attacks on Witch City. That made two things he did not know—which was two things too many. He felt the tide of his thoughts shift, and that gnawing uncertainty morphed into a growing fear for Etain's safety. It was likely he was being overly protective of his little witch, but he was unwilling to compromise when it came to her.

He would lock her in their tower if he knew it would not upset her. The thought lingered in his mind; it was tempting. Yet he did know, and it would, and did not think it was an option anyway. Not with her having control of the ring. She would never leave her witches to face a threat on their own. There was no doubt in Ciaran's mind that was exactly what it was.

A threat.

"This is a mistake," Anin said countless times in the last hour. She had not stopped pacing since she woke. Balthier and the group of Day fae he chose would be arriving in the next few minutes.

"It is not a mistake. You are going to do great," Kes said, as he had on repeat all night.

"I know nothing about planning an attack. How could I possibly do great?" She threw her hands in the air and stopped pacing long enough to glare at him. It was a struggle not to laugh.

"That's why you have me. I happen to know a little about planning attacks." He grinned at her, and she rolled her eyes, but he saw the smile threatening to make an appearance.

"What if I am not ready?" she asked, her voice growing softer. Now they were getting into the real issues.

"What if you are?" She stopped her pacing once more and held his arms open, inviting her to come sit in his lap.

She sighed and the second she sat, he wrapped his arms around her. "What is it really?" he whispered.

This was something they had not done in a while. Years ago, when she needed to talk about something, but really did not want to, they would whisper back and forth. Somehow, it made her feel better. It was like if she whispered the words, then she had not really said them.

"What if," she whispered. "What if I do not live up to the image the Day fae have created of me in their minds? What if I am a disappointment?" He thought this was where her mind might have gone.

"Anin, you do not need to worry about meeting anyone's expectations of you. The only thing you need to worry about is doing the best you can and knowing that it is enough." He caressed her arm in long, calming strokes as he spoke.

"No one is perfect," he whispered before he added in his normal volume. "Well, except for me, of course," she laughed, like he knew she would, and he felt some of the tension melt from her body.

"What about after?" she asked, no longer whispering. "I know nothing about ruling a court."

"While I have no doubts that you will do just fine figuring it out along the way, you do happen to have a best friend who also happens to be the only other queen in the realm." She smiled warmly when he mentioned Etain.

The witch had played one of the largest roles in getting Anin where she was now. Between the concoction she continued to make for Anin and giving her a safe place to say what she was too afraid to tell even him, made all the difference. He would always be grateful to Etain.

A scroll arrived. They both knew what it would say. She unrolled it, and they read Etain's neat, looping script.

They were here.

He gave her one last squeeze before helping her stand. "Are you ready?" he asked. She stood tall and gripped his hand.

"As I will ever be."

They ported to Etain's study, which they had determined would be the best place to hold the meeting. While the Night fae had come a long way and generally all accepted Anin, they had not wanted to take any risks with others. Witch City was the safest place for them within Nightfell.

Ciaran sat in a chair, looking as frightening as ever, while Etain was doing her best to make the three Day fae feel more comfortable. Even so, the newcomers looked terrified—until they saw Anin.

Their faces lit up, and the eyes that had only moments before been shifting, looking for an unseen danger, settled. They already trusted her.

It was awkward at first. Anin had no idea what to do when they bowed to her. Etain had everyone sit around a round table. It was a tight fit, but it meant everyone could see the center of the table for any references that might be needed. As soon as they began discussing the plan of attack, everyone seemed to relax.

Kes was impressed by the organization and the knowledge the rebels had. The first time he met Balthier, he was not sure the male was going to make it. It was good to see that he not only survived but that he stepped into his role and became the male he needed to be.

"We are not sure when, but at some point in the last few days, Tatiana placed a ward on the palace. Only she can port in and out," a female Day fae said. She seemed to know everything that involved the palace.

"I was able to get the most current map of the palace out, and I plotted the best path for you to the throne room. This is the path the lesser fae take to avoid as many high fae as possible. There are some new faces from the northern half of the court who enjoy inflicting pain on any lesser fae they come across," she said.

"Why are any lesser fae still entering the palace?" Etain asked. It did seem like abandoning the palace was the safest option.

"Anyone whose deal has dissolved no longer goes. However, there are still far too many with deals still in place. A few of us could not come because the deals they made prevented them from leaving the city," Balthier said.

Anin grabbed his hand under the table and squeezed. She carried a lot of guilt for multiple reasons, most having to do with the time it took for her to get to this point. She knew she could have had Tatiana taken out at any point after they had the bloodstones activated. Yet made the difficult decision not to, because she knew it was not what fate had intended.

Fate would get what fate wanted. That might include the possibility that whoever was sent to remove her would not return. That was something she was unwilling to risk. She knew it would be someone she cared for and felt guilty for choosing the few she loved over the many.

Kes thought it was the only choice. If she sent someone she loved to test fate, she would still be in the same position; only then she would be heartbroken.

"It will be the first thing I do," Anin said confidently. He knew, through the bond, that she was feeling anything but, yet she refused to let anyone else know. They all nodded.

"Tell me what you have at your disposal," Kes said. He needed to know what he had to work with.

"We have been hoarding as many weapons as we could over the past several years. Beyond that, we have knowledge of the infrastructure and how the high fae use it. We can make life very complicated," a male said, grinning.

Balthier rolled out another map. This one was of the entire city. They had come prepared, and Kes was impressed once again.

He stared at the map, studying it. He knew the basic layout of the city. He had been there several times and had even caused a decent amount of destruction in his quest to create chaos. However, now when he looked at the map, he was looking at it in a different light. He wanted minimal damage with maximum results. This was his mate's city—their city now.

"Do they not port?" Ciaran asked. Everyone turned to him; it was the first time he had said anything beyond the grunted greeting they all received. He was always on edge when someone new was around his mate.

"They do, but they have to make several trips to get transports of goods across." Kes liked this male. He did not back down in fear from the king of the Night Court.

Kes would make sure to get his name and remember it next time.

"How will that slow down attacks?" Kes asked. It was a good question—one he had been thinking about as well.

"Well, it likely would not. Everything we have done before now has been in an attempt to make their lives as miserable as ours," Balthier said. "We could not wage war, but so much in the city has depended on the labor of lesser fae that we saw an opportunity and took it."

"As you should have," Anin said. "Etain, is there anything the witches might know of to make porting difficult? Or even stop it altogether?"

"I am not sure, but I would imagine there is something. I will get back to you on that tomorrow," Etain said.

"Assuming the witches are able to find a solution, show me where would make the biggest impact. We need to slow them down and cause confusion," Kes said, once again staring at the map.

It took them a few hours, but by the end, they started to develop a solid plan. There were a few things they each needed to look into, and they would reconvene in three nights' time.

They planned a multifaceted attack to split Tatiana's troops throughout the city before Kes and the shadows arrived. He noted which teams he would position in each location, while the Twenty-Three would be with him and Anin as they took full control of the palace.

"There is another issue," Ciaran said. He was great at finding the weak spots in their plan. Some might be annoyed or think him negative, but Kes thought it was an invaluable skill. Of course, he would never say that to him.

"What do you see?" he asked his cousin.

"Any Night fae will be weakened in the Day Court, and their power will drain at a faster rate." That was a really good point, and one that Kes had completely overlooked.

"Now that, I know I have something for," Etain said, a huge smile spreading across her face. "It will only last a few hours, but if I get the covens on it now, we should be able to make more than enough within the next couple of nights."

"Wonderful, thank you," Anin said to Etain.

"Of course," Etain responded. "You are my family." The few Day fae around the table looked at the four of them. It was as if it just occurred to them that not only were they the king and queens of the realm, but they were also a united force.

"My love," Etain said to Ciaran. "Will you help me take them home?"

"You are not going anywhere near that court right now. I will do it," he said. Before she could say his name, he was gone, and so were the Day fae.

"One of these nights, he will understand the importance and necessity of farewells," Etain said, sighing and shaking her head with a smile. "That went well."

"I think so," Anin said. "It's really happening." The statement almost sounded like a question. Etain reached over and grabbed Anin's hand, giving it a soft squeeze.

"It is, my friend. In a few nights you will be Anin, queen of the Day Court, and you will be wonderful at it."

The two continued to talk, and Kes was grateful for

Etain reiterating the same thing to Anin that he had told her. His thoughts wandered as he considered the list of things he needed to get done within the next few nights. There were a few things he needed to ensure Anin knew how to do.

He had already taught her how to create a shield of pure power, yet it would not hurt for her to know how to do a few basic defensive maneuvers. There was not much time, but he planned to use every minute of it.

His mate was about to become the queen.

"It's strange not having Tyne here," Panella said when Ravyn entered the study on their floor of the home they now only shared with Lyra. Tyne moved with a quietness that was sometimes terrifying, unless she was at home; then she sounded like five witches stomping around at once.

"It's quiet," Ravyn said with a sad laugh as she took one of the seats across the desk from Panella.

"It's as though a whole horde of witches moved out when she did," Panella said as they both laughed true laughs, thinking about their daughter.

"Things are so different for the witches who grew up here," Ravyn said. "We never even dreamed of leaving our covens, and here she is, living in an apartment with two of her friends." They missed her, and she had only moved out a few nights ago.

While it's hard to watch your youngling grow up and reach maturity, it's beautiful at the same time. Being a parent is wanting to stop time so that they never grow up; yet, it's also feeling excited to see the being they become at the next stage of life. It's wanting to hold on as tightly as possible to them, while also wanting to see the amazing things they will do.

"I loved my younghood, but I would have loved growing up in the city even more," Panella said. "Although it's probably for the best; we caused enough trouble as it was. I cannot imagine what we would have gotten into here."

"You know," Ravyn said, standing up, "There is one positive to Tyne moving out."

"What's that?" Panella watched, transfixed by her bonded, as she slowly slid the straps of her dress down her shoulder and shimmied out of it until it pooled at her feet. She did not take her eyes off her for a moment as Ravyn took her time walking around the side of Panella's desk.

Ravyn dropped to her knees, locking eyes with Panella as she expertly untied the laces that held up her pants. Panella lifted off the seat when Ravyn started to pull them down. Once she got them off, she threw them to the side.

Her gaze never wavered as she wrapped Panella's legs around her shoulders and then grabbed her by the hips to pull her to the edge of the chair.

"This," Ravyn said, just before she slid her tongue between Panella's folds and gave her one long slow lick from entrance to clit.

"Fuck," Panella groaned, weaving the fingers of one hand through the silky black strands of her hair and resting her hand on Ravyn's head. She watched her lover as she flicked her tongue and sucked with the precision of someone who had mastered another's body. Goddess save her, but Ravyn between her legs was her second favorite view.

Panella was getting closer to the razor-sharp edge that promised pure pleasure on the other side. She gripped the hair between her fingers and pulled Ravyn into her harder.

When she reached the very peak of her pleasure, Panella plummeted into ecstasy. Her wet heat flooded Ravyn's mouth, who kept devouring her through her free fall.

Finally, she opened her eyes to see a smug smile on her bonded's face. Panella leaned forward and crashed her lips to Ravyn's. She kissed her breathless while picking her up and sitting her on the desk; then she leaned into her, forcing Ravyn to lean back on the palms of her hands and knocking the books on the ground.

Panella put Ravyn's feet on the edge of the desk and pushed her knees wide. She knew her lover would be dripping. She enjoyed giving as much as receiving—well, almost.

"Look at how needy you are," she said to Ravyn, her voice giving away her hunger. Panella put her head between Ravyn's legs and flicked her tongue over her sensitive bud lightly, over and over until Ravyn was writhing beneath her, searching for more.

"Panella, please," Ravyn begged.

Panella sucked hard on her while she entered first one and then two fingers into her wet heat and searched for that spot that... there it was. Ravyn's head fell back as she let loose a sound that was between a cry and a moan.

That right there.

That was her favorite view, Ravyn getting lost in her pleasure. If she saw it every night for an eternity, it would not be enough.

She could feel her getting closer, so she added a third finger. Panella moved her hand quickly while applying pressure to that spot inside her, all the while her mouth never relented. Ravyn clamped down tight on Panella's hand just as Panella sucked hard on her clit.

Ravyn's scream started low, from deep within. Her body tensed, lifting her feet and pulling her knees tighter in toward her chest. By the time she reached the end of the scream, it was silent; then her entire body went lax. She collapsed back onto the desk, breathing hard.

Panella pulled Ravyn's limp body off the desk and sat them both in her chair, with Ravyn across her lap. She ran the pads of her fingers up and down one of Ravyn's legs as her bonded came back to herself.

They sat there, holding each other for a while longer. Neither of them saying anything, just enjoying the feel of the other's soft skin against their own. It was the chill in the air that finally made them separate and get dressed again.

"Maybe we should have had Tyne move out sooner," Panella said, grinning at Ravyn. She laughed and shook her head as they both began to pick up the mess of papers and books scattered around Panella's desk.

Panella went to close a book so she could pick it up and add it to the stack when something caught her eye.

Even leaders must learn to find the balance between them, in order to…

The text had been rubbed away; however, she knew exactly where she had read that before. She scanned the page a bit more and there was something about the place where all meet.

"What is it?" Ravyn asked. Panella read a little more before lifting her gaze to her bonded.

"I know where they are."

Tatiana shook her head again, yet it did nothing to clear the flashes of visions that kept surfacing.

... a hand... a doll... singing...... running through a field of flowers... climbing a tree... laughing younglings... looking out a window...

They did not stop, nor did they linger on any image long enough to be truly seen. What made them even more disorienting was the way the visions layered over her actual sight.

... a lesser fae holding a youngling... hands... a goblet... laying in the sun... face after face standing behind the same desk... a small pool of golden blood dripping onto the floor...

"Make them stop!" she screamed at no one in particular. Her breaths were impossible to catch, and her head felt far too light. She needed more power.

If she had more power, she could stop the visions.

If she had more power, she could rule the realm.

If she had more power…

She would be loved.

"Show me where to find more power," she seethed at the *whispers*. They stayed quiet more often than not, ever since she discovered that blood magic does not work on the lesser fae. She had begged them many times in the past few days to show her where to find more. She was certain they knew and were keeping it from her.

"Show me!" Her scream echoed down the hall of which she had no recollection of walking. The last she remembered, she was in her chambers.

"I said, SHOW ME!" she bellowed so loudly that she tasted blood in the back of her throat.

"We have told you, there is no other source of power," the *whispers* finally said. It was the same answer they gave her whenever they chose to respond to her, that is.

"You lie!"

"Stop throwing a fit like a spoiled youngling. If you do not control yourself and stop acting like the mad queen the realm is calling you, then the gift we have given you will be wasted." She laughed. The sound contained not an ounce of joy.

"Some gift," she murmured

…standing before the closed doors of a ballroom… a hand gripping too tightly… white wings blocking out the sun…

She sat at the table in the council chamber with no recollection of how she got there. Her new council members were laughing at something with the few remaining members of her last council. The rest of them either sat rotting in her dungeon, waiting to be consumed, or had already been.

Directly following the incident, she sent out a message to the northern high fae city, Solarath, and the eastern city of Flarimmar. She requested the presence of all high fae who wanted to ensure that the lesser fae stayed where they belonged. The beings who responded had not disappointed.

No longer needing to control the golden army lessened the strain on her power. Since learning about the costs of using blood magic, she attempted to be more cautious, but was rarely successful. Relying on blood magic had become as natural to her as breathing.

It was not only used for controlling beings; there were many spells that incorporated its use, such as the spell she had placed on the hall that prevented the bird from reaching the creature she had locked away.

Until Raindal made the grievous mistake of allowing the nymphs blood to spill, thus breaking the spell. She glared at the male in question. She had refused to remove her hold on him; he was the only high fae she controlled all hours of the day.

Her new army savored drawing out the deaths of any lesser fae they encountered. They were precisely what she needed. Since their arrival, not a single gown had gone missing, and everything remained in its place. She felt as if she were in control again.

...youngling giggles... golden blood on a golden hand... swimming in the lake... golden blood on a golden hand... healing a youngling's wound... golden blood on a golden hand...

She clenched her eyes shut and willed the flickering visions to stop. Her vision cleared, mostly, and her hearing returned just as one of the new members spoke.

"No matter how many of them we kill and no matter how we do so, the rebellion only pushes harder," he spat.

"We need something bigger, something that would devastate the beings and make them incapable of organizing," another said.

"The younglings," Tatiana said in her youngling-like voice. Once all eyes were on her, she gave them a malicious grin. "Gather up all their younglings. Then, kill them. All of them. And make a big show of it. That will crush their wills."

The faces around the table did not look at her in disgust or as if the idea troubled them. They all returned her smile and nodded slowly. There was something about the gleam in their eyes as they contemplated Tatiana's idea that felt familiar to her.

It was a madness she recognized.

One that made her feel a little less crazy, even as fresh images flashed across her vision. Even as she wanted to scream and rip her hair out as her mind faded. Even as...

...a hand on a small throat... golden blood on a golden hand... a dusty table under a shattered cheek... golden blood on a golden hand... golden blood on a golden hand... golden blood...

After the meeting, Lyra could not help feeling excited for Anin while also dreading the changes she knew were coming. The last few years had been the best of her life, surrounded by her family, enjoying their company at any time.

That was all about to change. They would no longer live in the same location; they were all going in different directions in life. Panella had become the unofficial historian for the witches and had the massive task of searching through fae history to find theirs. At least she would have Ravyn with her.

Anin and Kes were going to rule the Day Court, and there was no telling how much time they would have for the rest of them once that happened. They had a lot of work ahead to rebuild the Day Court after centuries of chaos.

Even Tyne was making her own path in life, and Lyra was both horrified and grateful that she would at least get to see her niece regularly once she became an official member of the Silent Shadows.

Life had been great. Yes, change is necessary, but that does not make it easy. Even Lyra's own path was changing; Zandar had ensured that. He squeezed his way into her life and refused to leave, staying until she made room for him.

He was taking her on their date tonight; any minute he would be there to take her to… she did not know. He refused to tell her. It was well known that Lyra did not like surprises; she liked to be prepared for everything. Zandar was one big thing that she had not prepared for and it seemed there was no going back to do so.

The door opened, and his footsteps, which she knew so well, climbed the stairs. She had stopped yelling at him for not knocking; it never seemed to make a difference, anyway.

"Lyra?" he called. She pulled on her shoes and met him in the lounge.

"Do you always have to yell?" she asked, rolling her eyes and loving the way his eyes sparkled in return.

"You do not particularly enjoy listening to me, so I have to make sure I am loud enough for you to hear." She laughed even while attempting to sigh; the effect was no longer one of annoyance.

"Goddess, help me not kill this male," she said under her breath, loud enough for him to hear.

"Come, little terror, are you ready?" he asked, holding his hand out for her to port them to wherever they were going.

"Shut up, fae-fae," she said, grabbing onto his hand.

Lyra had never been here before; she had never even known it existed. It was a tree—not just any ordinary tree. This one grew three times as tall as all the other trees surrounding it; it was likely taller than any other tree in the realm.

"How have I never heard of this before?" she asked, swinging her feet that hung from the giant branch they sat on.

"Surprisingly, not many know—not even the Night fae." He shrugged.

"Sure, but how does anyone miss it?" There was no flying by the massive thing and missing it.

"They have forgotten," he said, as if it were common knowledge.

"What does that have to do with anything?"

"Once you forget about it, you can no longer see it."

"What?" she was seriously confused.

"There is lore," he started. "Which only exists in spoken form now, after the purge. Luckily, my mother was a keeper of tales—just like my grandmother and all the mothers before her, and now, just like my sister."

"You have a sister?" Lyra interrupted. He had never mentioned a sister or any family, now that she thought about it. He was slow to nod, as if admitting it brought him pain.

"Yes, but we have not spoken or seen each other in a few hundred years—maybe more. We had a… *disagreement*, and I left." Before she could say anything, he moved on.

"So, the tree." Lyra squinted her eyes at him but let it go; he would tell her when he was ready.

"The legend says that a different kind of fae—faeries—used to live in the realm."

"Like fairy tales?"

"Yeah, exactly. Anyway, there were no courts; there was one king and queen who ruled the realm. They are believed to have been buried underneath this tree."

"I thought fae did not get buried since they turned to dust," Lyra said, confused.

"Fae, yes. Faeries? No one knows."

"What happened?"

"They had three children. The son of dark took one half of the realm; a daughter of light took the other, and the third daughter wanted nothing to do with it, creating a home in the center of the realm with beings just like her."

"That's how the night and day courts were made?"

"Not exactly. They used to call the courts the Seelie, which means happy, and Unseelie, which means—"

"Not happy?" he laughed.

"Something like that. No one really understands what happened to the faeries; the stories are mixed. There is one tale that says there was a Great War, and they destroyed each other—which, in my opinion, makes no sense. The other one is more probable."

"Wait, you believe this?"

"I do. There are many things my mother was not wrong about, including this tree."

"Something went wrong—maybe it was magic, maybe it was power, or even the land itself. But I think they went somewhere else and took half of the realm with them: half of the sun, half of the moon, and half of the land. When they left, the realm changed: one half always in night, one half always in day, and then the realm created the fae."

"Perhaps it was both," she said.

"What was both?"

"Perhaps the war is what went wrong; your story does not mention the witches."

"Apparently, they are the only constant in the realm. It's likely because of the Many Faced Goddess."

"Hmmm," she said, thinking, "I bet they did something as a punishment; witches are the ones that keep the balance."

"And they can be pretty incredible." He leaned in to kiss her just as a scroll appeared between them. Lyra unrolled it and read the message; then she read it again.

"Shit."

Chapter 49
Balthier

althier felt as if all their suffering and hard work were finally about to pay off. They had the support of all the rulers in the realm, even the King of the Night Court. Although he knew that if it were not for his mate or his cousin, he would not lift a finger.

Balthier could not care less; it did not matter to him as long as he was willing to help, and he was. While it was clear that the Silent Shadows belonged to Kes, they remained the warriors of the Night Court. Moreover, his meticulous attention to detail caught any holes in their tentative plan.

In just a few more days, he would have his mate back in his arms. In that time, his best friend would no longer be forced to give her body to any high fae who would pay. They only had to hold on for a few more days.

A scroll appeared in front of his face, and he could not explain why, but dread washed over him as he reached for it. He did not know how he knew, but whatever was written on this scroll was not going to be good. The message was written in the frantic hand of Lorella, and it was worse than he could ever have imagined.

They are coming for the younglings.

No.

It was too soon.

They were not ready.

His limbs were frozen by fear, and his thoughts were all over the place and never complete. What could they do? How could they protect their young? They are no—

Calm down, Balthier.

He took several deep breaths and reminded himself that he did not have the luxury of panicking. There was already a plan in place for an attack like this, and he just needed to go through the steps. Too many lives depended on him not dissolving into a worthless mess.

He pulled out his scroll to send messages to every faction leader, but first, he needed to send one to their queen. They could not wait to see if she came; they needed to start the evacuation.

Years ago, he created a chain of communication that spread news within minutes throughout the entire Dayless Quarter. He ran to the hut of the being who was the first link in the chain and banged on their door.

"Balthier?" The pooka's face paled at the sight of him. "Is it time?" she asked, her voice shaking.

"Yes, activate the chain: full evacuation." She gaped at him and stood frozen. "Now!" he yelled, snapping her out of the haze of fear. She nodded, and he ran to the start of the next chain. He had to deliver the same message to two other beings, and then they would handle the rest.

He watched as the fae, fear clearly written on their faces, managed to stay calm as they went to their designated locations. It was working.

When they created the evacuation plan, they knew that not everyone could escape from the same location. It would be too slow and would make them too easy to target. They decided to create several hidden exits along the barricade they erected around their entire quarter decades prior.

Once they had the plan, they tested it repeatedly until the entire quarter knew their path by heart. It paid off because he could see the fear clearly on every face he passed. They did not need to think about where they were going; their bodies knew where to take them.

They had not received a warning like the one they had just gotten when Tatiana marched through the city. They had been clueless until someone saw the golden armor glinting in the sun. By that time, it was too late. They had been lucky, and he knew they would not be again.

When he was close enough to the entrance, he could see the magical barrier already in place and fortified. It would not protect them; it would only buy them time.

He hoped time would be enough.

Her body burned with the need Kes never failed to make her feel. He kissed her as if he were dying, as if it were the last thing he would ever do. It left her gasping each time.

He moved his mouth next to her ear so that when he spoke, his lips barely touched her. It always made her shiver.

"How does my queen wish to be worshiped today?" he asked as his hand trailed down her body, grasping her breast through the wings she had wrapped around her. She sucked in air and pushed herself into his hand.

"Does my queen want my hand?" His hand skimmed down to the apex of her legs, barely brushing her sex. Gods, how could such small touches make her feel so much?

"Or maybe my queen wants my mouth," he said, licking and nipping along her neck. She could only make needy sounds that made him chuckle.

"Or," he began, grabbing her hand and placing it on the

hard bulge between his legs. "Does my queen want this?" The "s" hissed as she squeezed her fingers around him as best she could with his pants in the way.

"All of them," she gasped when he nipped her ear.

He sat back, lifted one of her ankles to his mouth, and began kissing a painfully slow trail to where she needed him most. Just as he reached her inner thigh, and she thought she might die before his mouth ever reached her core, a scroll arrived in front of her.

"You have got to be kidding me," Kes groaned. "Leave it for now. It can wait." He continued kissing, but something told her to open it. She unrolled the scroll and immediately sat up straight.

"Oh, no," she said, covering her mouth with a hand to stifle the cry.

"What is it?" he asked. She passed him the scroll, and he took a few seconds to read it. He looked at her, his eyes frantic as they searched hers for what he already knew.

"We have to go now. It has to be now, not a few nights. Now."

"Fuck."

They ported to the armory, and Kes summoned his Twenty-Three. There was no time to organize the entire Silent Shadows as they had planned. She felt the weight of time wrap around her while duty rested heavily on her shoulders. Kes grabbed her hand, and she looked up at him.

"It will be okay," he said with such certainty that Anin felt just enough of her burdens lift, and she stood tall as she looked at the assembled beings.

"There is only one possible option," she said after they

explained what was going on. Kes looked at her, confusion warring with fear.

"I need all of you," she said before locking eyes with her sister and then her mate. "All of you need to go to the Dayless Quarter. Protect them. You only have to make it long enough for me to sit on the throne."

"Where will you be?" Lyra asked. Her sister looked terrified, not for herself but for Anin. She smiled at her and hoped it would tell her that she would be fine.

Everything would be fine.

They would all be fine.

"I have a long-overdue date with my sister." She was terrified of seeing Tatiana again and wished she had more time to prepare. Although she knew, no matter how long she had, it would never be enough. Perhaps it's better this way. She has no time to think about it and play out what might happen in her mind. Maybe it was always meant to be this way, fated even.

Gods, she hoped so.

"Who is going with you?" Kes asked, even though she could feel that he already knew the answer. She knew he would not accept this without a fight, and she hated that she was going to have to order him as his queen.

She told herself over and over that everything would be fine. They would all be fine. They had to be.

Right?

"No one."

"Good, you both are here," Panella said as she and Ravyn entered Etain's study. Ciaran hated that the witches walked in freely and never knocked.

"I know where they are," Panella said excitedly before Ciaran could explain the merits of privacy to them yet again.

"Where what is?" Etain asked, gently putting down the jar she had been using for a spell. She never knew when it would become unstable and explode.

"The books."

"Finally," Ciaran said, placing the book he had just been reading on the side table next to his chair. "Leave the location, and I will go tomorrow." Panella's excitement died.

"Ciaran," Etain admonished under her breath.

"Fine," he sighed. "Was there something else?" Etain

rolled her eyes and shook her head; he could be so dense at times.

"Yes." Some excitement returned to Panella's voice. "The realm was united at one point; both of the courts and the witches worked together, and the realm was peaceful."

"Sounds incredibly dull," Ciaran said quietly to himself. Etain had to pinch her lips together to keep from laughing.

"Sounds wonderful, if you ask me," she said, smirking at her mate.

"Well, there used to be a place where they would meet. It was in the very center of the realm. Under that building will be the entrance to the location hiding your books." Panella looked proud of her find, but Etain's mate barely paid her any mind.

"That's amazing! You must be thrilled to have solved the puzzle. Isn't that amazing, my love?"

"Yes, I am beyond ready to be done with it."

"I want to go to this one," Panella said, grabbing Ravyn's hand. "We want to go, too."

"Abso—"

"That sounds like fun," Etain said. She walked to the two witches and turned her back to Ciaran. "If you show me where we can port—"

"Little witch," Ciaran growled, and Etain winked at Panella and Ravyn. They managed to keep straight faces, even as Etain saw the mirth sparkling in their eyes.

"Oh! Ciaran, would you like to join us?" she asked as she spun around and smiled at him. He sighed, stood, and squinted at her as if to say, I know what you are doing.

"Where are we going?" he asked, defeated. Panella pointed it out on the map Etain had on the wall. Ciaran barked a laugh, making them all jump.

"I know the place." That was all he said before he ported them all to the ruins in the center of everything.

"How do you know this place?" Etain asked as they looked around to take in their surroundings. Whatever had been here had long ago fallen apart, except for the bottom half of a tower that still stood.

"This is where Kes met that fae from the Day Court while Anin was missing," he said, chuckling. "I love that he thought he was being so secretive; I don't think he knows that I know."

"You never told me that," Etain said.

"Sometimes I have to let Kes think he has secrets, or his feathers will get bent out of shape; no one wants to see that level of theatrics," he said with a shrug, making them all laugh. It was funny to Etain how they acted like they disliked each other immensely; they were fooling no one.

"What do you say we split up and search for the entrance?" Panella suggested. Ciaran grunted his agreement and began to walk away, Etain's hand in his. She looked at them apologetically, and they both smiled at her and winked.

They had been searching for a while and found nothing. Not that Etain was complaining; she got to watch Ciaran pick up ridiculously large pieces of rubble. The way his muscles moved under his shirt was enticing. She bet it would be even better if his shirt—Etain ripped her eyes away from him. She needed to quit fantasizing about her mate and help him look for the entrance.

"Little witch, I need to tell you something," Ciaran said as he picked up and moved another chunk of wall that had fallen eons ago. His words were so out of character for him that she looked at him in worry; usually, he would just say what was on his mind without a preamble, or more than likely, he tended to keep things to himself. It was something they had been working on.

"Is everything okay?" she asked tentatively.

"Yes, of course. Why would it not be?" His confusion erased her worry.

"You sounded so serious that I thought something bad might have happened," she said.

"Oh, no. That would have been preferred." He was entirely serious, which only made Etain laugh.

"All right then, what unfortunately not bad thing do you need to tell me?" He gave her one of his boyish grins, still wicked and far too wide, yet playful at the same time. It was her favorite of all his grins.

"Ever since we found out about the secret society, I have been following them. I had been looking forward to an excuse to finally end their inconvenient existence. Unfortunately, you were right; until tonight, all they had done was complain, and while that is reason enough for me, I knew it was not for you."

"I am impressed that you were able to stick to following them. Well done, my love." While he might have only spared their lives because of her, Etain was still proud of him. It was not so long ago that he would have acted first and then asked for forgiveness later.

"Well," he said, and thoughtlessly rubbed the back of his neck. It was a motion he tended to do whenever he felt her praise him through the bond. He loved it, yet had a hard time accepting it. "I did come close several times to being done with it and mounting their heads—

"—on stakes in the Great Hall? Yes, we know." She laughed, and then something occurred to her. "I have been meaning to ask you. How do you do it?" she asked.

"Do what? You will need to be a bit more specific, little witch."

"Get their heads not to turn to dust." She had wondered about it when she first learned that fae turn to dust and return to the realm when they die. Yet Ciaran had a collection of heads in the Great Hall when she first arrived in the Fae Realm. It had been like a disturbing piece of art that Etain never wanted to see again.

"It's a simple preservation spell that is meant for food… but works surprisingly well on—"

"Never mind," she said, with her nose scrunched up in revulsion. "Forget I asked." Ciaran laughed, picking up a giant boulder like it weighed nothing.

"Anyway, tonight—"

"It's over here!" Panella yelled to them. "Ravyn found it."

Etain was almost certain that she heard Ciaran grumble under his breath, "I wanted to find it." She giggled as she watched him throw the bolder he had picked up just before Panella called out to them. He might be pouting, but he looked good doing it.

"What were you about to say?" she asked him.

"I will tell you later. It's nothing important, just something I wished to know your thoughts on." He wanted her opinion, something he would never have thought to ask for decades ago. Not that he did not always value her opinion, but the thought to ask would never have occurred to him.

"Ciaran?"

"Yes, little witch?" Ciaran asked, looking down at her.

"I love you," she said, wrapping her arms around his waist. Ciaran gently held her face between his hands and bent down to kiss her tenderly. He pulled back far enough to rest his forehead on hers.

"Love is not a strong enough word for what I have for you, little witch." She sighed as heat crept up her cheeks. For such an oaf, he always knew just what to say.

She fell for him all over again.

Balthier had done all he could do. Now he waited to see what would happen. He should be at his designated place, evacuating with the other Dayless residents. Yet something held him there, sitting alone with a view of the entrance.

Hope.

It had only been a handful of minutes since he sent the scroll to Anin. They would need a moment or two to gather themselves if they were coming. It was not too late; there was still a chance they were coming.

"Whatever happens, Balthier, I will always love you. I will always be grateful for your friendship," Killia said as she came to sit beside him. She reached out for him to take her hand, and when he did, she held on tight. Her grip was the only outward sign of her fear.

"Always," he said, kissing the top of her head.

"Do you think they will come?" she asked.

"Time will tell," he said. Yet, even as he spoke, the hope

he had just been desperate to hold on to began to sift through his fingers.

"Then it is a shame that time is what we do not have. I do not regret the rebellion, and I definitely do not regret making their lives miserable—even if it was short-lived." Killia was speaking as if their deaths were assured; maybe they were.

"Nor do I." The only thing he regretted was not being able to hold his mate one last time: to have his voice be the last thing he heard before they both returned to the realm.

"There they are," she said as they watched Tatiana's soldiers port just outside their quarter.

He would forever be grateful to the strange silver-haired witch who randomly showed up and put a ward over the Dayless Quarter. She said only those who needed to would be able to port in, and any who meant them harm could not. No one knew who she was before she arrived, and no one saw her again after she finished.

They had made the barrier stronger than it had been a few days ago when Tatiana arrived. They had been forced to scramble to get that one erected. He knew this one would not hold indefinitely, but maybe long enough for the younglings to escape.

Off in the distance of the city, an explosion occurred. It momentarily drew their attention away from their attack on the barricade. He knew what was in that general location.

"I figured I would leave a little farewell gift," she said with a grin.

"I hear it's better to go out with a bang," he said, and

they both started laughing. The sound grew into something that resembled madness to him; perhaps it was. Any sane fae would be trying to escape, not have a front-row seat to their own death.

"Am I interrupting something? Shall I come back later?" a voice asked from behind them. They turned around, and Balthier scrambled to stand.

"You came." It was a statement, even though the disbelief in his voice made it sound like a question.

"We did. A lot less prepared than I would have liked. Yet I have always enjoyed going up against the odds," Kes said.

"I did not think…" Balthier's voice trailed off. He kept blinking, believing it was all an illusion created by his mind.

"What he is trying to say," Killia said, "is thank you."

"Where are the entrances?" a witch with dark skin and a wild mane of blonde curls asked.

"That's the only one," Balthier said, pointing to where dozens of Tatiana's soldiers were attacking the barrier.

"Why do they not port in?" the large grey-skinned male standing next to the witch asked. Before Balthier could answer, the witch beat him to it.

"I knew you were dense, fae-fae, but even a recruit could have told you there was a ward in place," she said. Her words were clipped and contained not an ounce of kindness. Yet the two were clearly in love, or something akin to love.

"Lyra, quit lying to the poor bastard," Kes said before he addressed the grey-skinned male. "I would not have known if she had not said anything; only a witch would know the work of another witch."

The sound of something cracking drew their attention back to where the barrier was about to go.

"That's the only entrance?" Kes asked, making sure he heard correctly.

"Yes." Kes grinned wickedly, showing razor-sharp teeth in response to Balthier's answer.

"Well, things just got easier."

"No." He would not let his mate walk into the palace alone. Who knew what she might encounter? He was going with her. There was no room for debate.

"Kes," Anin began softly, "I need you to protect the younglings."

"And I need to protect you." He was livid that she thought he would just go along with leaving her to walk into danger alone; she grabbed his hand and pulled him aside.

"I know this is not what you want, and everything within you is telling you not to listen. But, Kes, I know this is what's supposed to happen. I need you to trust me —not just as your mate but also as your queen." She looked at him with pleading eyes.

"So, this is an order? You are telling me, not as your mate but as your general?" he asked, and she nodded.

He released a long sigh. He could not go against her

first order to him as queen. Not only would it be disrespectful, but it would also weaken her confidence. On the other hand, if she did not make it out of this alive, there was no point in following orders.

"Please, Kes, I need to prove to myself that I am strong enough to be queen."

Fuck.

He held her head in his hands and brought her face down so they were eye to eye. "The second I feel you are in danger, I am porting directly to you; that is nonnegotiable," he said, relieved when she nodded in agreement.

"Okay, but give me at least a second to try to take care of it myself."

"Anin, you do not have to do any of this by yourself. You are not alone, and it does not make you weak to need your friends, your family, or me."

"I know, and I do need you—all of you—but I also need to know that I am no longer broken."

"You are not broken," he whispered.

"I need to believe it as much as you do," she whispered back.

Fuck!

"Okay, you get two seconds, starting from the moment I sense you're in danger. Not a second more, Anin," he growled.

"Thank you," she said, kissing him softly. "We have to go."

"We have to go," he agreed. "I swear to the gods, Anin: if anything happens to you, I cannot be held responsible for my actions."

"Deal," she said, smiling. He took a deep breath before

turning back to the room where everyone was trying to look anywhere but at them.

"Time to go! Twenty-Three, you are with me; we are porting here." He pointed to Dayless Quarter on the map of Daybreak—the one the Day fae had left with them. "And Night fae, for the love of all things wicked, do not forget that you will drain faster and be weaker in the Day Court. Adjust accordingly," he said before looking back at Anin.

"Be safe," she said.

"You first," he replied. "Let's go!" He ported away before they could say anything resembling a goodbye. He refused to tempt fate.

They had chosen the perfect place to port. It had a clear, elevated view of the entrance. Dozens of day fae attacked the barrier, which seemed to be holding for the time being.

He heard laughter and saw Balthier—and he could not remember her name, the female with the sad eyes. They were sitting just off to the side of where they had ported and had yet to notice their arrival.

Perfect.

After a quick discussion, they learned that it was the only entrance. They could bottleneck Tatiana's Day fae and pick them off as they tried to cross into the quarter. They needed to move quickly; the barrier was going to go at any moment.

"Spread out. Give yourselves enough room to work, but stay as close to the entrance as you can. The harder we make it for them to get in, the easier it will be for us."

They spread out and formed a semicircle with him in the middle and Lyra to his right.

"Want to bet I kill more of them than you do?" Lyra taunted.

"It's nice that you think you could even come close to beating me," he said, laughing.

"Just you wait, old bird," she replied.

"You in, Zandar?" he called to the male on Lyra's right.

"Nah, I learned my lesson a long time ago: never bet against this one," he said, grinning as he pointed at Lyra.

"Ha! I like him, little chick."

"Shut up, bird brains," Lyra grumbled.

"Did you hear that, little terror? He likes me," Zandar said, laughing when she said something low enough for him to hear. The barrier gave another loud crack, but still held.

"Get ready!" he called to his team. "Night fae, what happens to us in the Day Court?"

"We drain faster and are weaker!" he exclaimed, surprised that they managed to mostly say it together.

"Do not forget: it might cost you your life." He looked each of his team members in the eye before saying, "One last thing: do not die! That's a fucking order!"

Kes should be filled with fear—fear for his mate, for his team, and maybe even for himself. Yet he was not; he was excited. It had been a long time since he had a fight like this, and he was going to enjoy every minute of it.

There was one last loud crack followed by a series of quieter ones when the barrier finally fell. There was a pause as the dust settled. Everything was silent for two whole breaths. Then there was a loud roar from the other side—the sound of dozens of voices rushing into battle. His team knew better.

They were silent; no one moved a muscle. It was not until the first several cleared the broken barrier that they began to descend on their prey.

"Lyra!" he yelled.

"What?" she asked, clearly annoyed, which only made him grin wider.

"Cluck, cluck! Let's have some fun!" He could hear Lyra roaring with laughter as they all prepared for impact. He sent Anin one last "be careful" with their strange form of communication before blocking everything out around him.

It was time to play.

Chapter 54
Raindal

Raindal walked beside Tatiana, not of his own volition, just as he had for the past few decades. She had always been crazy, but somehow, she had become even more so since she imprisoned him with her blood magic. Most of the time, he tuned her out and got lost in his thoughts or memories.

However, recently he had begun paying attention. The rebellion had finally come into Tatiana's sight and had caused enough problems for her that she planned to do the unthinkable. Younglings should never be used as game pieces. He hoped the news would spread quickly, and they could do something to protect them.

When a lesser fae turned the corner and stopped in her tracks, her eyes wide, he wanted to scream for her to run. She just stood there. Had she not heard what Tatiana had him doing lately?

"What do we have here?" Tatiana asked in a disturbing, youngling-like voice. "Have you come to play? I know a great game. It's called 'Exterminate the Vermin.'"

Raindal began walking toward the fae he knew so well; she had been one of his longest spies. He wished he could close his eyes; normally, she had him use his fire, and it was over quickly. He could tell himself that it was better that way; at least they had not suffered.

The distance between them had already closed to just a few more steps. He screamed at Tatiana in his mind to stop while he screamed at Lorella to run. The moment she was within arm's reach, Tatiana made him close his hand around her neck. When he started to squeeze, she shoved something into his pocket.

Instantly, he knew he was free of Tatiana's hold and dropped his hand. He wanted to look at whatever that was that sat in his pocket, but it would have to wait.

"Raindal!" Tatiana screamed. "What are you doing?" He did not answer her and instead turned to his friend.

"How many more are in the palace?" he asked.

"Three. They should be here any moment," she said. He nodded, and as if fate had planned it herself, the three lesser fae came from the other side of the hall. They stopped, uncertain what they should do with Tatiana between them.

"You cannot leave, Raindal! I forbid it!" Tatiana began to stomp her foot like the petulant youngling she pretended to be. Although Raindal was not so sure it was an act.

"How could you abandon me? You love me! You told me you did!" That was a statement Raindal could not ignore.

"No, Tatiana, I do not love you. Just because you make me say something while I am under your control does not mean I was the one who said it. You said it to yourself through me."

"Yes, you do!" She stomped a foot with each word, as if that would change his mind.

"No, but I do have a lesser fae fated mate whom I love with everything I am. Everything has been for him and never for you." Her eyes went comically large, and her mouth opened and closed like a fish, but no words came out.

"Come on," he said to Lorella, and grabbed her by the hand to run past Tatiana. Just as they neared her, she reached out to grab him. He put up a shield of fire, burning her hand. She screamed and then sobbed, holding her already healing hand to her chest.

He wanted to burn her to a crisp, but his power was already low. He also did not know whether the blood magic would somehow keep her alive. Either way, he was not sticking around to find out; he had a mate to find.

The moment they reached the other three lesser fae, he grabbed on to all of them and ported everyone to the Dayless Quarter. The last thing he heard was Tatiana screaming at him to come back.

He had expected that when he ported to the Dayless Quarter, the place would be relatively calm. Instead, they were in the middle of a crowd of lesser fae, all moving hurriedly toward the back of the quarter. In the opposite direction of his mate.

Balthier was at the entrance, where any minute they would face dozens of Tatiana's new, ruthless soldiers. With no one to protect him.

Raindal had not been able to protect his mate for decades; he would not fail him again. He pushed his way through the crowd and then ported to where the bond pulled him. Balthier was never going to stand alone again.

That, he promised.

Chapter 55
Tatiana

"**M**y queen, the Night Court has arrived in the Dayless Quarter," one of her new, blood-thirsty council members said.

"They dare interfere in my court?" she seethed. "How many?" She was going to port to Nightfell immediately after this nonsense was taken care of. She would show them what happens when you interfere in others' business.

She bet Ciaran would think twice if she took that Walsh witch he had stolen from her. If she sacrificed her, Tatiana would have more power than she knew what to d—

... pulling on pants... golden blood on a golden hand...a hummed lullaby... golden blood on a golden hand... a ripped bodice... golden blood on a golden hand... angry-faced younglings... gold—

"My queen?" Tatiana blinked several times.

"What?" she snapped.

"What would you like us to do?" the male asked, concern on his face. She did not know if he was concerned for her or about her, but either way, she did not appreciate it.

"I asked you how many Night fae there were," she said. How dare he demand answers from her when he could not answer even the simplest of questions?

"Around twenty, as I told you several minutes ago," he said, the look of concern growing.

... a hand petting her head... a flash of—no... racing up a tree... a flash of—no, no, no... small arms wrapping around an ample waist... a flash—Stop! She refused to look... a fla—

"No!" she screamed, and the council member jumped.

"No, to what?" he asked, confused.

"Nothing, I was not speaking to you," she spat. The male slowly nodded his head.

"And your orders?" he asked, sounding frustrated.

"You will remember to watch your tone, or you will never do anything again," she said in that low voice that she hated. It made her dislike the male even more.

"Yes, my queen," he was quick to say. She stared at him for a while, waiting until he began to shift on his feet. Then she shifted her face back to the happy Tatiana.

"Twenty Night fae," she sang. "Weakened and losing power by the minute. It should not take long to get rid of them. Send everyone! Squash them! Let's see how fast this can end!" She smiled at the male when she finished her song. Her smile began to fall, and she cocked her head to the side.

"Was that not a good song?" she asked.

"What? Oh, yes, it was wonderful," he said and smiled at her.

"Then why are you not clapping?" she regarded him for a minute, as if he thought she might be making a joke. When she did not say anything else, he began to clap and did not stop until she raised her hand.

"Thank you. I am so glad you enjoyed it." He nodded at her again.

"Shall I go give the command to send everyone and end it before it even begins?" he asked her with a vicious grin. Maybe she did not hate this male after all.

"Yes, do it now."

"It's a mistake," the *whispers* said. She had been ignoring them as much as she was angry at them.

The male nodded and left the room to issue her command. She was alone; well, she was never truly alone. The *whispers* were always there.

"You are making a mistake yet again," they chided.

"No, I am not! You just wait and see!" As soon as they saw how quickly those Night fae were returned to the realm, they would beg for her forgiveness. Then they would take her to gain more power. She knew they were just testing her.

"Time and time again, you refuse to listen." What did they mean? She listened to them all the time. Perhaps if she had not—

... Tatiana in a field of flowers begging herself to hold on just a little while longer...

She shook her head. That had been different from the other visions. That one felt real, and she did not like it.

"*We have no use for a failed queen,*" they said.

...Tatiana in the same field telling herself to just let go; she can let go...

"You said you would never leave me!" she cried, receiving no response besides the fading echoes of their unsettling laughter.

They had promised her. She remembered that now. In the beginning, they had promised her. Yet, just like everyone else, they were gone; they had abandoned her.

No one wanted her.

Chapter 56
Ciaran

The stairs they descended were not unlike those under his archives. Both had an obnoxious number of steps and spiraled. Why did they always have to spiral?

"I cannot wait to see what waits for us at the bottom of these stairs," Panella said excitedly. Her enthusiasm only annoyed him further. He would have preferred to come alone.

"Do you think there will be historical artifacts?" Panella asked. When Etain cleared her throat, she realized that she was asking him.

"How should I know? I have never been down here either."

"Ciaran," Etain admonished under her breath. He sighed, then stopped to prevent them from continuing down the stairs.

"Look, I do not know what will be there. The temples held nothing but a stone box with a slip of paper. What I do know is that the temples hid traps meant to kill—not maim. So when we get to the bottom of the stairs, you should all wait so I can ensure it's safe." He cared only about Etain; however, she cared about the other witches, which meant he was supposed to as well.

"You never told me it had been so dangerous," Etain said.

"Are you worried about me, little witch?" he asked, teasing her.

"I always worry about you, mostly about your poor decision-making skills," she replied, laughing.

When they finally made it to the bottom, Ciaran inspected the hall of things. He cringed, knowing Panella's reaction to the place would be... enthusiastic. He almost wished he had found a trap of any kind so he could tell them it was too dangerous and that he would find the books and meet them back at the top.

Unfortunately, he found nothing, and if he tried to tell them he had, Etain would know he was lying immediately. He did his best to mentally prepare for the shrill sounds he knew were about to come from Panella before he gave the all-clear. It turned out there was no preparing for the screech that left her mouth and echoed throughout the long hall.

The walls had been built with warm-toned stones. The never-ending fire illuminated the space, making everything look nearly golden. He absolutely hated it. Golden tones were the bane of his existence. There was a reason any gold in Nightfell would be difficult to find: he much preferred dark stone, and if things had to be lit with the warm light of fire, at least the black would offset it and spare his eyes.

As if that were not enough, the walls were covered in hundreds of paintings and shelves of old books. It was going to take forever for Panella to get to the other end of the hall. He was tempted to go on without them. Then Etain eyed him, making it clear she knew what he was thinking. He sighed and looked around for a place to sit and wait.

He hated waiting.

Two golden statues sat on either wall, facing each other. One was of a female with long, flowing hair and a large crown on her head. Her rounded ears made it clear she was not fae—a witch, perhaps. The other was of a fae male, also in a large crown. The statue had wings similar to Ciaran's, and he thought it was the one redeemable quality of the horrific statue.

"Ciaran, this one looks like you," she said as she studied the face more closely. "He even has a mouth like yours."

"I assure you, that gaudy thing looks nothing like me," he said, disgusted at the thought of being compared to that travesty. Etain turned away from the statue to look at him, then promptly laughed.

"Oh, my love, nothing could ever compare to you," she said in a joking tone, but he could feel she meant it.

"Look at this," Panella said. Ciaran was surprised that she had quieted. Apparently, she was not capable of studying the objects while speaking. He was incredibly grateful.

"What is it?" Ravyn asked.

"It's a painting of the realm. At least that is what the shape of the land looks like; however, it's not the realm at the same time." Ciaran hated that his interest peaked. He went to stand next to her and looked for himself.

"There is no Day or Night Court, but I see what you mean. It's our realm, just not as we know it tonight," he said.

"What does that say?" Ravyn asked, pointing to the word at the bottom of the map.

"You cannot read it?" Ciaran asked, stunned. Witches stored all their past languages in their blood. If their ancestors spoke it, they could, too.

"It says 'Faerie.' What a strange word," Etain said. When they all looked at her, that beautiful red flush filled her cheeks. "I don't know how I can read it." She shrugged and turned back to look at the strange map.

Everything looked unfathomably old, yet the further they went, the newer things appeared—comparatively newer. Even the newer items looked older than anything Ciaran had ever seen.

"Oh, look, here is the realm we know. Well, at least the land is divided in the way we know," Panella said, more than halfway down the hall now. Maybe she would not take as long as he originally expected her to.

This map was nowhere near as old as the first one and yet it was nowhere near new either. It showed half the land in night and half the land in light. There were a multitude of cities he had never heard of everywhere, but nowhere did he see Nightfell or Daybreak.

"Look how many cities there once were in the center of the realm," Etain said from beside him. "It almost looks as though the Day and Night fae cohabitated." The thought alone made a shiver roll through him.

"It must have been some form of punishment," he said. "I can think of no other reason the two courts would want to share a space."

"What if their fated mate was from the other court?" Etain asked him.

He wanted to deny that ever being a possibility, yet his cousin had to go and disprove his argument before he could even make it. Ciaran made a noncommittal noise. He still thought it must have been some kind of punishment. Etain just laughed softly and shook her head as she laced her fingers with his, continuing a slow path toward the end of the hall.

When they reached the end, it opened up into a cavernous room. There was just as much stuff, if not more, lining the walls. However, the one thing none of them could help but stare at was the stone statue of a very large beast.

Ciaran had never seen anything like it and wondered if it had once roamed the realm. If it had, he was not sad to have never seen one. While spectacular, it was not something a fae would want to encounter alone. It was so large and far beyond his wildest thoughts. Ciaran could say only one thing, and it was not something he said often.

"Wow."

Chapter 57
Tatiana

"Please come back. Please," Tatiana sobbed. "I promise I will listen." She slid to her knees before her throne to beg the unseen beings.

"I will do what you say." She could no longer hold herself up right and fell over with her forehead to the floor.

"Please." Tatiana's words were full of desperation, even as her voice grew weaker.

"Please come back."

"Please, do not leave me alone." Her voice shook, and the last few words came out a mere whisper as she voiced her greatest fear.

There, lying on the floor, Tatiana had a thought: maybe if she proved to them that she could be powerful, she could do it. She could find more power on her own. Maybe they were just testing her; they promised not to leave her.

That's what it was, she decided—a test—all she had to do was pass it.

They will come back.

They have to come back.

They promised.

She slid back up to her knees, dragging her hands along the floor. She blinked several times before she could see through the haze of tears. One big, deep breath later, with a large smile plastered to her face, Tatiana knew what to do.

She would get them back; she would not be alone.

She was alone.

...a sobbing youngling, Tatiana, crouching in a corner with a blanket wrapped around her...

No!

That was not her!

She was not alone.

It was a test—nothing more.

There was only one way she could impress them enough. One way she could guarantee their return. She had to get all the power.

Every last drop.

Tatiana sent her power out, casting a net as far as she could, which admittedly was not as far as it used to be. She took all the high fae in the palace, every single one in her dungeon, and any stragglers she could reach just outside the palace. Once she held them captive and made them slaves to her will, she called them to her.

Every last drop.

Pass the test.

Pass the test.

Pass the test.

She knew they were watching her; they had not really left her.

It was only a test.

They had not left her alone.

Alone

Alone

Alone

...pleading with her eyes to her mother to save her... her father, too deep in his cups to pay attention to her distress... white wings blocking out the sun... golden blood on a golden hand...

She blinked as her knife went through another Day fae; the line before her was not nearly as long as she would have liked.

Pass the test.

Pass the test.

They will be back.

She will not be alone.

Alone

Alone

Alone

...youngling Tatiana and her friends climbing trees... youngling Tatiana swimming in the lake... a hand gripped too tight around her wrist... a heavy arm draped across her shoulders...

Another Day fae dropped dead before her. Bodies piled all around her. Multiple colors of blood swirled and mixed into new ones, yet no power filled her. Just like everything else in Tatiana's life, power abandoned her.

No.

Something was not right; power was still within her. She refused to admit how little there was. She would get more.

Pass the test.

More power.

Alone

Alone

Alone

... golden blood on a golden hand... hold on... golden blood in a small puddle beneath her wrist... hold on... glass breaking beneath her cheek... let go...

It was not working. She could not understand why she

did not feel the power burning through her veins. She was forgetting something, but what was it?

She needed to think.

There was no time to think.

She needed more power.

Alone

She needed to be wanted.

Alone

There was only one faceless Day fae left. One more sacrifice. One last chance to be enough.

Strong enough.

Alone

Powerful enough.

Alone

Just…enough.

Alone

She just wanted—no, needed—to be enough for even one being. She looked at the last fae that remained, and suddenly she could not breathe. Something snapped in her chest—something she should never have had again. They shared a gasp as realization dawned on them both.

"Thatcher?" Tatiana asked. Confusion and something else she could not name—wonder, perhaps—cleared her thoughts. It calmed the storm raging within her. The small voice she had neglected in the back of her mind for longer than she could remember was too loud to ignore any longer.

"Tatiana?" he asked, just as confused as she was. Yet the only other expression she saw on his face was horror. For the first time, she looked down at herself and saw a rainbow of death dripping from her. She thought it beautiful, even when she knew now it was anything but.

"I—I do not understand," she whispered to the male. She truly did not. Mate bonds only happen once in a lifetime; she had already had a mate, right?

A thought—one she had forgotten she ever had—danced across her mind: a memory, not a vision, of a desperate search in the archives; a way to save her from the thing she knew to be wrong.

Reminold.

That did not make sense; they had been happy. Flashes of what followed their mating ceremony—no, their bonding ceremony—assaulted her. She did not want to remember *that*. She never wanted to remember *that*.

It was not real.

It was not real.

It was…

real.

A sob escaped her. She reached out to the male she had raced up trees with countless times as a youngling, but then saw her hands. She did not want those hands to touch him.

"What…?" he said before pausing to collect his thoughts. His eyes slowly softened to her, and what she felt through the bond was everything she had ever wanted. He reached out and brushed a blood-soaked strand of her golden hair away from her sticky face.

"What happened to you?" he asked her. His voice was full of sadness, and it took Tatiana a moment to understand that it was for her.

He was sad for her.

The walls she had constructed around her true memories crumbled. They were not kind to her; each one was a knife in her already tattered heart. She tried to shove them back in, but she was hemorrhaging memories with nothing to help slow the deluge.

Pain.

Images of suffering sped by, yet not fast enough for each one to tear her open further. Suffering that had been caused not only by the male who had somehow faked the mate bond, but also by the fact that those meant to protect her never once attempted to do so. The agony of her parents' betrayal threatened to suffocate her.

She thought she was going to be sick.

Her eyes met his. She felt tears flow down her face—tears for the life she had willingly forgotten the day she gave herself over to the lies in her favorite field of flowers. The land had told her to hold on, to be strong. She had not been. It was too hard to fight alone, and she had been so very alone.

"Too much," was all she could get out with her tear-choked voice; it had barely been audible. Speaking those words acknowledged the truth of her past.

The truth of her own betrayal.

"We could have had a beautiful life filled with love and laughter." She felt the truth of his words.

"We still can," the words came out as a plea rather than the statement she had intended.

"No, Tatiana, it's too late for you—for us," he said, grabbing her hands. She wanted to pull them away to keep him from her filth; however, she was selfish and craved the touch of her true mate.

"No," she sobbed. "Please, I can be a good girl. I will be. I promise." Her words came out in gasps as dread wrapped tightly around every inch of her.

"Not in this life. You have done too much," he said with a gentle voice, and smiled sadly at her. "Perhaps in the next." He raised a knife—her knife that he had somehow slipped from her grasp—to his throat and sliced deeply into it.

"No!"

Chapter 58
Anin

Anin waited until Kes and his Twenty-Three had been gone for several minutes. She hoped they would steal all the attention. Knowing her mate, it was a strong possibility. Besides, an audience was not necessary for her to take her throne.

Her throne.

It was a strange thought that had always seemed out of reach. She had not even wanted to reach for it—not until Tatiana made it impossible for her to have a simple life. Contentment for her would have meant living out the rest of her nights with her family. Now, she would not get that.

Her whole family resided in Nightfell, and after tonight—*today*—she would live in Daybreak. She knew it was silly to feel sad about this. Porting took a second at most. Moreover, now that witches had their own form of it, none of them would be more than a second away.

There was something about sleeping under the same roof as them: knowing they were breathing the same air and walking the same halls, the possibility of running into one of them at any given moment. The little things were the ones that were going to change.

Anin checked the map one last time, committing it to memory before she ported to the side entrance of the palace. According to the information they had received, it was the least used. However, if someone did come, chances were it would be a lesser fae. Just as they had promised, there was no sign of life anywhere near the door she opened.

When she stepped over the threshold, the door shut behind her. It was the door closing on the life she could have had—the one she had been living. The clanging of the door vibrated through her with a sense of finality. Without looking back, she took her first few steps toward the life she was destined for.

It was eerily quiet in the palace. While she hoped not to run into a single being, she expected to hear them, at the very least. Life had sound; even in silence, and no one knew that better than Anin.

Following the route from the map, she turned down the hall and opened the third door on the right. It opened to the sideboard room, and she knew that if she took the door on the left, she would be in the dining room, which was just as empty as she was beginning to think the entire palace was.

She stood with her hand on the knob of the door and took several deep breaths. It led into the main hall that would take her directly to the throne room. Perhaps no one would be there, and she would be able to take her throne without any fuss, although deep down she knew that was where her sister would be.

Tatiana.

Just the thought of her made Anin's breath come faster. She truly did not know how she would be able to see her, face to face—she stopped. She had not considered the possibility that Raindal would be with her.

A big part of her wanted to run to Kes and let him fight every battle for her, just as he had offered. Yet, she knew she could not. If she were unable to look her tormentors in the eyes, how would she ever feel worthy of the crown?

No, she had to do this.

She had not truly taken note of the piles of dust she passed in the halls. It was not until she got closer to the throne room that she noticed the piles everywhere. They were impossible to miss. She knew what they were: the remnants of dead fae. She could not help but wonder if they would still be alive had she come sooner.

She was nearing the final junction between her and the throne room when she heard them: footfalls. Someone was coming. There was nowhere to hide, no doors close enough to sneak behind.

Shit.

Stay calm.

Anin readied her vines and raised the shield Kes had taught her to create. She hoped it would be enough. It would have to be.

When the fae came running around the corner and saw her waiting there, he stopped—momentarily stunned.

It was just a couple of seconds, and Anin intended to use them.

"Stop," she said, putting up a hand. "Leave, and do not come back," she added. She would rather not harm anyone, and she definitely did not want to kill another living being—no matter if they supported her or not.

The more she looked at him, the less of a threat she thought him to be. He seemed terrified, and she did not think it was her mere presence; something had happened.

"She—I just—she did not see me," was all he said as he sprinted past her. Anin could only assume the 'she' he spoke of was Tatiana. She did not blame the male for wanting to get as far away as possible; she wished she could do the same.

When Anin stood in front of the large, gilded doors that led to the throne room, she stopped. This was it. Once she opened that door, there was no going back. Although she thought she never truly had any other option—not when fate had already decided for her.

Her heart raced, the beating pounding in her ears. A few deep breaths later, she calmed herself—well, enough, at least. She listened to the room beyond the doors, hoping to hear it empty of life.

It was not.

She heard Tatiana speaking softly to someone. When no response from another voice came, she relaxed. At least she only had to face one of them.

She could do this.

She was stronger than her past.

She was a queen.

Placing her hands on the knobs of both doors, she

went to shove them wide open. If she was going in there, she might as well make an entrance. She smiled. Kes would be so proud of her theatrics. Anin took one last deep breath and pushed on the doors with all her might.

She could not breathe.

She gasped for air, but none filled her lungs. How was it possible? Oh gods, why had she not listened to Kes? She did not understand how it could have happened. Somehow, Anin was back in her cage at the temple as Tatiana massacred dozens of fae.

No, not again.

Not after everything.

She could not do this again.

Darkness seeped into her vision from the edges.

No…

Chapter 59
Kes

ozens of Day fae stormed through the broken barrier, their elemental magic flying. They were sloppy; Kes could tell they had never received any formal training. These were just bloodthirsty fae who enjoyed hurting others.

But so did Kes.

They all wore the cockiness of someone who had already won. One fae caught his eye and grinned at Kes as though he were personally going to take him down. He laughed at their false sense of security. Numbers could not compete with skill—a fact they were about to find out.

When the Twenty-Three launched their attack, it was just before the mob of Day fae came within range. Explosions went off alongside the elemental attacks, all at once. That was when the Day fae's inexperience showed.

Chaos erupted all around them, while the Twenty-Three continued their assault. At some point, the Day fae would finally push through, and they would be forced to fight up close and personal. However, for the time being, it was fun to watch them scramble.

Kes caught the eye of that same fae. Just moments ago, he seemed so sure of himself. Now, his eyes were wide with terror. Kes gave him the same grin—the difference was that he meant it and could deliver.

He pulled the wind toward him before he began to spin. He had not had the chance to use this technique in a while. Once he had built the cyclone up to the perfect strength, he gave the signal, and all of his Twenty-Three hit the ground before he stopped and flung his arms wide. A blade of wind cut through the entire first wave of Day fae.

"Little chick," he called. When she did not respond, he called even louder. "Little chick!"

"What?! Can you not see I am busy?" she asked, sparing him a quick glare.

"Yeah, yeah… but did you see it?" he asked. He loved to harass her while they fought. It always made her take her anger out on whoever was unfortunate enough to be in front of her. Kes found it hilarious.

"How could I not? Hot blood gushed over me, followed by a poof of dust." He could practically hear her rolling her eyes.

"A poof of dust? A poof? What is that? Some kind of unit of measurement?" he asked, verbally poking at her again.

"Yeah, it's how I'll be measuring you soon if you do not shut the fuck up," she promised. Kes roared with laughter.

"Hey, Zandar?" he called to the grey-skinned male next to Lyra.

"Nope. Are you trying to get my balls cut off? I know better than to anger the little terror," he replied. His tone suggested he did not actually know better.

"You both are going to figure out exactly what a poof is if you do not stop harassing me." She looked over at Kes, her eyes widening. "Look out, bird!"

Kes spun around to see absolutely nothing threatening coming his way. Lyra cackled. "You should have seen your face!"

They all laughed as they continued fighting. Everyone he saw had smiles on their faces. Well, the Twenty-Three he saw. The Day fae looked only terrified. Was it in bad taste to hope that they were saving the better fighters for later? Even if it was, he silently wished for it. This was a bit too easy for him.

Easy or not, Kes was having a great time. That was until he felt it; he stopped dead in his tracks, his wind dying around him.

Anin.

Chapter 60
Raindal

Raindal was desperate to find his mate. He followed the bond and let it lead him to Balthier. The moment he sensed he was close was the same moment he had to start fighting other Day fae to reach him.

There were so many of them, and his brows lifted when he spotted the black-feathered wings he recognized anywhere. If Kes was in the Dayless Quarter fighting for the lesser fae, did that mean Anin was…

No, he would not allow himself to get his hopes up. He had been disappointed so many times and was not willing to feel that again—not when his mate was somewhere close. The bond made it feel as if he were standing next to him.

He followed the pull to a side alleyway. Several Day fae were laughing as they strolled carelessly down it, which meant they did not see who they were stalking as a threat. Balthier.

The bond confirmed it, particularly when the panic

began to filter down from him. There were five of them and one of him, and he doubted they had spent the last few decades locked in their minds under the control of the queen—often forgotten and with very little food the entire time.

He was weak.

It did not matter.

He snuck up behind the five fae, and before they knew he was there, he threw his fire at them and ported in front of Balthier and Killia. There was no time to say hello. Two of the five turned to dust; however, the three remaining were enraged.

Raindal was getting very close to the bottom of his well. He threw more fire at them and put up a wall of flames blocking their path. One of them used their wind to step through, leaving it open for the others.

He engulfed the one with wind in flames. The moment his attention was diverted, the wall of fire closed and consumed the third member of their party. The two remaining began throwing their wind and water at him, and Raindal was forced to use his power to put up a shield. Every time they weakened his shield, he depleted his well a little more.

If this came down to who could outlast the other, they would win. He needed to end this before it was too late. He threw fire at them incessantly while coaxing flames to ignite beneath them. Everything he did, they deflected, and every second, his power drained a little more as he kept the shield up.

Finally, one of them missed his attack while putting out the flames of the previous one and immediately turned to dust. With one more to go, Raindal liked their odds even more. If his power had not been overused, this would already be over.

Just another reason to despise Tatiana.

She used his power, his magic… his body as she pleased. It did not matter to her if she never let his well replenish. The only time it had a chance to fill completely was if she happened to forget about him for an extended period.

He could not help but think of Anin in those moments of solitude. Had she also been relieved to be left alone yet filled with dread, having only her thoughts to keep her company? He felt disgusted by the things he was forced to do to gain Tatiana's trust while also putting him in a position to be in contact with Anin.

He would never have been able to reach her had Tatiana not wanted him there. She would still be there had he not known how to break the spell on the hall. He would never have found out had Tatiana not felt comfortable enough to confide in him.

Wind against fire: which would win? The male's shield was strong, and none of Raindal's fire was breaking through. His power—nor his magic—was going to win this fight for him. There was only one other option.

He had just enough power to port one more time. He gave no indication that he was about to move. He threw fire at the male's face to distract him and remove Raindal from his line of sight. Raindal ported just behind the male, wrapped his hands around the side of his head, and twisted. He pulled as hard as he could, and the head came off, turning to dust in his hands.

"Raindal!" Balthier yelled. Raindal was mildly aware that he was swaying on his feet and that his well had one single drop left. The moment his body used it to heal the minor cuts he had received was the moment he would be forced to sleep.

"Hello, my love. I—" Just as he feared a wound healed, he felt himself tipping forward. Two strong arms caught him. The last thing he saw before his eyes were forced closed was Balthier's beautiful face.

At least he got to see him again.

Chapter 61
Etain

"Is that a dragon?" Etain asked as she stared at the giant statue before her. When no one said anything, she looked at each of them, wondering if they had heard her.

"A what?" Panella asked after a few minutes.

"A dragon. Is that one?" Etain asked again.

"We do not know what a dragon is, little witch," Ciaran said. She was surprised that the Fae Realm had never heard about the fabled beasts.

"In the Human Realm, there are tales about these large, winged creatures with reptilian features. Apparently, they were notorious for stealing sheep and other livestock. There are also a few cautionary tales of villages that were demolished, and even some about humans being carried off.

One of my favorite stories is about this town that happened to be next to a dragon's den. The story goes that they would leave daily offerings to this dragon in exchange for it leaving the town alone. For hundreds of years, several generations kept the tradition alive, and the town became wealthy from the rich soils they farmed freely and the abundance of livestock, which was often used as the offering.

Well, after hundreds of years of cohabitating peacefully—"

"The dragon came and attacked the town?" Ciaran asked. She did not think she had ever told him a tale in which he was this captivated.

"No," she said, laughing. "A new leader of the town was appointed, and year after year, he became less generous with the offerings. The town used to give the fattest of its livestock when they were poor, and now it was giving its thinnest when they were at their richest."

"Figures, a human would do something so arrogant," Ciaran mumbled.

"So what happened?" Panella asked.

"The dragon flew down from its mountainous cave and gave them one full day. By the next night, they better have given their best offering, or he would end hundreds of years of peaceful coexistence."

"What did they offer?" Ciaran asked. "I would have just given it a few extra sheep; the creature was obviously not greedy."

"Well, as reasonable as that sounds, the leaders of the town were not. They decided to get rid of two problems at once.

You see, there was a woman who lived on the edge of town. She was not well liked by most of the townsfolk and a little too well liked by the male population. She rarely left her little cottage unless it was at night, just to avoid the unwanted attention."

"Ahhh, now I see why this is your favorite story, little witch," Ciaran said. He was not wrong. She loved this story, but this next part, along with the parallels between the woman in the story and Etain's life in her village, always felt familiar.

"Shush, you," she said, swatting at him playfully. "So, you might have already guessed, but the townsfolk went to this woman's cottage just before sunset the night the dragon's payment was due. They broke down her door and pulled her out by her hair while she kicked and screamed the entire time."

"Males," Ravyn scoffed, and they all laughed when Ciaran looked offended by the insinuation that he was anything like the males of the story.

"Well, they dragged her up the mountain to the place where they always left their offerings. The woman had never stopped fighting the whole way and managed to get a few good kicks in, bringing some of those men to their knees.

Once they reached the right place, a few hooks were driven into the stone for them to tie their offerings to. They tied her legs and arms in such a way that she made the shape of an X. The men patted each other on the back for a job well done and then turned to make the long trek back down to the village."

"Bastards!" Panella said angrily.

"They had not made it more than a step when the woman spoke. 'You will live to regret this! Mark my words!' They all thought nothing of it and even laughed as they disappeared from her sight.

The woman was exhausted. She had tried her hardest to get away. She never gave up, but in the end, it did not matter. Even though she wanted to cry and scream her rage simultaneously, she stayed silent. She would not give them the satisfaction."

"Impressive. Again, I see why you like this story," Ciaran said, grinning his too-wide smile at her.

"Well, the sun set completely, and the woman was unsure if she would freeze to death or if the beast would eat her first. She did not have to wait long to find out."

"Etain, if after all this the woman dies, I will be very sad," Ravyn said.

"Just listen," she sang to her friend. "The sun had not been down for more than an hour when the beast arrived. Or at least she thought she heard the sound of the dragon landing behind her. However, it was not a dragon that came to greet her. It was a man."

"Ohhh, I think I know where this is going. If you like this story, remind me to lend you a few books," Ravyn said, winking. Etain felt her cheeks redden.

"This man asked what she was doing tied to a mountain, and she looked at him as if he had grown another head. Then she said, 'Oh, I just thought it seemed like such a beautiful night to tie myself up. You should really try it sometime.' The man laughed and then offered to help her free herself, which she, of course, gratefully accepted.

He asked her again how she wound up there, and she told him the whole horrible story. She was so mad at herself when she let a tear drip down her face at the end of her tale. The male reached out to brush it away, and she nearly groaned at the heat that came from his hand alone. She was still freezing, after all."

"Etain, is this one of *those* stories?" Ciaran asked, looking at her suspiciously.

"I have no idea what you mean. Anyway, the man put his arm around her, and his heat chased her chill away. He offered to let her stay at his place for the night so that she would not have to climb down the mountain at night. She was wary of the offer, but she really had no other choice, nor did she plan to return to her village.

The man took her to a cave not far away, and her worry turned to alarm. 'You live in a cave?' she asked him. He smiled and said, 'Yes.' She felt her heart racing as she said, 'And you are very warm.' He smiled and answered the same way. She swallowed hard before saying, 'You arrived at the platform at the same time as the…' She feared asking her next question. 'Are you the dragon?'

The man laughed and said, of course he was, and she threw her hands up and yelled something about making it all the easier for him to eat her. Then she yelled at herself for being so stupid to just go along with him. Then he said," she paused and looked at Ciaran with a smirk.

"'While I would not mind devouring you, it is not in the way you are thinking,'" Etain said, saying the words in as deep a voice as she could.

"I knew it," Ciaran grumbled, which only made the three witches laugh.

"Needless to say, the woman was speechless and still freezing, mind you, so she may or may not have let him… warm her up."

"In more ways than one," Panella said, starting another round of laughter. Ciaran groaned.

"What happened with the village?" he asked, clearly trying to move past that particular part of the story.

"Well, the dragon was obviously not going to eat the woman. He had not been eating any of the offerings—well, at least not him alone. He had been taking them back to his people, several mountains over. The idea that they would offer a human woman to him, assuming he would eat her, was offensive, and what they did to her was criminal.

He went to the village with her flying on his back the very next day. She looked every single one of those men in the eyes while she pointed them out and said, 'I told you that you would regret it.' I am sure they did, but no one truly knows because in the next moment, the dragon had those human men for a snack."

"That's respectable," Ciaran said. He would think the dragon eating the men was the best part.

"What happened to the woman and the dragon?" Ravyn asked.

"Oh! Well, he took her back to his den and—"

"That's enough story time," Ciaran said.

"I will tell you all when we get back. I had no idea Ciaran was so… sensitive." She squealed, laughing, when he growled and tried to grab her. She stepped closer to the statue in the center of the room, and Ciaran stopped in his tracks, looking terrified. It was not an expression Etain could remember seeing him wear before.

"Etain, walk slowly back to me." His tone was too serious to think he was joking. The second she was a few steps away from the statue, Ciaran sped to her and then back to where Panella and Ravyn stood. Their eyes were wide and jaws slack as they stared at the center of the room.

"What—oh," was all Etain could say, because at that moment the statue in the center of the room was lifting its head—no, its six heads. What they had thought was stone was actually blanketed layers of dust. When the dragon shook its heads, dust went flying everywhere, revealing the red scales beneath.

It stood to its full height, and then all six of its heads snapped to look at them right before each head let out a roar so loud that the stone walls shook. Etain was certain of only two things.

Dragons were real.

And they were in big trouble.

Chapter 62
Tatiana

"No, please no," Tatiana begged, whoever was listening, as she fell to the floor with Thatcher. She wrapped her hands around his wound in an attempt to slow the bleeding. His eyes pleaded with her to let him go, but she could not do it.

"I can heal you," she said to Thatcher, the idea dawning on her just then. It had been so long that she had nearly forgotten it was the magic she had been born with.

She could save him.

Excitement filled her, only to instantly fade away. She had forgotten, like she had so many other things, what she had just read a few days ago: the cost. Blood magic stole her innate magic and depleted her well of power every time she had used it. A blanket of cold fear draped over her, the weight of it crushing.

He was fading. She could feel the slowing of his body. His blood was turning sluggish, and his once beautiful bronze skin was paling. She could not lose him.

Could not be alone.

Could not—

She reached for the once-familiar magic within her, the magic that had healed him once when they were younglings—something she had only just remembered. The magic that was so similar to blood magic, yet was on the complete opposite spectrum. Two sides of the same coin: one for good, the other for... she did not want to finish that thought.

She found a kernel of her natural magic; it was all that was left. It had once felt endless; it had been endless, but had been whittled down by her to nothing but a mere crumb. She gently reached for it, hoping it would be enough; it had to be enough.

Please let it be enough.

When she held it firmly within her, she used all she had left to heal him.

She pleaded with her magic to do this one last thing for her, begging fate to give her another chance. She would do anything—anything, if she could have just one year, one month, one day, one hour, or even one more minute of true happiness with him.

"Hold on, please hold on," she cried. She squeezed her eyes shut and willed that small remnant of the old Tatiana to be enough—just let it be enough.

Just let her be enough.

Please.

She felt a hand briefly brush against hers.

Please.

She opened her eyes, and a wail came from her— a sound she hadn't been aware she could make. The devastation and agony that filled every crack and crevice of her being had culminated in a sound of anguish. It began deep within her and built as it ripped its way out of her.

It was not enough.

Tatiana dropped herself over her true mate as he took his final breath. The bond within her burned away, leaving nothing but a husk of a female behind.

How could fate have been this cruel? She gave her a true mate, but also gave her to Reminold. The bond she had with him could not compare to the bond she had just lost. She could not decide whether knowing the truth was better or if never knowing would have been.

He would rather kill himself than spend one more second with her; he would rather be dead than be her fated mate. He—

He did not want her.

The mate bond had not been enough.

Her magic had not been enough.

She was not enough.

Never enough.

Chapter 63
Lyra

"Kes, stop fucking around," Lyra said. He had been acting like a fool the entire time; honestly, though, when was he not? He thought it was funny to stop and freeze in place.

Dumbass.

Without the wind circulating around him, the Day fae saw their opportunity to close in. Knowing him, this was exactly what he was hoping for. Any minute, he would shoot his wind out and do something gross, like cut off all their heads while using a preservation spell.

Disgusting.

When they got too close to him for comfort, she felt as though something was wrong. He was there, alive, and not actually frozen in place. Yet he was entirely focused on something she could not see. There was only one thing —or being—that could distract him this intensely.

"Kes! What is it?" she yelled as she began to fight off the fae that were far too close to him for comfort. Zandar came to help her, and with Kes not fighting and the two of them out of formation, things were bound to take a nose-dive soon.

It turned out to be much faster than she anticipated. One fae went down and turned to dust, while another looked very close to the same fate. They must have under-estimated the drain the Day Court would put on them. Their magic was weaker on this side of the Borderlands, while their power began to drain the moment they stepped foot into Day territory.

Good thing witches did not have to worry about that; they were carrying the fight, even as their supplies started to dwindle. Sometimes it's a slow descent when you fall from the top; others sneak up on you, and out of nowhere, you are on your ass. This was like the latter.

Lyra looked around at their team just as the first witch fell. She looked where the now crumbled barrier was still pouring Dae fae. The odds were suddenly beyond the scope of outnumbered and leaning more toward over-whelmed.

"Where are they all coming from?" she asked Zandar, loud enough for only his fae ears to hear. "I do not know, but I was just wondering the same thing. She must have sent every single fae she had at her disposal." It made sense; kind of. Actually, it was rather dumb.

By being more concerned with attacking them and killing the lesser fae, she left herself completely unpro-tected. Good news for Anin. She hoped. Based on Kes's face, she was not so sure. He looked like he was about to port at any minute.

If he left, there really was no hope for the rest of them.

They needed him to snap out of it if they were going to have even the smallest of chances to turn this around. As if mocking her, she saw another Night fae fall out of the corner of her eye.

Lyra looked at Zandar. He was still going strong, even though she knew he was wearing thin. His grey skin shone in the sun with perspiration. She should have let herself fall into him decades ago. At least they had the chance to go on a date; she wished they could have more magical moments like that one.

Another Night fae fell, and it did not feel like it would be much longer until they all did. They could port away, she supposed, but she would never leave Kes undefended. Not only did she reluctantly love the bird, but if he died, her sister would die. Lyra would never be willing to let Anin die in her place.

No, they were going to stay, and they were going to fight till the very end, no matter what that looked like. She thought she saw Kes stir out of the corner of her eye, but she did not have a moment to glance behind her.

"Hey!" Zandar called to her. "We are not dying anytime soon, little terror, so get that look off your face and be the badass witch we all know you are."

"Shut up, fae-fae," she said. She straightened her spine, and they moved back to back. If she would die, she was going to make it as difficult as possible.

Chapter 64
Anin

Anin was spiraling as memories reared their ugly heads one by one. It was a never-ending montage of violence at the bloody hands of Tatiana. There was always so much blood, which was not surprising considering her moniker: the blood queen.

Throats opened, pouring blood.

Fresh wings mounted to the wall.

The cries for mercy.

Tallon.

She squeezed her eyes shut and felt down the bond. It never lied. Every time she had an attack, Kes told her to feel for the bond. They had happened frequently and for such a long time that she was no longer aware of when she did it.

Kes was there, waiting for her at the other end, as he always was. She could feel the concern and fear he had for her; that was real.

He was real.

The fear that gripped her so tightly she could not

breathe started to loosen. It took a couple of tries, but eventually she was filling her lungs and releasing the air slowly. She counted her breaths until they came steadily on their own.

You are free.

You are strong.

You are not broken.

You are a fucking *queen*.

She opened her eyes, and the visions were no longer there—not gone, just put away back in their place. There was no hiding them; she had tried that, and it had not ended well for her.

Now she knew that to acknowledge them was to conquer them. Everyone wore the proof of their past—both good and bad—like invisible garments that only the heart and mind could see. There was no removing them, and there was no avoiding them. If you did not figure out how to wear the worst, it would always overshadow the best.

She knew that now. It did not mean it was always easy. Each time she woke, the ugly beast of her past was there. She looked at it, studied it even. Eventually, looking at it was no longer terrifying—mostly. There would always be times when the beast would win.

It had been the blood that set her off—a kaleidoscope of colors painted the white marble floor. It was horrifically cheerful, considering the medium. If it were not for the dozens of dead bodies—not dust—she might have been able to pretend it was paint. However, there was no pretending the smell away.

In the center, where all the blood pooled, was Tatiana

—her tormentor, her sister. She was draped across the body of a male, whispering nonsense to him as her body shook from the quiet tears Anin barely heard. It was not until Anin made it halfway across the room that Tatiana became aware of her presence.

She screamed at her—words Anin could not understand. When Anin only stared back at her, she tried to get up. She refused to let go of the male's hand still woven with hers, which made it an impossible task. All she managed to do was slip around and then fall back into the puddle of blood around her, screaming the entire time.

"I would have loved you," Anin said. Tatiana quieted and beheld her with wild eyes full of pain. "I would have been your best friend. We could have been a family." Tatiana blinked at her several times before she lay back down on top of the male.

Anin wondered briefly who he was and if Tatiana even knew she was lying on a dead body. She turned her back and took three more steps before she heard the soft plea.

"Please, help him," Tatiana sobbed. Anin had never seen her cry, and her voice sounded so different from the strange, high-pitched sing-song voice. She wondered if it was her true voice.

"Please."

Against her better judgment, Anin approached Tatiana. Her throne was right there, waiting for her. Yet she walked away from it and toward her sister. She told herself it was for the sake of the body lying on the floor, not the female who stroked his face gently. The closer she got, the better she could see the tears that left clean tracks on her bloody face.

Tatiana never took her eyes off the fae on the floor. Anin might not know who he was or what had happened, but she knew Tatiana had loved him—as much as she was capable of. Anin took one look at the male and knew for certain what she had already suspected.

He was dead.

His eyes were open and unseeing. No blood spilled from his wound. His chest never rose and fell with the effort of breathing. The only movement the male made was the hand Tatiana gripped.

"He's gone," she whispered, terrified of how Tatiana would react. She need not be. Tatiana collapsed on top of him again with a massive sob. Her pain was so visceral that Anin could not help the tears that sprang to her eyes. She did not want to feel for Tatiana, and she did not think her tears were for the bloody queen; they were for the sister she could have had.

"It was him, not Reminold. I was not enough. He did not want me," Tatiana said the words into the male's chest so quietly that Anin was not sure she heard her correctly. Not that it mattered.

Anin turned away from the strangely heartbreaking scene before her and closed the distance to the dais. The last time she stood at the base of the steps, it had been after Tatiana threw her down them.

She had surprised herself with the amount of strength she was able to muster to stand back up—even more so when she made it up each step. In that moment, she had been a peek at the Anin she would become.

The Anin she had become.

The Anin who picked up the shattered pieces of herself and reassembled them into something new.

The Anin who climbed the stairs and finally sat on her throne.

Chapter 65
Kes

Something was wrong; fear and panic gripped Anin as she felt her body shutting down from sheer terror.

She was clearly in danger, and Kes was having a hard time respecting her wishes to give her a moment to fight her own battles. He would not be able to port directly to her, not with the ward that Tatiana had placed on the palace. How long would it take for him to port to an entrance and race to find her?

Would it take too long?

Was he willing to take the risk?

He was deciding which entrance was closest to where she was, based on the map of the palace he had memorized. She was near or in the throne room, and one of the main doors was just down the hall. He was just about to port when he felt her.

She was feeling down the bond, searching for him frantically. The moment she felt him, the panic that had been all-consuming seconds before loosened its grip slightly. Something had triggered one of her attacks.

He was incredibly proud of her. Even a year ago, she would not have been able to work this quickly. She did exactly as they had practiced.

She felt for the bond, knew that whatever she was seeing could not be real, and then began to count her breaths. He could feel her calming more with every second, and Kes could finally breathe, knowing she was not in immediate danger.

From the moment he felt her fear, nothing else existed. The entire realm around him disappeared. He gave her his undivided attention. If she needed him, he wanted to ensure he went to her immediately. Even a single second could be too late.

That was why, when the chaos around him came back into focus, he found himself surrounded. Lyra and Zandar were overrun as they tried to be a barrier between the flow of Day fae and him. The surrounding fae had been attacking the shield he put into place at the start of the battle, and it was cracking. It would fall at any moment.

The moment it fell, the circling fae closed in on him. "Well, shit. I hate to break it to you, but none of you are my type. I know rejection can be hard, but there does not need to be any hard feelings," he said to them. When all else failed, his mouth never did.

He pulled wind to him as fast as he could use it, never able to gather enough to make a large enough impact. He sent wind cutting down on the one fae that seemed determined to drown him. Without waiting to see the outcome, he turned and blew the flames that had nearly charred him into another. The second that fae caught fire, the spikes of land that had forced him to dance around the edges of the tightening circle stopped.

While he fended off attacks and attempted to return his own, he tried to take stock of the rest of his team. He glanced around in time to watch three Night fae fall to dust almost simultaneously. Several more looked like they were not far behind.

Lyra and Zandar were back to back; Lyra threw her pouches and cast her spells, while Zandar created a barrier of fire around them, lobbing more at any fae that got too close.

Zandar was doing his best to conserve his power and mostly used the large ax in his hand. Considering the several piles of dust in front of him, he had already claimed many heads. It did not seem to make a difference; the skill with which he handled his ax and the speed at which Lyra cast her spells while throwing her staff around did not prevent them from being surrounded by as many Day fae as Kes.

Things were not looking good for them.

In a matter of seconds, things had turned drastically for them. If it came down to it, he would abandon the fight and find his mate. He would not risk her life for the sake of his pride.

Kes took one last glance at Lyra; he hoped he would be able to get her out alive as well. Anin would somehow blame herself, and he did not think she could survive the loss of her sister.

He was not certain he could either.

Chapter 66
Ciaran

G*reat.*

Naturally, a giant beast slept in the center of the underground archive. How foolish of him to think the challenge had been simply finding the place.

No, of course not.

"We should get out of here," Panella breathed.

"We should, but that's going to be a problem," Ravyn said nervously.

"What do yo—" Ciaran started, sighing when he saw a stone door slide the last inch into place, trapping them with the very angry beast behind them.

Great. Just great.

"Etain, in all your dragon stories, do any of them say how to defeat one?" Ciaran asked calmly. He did not know how, but they were getting out of there alive. He refused to have any other outcome.

How hard could it be?

"No, not that I can remember—Ciaran! Watch out!" Etain screamed as one of the six heads got too close to biting him. It reached out at them, snapping its massive jaws.

"We have to figure something out—and soon!" Panella said as the beast stepped toward them. It would help if he had any idea of what exactly he was dealing with.

"I have shadows, and most of my power would require me to be near it." He studied the dragon, absorbing everything he could. It was huge, but slow. The small space hindered both it and them.

"Ciaran, I swear if you get anywhere near that thing—" Etain squeaked, jumping out of the way of a snapping head.

"We are pretty much useless without supplies," Panella said regretfully. He had already assumed they would not be much help.

"Ciaran," Etain warned, as he stepped toward the beast.

"I have an idea," was all he said. The next time one of the heads came close enough, he shot out his shadows and sliced the head from its neck. The dragon screamed as the head bounced across the floor.

One down, five to go.

"I do not think that's going to work," Ravyn said, her voice trembling slightly. Ciaran looked to see what she saw and wanted to curse whatever god was responsible for creating something so ridiculous. The neck from which he had just cut a head was regrowing it at record speed. All he managed to do was make it very angry.

Very angry.

"Shit," he said, speeding around the beast as more heads snapped at him. Perhaps there was another way out of the back of the room.. He was not hopeful, but it was worth checking.

Just as he thought, there was only one entrance and exit to the space. Where the creature's body was slow, its heads were incredibly fast and agile. One nearly caught him, even at his top speed.

"Etain, can you hold it with your colors?" he asked. A plan formed quickly in his mind.

"I can try!" she called over another deafening roar. Blue and orange flowed from her, twisting and braiding together in an intricate pattern. Once she got it just right, she sent it toward the dragon.

Blue and orange wrapped around the red, scaly necks and twisted down the beast's body, wrapping around its legs. He could see the strain it was on her to maintain her power. The dragon roared and fought against her hold, causing Etain to grimace.

"Ciaran, I do not think I can hold it for much longer. It's too strong," she cried.

He did not wait a moment longer and shot out again with his shadows, making them razor-sharp. If he cut off all of their heads at once, that had to be the end of it. He knew of no beast that could live without a single head. His shadows arced and sliced through all six necks easily. Blood poured from the headless necks. Ciaran expected the creature to collapse at any moment.

He now knew of one beast that could live without a single head. Not even a second after all six heads bounced across the floor did new ones grow to take their place. If he thought it was mad before, it had nothing on the rage rolling off of it.

Etain was close to losing her grip on the beast, so he had to make this one count. He formed his shadows into a sharp tipped point and aimed at where he guessed the heart to be. Where his shadow blade had no issues cutting through its neck, his spear could not penetrate the scales.

Fuck.

Every second his little witch held on to the dragon was a gift. One he did not want to waste. He thought of another option, but nothing viable came to him when Etain screamed.

No!

Chapter 67
Tatiana

Tatiana laced her fingers with Thatcher's cooling tones. She could do nothing but sob over the dead body of her true mate—the future she had been meant to have. Cracks deepened in her mind as images of what could have been plagued her incessantly.

... Thatcher sitting next to her in the throne room, smiling at each other as the Day fae made their requests...

She did not want this life. She had made a mistake centuries ago, and now she paid the price. Her power was gone—every drop. The well could hold nothing. Her magic... her magic had been consumed by the blood magic.

...Arms wrapped around her, and happiness lit up her face. She was well and truly loved...

Magic that she could no longer use, even if she wanted to—which she did not. She did not want to feel blood magic ever again. Yet there was no escaping it.

...Meeting Anin for the first time and feeling overjoyed at finally getting the sister she had always wanted...

It was everywhere in her—in every pore, muscle, and bone in her body. It consumed everything good in her, leaving only the living corpse she had become. She rotted a little more with each passing second.

...waking in Thatcher's arms after a few hours of sleep that had come only after they had exhausted each other with pleasure...

Something stirred within her—something she had been feeling awaken for days. Something was coming for her.

...sitting on their thrones for the first time and being declared the true queen and consort by the land...

Tatiana did not want to be there anymore. She did not want to exist. Yet somehow, she knew that if she raised the knife to her own throat, the blood magic that had infused her body would never let her go.

It did not even let the dead go. Their bodies had to be burned to return to the realm. The knife, now several inches from Thatcher's body, was somehow responsible for the death and preservation of so many.

She wanted to go back to a time when she was truly happy. Had a time like that ever existed?

...standing across from Thatcher at their mating ceremony, knowing she could do anything with him by her side...

She wanted to hide in that dark place in her mind—so deep that she could never find her way out. She had done it to a different version of herself; she could do it again.

...Thatcher seeing her standing next to Reminold just a few short years after she had given up in the field of flowers. Yet she had not given up; she held on tight to her promised future. Their eyes met. She was struck by something far more powerful than the weak link Reminold had been masquerading as a mate bond.
She was finally free of him—especially when Thatcher killed him on the spot. When their mate bond snapped into place, he felt everything she had endured. The Land had not lied. If she held on, all her hopes and dreams would come true.
She was safe...

She was not safe. She needed to lock herself away, somewhere she would never emerge from again.

The Tatiana meant for Thatcher had died centuries ago. Born from her ashes was the Tatiana he could not bear to be mated to.

Had there ever been a Tatiana meant just for her?

She felt her mind fracture as she sifted through memories, looking for a time when she had been happy, stopping on one she had long forgotten.

Yes, that will do.

Her mind broke open completely—a gaping abyss to the nothing she desired. Tatiana did not hesitate; she jumped and let the darkness swallow her whole.

She smiled.

She was finally safe.

Chapter 68
Panella

E tain tightened her web of colors around the dragon; Panella had never seen her look so determined. Her hair stuck to her face, now damp with perspiration. She sent even more of her color power to wrap tightly around the regrown heads of the dragon.

Each woven rope of color gripped tightly as the beast thrashed, attempting to break Etain's hold. The blue seemed to glow brighter as it wrapped tighter around the dragon. Panella could hear Etain's grunts as her feet slid across the floor; still, she did not relent. Her feet slid faster toward the dragon just as one of its heads broke through her colorful net.

Etain released her hold on the colors just as Ciaran grasped her around the waist and pulled her back toward the far wall. Panella sighed in relief. She had dived for her queen, even knowing she would never make it in time. She never thought she would thank the Goddess for

Ciaran's existence.

"I do not think that will work," Panella said, admittedly stating the obvious. Ciaran glared at her, and she held her hands up in surrender. "I only meant the physical attacks. It seems impervious to it."

"What if we used the weaver?" Etain asked him. He looked at the amulet around her neck, seeming to weigh their options. Panella did not know what other options existed.

"We never really know what is going to happen, and I don't think several shadow Ciarans are going to help us in this situation," Ciaran said.

"Do something else," Panella said, earning herself another killer glare from Ciaran. "Try mixing different color combinations with his shadows."

"That takes time," he growled at her.

"I do not think we have any other options, my love," Etain said. It always amazed Panella how Ciaran immediately calmed whenever Etain placed one of her small hands on his arm.

"Fine, let's try it," Ciaran grumbled.

Etain threaded her violet and orange through the amulet while Ciaran sent his shadows. Before they could see what came of it, they both had to jump to separate sides to avoid the snapping jaws. The room shook as the dragon took another step forward.

They tried again, and this time they were successful; the colorful shadow swirled around the dragon, inspecting it—only inspecting it. At least it distracted a couple of the heads as they tried to snap at it.

"That's not very helpful," Etain scolded the darting

shadows of color. "I do not know what combination to try." She looked up at Ciaran, worry creasing her brow.

"Try them all," Panella said, and before Ciaran could land one of his chilling glares at her, she added, "Ravyn and I will distract as many heads as possible." She looked at her chosen mate, and she nodded her head with determination.

Panella knew that Ravyn was feeling just as useless as she was. They needed to contribute, and if decoys were all they could do, then that was what they would do.

"All right," was all Ciaran said.

"Ravyn," Panella said the moment Ciaran and Etain began trying a new combination, "I think we are going to have to split up. I will go to the left, and you to the right."

"Agreed; maybe throw whatever we can at it," she added, and Panella forced herself not to cringe. These were all relics from a past that none of them knew anything about; however, getting out of there alive was far more important.

"Be careful," she said before giving Ravyn a hasty kiss. One of the heads was about to go for Ciaran and Etain again. Just then, a book went flying and smacked the head before it got close enough to do any damage. It whipped its attention to Ravyn, so Panella began screaming and jumping.

"Hey, you ugly beast!" she screamed. All six of the dragon heads turned to Panella and glared. The look was oddly feminine, as if the dragon were offended that she had called it ugly.

A new combination of shadow and color shot toward the dragon. This one seemed to be hurting it somehow, but not enough to be anything more than annoying to it. However, between her, Ravyn, and the new shadowy colors, they were keeping it busy and away from Ciaran and Etain.

More books and shadow color combinations joined the fray. Panella was starting to think they might just figure it out when she saw Ravyn go flying. She smacked into a wall and slid down. The whole thing happened in no more than a second; it was the longest second of Panella's life. A few seconds later, Panella was unsure whether she had a life worth living anymore.

Ravyn did not move.

Chapter 69
Anin

"I have been waiting for you, Queen of Light," a voice that was not really a voice said just after a bright white light engulfed her the moment she sat on her throne. *"This was not how fate originally planned. However, when gods play with things they do not understand, it's always fate that must correct its mistakes."*

She wondered, if fate hadn't wanted this, then why had it happened? Fate always gets what it wants. So, fate must have wanted everything to happen just as it did.

"Ah, that's where you are wrong. Yes, fate gets what she wants in the end. Yet the journey is never a guarantee. Fate can only react when other forces change a being's path. One being can change the fate of many."

Anin did not think that was fair; it was selfish and harmful. Why should others pay the price for a single being's choices?

"Maybe so, but life is rarely fair. Not even fate can control the sands of time and is constrained by its rules. There are only so many paths available for each individual, and they all inter-

sect with other's paths, creating a complex web of life. When one path is removed, every other path that touches it is changed.

None of that matters for the here and now. What's done is done, and that has placed you—Anin, daughter of the lesser fae, sister of witches, and keeper of light—on the throne as the true Queen of the Day Court.

It has been a long time since the realm has been united, and even longer since a son of night sat on a throne of light."

Anin took a shaky breath. It was happening. She already felt the weight of responsibility and duty sink into every pore.

"The light has always been within you, waiting for this day to come and set it free. The power you have always felt just out of reach is that of sunlight.

Only once in its existence has it allowed a fae to access it before taking its throne. It heard your plea for the young witch and answered."

This was the power she had never been able to call on again, the one that spared Tallon a brutal end that no youngling should ever face. That was who had been listening.

Her power.

"Yes. Nothing like that has ever happened before, and I do not think it ever will again. Powers choose their keepers, and sometimes they regret their choices; others connect to their keepers on a deeper level, like yours."

Powers are sentient? That was something she had never heard before.

"Of course they are. Power, like everything else, cannot be created without something to create it from. Just as it cannot be destroyed, only changed."

What creates power?

"That is the question," was all it said in response to her thought. *"Now, your gift."*

She was shown a vision of herself pulling a ball of pure sunlight from the sky that detonated on impact. The power was too big to be used more than once. She wondered if it could only ever exist once or if it would take her entire life force to use.

"Balance always demands payment. Nothing is free, no matter how big or small. There is always a price, and someone must pay it."

She knew that better than most. She had paid the price for Tatiana her entire life. She had chased Anin out of the court she called home, hunted her incessantly, and then tortured her just because she could.

"Your life has not been easy, but neither was hers. Circumstances can fundamentally change a being; her price has been paid."

Anin could not see how Tatiana's debt could ever be paid, but who was she to decide such a thing? She glanced to where she still lay draped across the body of an unknown male, covered in death. She nearly looked dead herself; the only indication of life was the rise and fall of her chest. Yet Anin thought that perhaps Tatiana had died and left the creature before her behind.

"Death can come in many forms and sometimes it's welcomed. What makes life, life? Is it the basic needs of a body or is it the life that the being within lives?"

It was a good question, one that Anin did not think had an actual answer. She had not felt alive for the decades upon decades she spent in her tiny cage, even while she still breathed. There were a few times she had been weak enough to welcome death if it had come looking for her.

"There is greatness within you; all you have to do is rise to meet it. You are a cornerstone of the future, Queen of Light. Shine brightly, especially when things are darkest."

The voice that was not truly a voice that had filled her mind only moments before, left; however, not before it showed her a vision of herself sitting on the throne with a crown of pure light adorning her head. It was as if the sun rose behind her, casting its rays into the twisting shape she now wore. It was beautiful.

She looked beautiful.

She looked powerful.

Mostly, she looked anything but broken.

"Help me pull him in," Balthier said to Killia, indicating the door a few yards away. She grabbed his feet while Balthier lifted him under his arms.

The homes of the Dayless Quarter were insubstantial. All it took was one shove with his shoulder, and the door opened easily. Hiding in the empty hut would do nothing but keep them out of sight. If anyone discovered them, nothing would stand in their way.

"How long do you think he will sleep?" she asked.

"I have no idea," Balthier said, half paying attention to her and half watching what he could of the fight at the end of the alleyway.

"I have never seen a fae exhaust their power before." She picked up his hand and let it drop like a sack of rocks. "Huh. He really is out cold."

"Unfortunately," he mumbled. It was hard to see from the angle he sat, but he thought he saw a Night fae fall.

"Can you see anything?" she asked, sitting beside him.

"I am not entirely sure what I am seeing," he answered honestly. "It looks like…" He was terrified to say it out loud.

"Like?" Killia drew the word out as she looked at him.

"Like they are not going to win," he whispered.

"Shit," she whispered back, wrapping her fingers around his.

"I think being on this side of the Borderlands is weakening them more than they realized. It looks like mostly Night fae are falling." His eyes were scanning for black feathers, and did not find them.

"I really thought we had finally done it when they showed up. We were finally going to be free," Killia said. Her voice was sad, as if she had already assumed defeat. Balthier did not blame her. Hope was a dangerous thing to possess in the Dayless Quarter.

Finally, enough fae parted, and he caught a glimpse of Kes. He was surrounded, the numbers heavily skewed against him. He moved faster than Balthier thought possible, yet it felt like he was just slowing the inevitable. Every time a Day fae fell, three took their place. When a Night fae fell, there was no one to replace it.

"I thought so too," Balthier finally responded. He glanced at his sleeping mate, wondering if he would have the chance to wake. It was better not to wonder.

He looked back through the crack of the door and watched the scene unfold at the end of the alleyway. He was just in time to see another Night fae fall. There were too many of them. At least, no matter which way the day went, he would be free.

One way or another, he squeezed Killia's hand; they would all be free.

Chapter 71
Kes

At least half of the Twenty-Three had fallen. Kes took in the unfolding situation. He did not like what he saw.

They were more than outnumbered—odds he typically found exhilarating. However, he could see that the remaining fae were nearly depleted of their powers and were fading quickly. He hated that it had come to this, but they needed to fight another day, better prepared next time.

Just as he was about to call for a retreat, a blinding white light encompassed him. Time became sluggish, and the fighting nearly stopped. It still continued, but at such a slow speed that it was almost comical.

Every being around him looked toward him, not really seeing him through the bright light, with similar expressions of surprise slowly forming on their faces. Everyone looked surprised except for Lyra, who looked at the light with pride, knowing it meant Anin had taken her throne.

Her sister was a queen.

His mate was a queen.

"A prince of night you were born, yet a king of light you were always fated to become. Even in the dark, you have always held the light. Moonlight and Sunlight are the original lovers. Their power is pulled together by a force stronger than fate. Day and night, moon and sun, they are the perfect balance."

Kes had no idea what the voice—one that was not really a voice—was talking about. Was it a metaphor for him and Anin? A sound he could only interpret as a laugh echoed through his mind.

"In a way, yes, but mostly no. You are the keeper of the power of moonlight, your mate is the keeper of the power of sunlight. Fated mates or not, you would have been drawn together. The moment you both were chosen, fate wove you together in her tapestry of life. Better to embrace the choices power makes than to go against them and fail."

The way they spoke of powers made it seem as if they were their own entities; that he was simply a vessel they chose to inhabit.

"No, not a vessel. A partner. You were chosen by your power, yes; however, by choosing you, your power gifted itself to you. There is no power without the fae, and there is no fae without power. Balance."

He wished the history lesson would end. Although the fighting slowed dramatically, it still continued, and he was surrounded by more fae than he could count. His Twenty-Three were still dwindling, and he did not like the odds against Lyra and Zandar.

It was not looking good.

"You are the true King of the Day Court, and you hold the

power of moonlight within you; your well is nearly bottomless. Use it," was the last thing the strange not voice said. It sounded an awful lot like it was laughing at him.

The moment the light vanished, time resumed its natural speed. Several minutes passed by in the span of mere seconds. The light had been enough of a distraction for him to call the wind to him faster than ever before. He kept building more wind within him as it mixed with something new, changing his wind in a way that felt unfamiliar yet right.

On instinct, he spread his arms wide beside him; his fingertips nearly touched the fae surrounding him. He brought his hands together in front of him, and the moment they clapped, a deafening boom sounded. It sent a shockwave of wind, lit by a silver-white light, that turned the fae surrounding him to dust while knocking everyone further off their feet.

The odds were now more in their favor; Kes and what was left of his Twenty-Three demolished the remainder of Tatiana's forces. Once it was obvious to everyone who was going to win, the remaining Day fae fled.

Lyra stood before him, covered in blood and dust, with her hand on her hip and her head cocked to the side as she looked at him. Finally, she sighed and shook her head.

"You are going to be even more insufferable now." It was not a question, but a statement.

"You say insufferable; I say... kingly." Lyra groaned while Kes and Zandar laughed.

"As I said, insufferable." Lyra shook her head at him

again before she stared at something above his head, grinning.

"What?" Were his feathers in a riot from the fighting?

"Ohhh, nothing. I just like your adorable, shiny little hat," she said, cooing as if she were talking to a youngling babe.

Kes had forgotten that the land had likely given him a crown of its own making; the grin he gave her was one of the wickedest in his repertoire.

"Oh no," she said under her breath, and looked at him, already cringing. He placed his fists on his hips and puffed out his chest while turning his head to look toward the sun. He knew he had achieved the desired look when Lyra groaned again.

"I think I look rather regal. Perhaps I should try more poses?"

"Goddess, save me," Lyra grumbled, making Kes and Zandar throw their heads back in laughter. They would mourn the loss of their members later; until then, they let themselves be happy.

They had won.

Etain

Etain gasped as she watched her friend collide into the wall. Her heart pounded at the sight of her friend's limp form, and Ravyn made no attempt to move.

"No," she whispered.

"Little witch, we need to concentrate. The sooner we take care of our little dragon problem, the sooner you can help your friend," Ciaran said, grabbing her under the chin and forcing her gaze away from Ravyn to look at him instead.

He was right; she knew he was, so she did her best to push her still friend out of her mind and to focus on their task. She could hear Panella yelling obscenities at the dragon while calling out to Ravyn.

No. She could not think about that.

"I do not know what combination we have not tried

yet," she said, trying and failing to keep the panic out of her mind.

"All of them?" Ciaran asked.

"At once?" He nodded. She did not see how it could hurt. She began pushing all her colors—except for her green—into the weaver as Ciaran fed it his shadows. They watched them all form together, and then... nothing?

Oh no.

She watched as the blob began to pop and hiss. She knew what that meant and lobbed the mass of power at the dragon just as it exploded. It did nothing but daze it for a few minutes.

"You did not add your shade to it," Ciaran said. "Try that next time."

She was reluctant to add her shade to any combination of powers, especially when Ciaran's shadows were involved. They had never been able to create the same results twice, and it was very volatile. However, she did not see any other options at that point.

"Okay." She fed all her colors and asked her shade to join as Ciaran sent his shadows in once more. This time, when their powers mixed, the mass acted on its own. It sped toward the heads of the dragon and made it so confused, the dragon's necks wove together.

It did not last long. The mass began to bubble out, and then, a moment later, it exploded. This made the dragon shake its heads and forced it to take time to untangle its necks.

"What are we missing?" Ciaran asked. She was not sure. They had tried every combination... no, they had not.

"Shadows and shade," she said excitedly. She felt in her bones that this was the correct combination. Ciaran seemed to feel the same. He nodded, and one of his wicked grins stretched across his face, never ceasing to make her heart stutter.

She asked her shade to come out once again, and it readily agreed as Ciaran fed his shadows through the weaver at the same time. Hopefully, it was the last. What came out did not look like much; if anything, it just looked like a smokier version of his shadows.

They watched with bated breath as the smoky shadow rose to where the dragon's heads were finally untangled. It broke off into six puffs and then disappeared through the dragon's snout.

The dragon shook its heads and huffed out several breaths, as if it were trying to expel the substance. The heads roared, and the beast began to panic. It swung its head and took confused steps forward and then back.

A choking noise came from the heads as, one by one, they began to recede into the dragon's body that was also shrinking. Within moments, the dragon was no taller than Ciaran, and when the heads were only a few inches away, they melded into one.

No one spoke as they watched in disgust as the dragon's body began to bubble. Etain feared it would burst, so just to be safe, she hid partially behind Ciaran.

It did not burst, however. Its shape transformed, and just as it fell to the ground, it shifted into the shape of a woman—a very dead woman. The body rapidly decayed until all that was left was a pile of bones.

"Ravyn!" Panella screamed as she ran to her mate.

Ravyn had still not moved, and Etain was starting to grow nervous. "She's alive," the words came out with a sob.

Panella placed her hands on either side of Ravyn's head and closed her eyes. She had the color pink, which Etain was entirely envious of. Healing injuries and illnesses had always been very fulfilling to her.

Within a few minutes, Ravyn's eyes flickered open, and Panella pulled her into her arms and held her tight. Etain's eyes watered when she saw Panella shaking as she silently cried into her lover's neck.

"It's okay; I am okay," Ravyn repeated several times as she made calming strokes on Panella's back.

"I would like to get the fuck out of here, so if you two are fin—"

"What he meant to say was," Etain said, elbowing Ciaran in the waist, "We are very happy that everyone is okay. If you two are ready, we should find a way out of this room and go home." She elbowed him again, and she heard him sigh, just like he did every time she made him mind his manners.

"Yeah, sure. Whatever my little witch says." She laughed softly as he pulled her into him. Whatever she said, indeed.

And he better not forget it.

Kes ported to the main entrance of the palace that now belonged to his mate. He walked to the throne room and threw open the doors. The sight of her sitting on her throne, with sunlight shining upon her, stole his breath. He had always found her beautiful, yet at that moment, she was stunning.

His feet carried him to the bottom of the dais below her. He did not need to instruct his body to move; it was always pulled to her in a way that he neither could nor wanted to control.

Kes fell to his knees and looked up at his mate. She smiled at him as tears gathered in her eyes. He could feel her pride in herself and in both of them. It was an accomplishment she had thought impossible, yet there she sat upon her throne.

"I have always been willing to get on my knees for you, my darling nymph," he said, lowering his voice before adding, "My queen." He would gladly spend the rest of his life serving her in whatever way she might need. Her face heated as he sent her images of all the ways he intended to serve her.

"Kes, please stand. You do not ever have to kneel before me, bow, or do any of that nonsense."

"I do not know, Anin. I think it could be fun to kneel between your legs while you sit on your throne," he said with a devious smile.

She laughed softly and reached for him, inviting him to sit with her. He placed one foot on the bottom step and noticed her eyes moving to something in the back of the room. When he turned and saw Tatiana sprawled on the floor, covered in a riot of colorful blood as she petted the face of a dead male, he could only think of the promise he had made to kill the bitch slowly and painfully for everything she had done to Anin. Without further thought, he moved to do just that.

"No," Anin said. Her voice was calm, steady, and commanding. She sounded so sure of her decision, yet he could not comprehend it.

"Why?" he asked, rage making his voice rougher than he had intended as he attempted to kill the bitch with his look alone. The need to have her neck in his hands was visceral, and it took every ounce of self-control not to ignore Anin's command.

"I am not her," she whispered. He turned back to Anin and felt her need for him through their bond. In a few seconds, he was up the steps, scooped her up, and spun them so she sat on his lap as he held her.

"Of course you are not her. You could never be her even if you tried," he said, staring into her eyes as he pushed the truth of his words through their bond. She smiled and nodded almost sadly before her gaze returned to Tatiana.

"I had craved death—hundreds, if not thousands, of times. Each one of them denied. Death is an escape; she does not deserve to escape. However, I refuse to treat her the same way she treated me."

"Why?" he asked, baffled. "You have every right to and should." After all she had done to Anin, he could not understand how she could not want to get her vengeance.

"Maybe I do, but just because I can does not mean I should. I will not be another ruthless queen," she said, leaving no room for argument in her tone. He could not decide if he was proud of her or furious; that bitch deserved her reckoning.

"I am also not sure *that*," she said, indicating the fallen queen, "is the same Tatiana any longer. The Land told me she had paid her price to maintain the balance. I do not know what that price was, but the Land knows far more than the rest of us. If it says her debt has been paid, I believe it."

Kes found it hard to believe that, after all Tatiana had done, there was even the possibility she could ever have paid her price. Even if she paid it over the next ten lives, it would never be enough; she could never pay for what she did to his mate enough.

"Look," Anin said, watching the mess of a female on the ground. "That pain she wears is real, and it does not matter if someone deserves a lifetime of pain; I would never wish it upon them." He knew she could never; her kindness knew no bounds.

"I would," he grumbled. She placed her hand on his cheek, and he shifted his eyes to hers.

"There are parts of everyone's stories that we will never know. I think hers might have been particularly horrific to create the monster she was."

"She's still a monster," he growled. He would never think differently of Tatiana.

"Maybe," was all she said. They both watched the disturbing scene before them. The blood that covered Tatiana was drying, cracking along the lines created as she moved. She sat there, rocking the dead male's head in her lap as she hummed a lullaby. "Disturbing" might not be a strong enough word.

Kes was certain it was all an act, and he refused to trust her for even one second. His mate might believe it and be far too forgiving and good-natured to do what should be done, but he was not. While he would never go against Anin's wishes, he would keep a close eye on Tatiana. The moment she played her hand, he would be there to end her.

They watched her for a little longer, and Kes could admit that there was something wrong with her, beyond what they already knew. Who was the male in her lap? Was he someone to her, or just a body filling a role in her disturbing production?

"What the fuck is she doing?" The more he watched, the more disgusted he became. "What's wrong with her? Besides being a crazy bitch?" he asked. Anin was silent for a long moment as she thought about the female who should have been a sister to her.

"*She* is broken."

Ciaran was both exhilarated and enraged after fighting the dragon. He loved every minute of it, except for the fact that his little witch had been in danger the entire time; that was unacceptable.

He knew Etain was more than capable; if it had not been for the two of them being there, that dragon would not have been defeated. The combination of his shadows and her shade had created—*something*.

They had never been able to create the same results twice, particularly when Etain's shade was involved. He was beginning to think it created whatever they needed or desired most at that moment. However, that fog of death—or whatever it was—he would like to be able to recreate. That was unlike anything he had ever seen before.

"Ciaran?" Etain asked, sounding as though she was waiting for him to respond to something she had previously said. He had not realized his mind had wandered as he stared at the now-empty space where the dragon had once stood.

"What was that, little witch?"

"I asked if you knew what it was." She looked at the space he had just been staring at.

It was always times like this when their differences were made obvious: where he was thrilled and wanted to recreate it, she was terrified of it. He knew without asking her that she would not want to attempt that again. He loved death, particularly when he was the one doling it out. She abhorred violence in general. They could not be more opposite, but he thought perhaps it was for the best. They were each other's counterbalance, and fate loved balance.

"I am not sure," he said, trying to think of what to say so she would not continue to fear their creations. "However, it's lucky that we were able to create it; I do not think there was any other way to survive the dragon, if that's what it was."

"Oh, that's exactly what she was. She looked so familiar. I know I have seen her face before; I just cannot seem to remember where," she said, trailing off into her memories, searching for the face she had seen only for a brief moment. "It's bothering me."

"It will come to you when it's meant to," Panella said, holding tight to her bonded.

"I know, yet it's like when the word you want to say suddenly leaves your mind just before you say it," she said and then sighed. "Well, shall we find these books?"

Finally.

"When I looked for another exit, I saw no obvious contraption like the other locations had; that does not mean there is not one. As the dragon suggests, whoever set all of this up has an interesting sense of humor," he said with very little humor himself.

"I saw something on the walls earlier, but we were a little preoccupied with not getting attacked by that thing," Ravyn said.

"A task you excel at," he said, and was immediately elbowed by Etain as she hissed his name under her breath. He fought to keep his grin from forming. His little witch was so bossy.

"He means finding things, obviously, since you were the one to find the entrance," Etain said, squinting her beautiful, golden-flecked eyes at him. Then he scowled when he registered what she had said. He was still annoyed that he had not found it.

"Oookay," Ravyn drew out. "Anyway, I am going to go look now." Panella whispered something to her as they walked away, and both females laughed.

"Ciaran!" Etain whisper-yelled. "That was not funny."

"I thought it was," he said with a shrug.

"Really? Would you have thought it funny if someone said that after you had just thought me dead?" she asked.

"No. Of course not," he said, appalled that she would even ask.

"Then why would you think it's funny with anyone else?" she asked as she turned to walk toward the opposite wall that Panella and Ravyn were looking at. He caught up with her in two slides.

"Because they are not you," he said, shrugging. He thought the answer was obvious. She stopped and looked up at him, trying to stay serious, but he could feel through the bond how much she loved being the center of his everything.

"Oh, my love, what am I to do with you?" she asked with slight scorn.

"I have a few ideas, but none of them require clothing." He gave her the wicked smirk that always made the flush bloom on her skin. Gods, how he loved the color of it.

"We need to focus," she said, swatting at him.

"I am focused," he said, never taking his eyes off her. Finally, she lost the battle with her smile and her flush turned an even deeper shade of crimson.

"On finding those books you have been searching for. Did you not say you were tired of searching for everything? Well, this is it; then you are done," she made a good point. He never wanted to search for anything again unless it was on his mate's body.

"Besides," she added, "maybe you can redeem yourself for not finding the entrance." She laughed when Ciaran squinted his eyes at her and hurried the last couple of feet to the wall.

"It looks like a story, similar to the pillars in the temple Tatiana showed up at. Of what, though, I cannot figure out," Etain said, staring at several images in a row. She was right; it was impossible to read.

Unless…

"They are not in the correct order." Just like every other place he had gone, there was always some kind of puzzle to figure out.

"Yes," she said. "You are right. Look at it in this order." She pointed to the tiles the images were on in the sequence she thought made the most sense. It did. It was the story of a female with raven-black hair. She was given a task by what looked like fae royalty—something about hiding the past from the future to prevent repetition and keeping it safe.

They moved to the other wall to see stories about two other females with a similar narrative. None of it brought them any closer to figuring out where the books were or, even more important, opening the damn door. He might be able to get his shadows through to find the mechanism to open it.

"Oh!" Etain cried. "They move!" She excitedly began moving the tiles into the correct positions, and once the last one was in place, they heard a click. Lyra and Ravyn went to the other three images and did the same, followed by two more clicks.

Nothing happened.

"There's this strange combination of images as well. Yet none of it makes any sense...wait. Even leaders must learn." She moved two tiles into place: "To find the balance between them." She moved two more tiles, leaving only two left: "In order to protect the realm."

Another click sounded, and then the door opened while the wall at the back began to slide open. It revealed...another fucking box. At least it was a much larger one, and he dared to hope to find the books that had become the bane of his existence. Panella immediately began to study it, trying to figure out the secret to opening it.

Ciaran walked up beside her and sent his shadows into the lock. He had done the same thing at the other two locations, and they had each opened easily. The sound of stone grinding against stone told him it had worked again.

"Well, that's one way to do it. Although, it's not nearly as fun," Panella said, looking rather sullen. Ciaran just smiled his too-wide smile at her. She rolled her eyes.

"Why do I even try?" she asked under her breath.

"This is you trying?" he asked her, laughing when she glared at him. She opened her mouth to say something else, but then the box opened enough to peer inside.

"Finally," Ciaran hissed. There were the books, more than he thought there would be. He found the *Book of Shadows* and grabbed it.

"You can have the rest of them," he said, waving dismissively at the several other books in the stone box. Then he stopped.

Kes should have the *Book of Air*.

Why was he even contemplating this? It was not like he cared for his cousin. No. It's only because it would help him and Etain in the long run. Yes, that was it.

He turned around and reached back into the box, grabbing the stupid book for his stupid cousin. Etain saw the names of the two books he had in his hands and smiled. She opened her mouth, likely to convince him that he actually did care for Kes.

He did not.

"Not a word, little witch," he said. She closed her mouth and pulled her lips between her teeth to try to keep the words from spilling from her mouth.

It did not work.

"I told you!" she exclaimed, then smacked her hands over her mouth. It did nothing to hide the giggles.

He did not care about his cousin.

No, not at all.

"What will your first act as queen be?" Kes asked Anin. She knew what she wanted to do; she just did not know how to do it, which made her feel even more inadequate for the role.

"I want to end all the deals the high fae forced upon the lesser fae, but I have no idea where to start to do something like that," she said honestly.

"Hmm," he hummed, thinking about it for a moment. "Ciaran and I never spoke about what changed for him when he became king. Honestly, I do not even know if I ever acknowledged that he is king. However, I do know he seemed connected to the court, almost like little strands linking him to certain things within his half of the realm."

Anin was not sure if she had the same connection, yet she did not see the harm in looking for the strands Kes spoke of. She closed her eyes and felt for—well, she really had no idea what. Would it be a feeling? Something she could see in her mind? Or something else entirely?

She was beginning to feel foolish when she gasped. She thought the rays of light she saw might be what Kes had been talking about. Following her intuition, she reached out to touch the strands in her mind.

Some strands felt right, while others felt wrong, as if they were tainted in some manner. She touched one of those first and was heartbroken when she heard what the fae had been forced to make a deal for. The coercion was the wrongness she felt.

There were so many of them. Each one she touched shaped Anin's picture of the life the lesser fae of Daybreak had lived. She grasped several of them in her hand and, without knowing if she was doing it right, she pulled. Each one snapped. As soon as the strands broke, they dissipated into nothing.

She grabbed as many as she could in one go and ripped them apart. Pure satisfaction coursed through her. If she did nothing else as queen, at least she would always know that she had freed the lesser fae. In a manic flurry, she ripped every single one apart and did not stop until the last strand dissipated.

When she opened her eyes, Kes was staring at her with a small smile on his face. "You did it; I could tell the moment you figured it out by the shift in your face. Well, that and the wild glee flooding the bond," he said, laughing.

"It was far easier than I thought it would be. Unfortunately, I think I still need to have a discussion with your cousin," she said with a grimace, making Kes laugh.

Her joy dampened when she heard the quiet humming start up again. Tatiana was still holding on to the dead fae's body. There were so many bodies. She would need to have a pyre constructed so that they could be burned and returned to the realm.

"What are you going to do with her?" Kes asked, sneering at Tatiana. Anin sighed and considered her options.

"I suppose the only thing I can do. She needs to be locked away." Just because Anin was going to allow her to live, did not mean she wanted to see her wandering the halls of Daybreak.

"Perfect. Let's put her in the same cage she held you in," Kes said seriously.

"No!" she scolded him. "I already said I am not going to be the same kind of queen she was. She will be locked in her own chambers and confined there to live out the rest of her life, no matter how long." Anin had a feeling her sister was not going to be around for much longer. She looked like she had already deteriorated from the time that Anin first stepped foot into the throne room.

"Are you sure?" Kes asked, obviously not thrilled with the idea of Tatiana having far more luxury than she had given Anin. A large part of her agreed with him and wanted to toss her into the small cage and leave her there to rot.

"I am sure." A larger part knew that the Tatiana who had grievously hurt her was gone. She would never get to make *that* Tatiana pay for the crimes she had committed against her. Even if she could, she was not sure she had the stomach for it.

"Alright. Do you want me to drag her there?" he asked.

He looked hopeful that he would have the chance to inflict some form of pain on the female.

"No, I will do it," she said. She stood from Kes's lap and slowly made her way down the few steps to where Tatiana still sat. Anin stood next to her, and after a few minutes—when Tatiana had not noticed her—she crouched down next to her.

"Tatiana," she said firmly.

"Oh," Tatiana said, blinking her eyes several times. "Hello." Her voice was that of a youngling. Not the youngling-like voice she had tried to emulate; this was the voice of an actual youngling.

"It's time to go," Anin said. Something told her to speak to Tatiana as if she were a youngling.

"Okay," she said as she stood slowly, never releasing her grip on the dead male. "Can I bring my doll?" It took Anin several seconds to realize she was talking about the dead fae.

"Let's get you a new one," Anin said, trying to keep her disgust from showing on her face. Tatiana looked at the male, and fresh tears fell down her cheeks.

"I love this one, though." It was not said in the whiny voice of a youngling being told no; it was the quiet voice of a grieving youngling who was trying not to get upset.

"What makes you love this one over others?" Anin asked. She told herself she did not care, but she could not stop wondering who he was to her.

"He was made just for me," she said as more tears poured down her face. Anin was not sure what she meant by that. Tatiana looked into Anin's eyes, and Anin saw no recognition in them. "Must I?"

"Yes, he's broken, and I do not think there is any repairing him," Anin said.

"He must be made anew?" Tatiana asked in a small, sad voice.

"I believe so." Anin watched as Tatiana nodded and then detangled her fingers from the dead fae. They had gone stiff, making the difficult task even harder for her.

"Where are we going?" Tatiana asked after her hand was free, looking at Anin.

"You need to go to your room," Anin said. "Will you show me where it is?"

"Okay," she whispered.

They went down several hallways and through a few doors before entering a hallway that looked as if it had not been used in centuries. Neither of them had said a word; however, she caught the nervous glances Tatiana kept giving her. She would open her mouth, just to close it and look back down at the floor.

"Have I been bad?" she finally had the courage to ask.

"Very," was all Anin said. Tatiana remained quiet until they reached a white and gold door. When she placed her hand on the knob, she looked at Anin with fresh tears streaming down her cheeks.

"I did not mean to be bad," she whispered, opening the door and stepping into the dusty room meant for a youngling. She had brought them to her childhood room. The wall of half-decayed dolls that stared at the sisters from across the neglected space made for an eerie audience. "I am so very sorry."

Anin said nothing as she pulled the door shut and used her sunlight to seal it. When she finished, she heard

Tatiana say, "I will be a good girl." She turned her back on the door and walked away, hearing Tatiana humming the same lullaby.

For reasons Anin could not understand, she suddenly felt like the bad sister.

Chapter 76
Panella

Panella had returned with countless books from the archive in the middle of the Borderlands. Several were in that same language that only Etain seemed to be able to read. She translated passages for Panella. Through those translations, Panella was teaching herself the language—a skill she had never needed to acquire before, and she found it fascinating.

One of the books she brought back was relatively newer and written in a language she could read, yet it contained a history unknown to any of them. There was little Panella loved more than discovering a past long forgotten by time; it felt nearly fantastical.

The book spoke of a time when the realm was united as one, which she already knew. What she did not know was how interconnected the courts and witches once were. The map of their realm, with all the cities in the Borderlands, had been an accurate portrayal.

Most beings in the realm spent most of their time in

the Borderlands, although it was not called that until much later. It had once been called Middlerealm. The city that once stood atop the archives—and the dragon—had been the center of everything. They called it Corids, or "The Heart," and it was where the rulers of both courts resided.

The King of the Night Court and the Queen of the Day Court were often fated mates. In fact, it was not uncommon for a Night fae to be fated to a Day fae. The realm had thrived as a whole for hundreds of thousands of years.

It was not until one Day fae and one Night fae fell into an unnatural magic that preyed upon the witches and created a darkness of some kind that everything changed. Whoever wrote the book seemed uncertain of what to call it; however, they described it as a darkness that consumed the land and anything in its path.

Those two fae systematically divided the realm and caused animosity between the once-peaceful courts. The courts and witches came together one last time to fight for the survival of their realm, but the damage had been done, and they could no longer cohabitate. Thus began the end of Middlerealm and the beginning of the Borderlands.

Panella had the uncanny feeling that history was repeating itself and could not help but see the parallels between the past and the present. The realm was on its way to being reunited once again, and the blood magic Tatiana had used was undoubtedly unnatural. Between the search for the elemental tombs and Anin's journey to the throne, she had nearly forgotten about the darkness that spread across the southern part of the Day Court.

She hoped that with the downfall of Tatiana, it would stop its forward progress. It was entirely possible that Anin, sitting on the throne, would heal the land. If they were lucky, the darkness plaguing the Day Court would resolve itself. After the madness of the last couple of hundred years, luck was something they all deserved and needed.

The changes within the Night Court from Witch City being located within their capital alone had been massive. Relationships—romantic, platonic, and business—had been built, tying the two groups together. As much as the witches had changed the Night Court, the Night Court had changed the witches.

They no longer preferred the separation of the covens and the distance from the courts. Witch City was now their home, as was the Night Court that surrounded it. She wondered how Anin, as the Queen of the Day Court, would influence the continued evolution of the realm. She glanced at the book, where an illustration of the map that hung in the hall of the Corids archives had been rendered.

There was still a long way to go to achieve that level of unity. It would take hard work to dismantle the animosity that had built up not only between the two courts but also among the witches. It would take time as well, but Panella was hopeful for the future.

It was a future worth fighting for.

Chapter 77
Anin

I t had taken them almost two entire days to burn all the bodies from the throne room, and even more to repair all the damage throughout the city. She had learned her way around the palace quickly and was grateful to have Lorella to show her.

They picked their quarters, which felt strange; it was hard to think of anywhere but Nightfell as home. The moment the door to Tatiana's real room opened, she knew it belonged to her. Anin requested that the entire room be gutted and transformed into something else. When they asked her what she wanted it to be, she thought about it for no more than a second.

"Anything else. The only thing I care about is removing her traces from the palace." She had worked on that for the days they had been there, making new thrones for each of them from vines as a statement to the high fae.

After she broke the bond of the deals made with the lesser fae, several high fae stormed into the palace demanding an audience. She was surprised to see so many still alive in the city, as Tatiana had decimated the high fae population.

"You had no right to end the deals between us and our lessors!" one of them raged.

"Want me to kill him?" Kes asked under his breath, making her laugh.

"Stop. You cannot kill everyone who speaks poorly to me. There has been enough death."

"I can kill some of them, though. It will make the rest think twice," he practically begged. She laughed again and shook her head when he added a little pout.

"I have every right to do whatever I wish. Or have you forgotten that we are the true queen and king of the Day Court?" she asked, waving at their bright crowns.

She messaged Etain when they tried to go to sleep, and they had not disappeared. They were so bright that neither of them could fall asleep. Etain laughed and told them how to make them appear and disappear with ease.

It was embarrassing when she discovered that all it took was to imagine it gone and then back again. Neither her, nor Kes had thought it would be so simple.

"They made those deals with us under their own will!" someone else shouted.

"Interesting. Did you know I can see each deal? If I touch the strand of the bond, I can even hear the words of each deal? There is a certain oiliness to the deals made under coercion—those were the ones I broke."

"No! It was nothing like that! They had a choice!" a new face yelled. She grew tired of the yelling.

"The next one of you who yells will spend a week in the dungeons. Am I understood?" she asked them. They all nodded, even as they scowled at her.

"That was incredibly sexy, my queen," Kes leaned over to whisper into her ear. She swatted him away, even as her cheeks heated.

Once she got control of the room and followed through on her threat to have Kes remove the next one who yelled, they began to understand. She would not tolerate the abhorrent treatment of the lesser fae. Any violence against them would result in a punishment equal to the crime committed.

Changing the court after generations of operating one way would not be easy. She was determined, however. No matter what it took, she was going to unite her court.

"Balthier and his mate are going to be here to greet us soon. I imagine Killia will be with them," she said excitedly to Kes. She spoke to him through scrolls and learned about his mate being forced to sleep after draining his power to protect him and Killia. She would offer them all a seat on her council; they were the ones who made the rebellion the success it had become.

"Where are we meeting them?" Kes asked distractedly, as he inspected a painting in the hall. She had never known him to be fascinated by art.

"The throne room. I tried to suggest something less formal, but Balthier insisted."

"You know what?" he asked. She was certain he had not heard him.

"What?"

"I think I know who painted this," he said, squinting at the piece. Anin went to see for herself what had enthralled him.

"Kes, that is possibly the worst landscape I have ever seen." The colors clashed, and the entire piece was flat.

"Exactly. This little shit who used to kiss the ground my uncle walked on painted something similar that hung in the council room. I told him exactly what you said—well, maybe not exactly. It might not have been as nice."

Anin's laugh surprised her as much as his words. She did not know what she expected him to say, but that was decidedly not it. He gave her a wicked grin before holding out his hand.

"The throne room you said? To meet Balthier, his mate, and Killia?" he asked.

"You were listening," she said, honestly surprised. He leaned in and kissed her cheek as he ported them to the throne room.

"I hear everything you say," he said, his mouth next to her ear, making her shiver.

They had waited only a few minutes when the doors opened and a smiling Killia walked in. While it still did not meet her eyes, it was a step in a better direction. Balthier stood at the door, pulling on the hand of someone else. When he finally got that person to enter the room, Anin stiffened and her breathing became labored.

"What is it?" Kes asked as he placed his hands on either side of her face to look her in the eyes. She needed to breathe. She could do this. She was the queen, not the Anin from her cage.

"Nothing," she said hoarsely. She cleared her throat and glared at Raindal. Balthier's smile drained from his face as he looked between Anin and his mate. "It was you? You were the rebel leader?" Her tone was sharp as she bit off each word.

"Yes," Raindal said, adopting the expressionless look she knew all too well.

"You are the reason Kes was able to reach me?"

"Yes." She stared at him, and the silence was awkward. The three other beings in the room had no idea what was happening.

"You have been enslaved by Tatiana since I was freed?" She could do this.

"Y–Yes." She looked at him and Balthier, and understanding struck her. The pained noises he made... he had been playing a role—one that still tormented her sleep, and possibly his.

"Okay." She did not know what else to say. She accepted his answers and even understood them to an extent.

"Okay?" he asked.

"Yes. You will not be held accountable for your actions while you were...leading the rebellion." His shoulders relaxed, and for once she saw an actual expression on his face. He was shocked, and if she were honest with herself, so was she.

"However, I cannot bear to see your face without seeing the things you did." He nodded; she appreciated that he did not attempt to make excuses for himself. "You will leave the city and never return. Understood?" she asked.

"Yes," he said, grabbing his mate's hand.

"I do not understand," Balthier whispered.

"I will tell you everything once we figure out where we are going." He looked at her and nodded before he said, "Thank you." Then Raindal left with a very confused Balthier and Killia trailing behind him, and she was at peace knowing she would never have to see his face again.

"What just happened?" Kes asked, sounding just as confused as Balthier. Anin had never been able to tell him anything about her time under the palace. She sighed, knowing she needed to share some of her story with him.

"Come with me," she said, standing up. She took him to the hidden door behind the throne and down the path she had walked only on the day she was rescued. Even still, it was ingrained in her memory.

When they reached the long hall that led to the small stone room where her ridiculous cage hung, she had to take several calming breaths before taking the first step. She thought each step would get easier, but they did not.

"I heard you," she said. "When you tried to get to me."

"It was horrible to be able to get so close and leave without you in my arms," he said, squeezing her hand reassuringly.

When they reached the door, she desperately did not want to go through it into the room on the other side. She did not want to, but she had to. She closed her eyes and pushed the door open; the smell immediately made memories flash through her mind. She reached down the bond to keep herself anchored.

She gasped when she opened her eyes. Nothing had changed. The room had remained untouched for decades.

The only thing that had changed was the level of decay of her wings. Most of them were barely more than husks, and she did not know how they still hung on the wall.

Anin took a few steps to reach out and touch the most brittle pair on any of the walls. "The first time Tatiana cut off my wings," she began and did not stop.

It was the hardest thing he ever had to listen to, even harder to keep his mouth shut so Anin could get it out. She managed to get through it all without stopping, even as the tears started and never stopped.

He wanted to go to her and hold her in his arms, yet he knew that if he touched her, she would never be able to finish. She needed to finish, and the second she did, he was there to catch her. He held her as she grieved for the loss of her wings, the loss of time, and the loss of who she used to be.

There was no telling how long they stood in her old cell, holding each other. Eventually, she pulled away just enough to turn her head and look at the dozens of wings on the walls. They were a part of her, and leaving them there did not feel right to him.

"What do you want to do with them?" he asked.

"What do you mean?" She looked at him, her eyes still

swollen from crying, and her brow furrowed as she thought about what he had said.

"Your wings—I assume you do not want to leave them here?"

"No, I would like to not leave them. But what should I do with them? It never occurred to me that I could—should—do something with them."

"Do you want to keep them, or perhaps burn them and return them to the realm?"

"Yes, that one. They should be returned to the realm. It feels right." She gave him a watery smile, her emotions still raw. "Will you help me get them down?"

"I can get them all down if that would make it easier," he offered.

"No, I think I need to be a part of it."

She commented on random pairs and the variations she saw in them as they took each set down. As soon as one of them got a pair down, they quickly ported it to the pyre Kes hastily constructed. Neither of them thought they could handle being touched more than once.

They saved the oldest pairs for last, and Kes was not sure they would make it to the pyre. Anin gently lifted the last of them—the very first pair—off the wall. A good amount of the husk crumbled under her hands. They no longer resembled the beautifully vibrant things they had once been. Now they were nothing more than a black, flaking outline of what they used to be.

"These were my favorite. Of all the wings I have worn, these were the ones I loved most. I do not think I have allowed myself to think of them as anything but temporary," she whispered.

"Never again. You need never fear anything like that happening again. This I promise you," Kes said. Careful of the delicate wings, he wrapped his hands around each side of her head, as he always did when he needed her to know that he meant what he was saying. She nodded, the motion small. He only knew because he felt it.

They ported the final pair to the pyre, and one of his fire-wielding Twenty-Three set it ablaze. He watched her as she said her final farewell, not only to parts of herself but also to the life she had lived surrounded by them. The memories would always creep up to haunt her, but now she knew the room filled with her wings no longer existed.

It had taken everything inside him not to hunt down the rebel leader. Anyone who hurt her deserved nothing less than a long, painful death. Anin might be able to see how all his actions had been to get her on the throne; Kes could not. There had to be another way that did not involve putting his hands on Kes's mate.

It bothered him that none of the beings responsible for harming his mate, both physically and mentally, were being held accountable. This only showed how much better Anin was than all of them. It took a strength that Kes did not possess to offer compassion to those who did not deserve it.

As the flames died down and the last bits of ash floated away in the breeze, Kes felt her determination solidify. She was ready to take on the plethora of problems the Day Court faced. He would be there to support her in any capacity she needed. He was ready to watch her conquer anything else fate had in store for her.

He hoped that now she knew what the rest of them had known all along: she was not broken; she never had been. The Anin he pulled from the cage had become the version of herself she needed to be to survive. It had taken time for her to shape herself into that Anin, and he had known it would take time to reshape herself once again.

That never meant she was ever broken.

Chapter 79
Raindal

They decided to go to the northernmost of the lesser fae settlements, located in one of the abandoned covens. Balthier had taken time to process everything Raindal had done in the name of freedom for the lesser fae. Raindal had not kept anything from him, and he did not blame Balthier for being angry with him.

Later, Balthier told Raindal that he was never angry with him, only horrified by the life he felt he had been forced to live. Raindal explained that he never felt forced; it was a choice. Nothing had ever been more important to him than living a true life with his mate.

"Are you ready?" Raindal asked Balthier and his mother.

"There's nothing worth bringing with us," she said. "What more do I need? I have my boys, and—where's Killia?" Just then, the door opened, and the female in question walked in.

"Sorry, I had to help get a few of the others settled,"

she said. She had taken it upon herself to help the other victims of the brothels either find their families or set them up with a group they could belong to. She even petitioned Anin to give them jobs where they could heal in peace. It was no surprise when she readily agreed. She took it upon herself to personally place them all based on their wants and desires. She was truly a wonderful queen.

He had always known she would be.

Within minutes of her being crowned, she ended every deal to which any being had been forced. This included the high fae that Tatiana had forced. Then, when the fae who had held all the deals came down to the city to voice their outrage, she did not back down. They could either silence their complaints or explain the mansions they had built far enough away from the city to avoid Tatiana's grasp, leaving everyone else to suffer.

"Are we ready now?" he asked the three beings who made up his family.

"Yes, let's get out of here," Balthier said, and they all looked happier than Raindal ever remembered seeing them. Freedom will do that.

He ported all four of them to the northernmost coven. They figured they would be safest from the rot there. If the courts could not stop it by the time it reached them, there would be no realm left to live in anyway.

Falling Star Coven was a large stone tower—mostly. Witches always had a unique way with architecture. Not many lesser fae had made it that far north yet, so they had the entire place nearly to themselves, at least for the time being. He hoped the witches would be understanding if they returned; mostly, he hoped they would never come back.

Part of him was sad that he would not get to serve the queen for whom they had all worked tirelessly to get on the throne. He would have loved to watch the court become everything he had ever hoped for. The other, larger part was just happy to be done with it all. They had done it; they had suffered and survived, and now it was time to start their lives together. It was time for them to truly live until either the realm or the rot took them.

Until then, they would live happily ever after.

Chapter 80
Ciaran

"I cannot believe this is finally happening," Etain said as she flitted around their bedchamber. "The realm is coming together once again."

"I would not go that far," Ciaran said. Etain and Anin wanted to bring the realm back to the time when each court was apparently cohabiting and the rulers of the realm ruled together. Ciaran, on the other hand, was not looking forward to it.

The Night Court inhabitants had come a long way in accepting the witches, but more were still resistant than not. A fraction of the palace high fae had recently disappeared in what he assumed was a protest.

Not that he was complaining. It was the entirety of the secret society, which included Syndari. If he never had to speak to that shifting fae again, it would be too soon. He was only happy to have them all somewhere his little witch was not.

While he did not care that they had left, he wondered

if that would create issues later. If they pushed too much change on their court members, would that cause an even larger divide? However, even if it did, did he care? There was nothing they could do beyond complain. Would it not be better to have all the annoying members of his court in one location?

What truly bothered him was he had no idea where they went. It was as though they just disappeared. Ever since he had been crowned the true King of the Night Court, he had a connection to the land. If he searched for a being, it could tell him where that particular being was. This made following the not-so-secret society far too easy.

Yet when he searched for Syndari, there was nothing. He supposed it was entirely possible that they had left the realm, in which case he hoped they never returned. All he wanted was to live the rest of his life with his little witch and have the rest of the realm leave them alone.

Of course, that would never happen.

"Ciaran?" Etain asked.

"Hmm?" she sighed, as she had been doing a lot lately, and went to sit on his lap.

"Are you all right?" she asked once his arms wrapped around her and she settled into his chest.

"Yes, of course."

"It's just that you have been rather distracted lately." She pulled away from him enough to be able to look him in the eyes, concern swimming in her own.

"Little witch, you know that whenever you are around I am always distracted," he said as his hands wandered her small frame.

"Ciaran," she laughed, "I am serious. What is going on in that thick head of yours?" She looked at him with such openness and love that the full weight of his obsession hit him. It happened sometimes, and he nearly forgot to breathe every time. If something happened to her, he would never be able to survive even a second without her.

"I cannot find them, and I do not like it when there is something I cannot do."

"Oh, you mean you do not like it when there is something you cannot control?" she asked, trying to hold back her smile and wearing a faux serious expression.

"Little witch, are you teasing me?" he asked, glad for an excuse to shift the conversation.

"Me? Never," she said and squealed when he stood up, threw her over his shoulder, and marched her straight to the bed, tossing her onto it. They had time before they needed to go; besides, it was not as though they could start without them.

"It's only fair that if you tease me, I get to tease you," he said, his hands sliding up her legs and taking the skirt of her dress with them.

"Ciaran," she tried to admonish; however, the effect was lost with all her squirming. "We have to go; there is no time for...ohhh." Her complaints drowned out as they turned into moans of pleasure when his head dropped between her legs. There was always time to pull his favorite sounds from his little witch.

It did not take him long to have her nearly falling into oblivion, only to not let her fall several times before she begged him to give her the release she craved. When he finally did, her back arched off the bed, and her mouth opened to scream; yet no sound came out.

"Now it's time to go," he said, wiping his mouth with his hand and giving her one of his too-wide wicked grins, when she could only nod. "Are you well, little witch? Shall I message them to resched—" She threw a pillow at his face.

"You are not getting out of this meeting, no matter how much you try to distract me," she said. When she tried to stand, and her legs wobbled, Ciaran laughed, which only made her scowl at him.

"Fine then, little witch," he said, reaching a hand out to help her stand and then porting them to the ruins where they had fought the dragon.

It was decided—*not* by him—that they would meet where the rulers of the realm had once worked together as a symbol of their commitment to the new realm order. If it had not made Etain so happy, he would have declined the invitation. It seemed ridiculous to have something so formal when they had all shared a dining table just the other night. Yet he had not met anything he was unwilling to do for her.

Even more obnoxious was the long descent down the stairs to the archives, well below the ground. He had suggested that they build a structure above ground so that all parties could port in and out. The queens of the realm —a term that made him grimace—had quickly vetoed that in favor of a large round table where the dragon had once stood.

He was painfully outnumbered, with Kes being no help at all. Not that he was surprised. Kes had rarely ever done anything other than be a nuisance during council meetings. It was also possible that knowing Ciaran was forced to listen to Etain and Anin plot the future of the realm with such...*enthusiasm*, brought his cousin an untold amount of joy.

Ass.

"These fucking stairs. 'No, Ciaran, we cannot make it easy on everyone,'" he muttered under his breath in his best Etain impression.

"What was that, my love?" Etain asked from in front of him.

"Nothing," he grumbled.

"Hmmm, are you certain?" he sped around her to the stair below and blocked her path before caging Etain in between his arms and the curved wall of the stairwell.

"Should I show you just how certain I am?" It was difficult in the dim light to get the full effect of the flush that he never had issues calling forth from her on command. It was something he endeavored to do as often as possible.

"Ciaran," she gasped. "We are already late due to your...*certainties*."

"Well, one can never be too certain." He leaned in and brushed his lips against the shell of her ear before adding, "Can they?"

"I am certain I am going to vomit if I have to listen to my cousin's attempt at romance for even a second longer," Kes snarked from the bottom of the stairwell. "Etain, I will never understand what you see in him."

"You are one to talk, bird boy," Lyra yelled from somewhere deeper into the archives. Etain's laughter as she stepped under his arm prevented Ciaran from saying anything else. It was not a sound he was ever keen to interrupt.

They were the last to arrive, just the way he preferred it. Etain turned to look back at him as she found her seat, one of only two remaining at the table, and mouthed "late" to him. He smirked at her. Late was subjective. He did not hold himself to anyone else's timeline but their own; therefore, he could never be late.

He had not been back since they defeated the dragon and found the fucking books he had spent far too long searching for. It was difficult for him not to replay the way his shadows and her shade had mixed together.

Death like he had never seen it before.

It had been glorious.

The growing silence tickled at his awareness, and he shook himself out of the memory to find all eyes on him. He really needed to stop allowing his mind to drift. It created situations where he was caught off guard. It was not something he enjoyed. He sighed and looked at Etain.

"We all agreed that at least the palace of Corids should be rebuilt. This way, we can have a central location that is neutral to the realm for these meetings," she said. Ciaran looked around at the space they were currently occupying that already fit that bill.

"Oh, so now you want to build something that is easier to access?" he gave her one of his too-wide toothy grins before he waved to the rest of the table dismissively. "I could not care less about what building we meet in or where that building happens to be located." There was a brief moment of silence before the conversation picked back up again.

There were thirteen of them around the table. Ciaran had reluctantly invited his remaining two council members. Etain had brought Panella, Ravyn, and Galetia. Anin had two lesser Day fae with her that he could not decide if they were about to soil themselves or—one of them locked eyes for a brief moment with Ciaran. No, they were definitely going to require fresh trousers.

At some point that he had not been made privy to, the Silent Shadows had become their own entity. Kes, Lyra, and—fuck. He could never remember the grey-skinned fae's name. Unfortunately, "fae-fae" was the only name that seemed to stick. He still found it appalling.

"Several high fae have gone missing," Anin said. Ciaran's ears perked up, and he tuned back into the conversation.

"Ciaran was just mentioning something similar to me earlier," Etain said, looking at him and he nodded slowly while he decided how much he wished to reveal.

"Can you find them?" Ciaran asked Anin. She looked at him with her brow scrunched and her head cocked to the side. He sighed. She still knew nothing. "If you need to find someone, you should be able to think of them and find them within your court. You are now connected to each being that calls you their queen."

"Oh. I did not know." Her eyes grew distant as she attempted to locate any of the missing Day fae. Finally, she focused back on the beings at the table, yet the crease between her brow did not lessen.

"I could not find a single one. I thought perhaps I was

doing it wrong, so I searched for someone I knew was not missing and found them easily." He nodded. It was the answer he had been expecting.

"How many?" A flutter in his stomach surprised him. Something about the missing fae made him nervous. It was not a feeling he was accustomed to.

"Nearly all the high fae," Anin whispered. Ciaran was, once again, not surprised. Tatiana had wiped out a large chunk of the population as it was, and those left behind would not be thrilled about the changes she was implementing.

"We will look into it," Kes said as he wrote something on the parchment before him.

Was he taking notes?

He was!

Ciaran smirked at his cousin. Kes took several moments to feel Ciaran's eyes upon him, but his quill stopped abruptly. He lifted his head, his movements slow, and met Ciaran's gaze.

"What?" Kes asked.

"Oh, nothing," Ciaran said in a way that made it clear there was, in fact, something. "You just make a lovely secretary. Perhaps Panella could use some help keeping track of her research." Kes barked out a laugh.

"Cousin, have you not realized yet that I make a lovely everything?" Ciaran rolled his eyes and the twins groaned.

"Well, as entertaining as this has been," Ciaran said as he made to stand. "If that is all, I w—"

"I have one last thing," Anin cut in. "In three days' time, the first official mating ceremony between a high fae and a lesser fae will take place in the northernmost town in the lesser fae territory."

"That's wonderful!" Etain said. His little witch loved a love story.

"Yes, wonderful indeed," Ciaran said, deadpan. "What does that have to do with the rest of us?"

"I was hoping everyone would attend as a show of solidarity." Before Ciaran could object, Etain grabbed his hand and eagerly accepted the invitation.

For both of them.

There was nothing he would not do to make his little witch happy, even if he had to suffer through another mating ceremony and the blinding light of that horrid sun.

He sighed.

Again.

"Gods, it's so fucking bright," Ciaran grumbled the moment they ported between two buildings in the small lesser fae town for the mating ceremony.

"Here," she said, pulling out a pair of glasses.

"Little witch, I do not wish to see this atrocious ball of fire any clearer than I already must," he said. She had to fight the smile threatening to take over.

While he had become less murderous over the years, mostly because she demanded it, he had become incredibly grumpy. She thought it had something to do with the lack of torture he got to inflict. He reminded her of an old man from her human village that was always yelling at the children as they ran by with peals of laughter pouring from their mouths. The comparison never failed to make her smile.

"Oh, just put them on and stop acting like such a grumpy old man," she said, hands on her hips.

"What did you just call me?" he asked, squinting his eyes at her. Whether in annoyance or from the sun, she could not tell. Either way, she shook her head, laughing.

"Just put them on, my love. You will be much happier once you do." She had to turn away to hide her mirth when she heard him grumbling about happiness being impossible for him on this side of the realm.

"The things I do fo—oh," he said, looking around. She had to pinch her lips together between her teeth to keep from laughing. She had created the lenses to absorb the sun's rays and then alter them to appear like a near replica of the moon's light.

"See?" she asked, losing the battle with her laughter when he squinted at her again.

"Hmm," he hummed, scowling.

"Much happier?" she asked, cocking her head to the side, waiting for him to admit she had been right. Her eyes flew open wide when he slowly stalked toward her and lifted her in his arms before pinning her between him and the wall of one of the buildings.

"There is only one thing that could ever make me remotely happy on this side of the realm, little witch," he said as he nuzzled the crook of her neck.

"Oh?" she asked breathlessly. One word whispered along her neck—it never mattered what the word was, and she was putty in his hands. "And what might that be?"

"I will give you a hint: It has absolutely nothing to do with magical eyewear, no matter how genius they might be." His hands slid up the sides of her thighs beneath her dress as he kissed a trail along the column of her neck.

"Hmm, I cannot possibly imagine what it could be," she said with a moan when he dragged the tip of one of his sharp teeth across her delicate skin. His hands crept higher as one snaked behind her leg to find her center. She gasped the second his fingers made the barest contact.

"Mmm, always so ready for me. Such a good little witch—"

"Oh, good! There you both are," Kes's voice came from the front of the buildings they were hiding between. When she looked over at him, there was no missing the delight dancing in his eyes.

"I swear to every god..." Ciaran groaned into her neck.

"We should continue this when we get back to our chambers," she whispered to him. She heard him make several inventive threats under his breath as he lowered her to the ground and adjusted himself. She could not help it when her giggles finally broke free.

"Little witch, little witch," he said in a singsong voice from behind her as she made her way to where Kes waited for them. "We will see just how much you are laughing when we get back." He swatted her on the ass, leaving a stinging sensation she felt all the way to her core. When she gasped and then clenched her legs together, he looked down at her with one of his too-wide grins, one that promised to have her begging to leave as soon as the ceremony was over.

The town had gone all out for the occasion. Vines blooming with flowers of all colors lined every building and created beautiful archways leading to the edge of the town, which boasted a backdrop of rolling hills covered in fields of wildflowers. The warm light of the sun gave everything a dreamlike quality that stole Etain's breath.

"Is it not stunning?" Anin asked as she came to stand beside Etain.

"It truly is," the witch said before turning to her friend to hug her. "Sorry we are late. Someone took their sweet time getting ready." She looked accusatively at Ciaran. "Honestly, I believe even Kes could have gotten ready faster." The two females laughed, but Etain gasped when she caught the dark promise in Ciaran's eyes. She never could understand how he could build such an inferno within her with a simple look.

Before anyone could say another word, the music changed, and they rushed to find their seats—well, everyone but Ciaran, at least. The musicians were forced to play the buildup twice, and the high fae at the end of the aisle gave Ciaran a tight smile as he forced everyone to wait on him, including the Chronicler. Etain snatched his hand and dragged him to their seats.

"Honestly, Ciaran," she huffed under her breath. He opened his mouth to reply, but she shushed him with a finger over his mouth. "Not a word until the ceremony is over."

He stayed silent through the entire thing, yet that did not mean he did not punish her the entire time. His thumb dragged lazy strokes up and down the side of her neck while the rest of his fingers gripped gently around it. Each time he found a spot that caused a shiver to run down her spine, he repeated the movement until she was squirming in her seat, feeling the heat of her flush consume her face.

She struggled to focus on the ceremony. One look at her mate's smug smile stretched across his face told her he knew exactly what he was doing to her. As if it were not already obvious enough. When she crossed her legs again for the countless number of times, his smile stretched further.

Bastard.

Finally, as the ceremony neared its end and the blood exchange began, nothing could distract her. The male high fae and female lesser fae were undeniably in love, as anyone could see. Few things brought Etain greater joy than love itself. It was the greatest gift—being the center of someone else's everything and having them be yours, even if they were the realm's largest oaf.

When it ended, the entire town erupted in cheers, and the celebration began. Tables overflowed with platters of food, and fountains of wine flowed freely. The music transitioned into a lively song Etain had never heard before. Yet the Day fae flocked to the dance floor, laughing as they executed the same familiar steps.

"That was beautiful," Ravyn said, her eyes rimmed in red and a large smile on her face.

"It truly was," Lyra agreed.

"If you say so. The sun is miserable," Zandar said, squinting. She hadn't thought to make him a pair of the same magical lenses.

Ever since Kes became the king of the Day Court, the sun did not bother him, nor did his power drain. He belonged to both sides of the realm now—a fact he never let Ciaran forget. However, Ciaran was waiting for the perfect moment to reveal that he, too, was free to move through the realm without fear of his power dwindling.

Honestly, she was surprised Kes had not already guessed that the land would maintain balance. She was willing to bet that when Anin had the chance to visit the Night Court again, she would not feel the effects either. The land and Fate were nothing if not exacting in their never-ending quest for balance.

"Could not agree more," Ciaran said, sneering at the sun as if it were the most offensive thing he had ever been forced to endure.

The rest of them laughed while the two Night fae grimaced. Yet when Zandar's eyes soaked in the true joy that Lyra wore, his features smoothed, and the intensity of his love shone through. She knew that if she looked at Ciaran, she would find the same look directed at her.

Etain could not remember a day—or night—that felt this light. She was surrounded by her chosen family; only Galetia and Tyne were missing. Except for Ciaran and Zandar, every face boasted a smile, and laughter rang out everywhere.

"Apparently, I have the power of moonlight. I had always had it and only needed the Land to unlock it. How fucking ridiculous is that? That many faced bitch had me looking all over the realm for something I already had." Anin scowled at Kes the moment he spoke ill of Hecate, to which he rolled his eyes.

"Sounds like something the hag would do," Ciaran growled. He and Kes would never be fans of the goddess. Etain sighed and shook her head, but she could not stifle the laugh that escaped her. Every time Ciaran mentioned Hecate, all she could see was the goddess pinching his cheek and calling him a good boy.

"Etain," Ciaran said in a warning tone. He did not enjoy being reminded of that particular moment. She raised her hands in surrender and did her best to school her face. It was too late. Everyone knew the story, and choked laughter bubbled up from their little group. Ciaran's scowl deepened, and once again, she was reminded of the old man from her village.

The two recently bonded mates cautiously approached them. They relaxed when they saw the smiles directed at them—everyone but Ciaran. She did not think it was possible for him to smile at anyone but her and occasionally Kes.

"Thank you for taking the time out of your Da—Night to join us," the female said. She appeared to be some kind of winged, pixie-like creature. Her features were soft and round, with her eyes seeming almost too large for her small face.

"It truly means a lot to have the support of the rest of the realm, particularly when a majority of the high fae on this side of the Borderlands cannot seem to give theirs," the male said. His bronzed skin sparkled in the sunlight.

Neither lingered after they all gave their well wishes. Even Ciaran did, though she had to elbow him in the side to coax him into reluctantly congratulating them. She could tell he was reaching his limit and that they would need to leave soon.

"So you got sunlight, and you got moonlight?" Panella asked Kes and Anin.

"Yes. Although I am still not entirely sure what that means. If you can find any mention of it that might help me understand how it works, I would appreciate it," Anin said.

"I am sure we can fin—" Panella started.

"Little witch," Ciaran said suddenly. "It just occurred to me that you never told me what you were gifted." He looked horrified that he could have ever forgotten something as profound as a gift from the land.

"Oh," Etain said. "It had honestly slipped my mind. Life was a little chaotic for a while after we were crowned."

"Understatement," Kes said under his breath.

"So, what was it?" Anin asked.

"It was rather strange. The Land said I—" Screaming made Etain abruptly cut her words off, and they all jerked their heads toward the sound.

The two newly bonded mates were frantic. The female was screaming unintelligibly as the male begged her not to touch him. Something was crawling up his sleeve, but she did not listen and frantically brushed at his arm.

It took two seconds too long for Etain to realize that everywhere the black substance moved, it devoured everything in its wake. The male was disintegrating before their eyes. The moment the female's hands touched the black, syrupy substance, she too began dissolving.

"Oh gods," she heard Anin gasp.

"Help! Please, help!" the female screamed. Etain did not think she had even noticed that her arm was nearly gone. The pixie-like female had her entire focus on the male, who was nothing more than half of what he had been moments ago. The high fae bellowed as he watched the same thing consume his mate.

"What—" Panella gasped as she held onto Ravyn.

"The rot," Kes said in a way that Etain did not think he was even aware he had spoken.

The land had warned them. It had begged for their help, but they had been too focused on the Day Court. Etain had assumed the rot had been connected to Tatiana, and with her unseated from the throne, the land would begin to heal. They had all thought that would be the case, especially when the land did not mention the rot to Anin and Kes when they were crowned.

They had all been wrong. So very wrong. She sobbed as the female gave one last choked scream before the sound was consumed as well. The land was not healing, and the peaceful feeling Etain had just been basking in dissolved as quickly as the now-dead newly bonded mates.

The rot had arrived.

Chapter 82
Leona

Leona had listened to the strange, echoing voice whispering to her for decades. She destroyed what it told her to and left the messages exactly as instructed. It had been a bit of fun, but finally, it was time.

The *whispers* led her to a book and she set the spells exactly as it directed. Once she had placed the instructed number, and she added a few more just to be certain. Leona was nearly lightheaded from the thrill and excitement of it all.

The little bitch would finally pay.

"Leona, are you certain?" Trillda asked. The fae was one of Leona's more annoying followers, and she knew she would regret bringing her along.

"Trillda!" she seethed. "Do you not wish to be one of

us? If you are too scared, then turn your unfortunate-looking ass around. I do not need you. Can you say the same?" She knew her words were harsh—cruel, even—but Leona did not care. If anything, she loved seeing the flash of hurt her words caused, especially when their eyes welled with tears, just like Trillda's did.

"Sorry, Leona," the female said in a barely audible voice while she stared at her shoes.

"Good," Leona said. She knew her wicked smile could rival even Ciaran's.

It was only one reason she knew she should have been queen. She should have been mated to Ciaran; fate got it wrong. Even the *whispers* had agreed with her. It would not surprise her if that red-haired witch had manipulated fate somehow. She had tricked her king into a false mate bond. Leona wanted to wear the insides of the stupid whore.

Ciaran had been meant for her!

"Now, all of you run along. You know what you are supposed to do," she said to the handful of pitiful females who worshiped her as if she were the queen, which, in her mind, she was. She was the queen of the Night Court. It did not matter what anyone else said; her father had promised her she would be queen.

It was her right.

Of the couple of dozen high fae females in the palace who made up Leona's ladies-in-waiting, these were the only ones with the fire element. The three with air were already in their assigned positions, waiting for their signal. It was difficult for Leona to be patient and wait for the exact right moment; she would, though; she was not going to let this opportunity pass her by.

With the witch out of the way, she would be able to take her rightful seat beside her intended; that was all that mattered. She could see it clearly. She would sit next to Ciaran on her own throne, dripping jewels. He would reach over and grab her hand to kiss her knuckles, thanking her for freeing him from whatever curse she had placed on him.

Leona pushed open the door that led to the so-called queen of the witch's apartment. It was appalling that she thought herself too good to live in Ciaran's tower. She forced him to allow her to create her own city within his, ever since her filth had been bleeding into the rest of Nightfell. Others might have begun to accept them, but Leona would never.

Red hair caught her attention. Leona could see it just peeking out over the side of a chair she sat in. Leona triggered the signal as she crept up behind the bitch queen while silently pulling out the obsidian blade the *whispers* had led her to. She had to go all the way to the Day Court to retrieve it.

They told her there was no way for anyone to heal fast enough from a wound inflicted by that particular blade. It was dumb luck that Leona had come across her while she was napping in the large wingback chair that faced the wall of windows, which gave an unobstructed view of their horrid city.

Leona would hate for her to miss the show.

"Kill her. Then nothing will stand in your way," the *whispers* encouraged. This close to ending the female who

caused her entire life to be turned upside down made her nearly blind with excitement.

She could feel the weight of her crown already.

She could feel the weight of her king on top of her.

She could feel the adoration of the entire court as they gazed longingly upon her.

She could feel the future she was meant to have.

All she had to do was kill this witch. She had imagined this moment hundreds, if not thousands, of times. If Leona were honest, she would much prefer to wrap her hands around the bitch and watch her life drain from her ridiculous dirt brown eyes. Yet a blade would do just fine.

Just as the first explosion sounded, Leona brought the blade around the chair and stabbed it deep into the bitch's abdomen. She screamed as she stabbed again and again, blood splattering with each thrust of the blade.

"I wanted to make sure your last sight was one worth having," Leona said as she stared out the window and made her way around the large chair. The flames were already consuming the city as witches scrambled below to snuff them out. She laughed, knowing it would be next to impossible. The spells she had placed around the city would ensure the flames burned for a certain period of time—no more and no less.

"You should never have come here. If you had only stayed in the Human Realm, none of this would have happened. There is no one to blame but yourself," she said, standing next to the witch she could hear gasping for air as she choked on her blood.

Leona wanted to make sure that when she finally allowed her eyes to drink in the destruction of the small human witch's body, it would be a sight she would never forget. She wanted to give her enough time to be one thread away from death so that Leona could watch the light fade from her eyes just after it dusked on her; she was the one responsible for her death.

When the gasping grew fainter, she finally sucked in air herself and let the full extent of her wickedness show in her smile. She let her features take on the terrifying shape of a true queen of the Night Court before she finally let herself turn and see what she had been dreaming about ever since she first laid eyes upon the witch.

"No!" she screamed. This could not be happening. She had made certain she had everything correct. Leona had left no room for error.

Or so she thought.

Instead of Etain sitting in the chair, staring at her burning city with horrified eyes as blood spurted out of her, it was the other witch: the old one who called the bitch her niece, the head witch of one of the covens. It was the same red hair, but it was decidedly not the same witch she had been planning to kill.

Leona screamed again and pulled at her translucent silver hair, smearing the witch's red blood in it. The old witch tore her eyes away from the destruction happening just outside the window to finally look at Leona.

She was slow in her movements. Even the blood was beginning to slow as it spilled from her. It took her a moment—one of the few she had left—to understand that it had been her stupid niece whom Leona intended to kill.

Instead of dying with a look of horror, the old witch

died with a smile on her face. The last bit of light that went out in her eyes had been triumphant. She knew she had taken the place of Etain, and she was happy to do so.

"Oh my gods," someone gasped from the door. "Leona, what have you done?" She looked up to see Trillda, daring to look at her with the horror the witch's face should have held.

How dare she judge her!

She said nothing as she approached the female—not until she stood right before her. "Not what I intended to do, but this should make me feel marginally better," she said as she dragged the blade across the unsuspecting fae's throat before stepping over the fae's fallen body and making her way back down to the street.

While she was upset about getting the wrong witch, she had still set their entire city on fire. It was a start. There would be no stopping for Leona until her original mission was completed. She would kill that bitch who stole her life and then bathe in her blood.

Slowly, she walked down the main street of Witch City, basking in the heat of the flames that continued to rage out of control. Everyone rushed around her, frantic to extinguish the fire consuming everything in its path while she walked out of the city as slowly as a smile stretched across her face. At least this had gone according to plan.

"There will be another opportunity for your revenge," the *whispers* said.

"I do not want to wait!" Leona yelled through her teeth.

"You must; for now, it is time for you to join us." She

should be sitting on her throne now, not running away. However, she was smart enough to know that if she wanted another chance to reclaim her life, she would need a new plan, and plans take time.

Leona ported to the location the whispering voices had given her and was immediately surrounded by the blackest of night. Out of the deepest recesses of darkness, stepped a being.

"Welcome to the Court of Whispers."

ACKNOWLEDGMENTS

Well, here we are again!

Just one more book to go after this one, and then the Realms of Lore: Fae will be complete. I have to admit preparing to write the final book in the series is both exhilarating and crushing. I can't wait to have it all together and yet the idea of leaving these characters behind... Well, let's not think about that for now.

Per usual, I need to first and foremost thank my parents. I've said it before and I will say it again—without them, I would not be afforded the opportunity to chase this dream. They listen to me prattle on about random ideas that I get mid conversation, and they never make me feel guilty for spending as much time writing as I do.

Jess, the hotdog lady herself, reads everything I write as I write it and then convinces me not to delete it. My best friend of twenty-six years (cries in old) and sister friend for life, thank you for being the window to my wall. Skeet. Skeet.

Rebekah is seriously one of the kindest, most genuine humans I have ever had the pleasure of befriending. Our brain dumping sessions are literally my favorite part of every book I write. Thank you for gifting me the covers for this series and for teaching me how to create covers for others. She is literally "Rebekah My Hero" in my phone. It's not an exaggeration, she really is.

Roxann(e) might be the biggest cheerleader of them all. It does not matter what is going on in her life, she is always there to give positive reinforcement. I'm so glad you decided you wanted to know EVERYTHING, I desperately needed another person to bounce ideas off of. So thank you for taking one for the team. Thots and pears to the rest of y'all.

The rest of our Inkling family: Kim, Katherine, Veronica, Emily, and Amber (AP). It's wild to think that such a random chain of events brought us all together, but now I could never do life without each of you. From late night sprints, spending hours on a call without speaking, spending hours on a call without shutting up, encouragement to push further, a Dramione addiction, retreats, forced check-ins by our resident extravert, and to all the random shenanigans… the love I have for our little fam is immeasurable. Ugh, feelings. Whatever, y'all know what I mean.

Every time I write a new one of these, I'm reminded that there are so many people in my life to thank. I'm grateful to all of you who hype my books on socials, the book clubs that have featured my books, the readers who are genuinely excited to read whatever is coming next (still always a shock to me), fellow authors who know a rising tide lifts all boats, and bigger authors who refuse to let us babies be taken advantage of. All of you are who make the community I am proud to be a part of.

And now if you will excuse me, I am going to go and yeet my *emotions* off a bridge. Later Taters!

ABOUT THE AUTHOR

Hi! I'm Amber Thoma, the author of *Prince of Darkness* and *Heirs of Darkness*. I have been a reader for as long as I can remember. I blame personal-pan pizzas (IYKYK) for instilling an obsessive addiction to the many worlds books could take me to early in my life. I grew up in Northern Virginia and lived there until a few years ago, when I moved to a sleepy little college town in the mountains. I live in a 111 year old home with my dog, Lilith, and my cat, Kitten (very original, I know), and I am minutes from my family.

Like many people, lockdown made me reevaluate my life. For over a decade, I knew there was something I needed—a change. I played around with so many ideas. Like moving to a different country, going back to school, and starting a family. None of those felt right. The part of me screaming, "YOU'RE ON THE WRONG PATH," never silenced.

Listening to my intuition when the logical side of me was smashing the panic button was terrifying. That first step off the path was the most uncomfortable thing I had ever done. They say you have to get uncomfortable if you want to enact real change. Well, I got wildly uncomfortable and uprooted my entire life, and I will never stop being grateful for taking that first step.

If I had never taken that step, I would not have had a year of time with my niece before she suddenly passed away. I would never have taken the time to address my mental health. I definitely would never have sat down and written a book, and committing to a 5 series saga that will take me ten to fifteen years to complete would have completely overwhelmed me. I would have given up before I started, like I have so many times in the past. The folder of several dusty novel plans and intros can attest to that.

What is the moral of the story? Do not let fear keep you from taking that first step off the path you know you are not meant to be on. After all,

Fate gets what fate wants.

ALSO BY AMBER THOMA

QUEEN OF LIGHT

Realms of Lore: Fae Book Two

"It's okay to be scared, it does not make you less brave."

"I will come for you."

Trouble brews for the fae of the Day Court while witches are hunted in the Borderlands. Nothing is too far when it comes to love or power. New prophecies are given and promises are made. The beings of the Fae Realm fight for the fates they desire. However...

Fate gets what fate wants.